My Name Is Deliverer

TRUE STORIES OF BOB NICOL

ISBN: 978-1-64314-110-7 (Paperback)

AUTHORS PRESS

AuthorsPress
California, USA
www.authorspress.com

Contents

Introduction

How in the world do I get myself into these situations? Funny—my parents used to ask me the same thing, all too many times, while growing up. Guess I just have a knack for it! Even as an adult, here I am, wandering the dirt roads of a small village deep in South Sudan, well after dark, following a man that I just met. He could easily lead me to a spot where his associates are waiting to pounce on me and relieve me of my valuables (which aren't many—but they won't know that until it's too late). Not two minutes earlier, I was harbored safely inside a U.N. compound, behind two high walls with huge gates, guarded and locked. How did I come to be outside those walls?! And following this stranger to who-knows-where, trying desperately to recognize any landmarks, that could tell me if he was leading me towards the destination that I desired? I wish that I could tell you that I'm making this all up. But the truth is, I'm just not that clever or imaginative. Nope. I lived every story you will read in these pages.

It was February 2008, and I was nearing the end of my first trip to Africa. I didn't know it at the time, but this would be the first of many excursions I would make to the Dark Continent. As of today, I have made more than thirty such trips; I've begun to lose count. And each of these trips began by journeying first to Kenya—to the capital city of Nairobi, specifically. From there, I usually continue on to the coastal island city/port of Mombasa. During the past nine years, I have made seven excursion trips to Ethiopia, two to Sudan (now South Sudan), and single trips to Tanzania, Liberia and even beyond Africa to Iraq. This part of the world has become my second home.

Why do I go so often, you may ask? Originally, I went to Africa because a blind missionary asked me to. He asked me to accompany him to South Sudan—he said that he needed my help. Not so much to aid him in getting around (which I was glad to do), but to use my engineering experience to help him with a big project he was undertaking in the remote village of Adoor. But when I look back on it, I believe that, ultimately, he wanted me to find new purpose for my life. He knew me well enough to know that I was in a very dark place in my life, and this trip might be just the thing to bring me out of that darkness. Ironically, it would take a trip halfway around the world, with a blind missionary, to the Dark Continent for me to see the light.

In the following stories, I invite you to travel with me. Together, we will get lost at times, but never for too long, I promise. Hopefully, if my words are chosen well, you will develop a picture of your own that will better describe what I experienced. To help with this, I have included a few pictures—most are specific to the work I do here in Africa, which is to drill water wells and provide sanitary facilities in the villages. But some, like the one below, are intended to simply convey a sense of everyday life for the people that I encounter on my journeys.

Three Generations: The protective mom, the stoic grandmother, and the wondering boy.

One of the first photos I ever took in South Sudan, this remains one of my favorites. The mom watches carefully, making sure that I mean no harm to her or her family. The grandmother, like most older Sudanese women, will not pose or even look at a camera. Some of them, I am told, even think it is evil to do so. The young boy?—now there's a different story. This photo was taken outside a medical clinic next to a dirt runway; we stopped to refuel the small plane on our way from Kenya to the remote village where the wells were being drilled. This young boy probably had no idea what I was zdoing, holding up this black box and aiming it at him, while partially hiding behind it. His expression seems to say, "What are you doing, and how is it helping us?" I have enlarged and printed this picture. It now hangs on my apartment wall where I can see it every time I leave or enter. I look into those penetrating eyes and ask myself, "How am I helping them?" An unsettling question, to be sure, but it does help me stay focused on my new purpose in life.

It is my sincere hope that you will see how I responded to the calling I believe was given to me—that is, to use my training and experience as an engineer to bring water to so many who lack a basic necessity that we in the developed world take for granted. I am doing what I can to improve the lives of as many African people as possible. I certainly don't do it alone, especially now that we have our own drilling equipment and a team to do the drilling. It takes many hands to get these wells drilled, and I am grateful to so many who have put their trust and backing behind me and my efforts in this land. Without them, I could not have accomplished any of this.

But is it enough? Of course, the answer is an emphatic no. Even with so many humanitarian and faith-based NGOs working to bring water to the thirsty, there are still, by U.N. estimates, nearly a billion people without access to a ready and annual source of safe drinking water. How can this be? How can we in the developed world ignore that overwhelming cry for help? The numbers are staggering—every day, 4 to 5,000 people, the majority of which are children, still die from lack of water or polluted water, usually from lack of sanitary provisions. Yet we, as a country, can waste a purported $1 billion in a single presidential election and not think twice about it. Do you have any idea how many people we could provide with life-giving water with that kind of funding? Well, I do—roughly 100 million! For about $10 billion, we could solve this horrible problem worldwide, once and for all.

With the passion I feel for this issue, I wish this book could be a how-to primer for solving the world's safe drinking water problem. Sadly, even if I did write it, I doubt anyone would care to read it. Nor do I know the right people. It's not that those who I do know and who support me are not extremely caring and generous. On the contrary, they certainly are. I simply don't know enough of them. Perhaps this book will help in that respect. I pray to God that it is so.

So then, what is this book about? In the stories that follow, I hope to give you a window into my journeys and introduce you to the amazing people that have helped me along the way. You will see me struggle with difficult, sometimes scary situations—some I got caught up into, while others I managed to create for myself. But what I hope you see, beyond anything, is the way God traveled with me through all of these circumstances, and always helped me find my way out. Always. He was – and is – the one constant good in my life, and yours as well, I pray. Surely, I don't always acknowledge that. But that doesn't make it not true. He is there for all of us, whether we call on Him or not, notice Him or not, thank Him or not. Please don't miss that in all these stories. His guidance, His restoration, and His love is the reason I write.

Dedicated to Mom and Dad. Thank you for inspiring me to write. Your dedication to my spiritual upbringing and growth sustained me throughout my life, even though I was not always aware. I just know you're enjoying your new life with Jesus. That must be so awesome. I look forward to rejoining you one day and reveling with you.

With love, Bob

Lost in Sudan

"And I wasn't all things I tried to make believe I was. And I wouldn't be the one to kneel before the dreams I wanted. And all the talk and all the lies were all the empty things disguised as me."

"*Sympathy*" by The Goo Goo Dolls, from "Gutterflower" 2002, Warner Brothers ©

I had never seen so many stars. The brilliant points of light filled the entire expanse of my vision and extended all the way to the horizon. The Milky Way stretched longer, broader, and shone brighter than I could have imagined. But perhaps this was par for the course out here in the middle of nowhere—Sudan, to be specific, some 60 to 80 miles from the nearest town. I stood transfixed, gazing at the night sky, marveling that God simply breathed all this into existence.

Suddenly, reality shook me and interrupted my star-gazing. The questions that had haunted me for the last two hours rose again and rattled around in my brain.

"Where am I? What am I doing here? Where do I go?"

These questions didn't apply to the present situation only, but to my entire broken and hurting life at the time. Although I didn't have the luxury of soul-searching at the moment, the truth of the situation spoke deeply. Alone in the desert, under a blanket of beautiful but silent stars, I knew the answer. I was lost.

A year earlier, I had been as far from Sudan geographically as I was emotionally. I was living my American life and had never thought much, if at all, about the country. One day, Dean, a missionary friend of mine, brought a Sudanese pastor with him to our early morning men's Bible Study. Dean had recently returned from a mission trip to the village of Adoor, Sudan. Dean introduced his Sudanese friend, Wilson

Garang Chang, to our group and then recounted stories of taking large boxes filled with medicine to the villagers for a variety of sicknesses that stemmed from a polluted water source.

Oh, did I mention that Dean is blind? But that doesn't stop him from traveling the world and spreading the message of joy and hope in the name of Jesus Christ to everyone he meets. Well, Dean quickly realized that the most pressing need for the village was not simply more and more medicine, but for a safe water source. Though he knew nothing about well drilling, he vowed to (somehow, someway) provide a water well for Adoor.

This is where I came in. I am an engineer, and everyone knows that engineers, in addition to being able to fix anything that ever broke, also know everything there is to know about scientific matters. Naturally, being the brilliant engineer that I am, Dean thought surely I could figure out how to get a water well drilled and equipped with a pump at this remote village in the middle of nowhere, Sudan, Africa. Right? No problem! The truth was, I didn't have a clue how to even begin to accomplish this. But the challenge was so unique and intriguing, I couldn't help but give Dean an enthusiastic and confident yes, I'll help you! Once I was alone, however, I found myself thinking, "Now what?"

Fortunately, with a little bit of research, I amazed even myself by discovering and arranging for Living Water International (LWI), headquartered near Houston, Texas, to provide the drilling services for Adoor. Unfortunately, my exuberance was short-lived. Shortly after completing most of the arrangements, LWI elected to pull out of Sudan altogether due to the intense unrest and instability there following the recently ended civil war. Sudan has endured an intense civil war for most of the last 40 years, and even now is still in an "undeclared" war following an election to separate into the two countries of Sudan and South Sudan. Added to all of this, Adoor Village, the village in which we hoped to drill, was situated very near the war-torn Sudanese state of Darfur—one more reason for LWI to exit the project. For Dean and me, however, this only intensified our desire to find a driller and help the people of this troubled area.

Fortunately, soon after this first disappointment, Dean met two pastors from England who were trying to assist the same small village in Sudan. Tim was pastor of a mid-size church outside of London, and Harry was the lay director of missions for the entire Assembly of God churches in all of England. Harry and Tim had learned that the chief of Adoor Village had already managed to locate a driller from Kenya, Geoffrey Ndungu, who was in the general area, drilling wells for a worldwide charity, Save The Children. He was also available to drill wells in neighboring communities like Adoor. Coincidence? Or the hand of God?

Excited to have a driller on board, we began to work out the logistics. As it turned out, Adoor was not so small in reality. Stretching more than 6 kilometers wide, and with a reported population of nearly 2,000, we concluded that a single well would not provide enough water, nor lessen the haul distance, for many of its inhabitants. Tim and Harry offered Geoffrey a price to drill two wells for Adoor, and he accepted.

Dean's new team made plans to meet in Adoor in a few months. My brilliant engineering work had come to an end. Or so I thought. Dean had been hinting at another request recently, which he now asked outright: would I please accompany him to Sudan to oversee the drilling of these wells? I admit this possibility had been lingering in the back of my mind as well, but it was too strange, too frightening for me to allow it any real space within my brain's (admittedly minimal) logic matter. Surely I was not the person for this journey! However, getting out of it would not be so simple. How does one tell a blind missionary "no?" What would I say? That traveling to Sudan is just too hard, when Dean himself travels internationally many times each year?

In spite of this reluctance, I began to toy with the idea. The truth was, I needed a change. I had just come out of a difficult divorce. (Really, is there is any other kind?) The turmoil had left me, my two younger daughters, and, I suspect, even my ex-wife, in a very dark place. Even worse, my youngest decided to live with her mother, and my middle daughter went off to college. My oldest daughter was married and living happily in Connecticut. For the first time in a long time, I was alone. I was lost.

But I soon discovered that even in the worst darkness, God brings light. For me, that light turned out to be a blind missionary with a request. Not an easy request, but one I began to consider was packed with the potential for adventure, hope, and renewed life. At the same time, I had to face liberal bastings of uncertainty and doubt. Could God actually use me in this broken state? Did I have anything to offer, or was I just trying to run away from the pain? At this all-time low point in my life, I was beyond broken. I was truly shattered. But deep down, I also believed that the God of the universe could make something good come from these shattered pieces of myself. So, even in the midst of so much doubt and insecurity, I felt an emerging hope rising within me. In spite of my fears of inadequacy, I said "yes" to Dean's request.

As the days went by and I prepared for the trip, I began to experience a new enthusiasm for life and living. God had given me a part to play, however small it seemed at the time, in His great story. After all, I began to realize, this is really God's story, and we humans get to be a part of the story He is telling! It's like that scene in City Slickers, the one where Curly (Jack Palance) tells Mitch (Billy Crystal) that the secret to life is finding the 'one thing.' When Mitch asks what that 'one thing' is, Curly says, "Now that's what you got to find out." After so much pain and suffering, I felt hopeful that God was beginning to reveal to me my "one thing." I knew what I could do for the "the least of these" in God's kingdom; I now had a glimpse of what my purpose was – or could be! Not even on the trip yet, I was already starting to share this hope and joy with friends and family. I was brimming with new purpose! What could possibly go wrong?

Flash forward to the desert. Here I was in the middle of my new purpose, and I was feeling anything but hope. I was far from my mud hut and even farther from home. I had wandered off, gotten hopelessly lost in the darkness, and Dean, Tim, and Harry were fast asleep and wouldn't miss me until morning.

If only Dr. Isaiah Dau were here with me now! Dr. Dau, our friend and Sudanese pastor of a Presbyterian church in Nairobi, spoke fluent Dinka, Swahili, and English. He could have asked the locals for directions back to our makeshift village. Lost, and not speaking the local language: a double strike against me.

Or if only I had Joseph the Woodcutter with me! Now here's a most interesting chap. Joseph, a Kenyan member of Dr. Dau's church, had joined our group because he was very handy with a chain saw. His task was to teach the young Sudanese men how to cut wood to prepare their own roof support beams. I met Joseph the Woodcutter for the first time at Wilson Airport on our way from Nairobi to Sudan. He brought with him a donated chainsaw, spare blades, and fuel and oil for the saw. Actually, we had all brought an array of unusual items to take with us on the plane to Sudan: in addition to Joseph's hefty set of tools, the Brits had brought bundles of wood stakes and plaques to erect around the village, and we had carried a load of Bibles and other books, as well as more medicine. Although I had worried that it might not fit, somehow we managed to clear all this stuff, after weighing it and watching it closely as it was loaded.

It's just as well that this was my only worry at the time, and that I didn't know that the commercial flight was only the first part of our trip! It turned out that to get to Sudan, we would initially take a commercial flight on ALS from Nairobi to the border of Sudan. From there we would pass through Sudanese customs, then board a chartered plane to fly into Sudan. It's also just as well that I didn't know, at the time, that ALS stands for Aircraft Leasing Services—not really a moniker that carries a river of assurance to me! Fortunately, the charter plane would be manned by a pilot from AIM Air - African Inland Missions, a 100 year+ International Christian Organization, with their own air mobility unit. Learning that helped to calm my nerves just a bit. Andy, the kind and friendly pilot, would fly with us on the commercial flight to the "town" of Lokichoggio just inside the Kenya-Sudan border, then take us the rest of the way into Sudan.

We boarded the plane, and I grabbed a seat next to Joseph, eager to chat with him. He seemed tense and bewildered, and I quickly learned that this was his very first airplane ride! This Kenyan man in his 40s was flying with me for his first flight ever. I felt obliged to calm his fears. I immediately made up some statistics to assure him of the sheer safety of flying. Gems like, "You are 10,000 times more likely to be run over by a *matatu* in Nairobi than to meet your demise in an airplane crash." And you thought engineering was my only skill!

However, it wasn't my reassuring bedside manner but the view from the sky that truly quieted his emotions. We gazed down at large red-tile-roofed villas that gave way to smaller towns and villages and then to remote farms—a breathtaking tapestry of lush green fields, terraced hillsides, and tree-covered mountains. Suddenly, there it was, towering in the distance—the majestic Mt. Kenya. At 17,000+ ft., this peak is second on the continent only to the legendary Mt. Kilimanjaro. Joseph, now at ease, regaled me with stories, lore perhaps, but highly entertaining tales he had heard about this magnificent peak.

As we approached the northern extent of Kenya, the beautiful, lush greenery soon gave way to a vast and harsh terrain of treeless mountains and desert-like flatlands of mottled tans and grays. As we got closer to the Lokichoggio air strip, we could see a very large lake off in the distance. Lake Turkana, as it's called, begins within Ethiopia, but most of its 175-mile length resides in Kenya. It happens to be the largest saline lake in Africa and the fourth largest in the world. Other than this impressive lake, however, I have to say that I found most of this new terrain unattractive from the air. Even Lokichoggio, or Loki, as the Kenyans call it, was unimpressive as an entry point into Kenya. In fact, you may recall this "airport" from a 2005 movie called The Constant Gardener. Ralph Fiennes, the titular star, takes off from Loki on a UN plane (which we saw parked all over the tarmac) that was taking him into Sudan to investigate his wife's murder. Sadly, we didn't get one of those fancy UN planes to fly in. But we did have a nice one, just the same - a Cessna Caravan, which was parked nearby.

Although the Cessna looked small, all six of us, including all of our stuff, and Andy, the pilot, managed to fit with room to spare. The flight into Sudan took nearly five hours, plus a mid-way refueling stop at an extremely remote dirt airstrip next to a medical clinic. Andy had to make an initial low pass over the dirt "runway" to announce our arrival, and also to clear the herd of cows hanging out on the airstrip, scattering them with the help of our noisy engine. We landed and disembarked, stretched our legs, used the (natural) facilities, and waited as Tim and Harry toured the medical clinic for pointers in stocking the one in Adoor that they had built.

After refueling, we flew another two plus hours to the small, remote village of Melalcon. Here we were greeted by villagers who brought us chairs and lukewarm drinks as we waited for our ride to our final destination. Kind gestures, and much appreciated, to be sure, although I never could quite get a respite from the relentless heat. Even though we were several hundred miles south of the lower extreme of the Sahara Desert, it still felt really hot.

Two vehicles soon arrived, a land cruiser and a truck, owned by Save the Children, we learned, and driven by two of Geoffrey's workers. After bouncing over 60 miles of very bumpy dirt road, we headed down a vague pathway, which then faded to nothing at all. Our drivers navigated by dead reckoning, I witnessed, for the last several miles. We stopped more than once while they discussed which direction might be correct, as nothing around us even resembled a roadway, let alone a path. Just as I was beginning to suspect we might be lost, all at once we drove right up to a gathered crowd. We had arrived in the center of Adoor Village, our home for the next week.

At present, however, in the starlit night, I was far away from my *tukul* (mud) hut in Adoor Village, and wishing for the company of my new Kenyan friends and fellow travelers with us. Yes, if either Isaiah Dau or Joseph the Woodcutter were with me now, they could certainly ask for directions from a native speaker, and entertain me with stories along the way. Unfortunately, they were nestled safely in their own *tukul*, back in the village – where I was supposed to be! Regardless, I realized that, even if we could ask for directions, we would need to have locals to ask. I looked around and saw only cows and several goats in the expanse of open terrain. Seeing them, I had to wonder what other, not so friendly animals might be lurking nearby. I refused to panic, but I admit I was becoming alarmed at my situation, which seemed to be getting bleaker by the minute.

I glanced at the stars again, this time searching for help. If only I could use these magnificent stars to help me find my way, to gain some directional functionality from them instead of just gawking at them, wide-eyed and open-jawed. There! I could identify the Big Dipper and the Little Dipper. One's bigger, right? And there was Orion's belt, and that one seemed a familiar astral creature, as well. But how to use them to navigate was a total mystery to me. If only my older brother, Doug, were here with me! He may not be able to navigate by stars, but at least he could point out many of the constellations. He also speaks fluent Arabic, which would also come in quite handy, as it is a second language for many Sudanese after their tribal language.

As I wandered, I replayed the events leading up to getting lost out here in the African desert. It began innocently enough with a call to my parents using our satellite phone. I figured it would be a thrill for them to get a call from Sub-Sahara, Africa at their home in Back Mountain, Pennsylvania (aptly named for its geography). Plus, I had been dying to use our cool satellite phone since we arrived. To place a call on this hefty handset, the phone seeks out a number of satellites in orbit until it locks on to at least three of them, and the more satellites that it locks onto, the better the connection.

Due to the time difference, I had waited until almost midnight to place the call. Our tired travel group had long since gone to sleep. After a couple of failed attempts, I listened in awe as the call to "Smallville," PA made its way halfway around the earth, and nine hours behind. My 92-year-old dad answered the call.

"Hi Dad, it's Bob, calling from Sudan!"

"What? Is that really you, Bob?" Dad responded somewhat incredulously.

"Hard to believe, huh, Dad?"

"Wow! How's it going? What are you up to?"

The questions came flooding in faster than I could respond. It's safe to suppose that this was his first call from Sudan, or anywhere in Africa, for that matter. My brother had spent several years living in Cairo as a young man, but I don't remember any long-distance phone calls from him coming to the house. And if he called, it sure wasn't from a satellite phone!

"Let me get your mom," Dad said. "She's going to want to talk to you, too."

"Sure Dad, I'll wait."

"Bob?"

"Yes, it's me. Hi, Mom."

"Wow! How are you doing? Are you getting enough to eat?"

Similar questions, different perspective!

It took some practice and patience to get the hang of the five-second delay while our words traveled such a great distance. But we were all so excited just to be speaking to each other half a world away to care. It was an incredibly memorable experience for the three of us.

I finally hung up with Mom and Dad, but the thrill of the new toy had left me wide-awake. Not relishing the thought of sweating and sleeping in stagnant air, I decided against turning in right away. As I dropped off the phone at our hut, I heard singing and noise far off from our compound. In the distance, I could see a small light emanating from the sound of the singing. Curious, I grabbed my windup flashlight (or torch, as the Brits called them) and trekked off to join the festivities.

I waded into the night, winding my way around small brush and thorny bushes, following the general direction of the light and revelry. Having jettisoned my Boy Scout wilderness training skills long ago,

I paid no attention to visual landmarks that might have helped me get home. No, I was singularly focused on following the melodic, yet strangely distorted sounds.

As I walked, I thought about the men in the village I had seen earlier that week. Many of them had facial scars, obviously man-made by the point of a sharp tool, typically in the shape of chevrons on their foreheads or cheeks. I had found it a bit unsettling and unexpected, since I'd spent no time reading about the Sudanese culture. My preparation had focused on the regional geology and water availability studies—compelling enough reading for an engineer! Had I branched out and read about the Sudanese people, I would have learned that these facial carvings served to distinguish the men as members of certain tribes. The Village of Adoor was comprised solely of the largest tribe, the Dinka, so the facial carvings, for those that had them, were very similar. While Westerners may find this practice a bit strange, I likened it to the tattoos that gang members use to identify their affiliation. Not that tattoos are an option here, since the Sudanese people are very dark-skinned. Now that I thought about it, I had seen no tattoo parlors, whereas in the States, they pop up on every corner. Maybe the Sudanese had facial carving parlors?

The music was getting louder, assuring me that I was getting closer. I now heard the sounds more clearly—singing, yes, but also screaming and other loud noises. I might have been (maybe should have been) scared that it was some kind of ritual involving mutilation or spirits or even human sacrifice. But my curiosity had made me bold, eager to see the show.

Several times my torchlight faded, but each time I revived the little light beam by winding the gear arm. I was very fond of this handy tool. I wasn't so sure I wanted to give it up at the end of our stay in Adoor. You see, I was informed that we guests traditionally leave the torches and various items, including extra food (like breakfast bars, beef and bison jerky, dried fruit) for our hosts when we depart. Such things are either very valuable (like the wind-up lights) or delightfully unique to them, like the dried meat and fruit. I remembered the hungry eyes that had been watching my glorious little light this week, and I held it a bit closer to me as I plodded on.

All at once, I came upon the gathering. It took me awhile to process the sight. The women of the village, young, middle-aged, and even older ones, were engaged in a ritual song and dance, while all of the men watched from the sidelines. As the women carried on in the singing, some of the women formed a circle with joined hands and danced around one way, then the other, while the remaining women stayed inside the circle singing, screaming, or chanting and making other noises. Then, as if on cue, they would suddenly break rank, turn and run screaming up a nearby hill into the darkness. Then they would come running back down, screaming, chanting, and singing all the way. They repeated this several times.

Mesmerized, I stood watching this spectacle without another thought for more than an hour. The celebration seemed as if it would continue forever. Suddenly, the lateness of the hour hit me, and I realized I was very tired. I knew I had another long day in front of me, and I really should be getting some sleep. I looked around the circle to say goodbye, but I had only been in Adoor for a few days, and I didn't recognize anyone. They seemed to take no note of me, either, unique as I was in this group. So I turned and started off in the general direction of our village area. However, all the light was behind me, and without distinguishing landmarks, I wasn't sure where I was going.

After I had walked enough desert to reach our group of huts, I realized that I could not recognize anything that even remotely looked like our little temporary village with its thatched papyrus-like reed wall. I felt a prick of concern, but keeping my cool, I simply modified the direction I was heading and continued on. When I started to see a number of cows, I knew that I was in the wrong place. I stopped walking. I knew that I was in Sudan and somewhere near the village of Adoor, but that's all I had to go on. I admit that at this point, some measure of fear crept in, but I tried to stay calm and come up with a plan. I couldn't ask directions from any of the children and teens that I had passed. They spoke no English, and I spoke no Dinka or Arabic.

I had to admit it finally—I was lost. I knew no one, except those that I came with, who were right now out there somewhere in the blanket of night, sleeping safely in their huts. I was feeling more frightened by the minute. I was alone, outside, at night, in a foreign country; I couldn't ask directions, I knew no one, and I had only a small wind-up flashlight. I'd even left the satellite phone in the *tukul* on purpose before setting off. I tried not to think about the warnings I'd heard, the danger a person could encounter here in this war-torn place, alone and without protection.

The situation was bleak. So I did the only thing I knew to do in a desperate hour. I prayed, asking God to help me find my way back to our village, even if He had to send me an angel. I felt peace that He had heard me, and I began to think.

Could I find my way back to the music? I had no friends there, but all things considered, it seemed a better choice than wandering lost in the desert. Just yours truly and a lot of cows. I crept past the sleeping cows, trying to attract as little attention as possible as I made my way back through the low desert brush. I could barely see the distant light in the blackness of night. I trekked on, and soon I heard the music and found myself back at the ladies' celebration. It wasn't my village, but I felt a flood of relief at being out of immediate danger. Now all I had to do was find someone, anyone, who could lead me back home. Although I realized at that moment, it wouldn't help if no one spoke English. I tried not to panic for the fiftieth time.

I stood in the short light of the fire, keeping a calm exterior but furtively glancing around the circle for a familiar face. Suddenly, a man approached out of nowhere—our good friend and longtime contact, Moses Garang Chang! I was overjoyed to see him, relieved beyond expression. He greeted me warmly and took my hand in his, and did not let go. We stood there, hand in hand, watching the ladies continue their wild celebration.

I began to feel uncomfortable. No longer afraid for my life, I now felt merely awkward—holding the hand of another man deep in the desert of Sudan. Although I knew no one else around the circle, I worried what conclusions they might draw. However, when I remembered seeing men holding hands several times since I'd been in Sudan, I began to relax. More than fifty young pastors had attended the Pastors' Conference that Dean and the team were conducting while I oversaw the well-drilling. The men had traveled from all over South Sudan, some over hundreds of kilometers, and by a variety of transport modes that included the back of dump trucks. For days now, I had seen many of them holding hands while walking along throughout the vast village, totally caught up in their conversation and unconcerned about any (distorted) thoughts of observers. I knew, too, that Africans generally abhor homosexuality, so I began to conclude that this must be simply a means of displaying friendship, void of any sexual overtones. I later confirmed this with experienced African travelers, and I gained a new appreciation for this beautiful and innocent means of presenting an emerging or a rekindled friendship. As I reflected on our almost hysteric phobias in the west, I began wishing that we Westerners could un-learn some of these harmful biases.

So there I stood, hand-in-hand with Moses, my new best friend and guardian angel. (Thank you God, I remembered "snap-praying.") Feeling safe now, I observed the ritual dancing and singing with more intent. Since Moses spoke pretty good English, I asked him if the men would join in with the dancing. He answered quickly, "Oh no. Tonight is the women's night." I turned back to watch the women; there appeared to be no script, nor even a leader. They took turns creating dance steps as the music moved them, and the others followed. Yet for all its seeming improvisation, the dancing had a consistent grace and fluidity. The dancers seemed totally absorbed in the moment, carefree in their enjoyment. I asked Moses if they got to celebrate like this often, and he responded, "No, not often." This must be a special night, I decided, their own night to lay aside family and societal burdens and lose themselves in singing and dancing with each other.

Considering this event was so rare, I felt incredibly blessed to have happened upon it. This evening of frivolity and merriment felt so simple, so spectacular, so pure. It made me suddenly wistful with regret. My daughters had long since labeled me as "clueless"—and not without good reason, I was learning. Added to the pain I was swimming in after my divorce, I wondered if I had come too late to understand or appreciate women, and to honor them in an appropriate manner. My eye skipped from woman to woman, trying to capture a piece of the joy they felt in engaging with one another. They were performing for no one; I saw no interaction between the revelers and the observers. One would have thought that they were totally alone, and that no one was watching. I glanced at the men, who were watching without comment, but smiling and even laughing as they watched their wives and daughters and moms in their exuberance and freedom. I found myself feeling deeply happy for these beautiful creatures and honored to have been welcomed into this wonderful spectacle in the dark morning hours in the desert, even as all of my fellow travel-mates slept on.

When I could barely keep my eyes open from exhaustion, I finally told Moses that I needed to return to my *tukul* and try to get some sleep.

Without letting go of my hand, he said, "I'll take you back." Like a tired child, I simply let my guardian lead me home. I told him of my failed attempt to find my own way home earlier that evening. He became visibly uncomfortable, and he told me that I should not even have gone outside our village fence without an escort, as there were many dangers for a lone white man without protection. I thought of the soldiers we had seen that day. Fearsome men, with chevron mutilations on their foreheads, carrying AK47 rifles and crossed "ribbons" of bullets. They seemed to step out of nowhere as we met with a few of the village elders. I had asked Chief Michael, our escort, what they were on the lookout for, assuming that their focus was wild animals. Oh no, I was told, they're protecting against neighboring tribes and remnant Darfurian vigilantes, envious of Adoor's good fortune in securing strong missionary support. They were greedy for a share of the new schools, clinics, and now the well-drilling, or worse, they simply wanted to destroy it all out of jealousy.

I apologized quickly to Moses for causing him to worry, and even more, for making him leave the night of dancing early. Nonetheless, I confessed that I was glad to have ventured out because I had been blessed with a truly enchanting experience that I would never forget. Moses then relented at my unabashed enthusiasm and smiled. "Okay, Mr. Bob. I, too, am happy that you enjoyed watching the ladies' celebration." We reached our inner village, and at my *tukul*, he promised to come by first thing in the morning (only a few hours now) to wake us for breakfast. Nescafe Coffee and sorghum porridge…I couldn't wait!

You'd probably think, after my harrowing night of wandering off alone, that this would be the last time I would pull such a stunt. Surely I had been properly chastened by my experience and the worry I had caused Moses. Well, it would have been the last time, had my desperation not caused another hasty wandering. This would not be the only time God watched out for me in the middle of Africa! Not by a long shot.

On our last night in Sudan, we had the privilege of staying in the fancy (at least by Sudanese "bush" standards) UN compound. You see, one of Geoffrey's men had driven the six of us, crammed into Geoffrey's SUV, back through the desert and the bush for some 70 miles to the grass airstrip where we had arrived only six days prior. The flight back to Lokichoggio with AIM Air would leave very early the next morning, so we needed to stay close by to catch our flight. The compound was unusually luxe with its block wall buildings, elevated concrete floor, and—truly rare—electricity! The giant diesel generator, located outside, groaned on relentlessly and would rob me of any chance at protracted sleep that night. I was grateful for the benefits of the generator that evening, however, when we sat down to a hot meal of vegetables and meat, illumination by incandescent lighting, and miracle of all miracles—TV!

Yes indeed, we enjoyed live coverage, beamed miraculously into this tiny dot on the map of Africa, of a major 'futbol' match between two of Africa's better teams, Cameroon and Ivory Coast. This game turned out to be a major African playoff game leading up to the African Cup, the build-up to the next World Cup. Harry convinced us all to root for The Ivory Coast, as their star player was on Harry's favorite team in England, Chelsey, of the Premier League. Oh, and one final benefit of the electricity to crown our festive evening—cold beer! We hadn't had this extravagance since we left Heathrow ten days earlier. How funny, I thought, one night spent sweating profusely in our stuffy *tukuls*, and the next enjoying a cold Kenyan beer, a savory meal, and a fun futbol game on TV. What an array of experiences here in Africa!

Sadly, my relaxation was cut short when Harry suddenly asked to borrow my satellite phone to call his wife, and I couldn't find it. We did have a second Iridium, so I offered that one to Harry, then slipped out to search for the lost phone in the last place I had used it. I didn't dare tell anyone that I was leaving, because I feared they would stop me, and I hoped to fix my error with no one the wiser. So off I went, through two locked gates and into the dark night, endeavoring to retrace the path we'd followed earlier. Earlier that afternoon, the SUV had dropped Dean and me briefly at a compound nearby while Harry and Tim drove on to look for a place to spend the night. I remembered Dean and I had waited on some chairs, and I was fairly sure I had left the satellite phone sitting on one of these. What were the odds that such a valuable gadget was still sitting around in the open? My stomach sank as I strode away from the UN compound and into the darkening night.

Suddenly, out of the darkness, a fellow appeared. Startled, I suspected that he may have been looking to fleece me, but I had little to offer in the way of cash. He seemed more friendly than malicious, and he spoke pretty good English. It seemed he did actually want to help me, and I decided to trust him. After all, I had left hastily and didn't really have a clue where I was going.

To my surprise, he led me directly to the very place I was asking for. I banged hard on the gate to get the guard's attention. When I told him my trouble, he let me inside, but he made my "friend," whom he eyed quite sharply, wait outside. I quickly made my way to the area where Dean and I had been waiting before. Astoundingly, our chairs were still there, and perched undisturbed on the very seat where I had left it was the Iridium phone. I couldn't believe my good fortune. A new Iridium phone costs well over $1,000, and even used ones, as this one was, cost $700. I breathed a hearty prayer of thanks to God for this help, which I could not accept as mere coincidence or luck. Not everyone believes in His help in the small things, even if they believe in God, but I have no other explanation why so many things that should not turn out well for me somehow manage to do just that. I believe God is just as interested in showing us His hand in the little things as well as in the big things. (Although let me tell you, the possibility of losing a $700 satellite phone was not such a "little thing" to me!)

The guard once again opened the compound gate for me, smiling and nodding as I showed him my recovered treasure. My new best friend was faithfully waiting for me outside the gate, and as I needed to find my way back to the UN compound, I found myself, once again, needing to trust in this local man's direction. In yet another instance of God's great help, I realized that I was actually glad this man had befriended me, because as the evening turned quickly into night, I no longer recognized any landmarks. Several times I suggested turns that my friend dismissed as wrong. I decided to follow his advice, once more trusting that God had sent this man to help me and not to harm me. (Sound a bit like Jeremiah 29:11, maybe?)

Before long, I recognized familiar territory; sure enough, my friend had brought me safely back. To show my appreciation, I told him that all I had was US currency—would he accept that as a gift for taking such good care of me? He nodded and humbly accepted the money that I offered him. I thanked him and said goodbye, and turned to enter the UN compound.

I tried to slip in quietly to the room where my friends were watching the end of the soccer match, but my absence had not gone unnoticed.

In fact, it had caused quite a stir when they found that I had left the compound. They chastised me strongly for my careless behavior, reminding me of all the bad things that can happen to a white man alone in Africa. I have to say now, that I was secretly glad that I had never told them "all the details" (like getting lost) about that night I ventured out to see the dance and had to be rescued by Moses. I boldly responded that I had not yet found any part of Sudan to be as dangerous as they say. Yes, we must exercise caution in unknown situations, but at some point, I believe you just have to let go of fear and trust in your abilities and that your fellow man does not exist just to harm you. Above all, you have to trust God to "have your back," which I do. He has not yet let me down.

Midnight wanderings aside, you may be interested to know how the daytime work was progressing. While Dean and the other missionaries led the Pastors' Conference and Joseph the Woodcutter was teaching the young Sudanese men how to use a chainsaw without cutting their toes off, I was assigned to oversee Geoffrey, our well drilling contractor, as he drilled and completed the wells for Adoor Village.

On our arrival in Adoor, Geoffrey and his team had been there five days and already completed one of the wells. He was now preparing to drill the second well at the top of a small hill next to a small two-room medical clinic. Nearby and partway down the hill, a brick building with window and door openings but no roof was destined to become a schoolroom. The missing roof, it turned out, was awaiting Joseph's teaching and his chainsaw to prepare the roof beams. In fact, metal roof sheets would soon be delivered to complete this "modern" structure. This was an unusual fixture; in Adoor, most "buildings" were just a scattering of *tukuls*, one for most families, or two or three for the wealthy. For these families, the main *tukul* was reserved for sleeping and relaxing, the second was used for cooking and storing food, and the third for their livestock. In fact, I learned that the number of *tukuls* owned would be an indication that they were one of the "wealthier families" in the village.

We had not even seen a true building with walls and rooms and a roof since arriving in Sudan (and not again until we lounged happily in the UN compound on our last night in Sudan). Even the "town" where we landed on the dirt runway, some 70-80 km away, was nothing more than *tukul*-like structures or makeshift tents and canvas structures, occasionally with elevated wood floors. It was interesting to see how everyday life is lived in other parts of the world, and it also taught me not to take for granted the abundance we have in the States.

I began to shadow Geoffrey in his well drilling work. When he took a break from setting up the new drill site, I asked him to take me to the first well that he had already completed. I was surprised to observe that it was merely a kilometer or so from the second well being drilled on top of the hill. As we walked to the well site, we passed a simple hand pump well. Geoffrey said the men of the village told him it was drilled some years ago by the United Nations. However, when it stopped pumping, it was abandoned. That's crazy, I said; it can't take that much to repair it. He agreed, but said this often happens in remote areas throughout Africa. I told him about Living Water International in Houston; I appreciated that, besides drilling wells in countries around the world, they repair more existing wells than they drill new ones. No sense doing the same job twice, especially when so many areas have yet to enjoy even one well!

The new well site was empty when we arrived, but as we started pumping water, many people, mostly women and children, began showing up. The water was quite muddy at first, but the longer we pumped, the clearer it flowed. Geoffrey instructed the people to continue pumping as long as they could—take turns, he told the children, and pump as long as you can before tiring. Only then will the well clean itself and start pumping clear, clean water, which they could drink and take home to their families.

Over the next few days, I drove Geoffrey crazy with questions. While I had overseen a number of wells drilled in the States and had several geologists who worked for me, I had never seen anything like this. Drilling in developing countries was certainly a different affair. For one thing, there was a lot more manual labor involved. The drill rigs were much smaller. Most importantly, Geoffrey employed many different people. He had brought a team of three Kenyans with him, then enlisted the help of three or four men from Adoor Village. He also recruited some of the women to sift river gravel to be used later for the well screening material. He even enlisted some of the older boys to help with smaller tasks. The whole event really became a community project.

At the time, I could not have seen how much this method of operation in Sudan would impact me; however, to this day, whenever I drill a well, I try to incorporate as many of the local villagers in our drilling project as possible. This method truly builds a sense of community ownership of the water well, and by including the locals in the well construction, they become familiar with how this fairly simple pump works. Geoffrey also left them with spare wear parts, which was a brilliantly practical solution, as this would allow them to maintain their own well and not have to abandon it like the now worthless UN well. One final benefit of including many of the community residents in the work is that it provides them with some income, which they don't have much opportunity to earn otherwise. I have found that this community involvement method of well drilling is one of the most special opportunities that we bring to these countries, one that the community leaders and elders really notice.

We also make every effort to live in the communities where we drill, for the most important purpose of building relationships with the people, and introducing them in turn to the most important relationship they can have, Jesus Christ. Living among them gives us a chance to get to know the people, hear their stories, and to share our own. We have a tremendous opportunity to share Christ with these villagers because they are so grateful for the gift of water wells; as Dean puts it, we gain a "hearing for the Gospel." In the midst of drilling the water well, we tell the people about Jesus, the Living Water, and how they can have salvation through faith in Him. Some hear our story and choose to believe in Christ alone for their salvation. Then we get to use the fresh new water for its highest use imaginable—baptizing new believers into the Kingdom of God! That part just leaves me undone. To be used of God in this way simply leaves me humbled beyond measure. What an honor!

These insights were still to come as I was overseeing my very first water well in Adoor. The work was going smoothly, but even so, one question haunted me continually. Why this place, Adoor, and not others? What was so special about it that we would travel from overseas to this tiny village, passing up many villages and isolated *tukuls*, and many, many Sudanese families along the way? Who will provide for their water well? – for their medical clinic? – for their school? Why Adoor, of all places?

I discovered the answer when I was teamed up with an interpreter that week. I had been asked to present a water hygiene class for the ladies of the village so that they would avoid re-contaminating the water after taking it home. Most of the women only spoke Dinka, so my old friend Bishop Wilson stepped in to translate—the very same Wilson I had met in San Antonio when Dean brought him to our church that morning!

Wilson, it turned out, was the main reason we were in Adoor. It was he who had initially connected with the English missionaries to get them interested in assisting their village. He seemed young to be a bishop over this and several nearby villages, no older than mid-30s, but he has grown up very quickly. His story is quite amazing—he was one of the now famous Lost Boys of Sudan who as children traveled hundreds of miles into Ethiopia to escape the Civil War. Their story has been the subject of a number of books and several motion pictures, making them well known worldwide. I have since met several other Lost Boys, and their stories of survival and what they're doing now are always compelling. Each one I have met is giving back to a world that turned its back on them in their hour of greatest need, yet none seem to be vindictive in any way. On the contrary, they all seem grateful for having survived, literally, and want to help mankind move forward.

Wilson is no different in this regard, and his way of giving back involves selecting some of the more ambitious and hard working young men from each of the villages. He then sees that they get some initial schooling and basic Bible training in Sudan, and if they show great promise, he finds a way to get them to Nairobi where he provides for their formal education. They go on to Bible College, and finally, he places them back into various villages within Sudan where they can minister to their own people. It was a great undertaking that I wish I had invested more of myself into. What an amazing journey, to go from fleeing across two countries with other children while being chased by marauding bands of "soldiers" bent on destruction, or by wild animals, just to escape sure death back home, all the way to raising up leaders to guide your war-torn country years later.

Out of this concern for his people, Bishop Wilson had connected with Dean and the Brits and convinced them of the tremendous needs within the largest community that he was bishop over, Adoor. These missionaries were looking for communities to help and to spread the message of God's amazing love. The connection with Adoor was a God connection, I believe. The needs were great; I saw the number of Darfur region refugees—orphans, actually— grow from about 150 on my first trip to nearly 500 on my second and last trip to Sudan, just one year later. Dean and his ministry donors continued to support these orphans for several years and provided them with teachers, books, food, money, and much more, until almost all of the orphans were adopted by families within the Adoor community. It was wonderful to be part of bringing so much aid to such a troubled area of the world.

My part in this work in Sudan, the reason Dean had invited me, was to monitor Geoffrey and make sure that he was drilling good quality wells on behalf of the Adoor community. The only problem was that Geoffrey knew about a hundred times more than me about drilling and outfitting water wells. If he'd wanted to, he could have easily scammed us. Fortunately, God sent us not only a well-trained and gifted well driller, but also a deeply religious man who once served as a pastor in Kenya. He was concerned, as we were, for the villagers' eternal fate, as well as their physical survival through the gift of clean water. I learned a lot from Geoffrey on that first and a later trip. I may have even asked enough "semi-astute" questions to make him think that I was not totally ignorant of developing country well drilling processes. Nonetheless, I have to say that he was gracious and patient beyond belief to share with me so much of his 20+ years of well-drilling experience in Africa. We have remained close friends to this day, and there are many stories to come about Geoffrey and our developing friendship.

At the end of our trip, despite my dangerous wanderings in Sudan, I did make it out alive. More than that, I made it out with new life inside of me. The person I was before and after that trip are two different people. Looking back, when I said yes to Dean, to accompany him to Sudan, I didn't know what to expect. I had nothing to compare it to. The only developing countries that I had ever been to were Mexico and Peru, and those for sightseeing. Drilling wells in Sudan seemed entirely different and frightening in its unknowns.

As I prepared for the journey, a voice in the back of my head kept whispering that there were certainly more qualified people than me to accompany Dean on this sojourn. I began to feel woefully inadequate. But I refused to mention these thoughts to Dean. I was more afraid that he would agree and ask me not to go. Scared as I was, I knew for sure I didn't want to miss this opportunity.

I realize now that my trust in God and my willingness to step out on faith were being opposed by the Enemy—Satan. I should have been able to discern his meddling, since I was still in a very dark place after my divorce, and I had named him back then to many of my friends as a driving force in our breakup. We know "he comes to steal, to kill and destroy" (John 10:10, NIV). He seeks to destroy sacred marriages. So it's not a great stretch to realize that he must detest our gift of life-giving water to "the least of these" in the name of Jesus Christ, the Living Water. Why should I not expect some pushback?

Yet although I experienced feelings of fear, the Enemy was not successful in dissuading me from my purpose. I went with the full confidence that the God of the universe had my back. "If God is for us, who can stand against us?" (Romans 8:31, NIV). While my daily decisions may not have always been right on, I knew that He would remain faithful to support me, as long as my goals were aligned with His direction to love and care for my neighbor. This holds true, I believe, even if your "neighbor" lives halfway around the world, does not speak your language, and sports facial scarring to aid in his identity. He, too, is a child of God and deserves to be shown love. If not by me, then by whom? If I could carry this confidence into "enemy territory" in Sudan, then I was determined to do my part to help Dean and the team share the message of God's relentless love.

When I said yes to drilling wells in Sudan, I was a broken man, carrying baggage from the demise of a marriage I had been happy in, stumbling blindly and in pain to the next season of my life. I didn't know what I was getting into, much less how to prepare for it. It was truly in weakness that I set out on this trip. Yet in our weakness, God is made strong. I see now that even though I was not ready or equipped to set out on this unusual journey, God had enough of my heart and trust to know that He could work with me. He would make me whole once again, but this time to serve His purpose, not mine. Sure, I got lost a couple of times on this trip, and then found again by angels in disguise; however, my real lost-to-found story was being written in higher places. This new purpose would unfold in more stories to come.

I remember a conversation I had with Dean on our second 9-hour flight back home. I told him that I wanted to do what Geoffrey was doing—providing life-giving water to the world's neediest people. On a high from Sudan, nothing seemed more fitting for my time, my energy, and my experience and training. Nothing in recent memory compared to the joy I felt when I witnessed the reaction of the villagers, mostly women and children, when the fresh, clean water finally erupted from the earth and into to their waiting jerry cans, buckets, or open mouths. I didn't know where to start. I only knew that I wanted more of that feeling, over and over, again and again; I knew that I would never tire of it.

"Dean," I announced solemnly. "We're going to have to gather a lot of money."

"How much?" he asked.

"At least a million dollars, just for starters," I told him.

Dean grinned broadly. "I like the way you think."

I smiled as well. God was restoring my brokenness and giving my life new purpose. I now knew what I had to do, and I was excited for the future. Indeed, I was finding my place in His big story. This lost man felt found again.

> *"And today is all you've got now. And today is all you'll ever have. Don't close your eyes. This is your life, are you who you want to be? This is your life, is it everything you've dreamed that it would be when the world was younger, and you had everything to lose?"*
>
> "*This is Your Life*" by Switchfoot from "The Beautiful Letdown" 2008, Columbia Records ©

Stuck in Baghdad

"How long have I been in this storm? So overwhelmed by the ocean's shapeless form. Water's getting harder to tread. With these waves crashing over my head. If I could just see you everything would be all right. If I'd see you this darkness would turn to light."

"Storm" by Lifehouse, from "Who We Are" 2007, AllMusic ©

The ride to the Baghdad airport was only vaguely familiar, even though I had just arrived in Iraq just a week earlier by the same route. The landscape didn't offer much for a visitor to remember, with its oceans of sand and sparse vegetation, a scruffy thorn tree or two, a sagebrush-like shrub here and there. Then sand, more sand, sand in astounding quantities. True, I had encountered hundreds of miles of sand only six months before while flying over the Sahara on my first trip to Kenya, but that was from a view at 38,000 ft. On the ground, driving through endless sand, the experience was much different. Obviously, Toto, I wasn't in Kansas anymore.

The control tower for the joint Baghdad International Airport/U.S. Airbase soon appeared, and I chuckled at the name. With only three or four airlines—all Middle Eastern—using this airport, the name "Baghdad International" was only technically true. Although, I reflected, more airlines than this must have flown here before the war. This was July 2008, and many changes had blown through the Middle East in the past few years.

As we approached the air terminal, I mused on my arrival the previous week. Talk about a fish out of water! Flying from Dubai into Baghdad on Iraqi Airlines, I was one of the only men attired in the Western standard of long pants and a shirt. Not wanting to be profiled as a peripheral journalist—or a professor, perhaps—I intentionally rejected any notion of shorts. "Good call," I told myself. Incognito was surely the right choice in this environment.

The Baghdad airport was large and modern in an 80's sort of way with its sculpted concrete façade, yet largely out of use due to obvious war damage. Not understanding a word of Arabic, I followed the turbaned crowd to what (I hoped) would be baggage claim; after a moderate walk, we did, in fact, empty out into the vast baggage claim area. Standing around the conveyors, I suspected the baggage handlers were trying to imitate the Chicago O'Hare baggage claim sleepwalkers I had experienced one too many times, as it took an extremely long time before they began sending the luggage out. Only two or three flights land at BIA each day, so this delay could not have been caused by high traffic. I prayed they weren't rifling through my bags for souvenirs and tried to stave off anxiety as I waited alone at this desert airport.

Who would meet me once I walked outside, and where? I had only a name, Abdul Kassab, and no idea what he looked like. I had his phone number, along with an Iridium satellite phone; but beyond that, I knew no country codes or how to place that call. Brilliant, I know. Okay, so I wasn't totally prepared. I can admit that, as well. In a sea of Middle Eastern faces, I felt utterly alone. The longer I stood there, the louder a certain nagging question grew inside me.

Why on earth did I come to Iraq?

Was it the money? I was here to do engineering work, but I was only getting paid my regular engineer's fee, plus a 30% markup for what I called "hazardous duty"; reasonable, but no huge incentive to travel to a dangerous and war-torn country. Was I lacking for overseas travel? Hardly! In just another week, I would fly to Nairobi, Kenya, to meet up with a missionary friend and a mission team of twelve people from the San Antonio area. I had simply decided to leave ten days early to make a "side trip" to Baghdad (perfectly normal, right?).

I took this job in Iraq to help an engineering friend, Jack, who was under contract to Abdul's father's Iraqi construction company, Alemco. Hey, maybe that was it—I just can't say no to a friend. I hadn't been able to say no to Dean six months ago, after all, and traveling to Sudan had changed my life. But no, I knew it was more than that. In my heart of hearts, the real reason beat loud and clear—adventure! I had never served in the military, and this was a chance to experience a post-war rebuilding effort. Here I was, in the capital of a country that we recently crushed in a very short war and were now spending billions of dollars monthly to repair. The fact is, I had jumped at the chance to see for myself what I'd only seen on the news. I doubted I would lack for adventure with such a rare opportunity as this!

The luggage began churning out on the conveyor, and I breathed a sigh of relief. I just couldn't see myself donning one of those sack dress gowns the male passengers were wearing. Grabbing my two large duffle bags and backpack, I now followed the crowd toward what I hoped was the exit. By now, my mind was working overtime, anxious with thoughts. What if no one was waiting for me? All I had was a name Jack had given me before I left. If this "Abdul" didn't show up, I'd be stuck at the starting gate—knowing not a soul in the whole country!

Only a few months prior, Jack had called out of the blue. He needed help reviewing his scheme for a water treatment plant at the international Victory Base Camp (VBC) adjacent to the Baghdad Airport. He was working for the ultimate client, the U.S. Army Corps of Engineers (USACE), who wanted a third-party assessment by a licensed professional engineer. I agreed to help out, then enlisted another engineering friend, Mark, to assist me; in no time, we had our report prepared and submitted. Once this satisfied the USACE, Jack passed on a new request—would one of us be willing to fly to Baghdad to oversee the startup of this system? I quickly let Mark off the hook, insisting that since he was married and I was no longer, I could more readily take the risk. I don't remember him putting up much of a fight.

One strange sidelight to this story of going to Baghdad was that Jack had first brought this project to Mark and me while we were working on another crazy project—eliminating the discharge pollutants into a nearby river at a maze factory in Saltillo, Mexico, of all places. So there we were, running chemical and physical tests at this huge maze factory during the day, and evaluating Jack's design for a water purification plant in Baghdad from our hotel in Saltillo each night. Don't even try to connect those dots, it's simply too random!

It took me several weeks to gather all of my travel documents to send to the USACE director at VBC so that they could issue me a Common Access Card—or CAC card (the military, I learned, has a special love for acronyms). The CAC card gave contractors access to any military base on earth. After my application checked out, the USACE said they would furnish the CAC card to me when I arrived in Baghdad. (And yes, I realize that "CAC card" is redundant, but that's what they call it, I promise you.) All that was left to do now was make flight arrangements to the Middle East.

As it turned out, I had to fly into Dubai first, as only commercial flights from Jordan, Dubai, and Kuwait City could land in Baghdad at this time. To make it even more difficult, these flights could only be arranged in the country of origin; I couldn't just purchase a flight to Baghdad online or even through a travel agent. After suggesting Dubai as the easiest "launch" location into Baghdad, Jack had arranged for one of his foreign partners, Ibrahim, to meet me in Dubai and help me get a flight to Baghdad. I flew direct from Houston—14-1/2 hours, my longest flight up to that point. In Dubai, I met up with Ibrahim, a very nice Iraqi engineer now living in Brussels.

After a drive around this rampantly growing city where I observed a high-rise construction crane on nearly every corner (sending up more than a hundred skyscrapers, I had read), we stopped at a large Dubai mall to drink Starbucks coffee. I asked Ibrahim if he ever planned to return to Iraq. No, he said, it was far too dangerous for him and his family; in fact, he would not even travel there for work. This did not exactly boost my confidence. Still, I was scheduled to leave for Baghdad on Iraqi Airlines at 9:00 the next morning. I even had my hand-written airline ticket ready to go, complete with the carbon copy attached, for the one round-trip flight daily between Dubai and Baghdad.

Although Ibrahim was not able to drive me to the airport the next morning, I was determined to forge ahead confidently. I've traveled lots of times! How hard could it be? I would get to the airport early, I was ready with all my documents, and I was traveling in the service of the U.S. Military. How could it be anything but smooth sailing?

The next morning, as planned, I arrived at the airport well before take-off. After some difficulty navigating the unfamiliar grounds, I finally reached the Iraqi Airlines gate. When I approached the last of several checkpoints, the gentleman asked for my passport and my "Government card." Oh no, I explained airily, I don't have that yet. The U.S. Corps of Engineers would print it once I arrive. He stared at me, unmoved, and informed me that I was supposed to have it to enter Baghdad. My mind raced for an answer. This was not what the USACE had said, but surely they would know this protocol. After a few speechless moments, the guard relented and waved me through. I was relieved, sure that this had merely been a minor glitch. Had I known a "minor glitch" would become a major headache later, would I have stepped so blithely onto that plane? Ah, the 20/20 vision of hindsight! For now, I was glad to be on my way.

The long, winding corridor gave me time for a short but focused discussion with God. Whether missions or my job, I never travel without Him. I asked calmly for His protection, from whatever meant to do me harm, whether I recognized it or not. I felt confident asking Him for this special care, knowing that He is well aware that I sometimes do stupid things (as you may be catching on). I trust that He loves me and looks out for me, and I often sense an extra measure of assurance from God, particularly, and most profoundly, when I most need it. It was precisely that feeling of assurance that helped me step off the plane in Baghdad in confidence and expectation.

All worries of being abandoned dissipated immediately when I emerged from the terminal to see a young (much younger than expected) Iraqi gentleman walking toward me.

He stated my name as a question. "Bub Nicol?"

"That's me," I replied. "How did you ever pick me out of the crowd?" Abdul Kassab, fortunately, had a good grasp of American humor, and he laughed out loud as he shook my hand. I didn't ask, but I imagined he must have watched a few SNL episodes on his satellite TV at the base!

He grabbed my heaviest bag—the antique, without wheels—and led me to his fancy Toyota Helix pickup truck. I was delighted to find that he spoke excellent, easily understood English. I told him that I was surprised to be met by such a young man, since I knew that he is in charge of several very large construction projects throughout this immense base. His company, Alemco, he explained, was originally selected to build many of the roads and parking areas in the base. Upon successful completion of these projects, they were awarded the design-build contracts for a wastewater treatment plant and a water purification plant—the very one that brought me here.

The trip was short, since the huge International base is located immediately adjacent to the airport, and we soon arrived at the gate to the joint forces base. It seemed like an entire battalion was standing guard. A young American soldier stopped us and walked over to the window; glancing inside, he asked us to park and come into the building. Once inside, I was informed that, because I did not yet have my magic CAC card, I would be required to have a military escort whenever I left the Alemco compound where I would be staying. Once the Corps of Engineers issued me the CAC card, I would no longer need an escort. For the first time, I wasn't so sure that I even wanted this card. I was sure I was going to like this escort thing!

In the security building, I presented my passport and was given a visitor badge to wear that showed my expected departure date, approximately two weeks hence, which was intended to be a few days beyond my actual return flight date. Did they know something I didn't? I considered uncomfortably for a brief moment, before snapping back to the present.

I was still only semi-official without my CAC card, but I felt quite a sense of security as I looked around at the number of men with automatic weapons and an obvious abundance of ammunition. But this comfort, too, evaporated unsettlingly as I began to wonder why so much firepower was required. The actual war had long since ended, more than five years prior—hadn't it? Soon, I would discover the truth.

As I thought further about the security, I clearly remembered experiencing the stark difference in military base access after 9-11. Indeed, our own Army Base in San Antonio, Fort Sam Houston (or Fort Sam, as the locals refer to it) had become extremely tight, whereas prior to 9-11, one could simply drive across it—anytime, and through any of its many unsecured gates. Not anymore. My youngest daughter, Jacqueline, played in a soccer league on Fort Sam for many years, pre- and post-9-11, and I served there as a youth soccer referee for several years. Once the war started, we had to get special passes just to get through the now well-guarded gates. As an engineering consultant, I also visited many military installations throughout the country, and I found it so much more difficult and deliberate to gain access to all of them, even as a military contractor. I presumed that the security in a recent war zone would be significantly more robust. Indeed, it seemed to my civilian eyes to be all of that, and then some.

With my now semi-official access granted, Abdul and I headed out across the huge base. We passed mile after mile of "rolling stock," trucks of all shapes and sizes, trailers, tankers, construction equipment, cranes, tanks, and jeeps, both regular and Humvee. We passed large banks of huge diesel generators and tanker trucks by the hundreds. I had never seen so much equipment in one place. What wasn't parked on these enormous lots were being driven all over the (mostly dirt) roads.

I also saw palaces—so many palaces. Saddam Hussein's palaces. They were easy to pick out, since they were, by far, the largest buildings on the complex. All were unique in design, and all ornate. I found them architecturally pleasing, and yet hauntingly creepy, having heard reports of what occurred within at the hands of that sick madman. Our military had found them all abandoned, of course. Not wanting these majestic buildings to go to waste, they immediately co-opted the palaces that that lay within the base perimeter to use as offices and headquarters. I was told that they were, in fact, some of the most ornate and plush office space that our top-ranking military had ever had the pleasure of occupying. Maybe the only thing we can actually thank Saddam for!

One of the palaces had a large crane standing next to it and appeared to still be under construction. Abdul told me that a French contractor was building it when the war began. When the war ended, they asked the U.S. to dismantle and return the crane to them. (You may recall that the French elected not to participate with the Iraqi Freedom Coalition Forces.) It seems the U.S. response to the French was pointed—"If you want your crane, then come and get it." Five years later, there it stood. I guess they didn't really want it!

Abdul then mentioned that Hussein had named this uncompleted palace, 'Victory over America.' "Really?" I asked. "Hussein was crazy enough to believe that this war was going to end in his victory?"

"Yes," Abdul shook his head. "He truly was that crazy."

Among the lavish and appealing palaces, the largest and most majestic was now occupied by the American military command under General Petraeus. It was surrounded by a huge man-made lake and had a heavily decorated arched access bridge from the mainland. Not all the palaces were this impressive, however; in fact, one was even badly "shot up." It had obviously been heavily shelled during the war. Abdul recounted that the Coalition forces had a jolly time banging away at it, long after it was vacated, and well after the war had ended.

After driving for miles within the immense base, we finally arrived at the Alemco encampment. A high cyclone fence surrounded it, and the only access point was through a large, well-guarded gate. Inside were a number of housing trailers, a shower and toilet trailer, a high bay maintenance building, and a lot of roadway construction equipment. We were met by Abdul's right-hand man, Hakim, who was slightly older than Abdul and married, with children. Hakim showed me to my "home" for the next ten days—a squatty 16-foot trailer with one door, one window, a well-used desk and chair, a couch/bed, small refrigerator, TV, and a very noisy but effective window A/C carved clumsily into the end wall.

I dropped my luggage, since Hakim wanted to show me around the complex. One of the trailers housed a small kitchen and dining room. Several of the trailers were chock full of bunk beds; these, I learned, were for the Nepali workers who performed the physical tasks for most contractors. It turns out very few Iraqi citizens perform any manual work on the base, even though they hold most of the work contracts with the U.S. Military. All of the manual work, including the building of the water and sewer plants, is performed by imported, mostly unskilled, Nepalese workers.

The shower and restroom trailer, though minimal, was clean and included flushing toilets. So despite the rather primitive conditions, including having to walk across the compound to use the restroom at all hours of the day and night, I felt safe. I could deal with a lower level of comfort if it included a high fence and an armed guard for protection. (At least they didn't issue *me* a hand gun for protection! I prefer to leave the "carrying" to the professionals.)

After my tour, Hakim dropped me back at my cozy trailer to get settled. Shortly after he left, there was a quick knock at the door, and a young Nepali strode in with his arms full of 1-liter water bottles. He placed all of them into my refrigerator and disappeared out the door. How nice, I thought. They figured I wouldn't be accustomed to the intense heat, and they didn't want to lose me to dehydration! I thought the boy had brought me about a three-day supply of water, but I soon found out this stack of bottles was provided daily, and sometimes twice a day. The bottles were securely wrapped and topped with a tamper-evident cap I was familiar with, both as a consumer and as a water bottling consultant (and a one-time licensed bottling plant operator in the state of Texas). The only real difference was the absence of a label stating its origin. Hmmm. Mystery water. However, in heat that can soar to well over 120 degrees, you don't get snobby about water. I swigged a bottle, and found it to be cold, clean, and satisfying. It would surely do.

I locked up my trailer home (more like a small shipping container, with no wheels, no stairs, and set right on the sand), then headed over to Abdul and Hakim's trailer. It was twice as long and served as a home and office for Abdul, Hakim, and their young, pretty secretary. I was surprised to see a female in this compound and soon discovered that she was also Abdul's girlfriend. She was very pleasant but, alas, spoke almost no English. After a brief introduction, I continued in conversation with my two hosts.

Abdul and Hakim updated me on the status of the installation at the water plant. They were happy I was there, they confessed, as they were stymied with "some issues" with the installation. Actually, their engineers were stymied by much of the equipment that Jack's company had delivered and that they had begun installing in the plant. I would see all of this for myself when they escorted me to the plant for my first walk-through.

Yes, escorted—but only until I was finally furnished with my missing CAC card. I admit, after the Dubai Airport incident, I was growing anxious to have it in hand. At the same time, after meeting my escort, Sargent Joe, I wasn't exactly unhappy to have such a congenial and entertaining person accompanying me! Sargent Joe was in security, which meant that he was the first line of defense for the Iraqi contractors' personnel, including subcontractors like me. He was a well-trained, armed and dangerous soldier, and still only in his mid-30s. Having never been in the military myself, I enjoyed hearing his animated stories from his time on duty as we drove back and forth across the immense desert base.

I remember one story quite vividly, since it took place in another desert environment and involved well drilling. He was stationed in Djibouti, where he was assigned to lead a team of men in drilling a well in the desert. It was a long way from civilization, and when he described it, I was reminded of the wells we drilled in South Sudan. I was curious, unaware that the military ever drilled water wells, except for large military bases like the one that we were on. Most often, they contracted these services out. According to Sargent Joe, they had tried that, but there were no contract drillers anywhere near this location. So the army decided to do it themselves. The description of the jobsite sounded a bit harsher than mine had been in Adoor Village. He said that the temperature would soar to 130-135°F during the heat of the day! The men would have to start drilling after 10 p.m. and stop shortly after daybreak, as the sun was just too hot to work in the heat of the day.

Remote as the location was, they still had neighbors—Bedouins had set up their camp nearby the U.S. Army encampment. Sargent Joe wasn't sure if they were from Djibouti, Eretria, Ethiopia, or even Somalia—most likely Eritreans, he thought. The most dangerous part of the job wasn't even the heat. It was guard duty, particularly during the hours when they weren't drilling, when the soldiers were sleeping, exhausted from a harsh day (night?) of drilling. The Bedouins, they worried, would attack and steal their supplies, as they lived in tents and had to haul in all of their supplies, including food and water for drinking, washing, cooking, and drilling mud. Not only that, it was more than a day's drive to a port, and worse, due to the intense heat and hard work, many of the soldiers would get sick. But in spite of the heat, sicknesses, and threat of attack, they succeeded in drilling the well and finding water. I don't even remember if there had been a point to drilling the well—indeed, it may have been just another one of those harsh army survival training efforts. But hey, the Bedouins had fresh water now, right? And Sargent Joe had survived, along with his platoon, and could now recount this story for me all the way in Baghdad.

We crammed that day with stories, because his escort duty would be coming to a quick end, we believed. He was assigned to take me to the CAC card office at first light the next morning. According to emails I'd received from various Corps of Engineers staff and the head officer, the paperwork was complete and the application had been forwarded to the card-printing station. Ah, to be legal and allowed to come and go as needed! I was anxious to get this CAC card process behind me and begin work without any more unnecessary impediments. I set my trusty travel alarm for 5:30 a.m. and hunkered down in my cramped but cozy couch-bed.

Not long after drifting off to sleep, I was startled awake by the sound of intense gunfire, punctuated with a number of large explosions. I jumped from my couch, crawled to the tiny, dingy window, peeled back the heavy fabric curtain, and squinted into the night. Everything looked much the same as it was on my walk back from the restroom trailer the previous night— the compound bathed in glaring perimeter security lights. There were no vehicles or people in sight. Nothing. Yet the mass gunfire and explosions continued to split the night air for at least fifteen more minutes. Suddenly, all noise stopped and silence settled back in (except for the drone of my noisy window A/C). Wanting badly to find out the cause of this onslaught, but afraid to venture outside—even in the apparent calm that ensued—I decided to wait until morning to ask about it.

As the sun rose in its intense early morning heat, I noticed activity outside my window. Teams of men were loading pickup trucks and trailers in preparation for the work day. Seeing one of the Nepali work crew bosses I had met the day before, I slipped out to ask him about the midnight gunfire and explosions. He smiled, amused at the barely concealed look of terror on my face.

"Just over there," he pointed, "is the base weapons training area. And beyond it is the base landfill. On the edge of the landfill is an unexploded ordinance detonation area where they explode all of the collected UXOs."

"But we're safe here, right?" I had to ask.

"Quite safe," he responded.

"Even from Iraqi soldiers in training, just learning how to shoot?" I returned.

Now I could see him squirm a bit. "Of course," he responded, though somewhat less confidently. I smiled to myself. I knew that the U.S. Army would locate and orient a firing range to provide safe buffer zones, even for those with poor aim. The conversation was a stark reminder, however, that I was still in a war zone, and I needed to be cautious of my surroundings at all times, whether I had someone looking out for me or not.

It was time to head to the CAC card office and secure my new CAC card, which could be used to gain access on almost any military installation anywhere in the world. This should be a simple process at this point, since I was already in the country, ready to assist the military... or so I thought, and so thought Sargent Joe as well.

Not so, soldier. Not when the U.S. Army puts its carefully crafted, super high security plan in motion. You can imagine my shock when the nice lady at CAC Card Central, after asking all the appropriate questions, and after checking with the Major, informed me that, no, I would not be receiving a CAC card. First-time cards, it turns out, can *only* be printed at military installations in the U.S.

"I don't understand," I stammered. "Isn't this CAC Card Central? And what about that guy that just left with a CAC card?"

The Major stepped in. "We only print renewal cards here at CAC Card Central, sir. You should have obtained yours before coming here."

"Well, sir," I replied, getting hot under the collar, "that's a bit difficult now that I'm here, isn't it?" He agreed, but added that Iraqi security at the Dubai Airport should never have let me board without the card.

Now Sargent Joe was upset. "Major, if this concerns a breach of security, then I have to point out, sir, that since the gentleman is standing before you, our combined Iraqi-U.S. military security program appears to be the problem, sir—not Mr. Nicol."

"That does appear to be correct, Sargent" responded the Major. "Indeed, we will have to look into that."

It now looked like I was truly in a bind, and the military was continuing their tough stance. I tried to plead my case. "Major," I reasoned, "I could easily have obtained my card on any of four military bases, all within twenty minutes of my home in San Antonio. The Army Corps of Engineers' Chief sent me an official email directing me to come to *this* office and get my new CAC card."

"Yes," replied the Major. "It seems we will have to get the word out to those who may not be aware of our rules in this regard." He looked at Sargent Joe. "I'll tell you what I will do, Sargent. Seeing as how Mr. Nicol meant no harm to our base operations here—and, as you say, is here on a very critical mission—I will present this as a waiver request to the Base Commander, to see if he will make this one exception. However, I will warn you," he added, "these are rarely granted!"

My hopes sank. I seriously doubted that my waiver request would come up as a pressing concern for General Petraeus (or whomever the Major meant) to fix. Besides, I had heard right before I left the U.S. that a young senator from Illinois was also coming to the base this week to meet The General, since he was running for the very job that would put him in command of The General!

"Hey," I asked Sargent Joe as we left CAC Central, "I wonder if he has a CAC card? Maybe my situation will get my name in front of The General at a strategic time, and perhaps an invitation will shake loose to that big welcome dinner that they always have for visiting 'heads of state' and other important people!"

"I don't know that I would count on that happening, sir," Sargent Joe chuckled at my daydream. "But you never know." (In hindsight, I am certain the reason I never received my invitation to that fancy dinner is because the base mail system does not service 20 ft. shipping container "barracks" within remote Iraqi contractor compounds. Oh well, I didn't have anything to wear anyway, since I had not planned for any formal dinners when I packed. Still, their loss, right?)

"Well, Sargent Joe," I said, "it looks like we're going to be seeing a lot of each other."

"That's fine with me," he said. "And how 'bout you call me Joe?"

"Deal," I said, "as long as you call me Bob from now on. 'Mr. Nicol' is my dad." For the moment, I wasn't too upset about not receiving the card, since I had a constant companion who told great stories, and, no less important, would always be "packing." Who needs a stupid CAC card anyway? I wondered. Let the Army figure it out! I was already here and ready to work!

My new long-term escort and friend, Joe, then drove me around the immense base, pointing out all the military and contractor features. The two things that I most remember marveling at, besides the palaces, were how much surface water was there (in the form of rivers, creeks, and large lakes/lagoons) and how much "rolling stock" was on base. A lot of it was roving, creating mild grid-lock at several four-way stops, but there were also acres and acres of sitting vehicles and fixed equipment, both military and contractor-supplied, I gathered, by their color schemes.

Okay, I get it, the U.S. military believes in stockpiling a lot of equipment on their bases worldwide. You never know when you're going to need a couple hundred water trucks, right? But what I couldn't figure out was, where did all this water come from? I could see that it was not newly formed. It was either natural (if it's somehow natural to have large rivers in the middle of a desert) or the work of Saddam Hussein or another regime. Either way, it was an astounding spectacle, one I never expected to see in Iraq. The palace headquarters for General Petraeus was actually built on a small island, in the corner of a very large manmade lake, the source of which was one of several rivers that ran along the outer boundaries of the base. I later learned that these rivers were to be the source water for the water purification plant that I had come to start up.

I asked why they would not drill wells to use for drinking water, which were typically higher quality than surface water. An Iraqi engineer explained that they had tried, but the groundwater was far too salty to be of any use for drinking water. I found that amazing as well, as I did when I was taken to the water bottling facility on base, which was built and operated by a Qatari contractor. The only size that they appeared to bottle were the 1.5 liter bottles. None of it was sold, but it was merely distributed to anyone who needed it anywhere on the base. It was delivered to my host's compound by the pallet. Outside the bottling plant, thousands of pallets of bottled water sat languidly, the bottles shrink-wrapped to the pallets. Many appeared to be collapsing under their own weight in the intense heat.

Near the end of our base tour, Joe took me by one of the well-guarded entrance gates. He drove out, briefly, to speak to one of the guard chiefs. I noticed that all of the entrances had the Jersey barriers, similar to what they use now in highway construction to close a lane for maintenance or reconstruction. These portable concrete barriers were in a layout I was familiar with, having driven past them on many military bases in the states: they were laid out in a way that caused the driver to have to switchback and at a very slow pace. This, of course, would deter any vehicle from cruising through the gate, bent for trouble.

Joe came back and led me just outside the gate, pointing to a street sign that read "Route Irish."

"Sounds like the road to a good pub…?" I suggested.

"No, Bob," he explained. "This road is only about eight kilometers long and leads right into Baghdad City." He said it was considered the most dangerous road in the world at this time! "So don't," he warned, "let anyone talk you into going into Baghdad—at least not without an entire military convoy, complete with heavy artillery."

I assured him that this was not remotely in my plans.

"I mean it," he insisted. "If anyone, civilian or military, even suggests it – for whatever reason!—you just tell them no. No way, no how! No!"

I wasn't sure why he was telling me this. I already knew that Baghdad was a scary place, and I had no business there. Even so, I promised to remember this and definitely avoid traveling down Route Irish anytime soon. Joe's sternness did leave an impression on me, though, even if only for his significant change in tone when warning me. It showed me how little I truly know about the responsibility of providing security for another person in your charge, particularly in a war zone. I imagined it put tremendous pressure on guys like Joe. I knew that I needed to do my part; I would try to be a model "guardee"—or "subject of interest" (or whatever generic title they assign to the one being protected!).

As we re-entered the base, Joe announced that he was going to take me "downtown."

"Is this a test?" I exclaimed, the good student in me kicking in. "You just told me that I was never to go into downtown Baghdad!"

"Not downtown *Baghdad*," he laughed. "Downtown on the base. It's where the restaurants and banks are located." The thriving epicenter of "downtown" turned out to be a few American junk food joints inside trailers. McDonalds, Dairy Queen, Colonel Sanders Chicken, and a Pizza Hut attracted plenty of customers, both military and civilian. Many sat scattered around the grounds, eating their lunches on picnic tables. Some downtown! I scoffed. To be fair, to a fast food junkie, I'm sure the sight of these American eateries are a pleasant surprise. Personally, I'd almost rather have K-rations! I said "almost."

Early that afternoon, Abdul took me to the water treatment plant. On the way, he stopped by another construction site, the wastewater plant, where Alemco was also the General Contractor. Curious, I asked Abdul how much experience Alemco had in designing and building water and wastewater plants. "None," he told me unabashedly. The U.S. Army Corps of Engineers simply awarded them both of these contracts based on the competence they demonstrated working on several paving projects. I reflected on how I had worked for years pursuing similar contracts with the U.S. military back home for a company whose main line of work was the design and building of water and wastewater treatment plants. I told Abdul that we had had very little success in winning these projects, particularly from USACE. Maybe we should have tried road paving as a sideline!

Nevertheless, as we walked toward a very large metal building, I expressed my excitement for them, and that I was glad to have the opportunity to help them with this project. Abdul expressed his gratitude that I was there, as they were in great need of expert assistance to successfully complete this and the wastewater plant projects. Excited and ready to begin my work, I walked into the building; immediately, my excitement turned to horror. In the vast interior of this massive building, pieces of equipment were haphazardly set in randomly selected places, and a tire-mounted crane was busily setting more pieces of equipment in their designated locations. Having reviewed the plans thoroughly, I could see immediately that there were a number of equipment modules that still needed to be set in place.

I looked around the place, appalled. "Abdul," I asked. "Where is the piping?" It had been ordered, he assured me, but it hadn't yet arrived on the Base.

"And what of the electrical—the cable, conduit, and controls?"

"Same thing," replied Abdul. "Soon they will be here."

"Abdul," I said as calmly as I could. "I'm only planning to be here for seven or eight days. You know that, right?"

"Yes, Bub," he responded, "but we really need your help every day that you are here to help us get ready to start up. The U.S. Army Corps is anxious to get this plant running, to make water."

I pushed aside my shock and assured him that I would help as much as I possibly could. "But without pipe or electrical, there is no way this plant will be ready in a week—maybe not even in a month," I insisted. "It will depend solely upon how soon the missing materials arrive and how quickly your Nepali workers can install them."

Abdul raised his eyebrows, catching on to how far behind the project was. "Can you come back here after you travel to Africa?" he asked. I guess Jack had told him that I was flying direct to Ethiopia and on to Kenya after I left Iraq.

"I suppose that's possible," I responded, "but there will have to be significant progress made this week."

He nodded in agreement. "First things first," he said. "Our engineer needs your assistance. He is having some disagreements with Jack's engineers—the ones in India. Perhaps you can speak with him and then call them after."

"Oh, and Bub," he added, "my father, the president of Alemco, is coming here tomorrow. He wants an honest assessment of our progress from you." I gulped as I envisioned a heavyset man with an enormous sword chasing me around the water treatment building, his belly sweating profusely, and his thick, black beard and dangly gold earring shaking as he yelled at me. Obviously, I had watched too many Three Stooges shows as a kid!

I snapped back to reality. "Ok, Abdul. Now let's go talk to your engineer."

Over the next few days, I spent most of my time on the phone with the engineers from India and with Alemco' engineer on the base. We did eventually work through all of the problems in communication, though the pipe and conduit had yet to arrive. When Abdul's father arrived at the site the next day, I met him at the treatment building. I showed him what needed to be done and admitted that it all hinged on the receipt of the missing pipe and electrical components. He then turned and hollered at Abdul to have all of it delivered by tomorrow. Ha! So much for chasing me around with a big sword! I did get one thing right in my daydream, though—he was a very rotund man, and he did have a beard. Also, he did yell, but thankfully not at me!

As I worked the days away, my gracious Iraqi hosts tried to keep me well fed. They constantly brought me food from "downtown"—burgers, fried chicken, pizza—food I, honestly, rarely ate, even in the States. They quickly observed that I was reaching my limit of fast food. Hakim asked me tentatively, "Would you like to try Iraqi food?" I agreed immediately.

We walked toward the kitchen trailer I vaguely remembered from my first day. It was merely a small, single oven gas stove with four burners, like something from my college days. On the side wall was a tiny refrigerator/freezer next to a sink filled with dirty dishes (also very reminiscent of college living). In the middle of the trailer was a small enamel table, where Abdul's secretary-girlfriend was seated. She immediately arose when we entered the trailer and began washing the dishes. I assumed she was getting ready to cook for us, but when she had washed and dried all of the dishes and cleaned the workspace, she left. That's when Hakim went into high gear, expertly preparing and cooking the food. I can't remember names or ingredients of anything I ate for the next several days. All I know is that it was all quite tasty, some dishes spicy, others not. And a welcome relief from the nonstop glut of fast food!

Abdul and Hakim were thrilled that I enjoyed their cooking, and each strove to outdo the other in delighting me with their culinary talents. This new mealtime gave me the opportunity to engage them in conversation and ask them about living through a war in their own country. When I first learned that I would be living with an Iraqi contractor on Victory Base Camp, I had been eager to hear a firsthand account of the war. And although I was in Iraq to work, deep down I was hoping that I could be used for a higher purpose in this scarred and troubled place.

I didn't know what I, an engineer working with a water plant, could bring as far as "higher purpose," however. At that point, I had only been on one mission trip to South Sudan, just six months prior. But since then, I had been consumed with my new mission to provide clean water for needy people in sub-Saharan Africa. Here in Baghdad, I was getting paid well to set up a water system for people who could more than afford it. What could possibly be my "mission?" That is when I made a deal with God. I would do the engineering work with Alemco at the water treatment plant, but I would stay open to opportunities for Him to use me for another purpose—His purpose.

This became my routine for the next couple of days. I would be driven to the water plant building where I would assist the workers in the equipment installation and then make-ready for operation. When I wasn't with the workers, I'd be on the phone with Jack in Atlanta or one of his engineers in India. Slowly, the equipment installation started to come together. However, the pipe and electrical components did not arrive. As my departure grew closer, I pestered Abdul with our need for these materials—like, *now*. Every day, it was a different story as to why they were not there yet. Eventually, I gave up and stopped asking. It was clear at this point that start-up would not occur anytime soon. When everything was finally ready, I would have to make a return trip from the States.

If I remained in the compound through midday, Hakim or Abdul would invite me over to the kitchen trailer for lunch. And each evening, I enjoyed dinner with them as well. No more fast food for me. Hooray! Indeed, this was quite the opposite of "fast" food—my hosts were never in a hurry to prepare the meals or eat them quickly. Thus, we had hours together to chat and get to know one another better. Sometimes even Sargent Joe, my driver and my protector, would join us.

Usually, Hakim did the cooking, so he and I had the most time together. I asked him the question that had been burning in my mind: what it was like for him and his family during the invasion of his country by my own country and the Coalition? I braced myself for the harsh response but was surprised at his answer. He said it was frightening, of course, for his entire family, but that they were grateful for the invasion.

"You mean you didn't see the Americans as your enemies?" I asked incredulously.

Quite the contrary, he explained; they considered our armed forces as their liberators. "You freed us from the atrocities of a terrible regime, that of Saddam Hussein and his evil family. We were a country of people without hope. Unless you were part of that evil regime, there was no hope for your family. There was no formal education, no chance for advancement, not even opportunities for business. We were all just trying to survive. That is why we, as a country, welcomed the American-led Coalition Forces with open arms."

I mentioned that our news stations constantly decried the mounting number of civilian casualties. He then told me the most astounding thing I have ever heard about this war. He said that yes, the number of civilian casualties *were* increasing. But most of the victims were being killed by other Iraqis—remnants of the Saddam regime—just to make the numbers of civilian casualties look worse! I felt sick to my stomach. "That is simply barbaric," I said. "Who would do that to their fellow countrymen?"

"Animals," he said. "They are scared, heartless animals." With pain in his eyes, he continued. "We are all Iraqis, fellow countrymen, it is true. But we are from different tribes. It's not that Sunnis and Shiites hate one another; we just find it difficult to get along, to share power. The oppressive Sunni rule of Hussein and his predecessors has not helped. And now," he added, "the remnants of that regime have vowed to kill anyone who works for the Coalition Forces. I am afraid to go home for fear that they will discover where I live and kill my wife and children."

I shook my head. "But you are all Muslims, are you not?" I asked. "In my limited knowledge of Islam, the Sunni-Shiite split seems like the differences within our Christian faith. Different groups have different theologies, or ways of interpreting the Bible. We might argue, or split off from one another, but we don't kill each other over our differences. And the only reason we can do that without violence, I believe, is Jesus Christ."

Hakim furrowed his brow. "I have heard of Jesus. But I don't know much about him."

"Okay," I responded. "Here's my best shot at an overview. Christianity teaches, and I firmly believe, that Jesus is the Son of God. Our Bible teaches that he lived as a man on the earth for about thirty-three years. In his last few years, he healed many people, even raising some from the dead. He preached sermons that people crowded to hear about the kingdom of God and about love. He taught that people were to love everyone, even their enemies, and to forgive them for hurting them, or even killing their friends or family members." Hakim looked shocked. I went on. "Jesus said a lot of wonderful things, but more than that, Scripture says he died to take away our sins. He gave us all—you too, my friend—something that we could always believe in and trust to be true. There is no one like him, not then, not ever—not even Muhammad."

Hakim narrowed his eyes. "How do you know that?" he asked.

"Well," I responded carefully, "Muhammad may have done some amazing things, too. I can't say that I know much about him. But I've never heard of him healing people, or raising them from the dead—Jesus did those things, too—or walking on water, calming giant storms, even feeding thousands of people with a couple loaves of bread and a few fish. Besides that," I concluded, "eventually Muhammad died. He has a tomb, right?"

"Of course," said Hakim.

"Well, Jesus doesn't! He was crucified on a cross by the authorities at the time, the Romans. But unlike the Prophet Muhammad, Jesus didn't stay dead. He came back to life after three days, just as our Bible predicted hundreds of years earlier, and hundreds of eyewitnesses saw him. Then he rose into heaven, where he still lives today with his dad—God."

"How can you know that is true?" Hakim asked.

"It's all there in the Bible," I said. "You can read it for yourself—in English or Arabic, or any one of hundreds of other languages."

I could tell that this had been a lot for my new friend to swallow. I let the conversation move on to other topics, like food or life in America (which people all over the world always ask me about). I sensed that I needed to move out of the way for a while and let the Holy Spirit work.

I had planted the seed. I knew that God would water and tend, and in time—His time—He would make that seed grow.

Hakim and Abdul invited me to lunch every day, and we continued to have hot meals and lively conversation. They truly seemed to revel in my enjoyment of their culinary talents. Now that the "religious" ice had been broken, they asked more questions about "this Jesus of mine." I was learning that Hakim was more of a practicing Muslim than Abdul, and he seemed most affected by our conversations. Abdul, I sensed, had other things on his mind, but he relied greatly on Hakim; perhaps he would ask Hakim more about it once I was gone.

All too soon, my time in Iraq came to a close, and I began to make plans for my departure. On the night before I was to leave, the three of us enjoyed a wonderfully tasty fish dinner. Hakim seemed quieter than usual. Finally, he spoke up.

"So. I'm not saying that I am ready to accept your Jesus for myself. Not yet, at least. But I have to say, your presentation of him causes me to want to know more." He looked at me intently. "I can tell you that I am not at all happy or content with Islam. It leaves me cold, and I find no comfort in its teachings. But," he added, "you must know that converting to Christianity can have serious repercussions within the Muslim community." He leaned back in his chair. "However, I must admit, I like everything that you have told us about Jesus. And we can see that he has had a very positive effect on you."

As we finished our meal, I thought about what Hakim said. I was surprised by his observation. I wasn't aware that I had presented all that much of a Christ-like demeanor! The Holy Spirit must have caused my friends to see something of "Christ within me." I glowed inside with joy at the compliment, pleased to have been used in any way to show the light of Jesus to others. What wonderful affirmation here at the end of my trip, evidence that God had used me for His higher purpose, just as I'd asked! My work here, for now it seemed, was done.

Abdul helped me make plans for my transport back to the airport in the morning, arranging both a vehicle and driver, and an escort, which included Sargent Joe and Diendi, the leader of the Nepali workers in the Alemco camp, to my great delight. Diendi was my constant driver and escort on my trips to the water plant. I had even persuaded him to drive me around for a closer look at some of the palaces, especially the U.S.

military headquarters palace. I know this made him extremely anxious, especially when I asked him to stop so that I could snag photos with my Nikon camera and new telephoto lens (a pricey toy I had justified buying at the mall in Dubai for the once-in-a-lifetime African safari I'd soon be enjoying in Kenya).

The morning I was scheduled to leave, Joe arrived early and Diendi helped me with my luggage. I decided to leave one of my bags and some work clothes, as I figured I would not need all of them in Kenya. I was certain that I would be returning in a short time to complete the system startup. My goodbyes to Hakim and Abdul were more like "see you soon," as we all assumed I would be back in less than sixty days.

We slammed the trunk shut and drove away from the compound. After a brief stop at the perimeter gate to turn in my visitor badge and sign out, we started out on the ten-minute drive, sailing through the endless stretch of sand I had not gotten used to.

So here I have finally arrived, back to where I originally started this ever-expanding story. This should all soon be over, right? Yeah!

As the control tower for Baghdad International Airport came into view, Sergeant Joe told me he and Diendi would accompany me through the check-in process as far as possible. I was relieved to hear this; in the back of my mind, I kept thinking about my missing CAC card. By a fluke, I had been let into Iraq; now would they let me out?

Few passengers dotted the terminal at first, but as I moved further along, a crowd started to build. I was glad we had gotten there early, and I pressed on through the initial checkpoints and the baggage x-rays. At this point, the airport personnel stopped my escorts from coming any further. I said goodbye to Joe and Diendi—again with promises that I would see them soon—then headed off with the other travelers. I remember looking back somewhat anxiously as they disappeared behind a wall heading toward the terminal exit.

I fidgeted with my flight ticket, the old-fashioned handwritten ticket with a carbon copy. The date, flight number, and time were legible, and I matched it to what I read on the (scant) departure list hanging on the wall. I felt reassured and handed the ticket to the attendant. She found it all in order, verified my name with my passport, and handed me a boarding pass. It's going to be fine! I cheered silently.

When I stepped up to the passport check, the gentleman there perused my passport and asked for my CAC card without even looking up. Obviously, he could tell that I was not military. "Oh, I don't have one yet, you see." I launched into the sordid details, but he was unimpressed. He summoned his manager over to his booth, explaining the situation to him. His manager asked me for my CAC card. I repeated my story, more urgently. He politely allowed me to finish and then, just as politely, informed me that I should never have been allowed into the country without the card. Now, he explained, I could not leave without the card.

"That's just the problem," I explained, sure that reason would win the day. "The head of the U.S. Core of Engineers assured me that I could get this card here, at the Base. That turned out not to be the case. They've even asked the General for a waiver to print my card since I was already here and all of my papers were in order. After all," I emphasized, "I was here at the special request of the U.S. Army. Unfortunately, the waiver request was denied. But I'm sure you can understand, after all of this, I'm just trying to go home so that I may finally obtain this card and return in a few weeks."

Unfortunately, reason would not have a place in the win column this day. In short order, they escorted me back to luggage drop-off, retrieved my bag, and handed it back to me. Then they escorted me out of the gate check-in area and left me there, alone in a strange country.

Now what was I going to do? Sergeant Joe and Diendi had long since left the airport, and I did not know how to contact them anyway. I had no idea how to get back to VBC on my own, and I couldn't just grab a cab like I could do anywhere else in the world—even in developing countries like Kenya, for heaven's sake!

I suddenly remembered that Ibrahim had given me Abdul's cell number before he left me in Dubai. I glanced at my satellite phone. I would need a clear path to the roving satellites in the sky, so I would have to look for an exit from the terminal and then try to place a call. I dug up Abdul's number, then located an exit that looked relatively safe (like I could tell the difference). I began dialing the satellite phone, but was stuck when I couldn't figure out the country code. With each try, I heard the dreaded computer message asking me to please try again. I tried not to panic as I tried every number combination I could think of. Finally, an airport employee saw me struggling and asked me, in pretty good English, if he could help me. I told him what had happened, and he offered to call the number for me on his cell phone. I thanked the Lord for this guardian angel.

Abdul could not believe his ears. "Bub," he said, "Go back inside the terminal and wait for me. I will come and get you as soon as possible."

"Okay," I said, "but how will you find me?" I tried to describe for him the gate that I was now at. If he would drive up to this gate, I would stay inside and watch for him. He agreed to try, but warned me not to come out until I saw him give a hand signal. I'm not sure what all this was about, but I complied, because I did want to get away from this terminal in the same condition that I arrived.

I found a bench with a view of the gate, and I sat to wait for Abdul, dejectedly. I was supposed to be on a plane right now to Dubai, and then on to Addis Ababa, the capital of Ethiopia. I was scheduled to meet up with CrossWay's Ethiopian Field Director, Melaku, when I landed. I had his number, but I had no idea how to call him. He would be waiting at the airport for hours for my plane to arrive, and I wouldn't even be there. I didn't know, as I do now, that he actually wouldn't even be allowed inside the terminal to wait, since visitors are forced to wait in a parking lot far from the terminal entrance. It was best I didn't know this at the time. I felt bad enough for Melaku, who I had not even met yet, and bad for me, who would be letting him down through no fault of my own.

The terminal was quite void of travelers while I waited. The eerie emptiness was vastly different from any airport I had flown out of in the States, or even the few I had experienced in other countries. Then again, none of them had been recovering from a war. At this time, only Iraqi Airways, Royal Jordanian Airlines, and a handful of smaller commercial airlines would risk flying into Baghdad. No U.S. or European-based airline would attempt it for a few more years. I didn't even recognize the names listed on the Departure/Arrival Board, other than the two nationals. Hence, not much activity in this ghost town of a terminal. In the undisturbed quiet, my gloomy thoughts seemed amplified.

It's no stretch to observe that when one is in a situation in which one has absolutely no control, it is easy to start feeling sorry for oneself. The "why is this happening to me?" syndrome, I like to call it. Indeed, I did not feel at all responsible for my predicament. The U.S. Army, for crying out loud, were the ones that brought me here. Did they really not care if their failure to understand the rules of conduct and operation for this base, as they were, would not permit me to be here without proper documents? Was I, civilian engineer Bob, supposed to know that I needed this magical entrance ticket in order to come help them achieve their purpose? No, the answer was simple. They had messed up, not me. And now I was having to deal with their failure. Did they even care?

Knowing the short trip between the airport and the Alemco compound, I expected Abdul to arrive in less than a half hour, even allowing for high traffic on base and backup at the gate. After more than forty-five minutes had passed, my anxiety flared up again. I remembered Hakim's story of sneaking home under cover of darkness to protect himself and his family from harm, even murder. "Just a statistic," he would say, but the danger was still apparent. I thought further of the numbers of innocent Iraqi men, women, and children, who had no part in the Hussein regime other than to fear it, forced to endure a blitzkrieg war right in their own neighborhoods. While this didn't relieve my situation, it did give me some perspective and stop my worry. I even felt a bit embarrassed for entertaining such fear. Surely, my situation was unfortunate, but dangerous? I think not.

After more than an hour, Abdul's shiny Helix pulled up outside the terminal doors. I waited for him to emerge or signal; instead, Sargent Joe and Major Elizabeth Jenkins, my USACE main point of contact, both jumped out of the truck in full assault gear. Both were, quite obviously, carrying. Maybe I was wrong about this situation being low danger level! I cleared the doorway of the terminal and started to walk toward them, but they ordered me to stop and wait. I complied, glancing around to observe any obvious danger—like I would know! Then again, I thought with absurd bravado, of course I would! I imagined Jason Bourne swooping down from the airport superstructure and annihilating any would-be assailants without so much as a sound. I'm all over this!

My fantasy continued as I prepared for them to tell me to zig-zag erratically enroute to the truck, then drop and roll before entering the back seat in a tight crouch. My muscles tightened, ready for the maneuver, but instead, they each grabbed one of my bags and one of my arms, and together we walked, closely and swiftly, to the door of the truck, where they essentially shoved me into the back seat. As Abdul pulled away, Major Johnson observed my confusion over this strange extrication.

"Bob," she shook her head. "We are so sorry for all of the trouble you are going through because of this messy CAC card thing." I nodded, but what I really wanted to know was, why all the drama? "This is simply Army protocol," she explained. "The airport, unfortunately, is considered unsafe."

"Unsafe?" I asked, glancing at Abdul.

"Yes," she replied. "Abdul could have picked you up as he did a week ago. But our commander, the Colonel, demanded that I come here personally, with Sargent Joe, our security officer, in accordance with Army protocol. We are trained to be prepared for the worst-case scenario."

I glanced at her weapon and grinned. "Well, Major, thank you for coming to get me. I am very impressed, I have to tell you. I have worked with quite a number of Corp Engineers in my career, both men and women, but I have never seen any of them don assault gear and holster a weapon. You guys scared me a bit back there! But, I have to admit, you also made it a lot more exciting for me."

Major Johnson smiled, relieved that I was in good humor. "You're welcome, Bob. Now, Abdul will take you back to his compound, and Joe will be over a bit later to bring you back to headquarters. I have one of our guys working on alternative plans to fly you out of here."

As we drove to USACE headquarters, I told my rescuers the entire ordeal at the airport, in as much detail as I could remember. Then Abdul drove us back to his compound, where Hakim and Diendi were waiting at his office. I recounted the whole episode for the three of them, realizing that each time I told it, it seemed even more bizarre and surreal to me. I understood the facts of the matter, the security that was necessarily put in place by both the American forces and the Iraqi government. But surely waivers had been granted in the past. And I obviously wasn't a threat to anyone! So why couldn't they just look away and let me go through security?

On top of all that, there was no paperwork that traced anywhere, so no one was held accountable. I truly believed that it was causing more of a mess for everyone, Iraqi security included, to be detaining me here than if they'd just relent and let me go. But no, I would not be getting out of Iraq the easy way. I knew that now. There must be another reason for this, I concluded. One on a much higher plane. Maybe, just maybe, the real purpose for extending my time here in Baghdad was because of some "unfinished business" with Hakim and Abdul.

Later that day, Sargent Joe escorted me to Major Johnson's office. She had been looking at options to help me get past the Iraqi passport checkpoint, and she admitted that the best way to do that was, naturally, to obtain a CAC card. "Unfortunately," she sighed, "we've been down that road, and that's not going to happen."

She then introduced me to a civilian employee on her staff, a structural engineering specialist named Ivan. Ivan had made a number of flights out of BIA over the last two years, prompting Major Johnson to ask for his help. I shook his hand, and we sat down. Ivan told us that we had two options. The first was to return for the same flight tomorrow. "But this time," he said, "have some cash ready to bribe the passport checker. A hundred U.S. dollars should do it."

I shifted uncomfortably. "What's my other option?" I asked.

"Gryphon Airlines," he said. "They fly civilian and military personnel from the military side of BIA. And unlike Iraqi Airways, you can purchase flight tickets online." However, he explained, they only flew several times a week, and only direct from BIA to Kuwait City.

"Okay," I nodded, hopeful with this new plan. "I'll see if I can get a connecting flight from Kuwait City to Kenya."

Ivan offered to drive me to the airport if I got a ticket lined up. Major Johnson asked me to keep her informed. "If it turns out that you have to stay here for a day or two longer, I could use some help with some options that we're looking at for that water plant you're working on."

I told her I'd be glad to help; then I went back to my trailer house and got online. Ivan was right; Gryphon only flew into BIA twice a week, on Wednesdays and Sundays around 8 p.m. Since it was now Monday, I would try to arrange a flight for this coming Wednesday evening. Interestingly, I discovered that the airline was in a partnership with U.S.-based United Airlines, which gave me some degree of comfort. It turns out United was striving to become the first Western airline to offer commercial flights to BIA, once the U.S. military declared it to be safe again.

It took me most of the day, but I finally secured a seat on the flight. I called Major Johnson and told her I had about two and a half days available to help her. She apologized again for my delay but eagerly asked if I would stop by her office to look at options for the water plant. I said I would get Abdul to drive me over so that he could participate in the discussion. "After all," I said, "he is the one that has a contract with you."

I spent the next few days assisting Major Johnson with her idea to expand the capacity of the water treatment plant. While not part of my assignment, it did give me something to focus my mind on while I waited to get out of Baghdad. Jack and Abdul, too, were excited for the opportunity to increase their scope (and, naturally, their fees).

As before, I was graciously invited to mealtimes with Abdul and Hakim. We continued to chat endlessly on all our usual topics. When we would exhaust our discussion on life in Iraq—something that I never tired of hearing about—the pendulum would swing to their myriad questions about life in America: what was it like growing up in America? Going to school? All schools, elementary to university? What were the cities like? The farms? The countryside? Like me, they had some insight into life in America from watching world news like BBC or CNN.

I confessed that CNN was our only real source of knowledge about life in Iraq as well, and that we Americans watched the entire U.S. invasion of Iraq right in our homes on our TV sets. It had reminded me of past wars that came to life on our TVs, like Beirut, Lebanon, and more recently, the West Bank, Gaza Strip, and in the oil fields of Kuwait. But none of these, in my view, remotely compared to the onslaught by the U.S.-led forces on their country, particularly on Baghdad. While most Americans supported the takedown of Saddam Hussein, the war was brutal, and I told them how frightened I had felt for the people of Iraq. However, after the troops routed the Iraqi forces, we watched the destruction of the giant statue of Hussein in downtown Baghdad by that American tank—to the utter glee of the large Iraqi crowd witnessing it firsthand. If I'd ever doubted our need to join this fight, all uncertainty vanished at that moment. Smiles lit up their faces. "We, too, enjoyed that moment, Bub."

My days working with Major Johnson and my nights enjoying the company of my Iraqi friends quickly came to an end. It was time, at last, to plan my "escape." I met with Engineer Ivan, who informed me that, for this flight, we would not even enter the commercial BIA. Instead, we would drive to the parallel runway side, which was controlled by the U.S. Air Force, and park in a lot next to the tarmac. He would accompany me right up to the plane, where I would show my passport and E-ticket information. I could bring a small carry-on bag, which they would carefully check at the plane, and my luggage would be dropped by the plane stairway where it would be taken to screening and loaded onto the plane. "Wow!" I laughed nervously. "That all sounds too easy!" Though I was smiling, I felt a certain uneasy feeling at the same moment and almost wished that I had not said it. I didn't know why at the time, but I would soon find out!

Ivan asked me to return to Corps headquarters at 1730 to make the 2030 flight. Although the airport was nearby, I was relieved to have plenty of time to make this flight. Diendi offered to drive me to headquarters; he and I had become quite familiar, as he drove me across the base to the water plant several times a day. He supervised all the Nepali laborers in the compound who worked for Alemco, and had actually recruited them and arranged for their transport from Nepal.

I asked Diendi what brought all of them so far and to such a dangerous place to work? He told me that there was almost no work in Kathmandu, his hometown. He and his men had enjoyed steady work here at the base for more than two years. Did he ever return home to Nepal? No, he admitted, he would not leave for fear of losing his job. He would only leave after the job was complete and they had no more work for him. For now, they were just thankful to have steady income. I was shocked to discover that these "attractive, steady wages" amounted to $1,000 USD per month, and that was for working six 10-hour days a week. I wouldn't tell him, when he asked, that I was making much, much more than that in my short trip to Iraq. I couldn't imagine having to leave your family for years just to scrape out a living to support them. I felt a new gratitude for the steady work opportunities I enjoyed back home.

He also asked me what I could tell was a burning question, one he'd saved for last: would I help him get to America and find a job? I felt terrible having to tell him no, but I reminded him that it would take him even further away from his family, which I couldn't bear. I also tried to buoy his spirit a bit by telling him how important he was to Abdul and Hakim—they had told me so more than once. He seemed genuinely glad to hear that.

Diendi handed me off to Ivan, who was waiting for me in the parking lot at USACE headquarters. I said goodbye to Diendi, yet again (I seemed to be doing that a lot lately), and we headed off. On the way to the airport, Ivan said he wanted to stop "downtown" for a quick dinner. Feeling a bit at his mercy, I didn't protest, although I had enjoyed avoiding fast food for the past week. We grabbed a burger and fries and found an empty picnic table under the shade of a few scraggly trees. While Ivan devoured his food, I asked him if he was concerned about the time. "I don't have to tell you that I really don't want to miss this plane," I said nervously.

"Don't worry, Bob," he assured me. "This won't take any time at all." I figured he knew, with all of his previous flight experience with Gryphon, so I relaxed while he finished his burger. I barely touched mine.

We jumped back in the truck and headed out from this center of the base towards the "airport" on the perimeter (hardly more than a runway). It was getting dark, and I tried not to display my growing concern. I didn't recognize anything on this route, though I could see the control tower off in the distance. Soon, we came to a checkpoint. My old fears returned as I thought about my lack of a CAC card.

"You don't think I'll have a problem with checking in, do you, Ivan?" I asked.

"Umm…I don't think so," he responded. This did not exactly buoy my confidence, I must confess.

My question was answered fairly quickly. As soon as we handed the guard-soldier our documents, he looked at Ivan's very quickly, and then at mine. Then he asked the question I was really starting to hate.

"Where is your CAC card?"

This time, Ivan launched into the familiar explanation, but the soldier quickly cut him off. He directed us to drive to a distant building to our left, park, and wait. "We will have to conduct a complete search before we can let you into the airport," he said.

"What airport?" I wanted to yell in frustration. "It's just a runway, for crying out loud! Just let me run away already!" But I controlled my mounting impatience.

Another soldier met us at the second building, which was a drive-thru, not unlike the drive-thru beer stores we have in Texas. He promised someone would arrive soon to search us. I consoled myself with the fact that the Gryphon Airways plane had not yet arrived, so I estimated that I should still have a full forty minutes to get through this snafu, park back at the lot, and then walk across the runway to the plane. I had read online that the walk to the plane was pretty long—over a quarter of a mile. Still, with this frenzied energy coursing through my veins, I was sure I could book it pretty quickly. If only the inspector felt the same urgency to book it to the search station…

The "short" wait for someone to come and search us stretched to ten, fifteen, then twenty minutes. Meanwhile, the Gryphon plane—MY plane—landed. Sitting helplessly on the bench in the drive-thru, I imagined the passengers deplaning and receiving instructions on claiming their luggage, since there was no baggage claim. No terminal, for that matter, and we couldn't even see the runway from inside the inspection building. I could only try to picture it in my head. Just then, I flashed back to an earlier vision I'd had of Ivan and me sitting in the parking lot watching the plane land. Things were not exactly going the way I had expected.

Finally, two soldiers arrived, one male and one female. I felt a glimmer of hope that we could still catch the plane. But once the soldiers started their search, all hope flamed out. They began by sending Ivan and me to separate rooms and, no joke, ordered us to strip down to our shorts! Next, we handed our clothes through a small window so a guard could check our clothes thoroughly. Then the male soldier did a thorough pat down—everything short of a cavity search. Finally, we were allowed to dress and come out to the truck. I had assumed by now they had searched my bags and the truck as well. Not so, Kemosabe. They had not even started. Ivan and I had to remove our bags from the truck ourselves, and then one by one they began slowly piecing through them.

At this point, I heard the plane's engines restart, and I knew it was over. I would not be in Kuwait City tonight. Still, when they finally released us, Ivan drove us like crazy out of the beer stand, raced to the parking lot, and we grabbed my bags and ran. We found a tent on the edge of the tarmac with tables inside and a whole crowd of people waiting for bags in the makeshift baggage claim. These passengers had just flown in from Kuwait City on My Plane—the plane that was at this moment flying swiftly back to where it had come from. Ivan and I turned away miserably and headed back to the truck.

On the drive back to the base, Ivan apologized for stopping for dinner. "No, Ivan," I sighed. "I can't let you take the blame for this.

You had no way of knowing that the CAC card would cause us such a huge delay. And if the Army had even a halfway responsible inspection program, I still could have easily made it. I mean, c'mon—they have two commercial flights a *week* to deal with! No, this is not your fault, my friend. This is just one more example of either a poor process or horrible implementation. Either way, this is all on the Army, once again. They have caused me untold problems ever since I landed at VBC."

"Well," Ivan stated, "you will be my guest tonight in the new Corps dorm. That's the least I can do. Besides, it's too late to take you back to the compound anyway."

We drove the rest of the way in weary silence, and by the time we reached the dorms, it was almost 10:00 PM—er, 2200! I had never been outside the compound after dark. As late as it was, the whole base seemed to be buzzing. Tons of military vehicles clogged the roads.

"Something is brewing," Ivan said. "This is not ordinary traffic."

We lugged my bags up to Ivan's room on the third floor. The entire dorm had been newly built and was very comfortable; it reminded me of my college dorm, only much nicer. I set my bags on the floor as Ivan ducked into his refrigerator. "Now for a treat, after all you've been through." He pulled out orange juice. He then uncovered a bottle of contraband. Vodka!

"Where did you get that?" I grinned. "Or maybe I should ask, *how* did you get that?" Ivan just stared at me. "Forget it," I said. "I don't really want to know." We both laughed.

He grabbed a couple of tall glasses, filled them with ice, and prepared our drink treats. We took the stairway up to the roof, where Ivan had a couple of cheap folding lounge chairs. From the roof of the three-story building, I could take in a great view of this portion of the base. I walked around the edge and surveyed the action below, amazed by what was happening right outside the dorm. The traffic we had seen earlier had formed itself into a long convoy on the main road leading towards the gate. Humvees, assault vehicles, even tanks were lined up, and helicopters buzzed overhead.

"What's going on?" I asked Ivan.

"Looks like a major convoy is deploying to one of the other upcountry cities," he responded.

"Does this happen a lot?"

"Yeah, but usually not this big. This must be in response to the escalating fighting over there." After several hours of mobilizing, we watched as they moved out. What an impressive display of force, I thought. And I got to watch it all from our rooftop perch.

At the same time, I observed what looked like fireworks way off in the distance and at various points in most of my 360° view. "What are all those explosions?" I asked.

Ivan squinted. "That's the enemy lobbing mortar shells over our perimeter fence. Most of the explosions that you see are our anti-ballistics, shooting down their mortars before they reach the ground." We watched as several more explosions went off.

"Man," I said, "that's a lot of mortars."

"Not sure why they do it," he mused. "Seems like a huge waste of resources to me."

Finally, after the convoy had moved out and the perimeter mortar explosions had subsided for the night, Ivan and I retreated to his comfy dorm room. As I prepared for bed, I thought of a question Ivan had asked me earlier, why I had opted to stay in the Iraqi contractor's compound. "You could have a room up here like most of the consultants that come and go. There are always plenty of extra rooms available, and way more comfortable than the compound."

"These dorm rooms are nicer," I had to admit. "But my place is fine. And the food is excellent."

"Really?" he asked. "Where do they get their ingredients?"

"I don't know, but Abdul and Hakim bring it in fresh from the outside and cook it up for me every night. All kinds of Iraqi specialties, different menu every meal."

"Wow. They must really like you. I've never heard of that happening before."

"Well, I like them, too. They're really great people. And they're trying real hard to do a good job for you guys."

Ivan nodded. "My associates have told me the same thing. I have not worked with them personally."

I was glad to hear the Corps thought highly of my friends. I felt a new gratitude that I had been assigned to the compound and gotten the chance to befriend these Iraqis that I could have easily missed getting to know.

By the next morning, the Corps folks were well aware that I was still on base. Abdul picked me up and drove me to headquarters, and Major Johnson greeted me immediately, apologizing once again for the CAC card debacle.

"I'm guessing that you don't want to stick around for the next Gryphon flight on Sunday, right?" she asked.

"Yes, Major, you're absolutely right on that," I responded.

"I've got someone on my staff working to get you the absolute next possible flight on Iraqi airlines," she assured me. "However, this time, it may require—"

She broke off. I filled in the blanks. "Ma'am, at this point I'm willing to try anything," I said.

"Obviously," she stated quickly, "I can't officially instruct you to use bribery." She glanced around and added, "If you plan to do it, though, you should probably get Ivan's help."

As we waited for Ivan to arrive to help plan what would be my *third* attempt at an escape, Abdul apologized, too, for my ongoing struggle to depart from VBC. "I want to help make this next attempt your final one. So please, I want to give you as much money as you need—to cover all costs, and to cover the Gryphon Airways flight that you missed, plus any extra spending money that you might need. I hope that your experience here will not keep you from returning again, soon. We really value your assistance."

"Thank you, Abdul," I responded. "I appreciate your offer. And I do plan to return to Iraq. I promise you, though, my friend, I will get a CAC card as soon as I return to Texas!"

Ivan arrived at the office, and I asked if he was still willing to drive me to the airport. "Sure," he said. "I feel confident that I can get you – by the other method that we discussed earlier. With my credentials, I will be able to take you right up to the passport booth and even talk to the checker there."

While we were discussing the details of this plan, Major Johnson came in with the news that they were able to book a flight for me. "The flight leaves tomorrow at 1100. I'll get you the information, but you'll have to go online and finish booking."

Confident in our new escape plan, I thanked everyone and smiled. "Now, since I have yet another full day here, Abdul and I will get back to work with Jack on the treatment plant expansion equipment costing." I turned to Major Johnson. "Hopefully, we will have some answers for you before I leave."

"That would be great," she responded. "Thank you so much for doing this."

"It's no problem. Ivan and I have already worked out the plan for tomorrow."

"I sure hope this plan works. I'd hate for you to have to stay 'til Sunday and take that next Gryphon flight."

"Me too, ma'am," I replied. "I'm already several days late to meeting up with my mission team in Kenya."

Major Johnson sighed. "I am truly sorry about that, Bob," she responded. "I want you to know I really appreciate your attitude and your calmness in dealing with this whole crazy issue. You have every right to be upset with us and with this situation, none of which is of your making. And I'm sure you are. But you don't show it."

"Well, thank you, Major. But I see no benefit in getting upset, as it won't help my situation. And I know you're trying everything to help me get out of here. Hopefully this will work!"

My mind's vivid imagination kicked in just then, conjuring up scenarios involving my next confrontation with the Iraqi passport/CAC card watchdogs. Having Ivan there with me as I tried, yet again, to explain my sad CAC card story could only help, I thought. Then I forced myself to stop thinking about it and focus on the work at hand. For another day, I was still "on the clock."

I stayed busy with phone calls and emails to Jack in the U.S. and his engineers in India. I felt confident that I could give Major Johnson a detailed scope and budget for her requested expansion scenario, especially when the costing pieces began arriving. I would be able to present her with specifications, at least, accompanied by our "best guess" first estimate. The plan then called for Jack to follow up with the Corps within a few days with a detailed cost estimate. Happy to be busy, the day passed quickly by. Before long, Hakim was summoning me to dinner.

As I strode happily off to dinner, I had the feeling that this would be my last meal (for this trip, at least) with my new friends, Abdul and Hakim, and that the next day's flight would be my "escape" from Iraq.

But then again, I had felt that same confidence at least twice before—and here I was, still in Iraq.

While I was excited to finally catch up with the mission team in Kenya, I felt a strange ambivalence. Where in the world is that coming from? I wondered. Was there yet more work to be done here in Iraq? For days, I had spent every idle hour thinking, dreaming even, of finally getting out of here. But I also hadn't been able to escape thoughts of the purpose of this extended time. Was all of this just an unlucky chain of events? Or did God want to extend my stay here for His purpose? Were there, perhaps, more seeds to be cast in this rocky soil of a place? Could I be used to somehow make the ground more fertile? What would that look like? Good questions, I thought, but none of which I had earthly answers for. Maybe that's the point, I thought. Earthly answers don't exist in this strange, inexplicable delay! "So just be open, Bob," I told myself. "Put on your listening ears and speak as little as possible. Answer their questions as best you can, and let God do the rest."

That evening, Hakim did most of the talking and asked me a lot of questions. He was struggling with his understanding of Allah, God, and his purpose in life. The Muslim faith seemed to have no answers for these major questions in his soul. Abdul was listening quietly, but I could sense that seeds had been planted, and fertilizer was being applied. I felt certain that God was working greatly in this situation. I don't remember the meal we had that night, but it had to have been tasty. Indeed, what meal had I enjoyed with my new Iraqi friends that was not?

At last, the day of my escape dawned bright and early. I straightened up my little trailer home, grabbed my travel pack, which had remained unopened for the last few days, and headed to Abdul and Hakim's office trailer to wait for Ivan. He arrived shortly after, and there was a bittersweet departure scene with me and my friends. While I stopped just short of the familiar Arabic dual cheek kiss, I did hug them both heartily, and we exchanged firm handshakes as we said our goodbyes. Today was the day, we all sensed strongly, that I would indeed escape. "It's not goodbye," I called out as Ivan and I walked to the truck. "As God allows, it is only 'see you soon!'" They waved to me one last time, and we were off.

Ivan and I drove out of the base gate for what was my third time in four days. I could tell that some of the gate guards were beginning to wonder about my comings and goings! We left the gate area and got onto the highway leading to the airport, and Ivan decided to rattle me slightly with a strange comment.

"You know, Bob," he said, "as soon as we left that gate, we're no longer within the protected area of the base." Surely I had known that was the case, but no one had ever said it out loud. "Also," he went on, "this all-white truck with the bright red Corps of Engineers' insignia on the doors...well, Bob, it may as well be a target!"

I felt vaguely nauseous. "You mean there could be some enemy lurking out here that would shoot at us or blow up this truck?"

"I'm not saying they would, but they could!"

"But why?" I argued. "We're not military."

"Doesn't matter," Ivan said. "To the Sunni Arabs, we are the enemy! They might feel good about taking out a couple of Americans."

I flashed back to all those mortars that we watched our ever-vigilant military shooting down around the distant perimeter just two nights prior. All of a sudden, that fireworks-like display didn't seem so cool anymore. Truly, any one of those mortars could take out this truck and blow us up with it—serious explosives meant to kill, maim, and destroy military personnel and property. I was instantly reminded of John 10:10: "The enemy comes only to steal, to kill, and to destroy." (John 10:10, NIV) This was enemy territory. No, I was not a soldier, and neither was Ivan. But in this violent land, we were still considered a target. Who knows what blowing up a truck and taking out two engineers might do for the enemy's confidence?

Ivan and I didn't talk for the rest of the trip to the airport, but it did seem that he accelerated just a bit after that. For my part, without being too obvious, I began to scour the landscape for anything that moved or looked out of the ordinary.

My ominous thoughts retreated somewhat as we pulled up to the airport, but I wouldn't be at ease until I was safe inside. Wanting to put as much real estate between myself and the "targeted" pickup truck, I moved with surprising swiftness, considering my bulky load. I didn't care to look back (surely they wouldn't shoot an unarmed man in the back!), even though I knew that I had left Ivan seriously in my wake. After reaching the terminal doors, I finally stole a glance back at Ivan. "It's okay, Bob, the enemy can't get us here," he laughed. "There's no way they can get this close to the terminal." Had I been that obvious? I thought sheepishly.

When your mind is on alert for "who knows what," it can create a world of tension, even when danger may not actually exist. I, however, was not ready to talk down that wildly uncontrollable portion of my brain just yet. Nothing against Ivan—he was nice enough and very helpful. But he was no Sargent Joe, and more importantly—he wasn't pack'n! But here we were, both safely inside the airport now. It's funny, I thought, this building that only a few days ago felt so scary just turned into my safe haven.

Now it was on to the next mission—get me on board the next Iraqi Airways plane heading for Dubai! Ugh. My excitement evaporated as I envisioned approaching the passport check without the magical Get-Out-Of-Jail-Free CAC card. I couldn't bear the thought of being refused one more time. I knew that I could, of course, with God's grace. I was just really hoping God's grace would let me pass on through this time!

I tried to run over my plan in an effort to gain my bearings. Let's see. Bribing 101. How should I act? What should I say? How and when is best to present the money? Was $100 enough? Too much? The more nagging question was why did Ivan and I have to be the ones to figure this out? "Shouldn't the military have a procedure for this?" I asked, irritated. "They certainly have procedures for everything else."

"Oh, come on Bob," Ivan chuckled. "This is the Corps of Engineers, not the CIA. We're just a couple of knucklehead engineering contractors, not soldiers of fortune!"

Still, I was certain that the military most likely did have procedures for these kinds of situations. They're simply on a need-to-know basis, and I suspected I didn't exactly fit in that category. Thus, it was up to me and Ivan to navigate these uncharted waters. I felt so uncomfortable in the world of "espionage!" Maybe I should have checked YouTube for a "how to" video on successfully bribing your local Iraqi Airport security. Too late now. I was going to need to depend on Ivan's direction to cover my utter lack of knowledge.

At least we had some time for focused planning, as I was early for my flight, and there were still very few passengers in the terminal. We found a table and chairs just outside the check-in area and strategized for my, I hoped, final escape attempt.

"What do I do if the guy finds the money and looks at me?" I asked nervously.

"Well, we don't want him to do that," said Ivan. "What I'm hoping for, and what I suspect he will do, is just pocket the money and stamp your passport. I haven't tried it myself, but I know guys that have, and with good success." I shifted uncomfortably in my chair. "Don't worry," he assured me. "I'll be standing right beside you, and if there's any trouble, I'll pull out my contractor ID." He winked at me mischievously. "Due to a lucky mistake, I am designated as the equivalent of high ranking military."

"Well," I conceded. "I guess this is the best we got at this point."

With the plan in place and my confidence somewhat boosted, we headed off to start the clearance processing. As before, I passed smoothly through all initial checkpoints. Then, ticket in hand, I took a breath and stepped into the line at the passport check kiosk. This time, at least, I had a friend by my side. I felt much more at ease as I compared it to my last attempt, in which Diendi and Sargent Joe could not accompany me.

As we waited, I suddenly panicked about leaving the hundred-dollar bill in the passport pages. I slipped it out of my passport and into my upper shirt pocket. Then I surreptitiously showed Ivan what I was planning to do and whispered to him to signal when he saw a good opportunity to slip the agent the cash. He nodded.

Just then, we were summoned forward by the man in the passport booth. We approached the glass-enclosed booth with a single Iraqi security agent inside. Ivan began speaking to him as he pulled out his high-level CAC card. Before he could show the man the card, another security guard appeared out of nowhere and grabbed Ivan by the arm, forcing him away from the booth and from me.

I suddenly felt defenseless, and the next moments happened in a blur. The security agent barely looked at my passport before asking to see my CAC card. I looked desperately for Ivan, who was trying to make his way back to where I was standing. I could hear him explaining furiously to his security guard that he, a representative of the United States Army, was responsible for getting me on this flight.

"Sir," the agent in the booth repeated to me. "Your CAC card."

Before I could answer him, Ivan rushed to the booth, security agent in tow. Now four of us stood tensely around the booth, Ivan and I, one agent outside of the booth, the other inside. Ivan was talking a mile a minute, flashing his high-level CAC card, but I could see that these agents were having none of it. The faster he talked, the louder they shouted that I could not board the plane without my card. At a distance, I could see two security guards begin to press toward us—and they were packing! Ivan's security agent met them halfway, speaking in heated Arabic, and then the officers made a beeline for us. I knew now that this third attempt, too, was over. In very broken "Engl-abic", they informed me that I would now be escorted out of the check point area.

Ivan was still arguing with the passport checker, telling him he'd be in big trouble with the U.S. Base Command for not getting me on this plane. But by now the guards with the holstered guns were pushing us away from the booth and towards the exit. Not only was this exit attempt a failure, it was the most aggressive I had encountered yet. Ivan and I trudged towards the terminal exit where we had only recently entered. It may as well have been miles long. We were both shaken and upset, he even more so than me.

"What in the world is going on?" I fumed silently. Everyone involved in this debacle kept saying the same thing—that I had done absolutely nothing wrong. But that hadn't stopped this madness from happening. I knew it wasn't my fault, and I was certain that the Corps of Engineers had nothing against me. Certainly the "military at large" was not running a secret mission to keep me in Iraq, since I had nothing of value to offer them. Why couldn't I get out of Iraq? The only conclusion I could draw was that it must be God's mysterious purpose. Whether it was for my sake, or the benefit of my new Iraqi friends, I had no answers. But then, who can understand God's ways?

Yes, even in the midst of my frustration, I still clung to the belief, in my heart of hearts, that it would all somehow work out for good. I knew I could trust the Scripture that says, "God makes all things work together for the good for those who love him." (Romans 8:28, NIV*)* I knew, too, that I had to fight the feeling of self-pity or being "put upon." Perhaps God was using my predicament to reach others somehow. I needed to quit worrying about my own well-being and be willing to let God work.

As I began to encourage myself, I even felt honored—honored that God would choose me to participate in His higher purpose. I didn't know if I'd see Abdul or Hakim again, or even how I would finally get out of this country. All I could do now was hope...and pray.

Still in a daze, we plodded the long distance back to the white Corps truck and buckled up in silence. Instead of going back to the base, however, Ivan took a sharp turn past the airport, rounded a rusty junkyard-like fence, and pulled up outside a dilapidated group of trailers and converted shipping containers. He explained to me that this was a cheap hotel where foreign workers would stay while waiting to get work on the base. "Believe it or not," he said as we got out of the truck, "we can actually get a decent meal here. And best of all—cold beer!" My spirits lifted. Hey, if I couldn't leave Iraq, at least I could get some hot food and cold brewskies to take the edge off!

We walked into a restaurant made of several mobile trailers fused together, with their wheels removed. The place looked empty except for a bartender. "Let's have two cold beers and a couple of menus for me and my friend," Ivan hollered as we made our way to an empty table. As we sat down, I suddenly noticed a gentleman sitting alone at nearby table, talking on a cell phone.

Two cold bottles of beer arrived at our table, and Ivan and I began to relax. He told me I was smart to have removed the bribe from the passport. There had been no opportunity to present it, and he was sure that, had we tried, the man would have pocketed the money and ignored me—or worse, had me arrested! I could tell he was struggling with the failure of the bribery deal, and he admitted that he really needed more details from people that had actually succeeded in pulling this off. I didn't know if I felt worse for myself, that I was still stuck here, or for Ivan, whom I knew was feeling dismal about failing to get me out of Iraq one more time. I told him, of course, that I didn't blame him, but his discouragement lingered as he swigged his beer.

While we enjoyed our cold beers and food in relative silence, we listened to the phone conversation of the gentleman sitting alone. His accent was obviously American, and I noticed a company name on his polo shirt that I had seen on a number of helicopters at the airport. I pointed this out to Ivan, and when the man finally finished his conversation, he noticed us looking at him. He waved in acknowledgment, and Ivan invited him to join us.

Randy, it turned out, was the president of a transport company that was moving goods and people around the country. As Ivan and I finished our meals, he dazzled us with stories about his company's work. We wondered how safe it was for his helicopters to be moving about the country, but he assured us that the military kept a good watch on them and provided armed escorts whenever they deemed it necessary.

After another round of beers, just as I was resigning myself to remaining in Iraq a few more days, Ivan surprised me with his sudden question to Randy.

"I wonder if you could help my friend get out of here?"

He told Randy about our three failed attempts to get me out of Iraq, including the debacle we'd just encountered. To my utter astonishment, our new friend responded, "Let me see what I can do."

He pulled out his phone and quickly dialed a familiar number, excusing himself from the table. Ivan and I stared at each other in amazement. In no time, he returned to our table and said, "I'm just waiting on a call back from my airbase manager. He's going to look into finding a flight and get back to me."

Ivan raised his eyebrows. "You mean today?"

"Yes," Randy replied, quickly becoming my new *best* friend. "This is my very best man whom I trust with the most important tasks that we receive. He literally knows everybody at the airport, as well as many of the officers at the base. If he can't get you out, then no one can." I'm sure I had a smile as wide as the moon at that point.

Randy's phone rang, and Ivan and I held our breath. After a brief exchange, he covered the mouthpiece and looked at me. "Do you have cash for an airline ticket?" he asked me.

My heart beat faster. "Depends on how much it is," I replied.

He got back on the phone, then said, "About $600?" Relief flooded through me.

"Yes," I said. "I have the cash."

"Okay," Randy said, pocketing his phone. "It's settled. We'll meet my guy at the airport in thirty minutes. He will escort you right through check-in and passport." I shook my head in shock, certain that I was dreaming. Somebody pinch me! Could this really be my ticket out of Iraq at last?

We continued chatting for a while, but I barely heard a word. My thoughts were far away, in Mombasa, Kenya, where I would soon join my associates on their initial African visit. I really didn't know any of them well, since none of them attended my church. Several of the youth were classmates of my daughters, however, and I had grown to know them better as we had prepared for the trip over the past several months. I knew by now they were well into the mission work, and I was aching to join them. Not only that, but the thought of jumping waves in the Indian Ocean, after enduring the miles of sand and dusty heat of Baghdad, made my head swim with delight. I knew I'd still have to pass through Dubai and spend one more night before heading on to Kenya, but even that couldn't quench my enthusiasm. I was finally leaving!

Finally, we headed to the pickup truck, and Randy instructed us to follow him to the airport. For the first time, I had not one thought of my missing CAC card. I thanked God for His timing, His favor, and for sending me an angel in the form of Randy and his connections. When we arrived at the airport, our "two vehicle convoy" was waved right on through to a private parking area and nearby entrance gate. This time, there would be no ducking and running to the entrance door, no sir! Ivan grabbed my heavy travel bag, leaving me with only my light backpack, and I felt like skipping to the door. I did manage to restrain myself, however, so as not to embarrass my friends.

A quiet and imposing gentleman approached us, and Randy introduced us to "his best man," Vingali. An Iraqi businessman before the war, Vingali now worked for Randy's company. After we had exchanged introductions, Randy shook my hand and told me that Vingali would now see me safely onto a plane leaving Iraq.

"How can I ever repay you?" I asked.

Randy waved his hand. "No need. I'm always glad to help a fellow American, especially one who's been traumatized like you've been. I hope that the rest of your journey is much smoother."

Ivan now said his last goodbye, too, but he was uneasy and apologetic. "Ivan," I assured him, "I blame you for none of my departure problems. Without your help today, who knows, I might have been detained by the Iraqi airport police. Your request to Randy for help has turned into a minor miracle for me. And I'll never forget your hospitality, watching that impressive military convoy buildup and the 'fireworks' from the dorm roof. I have nothing but gratitude for you, my new engineering friend."

Ivan looked relieved. "Well, you are very welcome, Bob. And I hope to see you again. Not on this visit, of course!" he laughed. "But when you return—with your new CAC card."

I laughed, too. "Ah, the elusive CAC card! I just might send you a picture of it when I finally get back to San Antonio."

"I'll be looking for it!" he said, and he turned to leave. Vingali grabbed my travel bag and we headed off down that familiar terminal corridor, one more time—hopefully, I prayed, the last. As gregarious as Randy had been, Vingali was quite the opposite. He was all business. I was fine with that, as I had little capacity for small talk at this point.

My mind was engaged elsewhere at this point, taking two simultaneous paths: On the one hand, I was dreaming of being airborne over Iraq, with Baghdad disappearing below. On the other, my thoughts were wrapped up in wonderment over why this had all happened. What was God trying to tell me in all these crazy events? I still didn't know for sure. One thing I did know for certain—I had not once been harmed during the entire trip. Any danger I might have faced may only have been the result of an overactive imagination, surely enhanced by all of the warnings I'd been given. Still, why the great difficulty in getting out?

I was still mulling over this mystery as "Vin" guided me through the now too-familiar airport checkout process. All of a sudden, there it was—the passport kiosk—looming before me. My first instinct was to turn tail and run. However, I suppressed that knee-jerk reaction and waited for Vin to take charge. I wondered if he'd shoot his way through, or wrestle some agents to the floor, but instead he quietly escorted me well away from the passport booth to a vacant wooden bench. Then he asked me to give him my passport and wait. Normally, I would never have turned over my passport to a near-stranger, unless they were seated in a passport check booth or airport police station. But I was so confident that Randy and Vin had been angels sent by God to lead me on my Exodus out of Iraq that I gladly handed Vin my passport and slumped onto the bench with my luggage.

I watched him walk away, calm and controlled. I noticed, for the first time, that he had (purposely, no doubt) led me far enough away from the passport booth that I could no longer see it. Thus, I was free from worrying about passports, CAC cards, or even flying out of there. In my newfound relaxation, I allowed myself a smile, even, as I took in my new surroundings. A mom, alone, with two young children, pushing an overloaded luggage cart, an older, poorly dressed man gesturing wildly in heated Arabic to a younger, more polished-looking "businessman"—his son, perhaps. I noticed a middle-aged Eastern couple staring in bewilderment at the Departure screen. I wondered how many of these people would be on my flight. Look at me, I thought in amusement, already this had become "my flight!"

Panic suddenly gripped me as I realized I didn't even know which airline I was flying. And where was Vin? Was it supposed to take this long? True, he hadn't been gone *that* long, but fear began to rise up in me again. Right then, I closed my eyes and prayed to a God who always listens, no matter how insignificant our request. "God," I whispered, "you brought me here to this place, at this time, and in a most unusual route. And now it seems I am finally about to leave. I enjoyed my time with Hakim and Abdul, and I leave them in your capable hands. I know that you'll guide me back here if there is more for me to do. But right now, Lord, I would really (*really*) like to join my team in Kenya. After all," I reminded Him helpfully, "We're there to do your work, to assist 'the least of these,' and to spread your Gospel message. I know those are important things. Will you please, please, get me on whatever plane it is that will carry me away? Today, if possible? I would be ever so grateful. You'll see. Thanks. In Jesus' name, amen."

Confidence returned. I looked for the arrival/departure screens. Those were quite sparse, so it was easy to find my flight to Dubai, UAE. Only one left on this day, since my original flight on Iraqi Airlines left hours ago. A direct flight on Jupiter Airlines. Never heard of 'em. However, by now I'm ready to fly on "Flying Carpets Airways!" Anyway, if I've never heard of them, that means that they don't have a crash record. If they did, I'd know about them, right? Things are looking good!

At that moment, Vin appeared at my side and said simply, "Let's go. It's all set."

"What? Just like that?" I asked in bewilderment as I got up to follow him toward the dreaded passport kiosk. He assured me that he did not do anything illegal or was not required to pay any sort of bribe, which he also indicated, would not have worked. "Ha! I was right about that, at least," I silently whispered to myself. "All I really had to do," he told me, "was to find the person in charge and tell them your story. Once I did that, there were no problems getting your passport approved without the CAC Card."

This time, we didn't even stop.

"I have already cleared your passport," he said over his shoulder. Too stunned to speak, I simply followed my new guide in silence. As we walked past the kiosk, I stole a glance at the passport checker. Sure enough, it was my "friend" from earlier. I broke out in a sweat, certain that he was going to pop out of his booth and grab me! Instead, to my utter amazement, he looked up and smiled with a knowing nod of his head. This Vingali—he's got these guys eating out of his hand, I thought. I really, really like this guy.

Next, we passed the two thugs with the guns, who looked expressionlessly at me, as if they hadn't roughly thrown me out only hours before. At the ticket counter, Vin handed the Jupiter Airlines operator my passport and my ticket. She checked it, handed me my ticket receipt, my boarding pass, and my passport, all with a smile. I grinned back like the Cheshire Cat, trying my hardest not to burst out laughing. I remembered that Randy told me it would happen just this way back at the restaurant. But after my previous attempts, you have to know I still had my doubts! I'm leaving! I thought exultantly. It's really happening. They can't stop me now!

Vin directed me to a nearby lounge and handed me my backpack. "The flight will begin loading in thirty minutes," he said. My head immediately flooded with joy and disbelief. Was I dreaming? I shook my head back and forth. I just knew in a moment I would wake up, back in my little trailer in the Iraqi Contractor's compound.

Vin extended his hand and told me goodbye and good luck; I smiled broadly and shook his hand exuberantly. "Thank you for everything, Vin," I said. "I really am amazed how you made this happen – and thrilled." I'm actually leaving. I can't believe it."

He nodded his head in his calm, stately way. "It was nothing," he said. "You just have to know the right people – and help them to understand that there is really nothing illegal that we are doing."

"I guess so! And I'm glad that I now know you and Randy. You guys are awesome. Who knows, I may be back again soon. But under no circumstances will I return without a CAC card. That will be my first priority upon returning to the U.S."

"Yes," he said, as he walked away. "That should save you from any future trouble with entry or departures."

"I certainly hope so," I wanted to shout back to him. But I did not want to draw ANY attention upon myself.

Just like that I was alone at the airport. This time, I felt no fear. I had my stamped passport and my boarding pass, and it matched the information I read on the marquee over the gate counter. My mind raced ahead to my arrival in Dubai. I would have another layover before flying direct to Nairobi, Kenya, the next morning. There would be no Ibrahim to greet me this time; I would be on my own. I felt a little nervous, but I also knew that the God who had brought me this far would see me on to my next journey.

At last, they announced that the plane was loading. I joined the line and happily brandished my boarding pass to the airline attendant, who welcomed me aboard, wishing me a nice flight. "Thank you!" I beamed. "I'm sure it will be." Then, dream of all dreams, I walked out of the gate and climbed the stairway into my plane. I found my seat by the window and settled in. Before long, pre-check was complete, and they announced that the cabin doors were closing. The engines roared to life. As we taxied to the runway, the sky was growing dark, and we lifted off to meet the approaching evening.

A peace and a joy beyond words flooded my soul, and I thanked God for finally delivering me out of Iraq. I thanked Him specifically for Randy and Vin, and Ivan, too, who had been my heroes—my angels—that day. As we ascended, I stared out the window at the VBC below. The base looked enormous, stretching out for miles in every direction. I could make out the well-lit roadways and many of the buildings, including the palaces. The lights were bright and dazzling in the dark of night. By contrast, I could hardly see the city of Baghdad, which was barely lit at all. I remembered reading that the city was still trying to rebuild the power plants that had been bombed during the war. I looked back at the bright lights of the military base that had been my home for the last week and a half, and I prayed for all the friends who would still be there tomorrow morning, continuing their lives and their work in Iraq. I prayed especially for my new Iraqi friends, Abdul and Hakim, that they might continue in their questioning of their Muslim religion, and in considering this "new Jesus." Then, surprising myself, I prayed that I would return to Iraq one day. Despite the ordeal I had faced, I sensed that my work there was not quite done.

As I finished the last of my prayers, I began to doze off. The quiet hum of the plane and the weariness of the week's events lulled me into blissful unconsciousness. Dreams of the happy reunion with our mission team and of far-off coastal Kenya carried me away to blissful sleep without a care in the world. I knew when I awoke, I would carry on, refreshed and ready for my next adventure.

> *"Why are you striving these days? Why are you trying to earn grace? Why are you crying, let me lift up your face, just don't turn away. Why are you looking for love? Why are you still searching, as if I'm not enough? To where will you go child, tell me where will you run?"*
>
> "*By Your Side*" by Tenth Avenue North, from "Over and Underneath", 2008, AllMusic ©

The Motorcycle Diaries

"I'm falling apart, I'm barely breathing, with a broken heart that's still beating. In the pain is there healing? In your name I find meaning.... I'm hangin' on another day, just to see what you will throw my way. And I'm hanging on to the words you say. You said that I will be OK."

"Broken" by Lifehouse, from "Who We Are", 2007, Geffen Records ©

DAY 1:

Welcome back to Kenya, Bob. Land of challenges and unexpected puzzles to solve. For example, how do you propose to get around this massive fallen tree in the middle of a mud-packed path flanked by deep lakes of water on either side? Years of engineering have not prepared me for this particular quandary!

These were the thoughts going through my head today as I naively set out for the school. This is only my third trip to the tiny community of Mtepeni, just up the coast and inland somewhat from Mombasa, Kenya. I have never driven there myself, and now here I was, driving, of all things, a motorcycle. When Emanuel (nice Christian guy who leased me the bike) handed me the keys today, it dawned on me that I have not ridden a motorcycle in over twenty-five years. Not only that, but Kenya is right now in the height of the coastal rainy season! Up until I faced this tree, I had managed to avoid the slick streets and the crazy, kamikaze lorry and *matatu* (van taxi) drivers in town, as well as the giant lake-like water hazards that consume entire roads in this wet world. But my luck had run out. I was totally unprepared for the unique barricade I found myself facing—a massive felled tree covering the entire road out here in the "bush."

I was already struggling to navigate the strange terrain—not quite jungle, but certainly not city-like or even rural—while maintaining my balance on the unwieldy machine. I had managed to avoid sliding or tipping over, though I had come close several times. Also, no surprise here, I was lost. Oh well. While I may not be exactly sure where I was, at least I could say with confidence that I was not going in circles—this was the first time I had encountered this giant tree. Now how to get around it…

As you may recall from my last story, I was here in Kenya just fifteen months ago for the first time with a mission team from San Antonio. We had a great bus driver who shuttled us everywhere, so I didn't pay much attention to directions. My second trip to Mtepeni was by myself about nine months later, and I hired a driver with his own car to take me to and from my hotel. I was there to assist the community in extending electricity to the church from about one quarter mile away, and I only needed to travel there three or four times to complete that job. However, this trip is quite different. I am overseeing the digging of a water well at a school in Mtepeni, and I need to check in every day for more than a week. The cost of a car and driver was too much for my budget this time.

I considered using public transportation, but it would have required a combination of taxis, a 14-passenger *matatu*, and a motorcycle taxi. The degree of difficulty that this posed, along with questions of security, kept me looking for options. I was finally left with two choices: rent a car or rent a motorcycle.

My problem with renting a car wasn't the cost—it would be more expensive than public transportation but still within my budget. No, the problem was slightly more daunting for me. You see, Kenya was once an English colony and in fact only gained its independence in 1963. Because of the British influence, all vehicular traffic in Kenya is identical to that of Great Britain: that is, they drive on the left side, while the steering wheel is located on the right side. I could just see myself getting totally disoriented and pulling out into the wrong lane and into oncoming traffic! I wasn't too keen on paying for damaged vehicles for them and broken body parts for myself.

I easily chose the motorcycle. However, I didn't count on slipping and sliding through the rainy season, nor encountering massive fallen trees along the way. Somebody forgot to mention these hazards to me. I'm not sure who to blame, though, so back to simply dealing with it.

Anyway, my dilemma of the day was figuring out how to get around this huge tree without tipping over. In the dry season, I could simply drive around it, but with the incessant rain, the adjoining field that I would have taken was now a swamp. If I tipped the bike over, the engine would certainly flood; then, not only would I be lost, I'd be pushing a motorcycle! The threat of this made me search intently for a solution.

While I pondered, my mind drifted back to that old tree-trimming gang that worked with me one Christmas break during college. I was a one-man survey crew with the assignment of pioneering an electric powerline right-of-way through a forest in Northeast Pennsylvania. Once I had set up my transit and identified the direction to proceed, the crew would deftly cut down everything in the way, whether small bush or gigantic tree. Out came the chainsaws, and in minutes I had a clear path to set my right-of-way stakes. I so wanted those guys with me today!

In lieu of having my Dream Team, I consulted the more practical (and smaller, I suspect) part of my brain, and forced myself to attend to the matter at hand. I decided to brave the adjoining field after all, since it was the shortest route available, and meet back at the road beyond. Although there was the threat of getting stuck in the "lake," this really seemed to be my best option.

I tightened my backpack straps and set off with both feet extended to assist in balancing. That turned out to be a very smart move. More than once the bike nearly tipped over, and on one occasion, I even felt it start to slide out from under me on the slick mud below the water line. If I hadn't quickly set both feet on the ground and cut the engine, I would have gone over for sure.

During this tenuous journey, I sent up a number of "emergency prayers." The kind that consist of two words: "Lord, help!" I didn't have the time or focus to pray more than that, but I figured He knew what I needed in this predicament.

He did, I'm happy to report, see me past this giant tree, through the swamp, and back onto the muddy road again. Then I was back to the lower threat level of merely being lost. My new plan was to find a friend to guide me. There was just one problem—I wasn't even sure where to tell someone that I was going! I knew that the community was called Mtepeni, but I wasn't sure exactly where it was in relationship to the church and fledgling Christian school where I'd be spending most of my time. Just then, I remembered visiting the local Mtepeni Primary School on my last visit here. If I could find my way to that school, I felt certain that I could then find my way to the church. Okay then, I would ask for directions to the Mtepeni Primary School! Now I just needed to find a human being.

The first person I encountered was an elderly gentleman. Middle-aged and older men and women living in the bush, speak very little, if any, English. Fortunately, I did seem to get him to understand "Mtepeni Primary School," and I got enough from him to determine that I was generally headed the right way. At least I didn't have to turn around and go back to the fallen tree.

I drove off in the general direction that he had pointed, and I continued to look for someone a bit younger who might give me more specific directions. I happened upon two young boys, who, when I asked them for directions to the public school, pointed in opposite directions. I thanked them and left them arguing with each other as I drove away. Finally, I came upon a teenage girl. She seemed to understand me well enough and gave me promising directions, including turns and landmarks to look for. "*Asante sana*," I told her, using one of my few Kiswahili terms ("Thank you very much"). She smiled broadly and answered with the familiar multi-use word, "*karibu*" ("welcome").

Thankfully, I started to recognize some familiar landmarks, and sure enough, the girl's directions finally brought me right to the Mtepeni Primary School! Hooray! Now I could rely on my memory to find my way from here to the church. In less time than I expected, I zoomed along the muddy roadway, deftly circumventing all the large puddles, until I arrived at a familiar site—the MBEWAU church and school near Mtepeni. My muscles finally relaxed—I made it!

I entered the school ground and drove up to the familiar large mango tree in the courtyard. The church elders heard me drive up and scurried over to meet me. My two very special friends, Jackson and Justin, whom I had come to know quite well from my two previous trips, were the first to arrive, followed by Pastor Nzarro and another young man, Titus. One by one, they greeted me with the familiar kiss to each cheek and hearty hug which I had come to know as their show of warm friendship. (Once you get over the discomfort of that strange first encounter, believe me, you begin to look forward to the experience. Westerners, I believe, could stand to let down our guard more often and experience the joy of friendly contact, beyond that of an arms-length handshake. Maybe the world could more easily receive us as "*rafiki*"—friends and companions. Wouldn't that be novel?)

I hugged my friends with equal warmth, flooded with excitement and relief at having arrived here in one piece. They were surprised to see me on a motorcycle, and when I tried to explain to them the route that I had taken to come here, they were amazed at my success. "I know," I said with a hearty laugh. "You'll have to give me better directions for my return trip."

While we were still gathered under the mango tree, I heard a loud engine noise and looked across the soccer field at an unexpected sight. There was some sort of large contraption attached to what sounded like a diesel engine with a high tripod on the end. The entire machine was engulfed in a huge plume of blue-grey smoke. I turned back to my friends slowly.

"Is that the drilling rig?" I asked hesitantly.

"Yes, Bob, that's it," came the response, followed by an eruption of laughter. "They have been pounding away for several days now."

"Well, how deep are they at this point?"

"About 12 feet, they estimated," came the answer.

"Oh brother!" I thought. "I guess that's what I get for going with the 'low bid.'" Looked like one more challenge I'd be facing here in Kenya.

I had been in negotiations with a local well driller for the past several months. Unfortunately, my first choice was a company that I didn't feel certain I could trust. They were insistent on drilling deep, while I had been advised by my hired pump system contractor to drill no more than 40 meters deep this close to the coast. Anything deeper, they warned, could lead to saline water. The first company continued to insist on drilling 70 to 80 meters, so I was forced to look for other options. That's when I found Earthcore Drillers. Their price per meter was less than the first guy, and they would drill to whatever depth I specified. More than that, I liked their positive and responsive attitude in our email exchanges. Today, it seemed I was about to find out if they were truly up to the job.

After the reunion under the mango tree dispersed, I wandered over to see this curious machine. What I saw, quite frankly, appalled me. I will now attempt to describe to you the scene that is still embedded in technicolor in my mind's eye.

There was a steel platform lying on the ground with a diesel engine perched on one end. The weighted drilling platform was elevated on the opposite end and there were two large belts, each more than 6 feet long, one connected to the engine's turning spindle, and the second one from a dual pulley where the first belt ends, transferring the circular motion up an incline and connected to the drill platform pulley.

Now, that second large belt transfers the motion from the first pulley to a gear box below the drill platform, thus causing the rotation of the drill pipe into the ground. At the lower end of the drill pipe is a cylinder with cutting "teeth" in the end, to "chew" through the earth, creating the well borehole. This cylinder, which was around 4 feet long, would fill with dirt and mud from drilling. So the operator would regularly have to winch the pipes back up and dislodge the dirt and mud from the cylinder.

Also, there was a 15-foot high tripod that came to an apex directly above the drill platform. This tripod supported a pulley at the apex, which contained the wire rope used to winch the drill pipe up and down the borehole using a hand crank.

The whole process would begin with the operator hand cranking the diesel engine (that's right, hand crank!), which eventually started the engine, albeit after much "coughing and wheezing" and the expulsion of a significant cloud of blue-grey smoke that engulfed the entire contraption and its two-man crew. While the operator was crank-starting the engine, a helper would stand by with the upper end of the inclined belt until it would just start to run on its own, then deftly push it onto the upper spindle to transfer the rotation to the gear box under the drill platform. Then, as he was completely obscured by the smoke, he would climb up onto the drill platform and stand on a small plate, barely large enough to contain his bare feet. Unbelievably, between his feet and legs ran the rotating drill pipe! I guess they wanted to take advantage of his 150 pounds or so to help drive the rotating cylinder at the bottom of the drill pipe further into the ground! I cannot begin to count the number of OSHA guidelines this rigging utterly trampled upon.

Oh, did I mention the fuel tank? It was a gallon cooking oil container mounted on top of a stick, stuck in the ground behind the engine, with a dangling plastic hose connected to the engine. Gotta love African engineering! Simple yet effective.

As I was watching their progress plod along—maybe an inch every half hour—they would stop the engine and begin winching the drill pipes up out of the borehole. These drill pipes were just 10-foot sections of 1-1/2" galvanized pipe, threaded together. Thus, for every 10 feet of depth reached, they would have to unscrew the pipe using pipe wrenches, two of only four or five hand tools that they had available. Obviously, the deeper they drilled, the longer it took to get the pipe out of the borehole and back into it.

When the drilling got slow, they would winch the pipes to the surface to retrieve the cylinder drill bit. After removing all the stones, mud, and soil inside the cylinder pipe, they would cut new teeth into the end of the pipe using a hand hacksaw. The frequency of having to cut new teeth depended on how hard the soil or soft the stone was. This process increasingly worked against them, as the shorter the drill pipe became, the more often they would have to stop and winch it all back to the surface. Not only that, but the deeper they dug, the more pipes had to be added as they went down and removed as they pulled the drill bit back up.

In fact, over the next few days of drilling, I would witness this cylinder drill bit whittle down until it was less than 2 1/2 feet long. Needless to say, this was an agonizingly slow process. In the process I began to admire these two hard-working young men more and more. Indeed, they seemed undaunted, not only by the hard labor, but also by the rains that poured at least once a day, followed by long periods of intense sun and heat. While I would often seek shelter from the rain, I only recall them stopping twice during the ten days that I observed them. And both times, the rainfall was torrential. However, as soon as it would slow down, but well before it stopped, I would hear the diesel engine cranking up once again. Cough, cough, sputter, bang, sputter... here comes another cloud of dark smoke, and a thin young Kenyan, dressed only in his slacks and a T-shirt, emerges from the smoke cloud, perched on his tiny platform, trying his best to make himself heavier than 150-odd pounds to increase the downward drill force of the heavy steel drilling platform. On and on this went, day in, day out. Never mind that they had very primitive equipment and almost no hand tools to work with, nor any sort of protective clothing. They were being paid to do a job—to drill our borehole—and they would not stop until it was complete.

So what was I doing, you ask, while this drilling process was trudging along? Well, originally I was closely monitoring their progress on an hour-by-hour basis. But this simply became too tedious for me to continue. Being an American used to more sophisticated drilling apparatus, I found it exceedingly difficult to stay focused on this peculiar drilling process once the novelty of it wore off.

Fortunately, school was in session, so there were about fifty kindergarteners around today. Some of them remembered me from my two previous trips, and the rest warmed up to me when they saw their friends playing with me. I was quite a novelty for them. As I sat on a bench under the mango tree, observing the snail-paced drilling from a distance, they would climb on me and pet my hairy arms, legs, and even my hair. Most of the kids' heads are clean-shaven, both boys and girls, and Kenyans do not have much extremity hair to begin with! I was like a big furry stuffed animal to them. They began calling me "*Babu*," which is Swahili for "grandfather." A few remembered from my November 2008 trip, almost a year ago, that my oldest daughter had just given birth to my first grandchild. So now I was in every way "Bobu." (And in fact, that is what my grandchildren now call me here in the U.S.)

I had assumed my adventure for the day was over, having braved such a harrowing trip to the school. But late that afternoon, Nzarro, the church pastor, came to me and asked if I could take him and his 2-year old daughter to the medical clinic in town on my motorcycle. I cannot describe the fear I felt at the thought of driving him and his tiny daughter on this precarious machine in such conditions. I knew that he could drive a motorcycle, as I had loaned it to him earlier, so I suggested that he drive and that I would hold Michael in the back. But he reminded me that Michael was extremely afraid of all "*mzungus*" (Caucasians) and would never let me hold her.

"I don't know if I can do it," I worried out loud. "I had a hard enough time driving myself here this morning, as you know. On top of that, Michael will probably be too scared to ride behind me, even if you're holding her."

"Well," he insisted, "I will make her understand. We will both be fine once we get started." I didn't know how to tell him that was the part I was most worried about—getting started! That, and the mud and huge "lakes" covering the roadway. But he was desperate—he suspected she may have pneumonia and needed to see a doctor and get medicine right away.

Seeing his awful predicament, and finding no better option, I agreed to take them. He assured me that he was confident that I could drive them safely into town. I couldn't bring myself to tell him that this did not ease my stress at all. Not knowing what to do next, I began praying mightily. I remembered the verse, "I can do all things through him who gives me strength." (Philippians 4:13, NIV). To that I added, "Let it not be me, but you, God. I'm just here to steer and operate the throttle. It's all on you to keep us from falling over, or crashing, or (the "small lakes" came flashing across my mind) drowning."

With that, I climbed on the bike and started it up, then waited as Pastor and a screaming Michael climbed on the back. Soon we were off, meandering rather erratically at first, until my balance started to improve. "I can do all things through Christ who strengthens me," I repeated in my thoughts constantly. And, "Not me, but you God." The muddy dirt road back to the paved road was only about 6 km, but it seemed like 60! At least I remembered the road, and where to go from there. It all came back to me as I drove. Yep, this is the route that I meant to take to come there (in reverse, of course), instead of the extensive journey that I took earlier simply because I could not find the right "take off" point from the tarmac road.

With each challenging obstacle, I prayed ever more intently, and to my great relief, we overcame them one by one! When I say "we," I mean me and God—me doing the steering and God doing all the rest. As I continued to see each barrier overcome, I gained new strength. At some point, I even started to think, "Yes, I can do this!" (with God's strength and guidance, of course). Now that I'm writing about it, I'm reminded of the aptness of 2 Corinthians 12:9—"My grace is sufficient for you, for my power is made perfect in weakness." (NIV)

His power in my weakness. How else could I have possibly navigated the treacherous, muddy paths, barely as wide as my tires, with slick drop-offs on both sides?! I'm just not that skilled, nor experienced enough, to have ever accomplished that on my own. And certainly not while transporting a desperate dad cradling his wailing little daughter and trying his hardest to comfort her. No, that simply wasn't my doing.

But we weren't in the clear yet. Suddenly, after what seemed like hours of clenched muscles and thousands of kilometers later (but only about twenty minutes), we were confronted by "the lake." An ominous body of deep, dark water engulfed the entire roadway for more than 100 feet, with no visible detour around. I stopped some distance from the "shore" and turned to Pastor.

"We don't have a choice, I'm afraid, Pastor. We have to drive through."

Pastor nodded immediately. "Let's go, Bob. I know you can do it."

The insecurity started to rise up again, but I reminded myself how far God had already protected us. "Okay," I said. "Hold tight to Michael." I glanced at the little girl. She had finally stopped crying and just stared at me with pathetically dreadful wide eyes. I wanted so much to assure her, but she was way too young to understand even a word of English. I turned back to face the lake. "I'm going to drive straight through. Hopefully, the water won't get deep enough to flood the engine or the exhaust pipe, either one of which could stop us in our tracks. I'll try not to steer much to help maintain balance if we start to slide." I braced myself, revved the engine, and said over my shoulder, "Just keep praying, Pastor. God will see us through this as well, I am sure."

I took off into the water. I don't remember sliding once, nor did I ever feel that we would tip over. But the lake was deep in the middle and began to cover my feet and lower legs. However, it never reached the engine nor the exhaust, miraculously. Finally, we emerged on the other side, and I drove on, not wanting to look back or even have to stop again.

We quickly arrived at the tarmac road, and I hurried on toward the town of Mtwapa and the medical clinic. Just as I started to relax from the treacherous dirt road drive, I was abruptly confronted with the crazy Mtwapa traffic—large trucks, crazed *matatu* drivers, and hordes of motorcyclists, not to mention countless pedestrians and the ever-present herds of cows, goats, dogs, donkeys, and horses! All ran wild through the town. There are no traffic lights, and the few policemen are usually on foot and not paying much attention to traffic. It's pretty much the Wild West—every man for himself! Having escaped the fiery furnace, I felt I was now heading into the Lion's Den.

My motorcycle magically managed to dodge all of these opportunities for disaster and wove its way into the heart of the city. Pastor alerted me, and I stopped across the street from the clinic. I asked him if I could help further; he said no, but he was immensely grateful for my willingness to navigate such a trail to bring him and Michael here. I asked him how he would get back, and he said that he would take a taxi. I gave him money for the taxi and also to help out with the doctor, then said, "I'll see you tomorrow at the school, and I will definitely pray for Michael's recovery."

The remaining 16 km of my journey back to my hotel happened without incidence—thank you, God, yet again. I also managed to arrive before dark, one of my main goals. I had made it, safe and unharmed.

Tomorrow will be better. I will not get lost tomorrow. True, I will still have to deal with the mud and the major water hazards—they're not going away anytime soon. The rainy season is here to stay. I've not driven yet through the rain, but I know that is coming. After all, I'm not here to sit in my room, or out in one of the covered areas overlooking the beautiful Indian Ocean. I'm not here "on holiday." I am here to work, and that work requires my presence at the remote school, overseeing my drilling contractor. And oh, the drilling. That is going to take time—a lot of time, I realize, based on what I've seen today.

Well, I've had enough adventure for one day. I'm turning in. It has to be all downhill from here…right?

DAY 2:

The dawn awakened me with a gentle soaking rain. I was hoping to see the sunrise over the Indian Ocean from my hotel window, but it was not to be this morning. All was shrouded by rain clouds. I asked the young lady at the front desk if she believed that this would be a sustaining rain. "I don't think so, usually it is not," she answered with a smile—always with a smile. Kenyans have such wonderful smiles. Indeed, most Africans do. But Kenyans' beautiful smiles seem to emanate from their delightful hearts and spirits. I think this is a key reason that I am so drawn to this country. I simply delight in its people.

I was hotel bound for the morning due to the rain, but as soon as it let up, I headed for the church. I took it slow, as the roads were still slick from the new rain. I had every reason to be further on my guard as I pulled off the hardtop road and began the 7-km trek up the dirt road, a.k.a. mud-way. The further I rode, the worse it got. But once again, God kept me upright on my rented machine, and I made it without a mishap—just a bit muddied from the experience.

The drillers were making progress—after a week, they had successfully reached a depth of 45 feet out of an anticipated total of 150 feet. But then came more setbacks. Groundwater began flowing into the borehole as they drilled deeper. Not enough to be useful, mind you, for capturing in the completed well. Just enough to be a real nuisance. Finally, the drilling foreman decided that it was too much; they would have to insert surface casing. They contacted the owner, with whom I had spoken on the phone and through email. I had yet to meet the gentleman in person. It seems he was drilling another borehole several hours away, which was apparently overwhelming his work schedule (or "eating his lunch," as we would say!).[1]

The drilling is progressing, but it is painfully slow. I'm wondering how this is going to work. I'll update you tomorrow.

DAY 3:

I could see evidence that the owner came by—there was a pile of 6-inch surface casing (lightweight PVC pipes) near the borehole location that was not there when I left last night. The team had already hooked onto the first pipe by the time I got there and were lowering it into the borehole using the drill rig winch. This first pipe slid down into the earth quite easily. They still had a hold of it with the winch to keep it from falling below the surface. They then latched onto a second pipe and were preparing to connect it to the top end of the first pipe that was sticking up out of the ground.

I watched them struggle with the second 10-foot piece of pipe in an effort to line it up with the first piece. It was obviously more than a two-man job, so I jumped in and assisted. The three of us were able to line up the second pipe and insert it into the top of the first pipe. What happened next was perplexing, sad, and frustrating all at once. I could see that the lower pipe had three small holes near the top around the circumference, while the upper pipe that was inserted into it had none. Since they had no drill of any sort, they were using one of the small screws to try to make a hole into the second pipe through one of the holes in the lower pipe. This was not working at all. The pipes were just too hard and continued to thwart all of their best efforts to either screw or pound the screw with a hammer into the sidewall of the pipe. It was difficult for me to watch them try so hard with so little to work with.

I was sorry I didn't have a drill to loan them, and I was mad at their boss for not providing them with the necessary tools. Compounding

---

[1]The owner was not completely absent. He did visit our site several times; I could always see evidence of that on the following mornings. But it was always well after I left in the early evening to beat the approaching darkness. Indeed, we had made plans to meet as well, on more than one occasion. But each time, without the benefit of daylight savings, darkness would be fast approaching, and I'd be forced to grab my motorcycle and depart.

my frustration was the fact that he had just been here the night before, delivering the surface casing pipes and the screws, yet failing to provide the tools they would need to connect them. Mostly, I pitied these two young men who were struggling with all their might to complete what should have been a simple task. And now I was struggling with them, since two of us, the assistant and I, were still holding the upper pipe in place, laboring against gravity to keep it aligned. Finally, I could take no more. I said to the other young man, "Take my place here holding the pipe. I'm going to see if I have something in my backpack that can help us."

The only thing I could possibly have was my trusty pocketknife. It was a keepsake—the one and only present from my former father-in-law that I actually found any use for. Indeed, Grandpa Farmer (as my daughters had appropriately named him since he lived on a real farm, with a tractor and real cows, but no chickens) was a most generous father to his five kids and ever-growing list of grandchildren. But when it came to Christmas gifts, he had a real obtuse concept for what we all could use. Like the year he bought all five of us each a set of full-size stuffed Santa and Mrs. Claus figures. Really? What do you do with them after five minutes when the novelty wears off?

This awesome pocket knife was the exception to those strange gifts. It amazed my father-in-law that, years after he handed them out to his sons and to me, I still had mine, and every time he asked, I would pull it out and show him. You see, he also knew that I had a propensity, indeed, a near-passion you could say, for losing the most precious items I was given. Like the time I left my brand-new basketball at the local YMCA less than a week after receiving it for Christmas. I ask you, who goes to a gym to play basketball and then forgets to bring home the one thing that he brought to play with? Yes, I continue to amaze my friends and family, particularly my three grown daughters, with my incredible ability to forget or lose things. I have made an art form of losing important things. Don't even ask me about cell phones!

So while I knew that I had brought my precious knife with me to Kenya, I wasn't sure I had remembered to transfer it from my checked luggage into my backpack—what a surprise, right? As I sifted through the menagerie of stuff in the backpack, I sent up a quick prayer to the one God that hears all requests, from the truly significant to the seemingly mundane. And even though I do not remember in the least having placed my pocket knife into my backpack, miraculously, there it was. Awesome God! *Asante sana*!

Running back to the drill site, I handed the knife to the foreman. Both men broke into broad smiles and started jabbering to one another in their tribal language. I regained my place next to the assistant and continued holding the upper pipe as the foreman skillfully carved a small hole in the second pipe with the sharp tip of the pocketknife. After he had done this three times and then inserted and tightened the screws into the pipes, we were finally able to let go of the upper pipe (but not before we removed the winch cable from the lower pipe and attached it to the upper pipe).

We were now ready to lower both pipes together into the borehole. As the assistant and I guided the pipe downward, the foreman cranked the winch. Just as the second (upper) pipe was nearing the top of the ground, it stopped, and slack came into the winch rope. It appeared to be stuck, or at least stopped. We tried pushing it down and then picking it up with the winch and "dropping" it, but nothing was working. We decided to take a break and seek shade from the now fully exposed and relentless sun, and to rehydrate as well.

While on break, I asked the foreman what he was planning to do now with this surface casing that appeared to be planted in the borehole. While we expected that we could get it out with the winch, we really needed to push it farther down the hole and add more casing pipe. But it was obvious that the borehole wasn't big enough. He showed me his plan to enlarge his core drill bit by welding sharpened "ears" to each side. That seemed like a good idea, I said, but how would they accomplish that? He asked if he could borrow my motorcycle and take the core bit into town to a welding shop. I agreed, and just like that, the assistant grabbed the core bit (sawtooth pipe), and the two men jumped on the motorcycle and headed off into town—weaving noticeably, I couldn't help but observe. Note to self: if someone asks to borrow your *rented* motorcycle, test them first to see if they really know how to ride!

While the drillers were off getting their drill bit enlarged, I went to see what the church elders were up to. I found them, along with the pastor and a young man named Titus, building a perimeter fence around the church yard. I asked them if they could use an extra hand, and they readily accepted. They were digging holes and setting fence posts in concrete. Given the choice between digging the holes or making the concrete, I chose the latter. Besides, after watching them excavate those narrow holes with their ever-handy *jembe* tool (a small, short-handled hoe-like tool, generally used for digging small holes), and a *panga* (machete), I quickly surmised that mixing concrete was the only viable work option for me in this situation. It was truly amazing to watch how quickly they could excavate in nearly perfect symmetry a 6-inch diameter by 2-foot deep hole.

The fence posts were cut from mangrove wood, which I had not seen before in Africa. Apparently, it is readily available here, and often used for fence posts. Compared to the light-weight cedar that is used throughout Texas, mangrove branches make significantly stronger post material, as they are quite dense. I noticed they had painted the bottom 2 feet of the posts with a thin, white, paint-like substance. They told me that this was poison to keep the termites from destroying the posts underground. How hardy these termites must be, I marveled, to attack this extremely hard wood underground—and embedded in concrete, no less! Now there is a varmint I would not want anywhere near my house.

Watching them mix concrete, I learned a new way to perform a common task. I had often mixed concrete for my own home or church projects, and while I estimated that I had managed more than a million cubic yards of concrete placement during my engineering career, I had never before seen concrete made this way. They would start with a pile of sand and add a bag of cement, mixing thoroughly with a shovel. Then they would form it into a volcano-looking circle, and into the crater of the volcano they would pour a bucket of water. Then one or two of them would mix this concoction with shovels, turning it over and over until it eventually became mushy concrete. All this was done right on the dirt ground. Next, they would shovel the mushy concrete into buckets and haul these buckets to the work site. If this sounds like laborious work, well, it is. I wondered if they would add any aggregate (fancy engineering term for gravel, stone, or rock) to the mixture to give it more strength. That was soon answered when I assisted in gathering small, hard coral rocks, which were tossed into the concrete mixture after pouring it into the hole. Brilliant! The rocks added strength while displacing concrete (mortar), allowing the concrete mixture to "go further."

Looking around, I discovered a small, broken down wheelbarrow, which I had happened to use to haul rocks when I was here a year ago with the mission team. I had fixed this exact wheelbarrow then, and here it stood again, with the same problem—the wheel had come off the axle. I managed to find some metal "parts" and was able to sort-of fix the wheelbarrow wheel. This, I hoped, would at least make our drudgery somewhat easier. I would now have my chance to show them what a help I could be!

When Titus did not come back with his bucket for more concrete, I figured the haul had gotten tiring, as it was completely on the other side of the property from where we were making the concrete. So I decided to fill the repaired wheelbarrow and haul it to where they were installing the fence posts myself. As I well knew, filling the wheelbarrow was the easy part. The difficulty lay in pushing it to the work area. When I finally arrived, they were excited to see me—no one more than Titus!

I helped drop some of the concrete into the hole, tossed in some coral stones, and mixed it with the help of a straight, long tree-branch. Then we pushed the fence posts down into the softened concrete. As someone held the post plumb, the rest of us shoveled concrete into and around the post up to the surface. Using this process, we were able to install all of the fence posts on one of the remaining two sides of the property. It was hard work, but it gave me great satisfaction to be of assistance to these, my friends. It also, thankfully, gave me something to do instead of sitting around watching the laboriously slow drilling process. I was grateful for the chance to get to know my friends better and contribute toward a vital project for the church and school.

When the men returned from the welding shop in Mtwapa town with their new and improved core bit, the drilling team went right back to work. I was impressed to find that the simple, yet ingenious design worked well. The new drill bit easily widened the hole, allowing the surface casing to be much more easily inserted. This greatly increased their progress. My hope is renewed for seeing the project complete before I have to leave Kenya! (I'll be traveling next to Ethiopia to meet up with Dean and his medical team at a new school plant.)

I'll keep you in the loop.

DAY 4:

Today, I found the team still working on the fence posts, but this time at the front of the church next to the road. The team at work was Justin, Jackson, Pastor and me. At one point, I found myself working alone. Just as I was beginning to wonder where everyone went, I heard a commotion, and Pastor's wife came running towards me, yelling frantically. Somehow I managed to cobble together from what she was trying to convey, with her few words of English, that one of the drill workers had been injured. I ran to the drill site and found the foreman hovering over his friend, who was lying on the ground. The bottom of his trousers were badly torn, and a gash on his leg was bleeding badly. I ran back to my backpack to grab Band-Aids (the only first aid item I had), and I also brought a small soaked towel to clean off the wound. It didn't appear to my untrained eye that there were any broken bones, so after washing off the blood, I covered the gash wound with the Band-Aids. Then the foreman told me the story.

While the assistant was at his usual perch above the drilling spindle, his pants leg suddenly got caught in the rotating drill pipe. The loose material started wrapping around the pipe, but the assistant didn't realize it at first. He suddenly screamed in terror and pain when it began tearing into his leg. Had it not been for the lightning-quick action by the foreman, I am certain his leg would have been badly mangled, possibly even severed. Thankfully, as soon as the foreman saw his assistant's pants twisting around the drill pipe, he grabbed a nearby length of pipe and knocked the rotating belt off the spindle, which immediately stopped the drill pipe from turning. Then he helped his friend get loose from the pipe and set him on the ground nearby. Incredible!

With the foreman as my interpreter, I told the young man that God had spared him from a very bad injury through the quick action of his boss, a.k.a. his guardian angel. I commended the foreman for his quick, decisive action. The assistant stood up and slowly put pressure on his leg, then started walking. Next thing I knew, they were starting the drill machine all over again, and with the roar of the engine and the familiar engulfing cloud of blue smoke, the assistant once again climbed on top of the drill platform. This time, however, he had trimmed off both of his pant legs!

I was glad to have been able to speak freely about God with these men. I knew that both of them were not Muslims and that we could talk openly about their faith. Up until the previous Sunday, I really wasn't sure. I was surprised to see them in church here at MBEWAU. The entire area of Mombasa is predominantly Muslim, and in particular, a good portion of the businesses, so it seemed reasonable to expect that this contractor and his men would be Muslim.

Justin later told me that not only were these two drillers in church that Sunday, but in fact they slept each night in the church on pads on the floor. And here they were on Sunday, their one day off, singing praises and praying along with the congregation. I was heartened that God had led me to this contractor with these committed Christian workers. Despite the antique equipment and lack of tools, I know that they will see this well project through to completion. Maybe not before I leave, but that is okay—God will surely help them drill this borehole.

I just now realized that I have forgotten to explain what this name MBEWAU means. Or, how to pronounce it either. So sorry for the oversight. It is an acronym for *Mtepeni Baptist Elders Waking Up*. I kid you not. And it is pronounced, "M-bay-wow." As with a great number of communities, schools and other institutes, the name represents a condition or may even tell a story. In this case, it is a name adopted by these Baptist Elders for both their primary school and church, to present their current view of themselves. Total honesty and transparency—not at all uncommon in rural Kenya, particularly in Christian communities, yet too often lacking in western culture, where we may sometimes even tend to boastfully proclaim ourselves to the world with our selected monikers. It's as if they are saying that they are emerging from the darkness in search of the light—the light of Jesus' love, that is, that they intend to present to their students and to their congregation. I don't know about you, but I admire that greatly.

The remainder of the day, thankfully, passed without further incident. As daylight gave way to dusk, we were finishing up the last of the perimeter fence posts. I immediately began gathering my things to set off for the hotel before darkness set in. Just then, Pastor stopped me to report that the ladies had prepared chai and invited me to join them. I didn't want to drive the motorcycle home in darkness, but I truly did not want to offend these ladies. I knew that they had gone to no little trouble in preparing the chai.

You see, it's not quite as easy as filling a tea kettle and turning on the stovetop like we do in the States. These women must start by collecting firewood with their own hands, then slowly build their fire to the right temperature. Not only that, but the milk for the chai had to have been sought out earlier today at a store in town or a neighborhood *duka*. For me to decline the invitation would be, frankly, like a slap in the face to my friends. I determined to stay and enjoy the chai and tasty biscuits to go along with it, as well as the wonderful conversation. It was not a disappointment!

When I finally said goodbye and set out on my motorcycle, darkness was quickly approaching. I had to stop briefly to figure out how to turn on the headlight (first time using it). With that accomplished, I drove gingerly down the miles of dirt road, with plenty of water hazards popping up that I was forced to maneuver around. Eventually, I made it to the hardtop paving and drove on into Mtwapa. The last dozen miles or so of the trip were spent hugging the side of the road while deftly watching for invading *matatus*. More than once, I was forced off the road and into the ditch to avoid being run over as the crazy drivers bore down on me with their lights flashing and wild music blaring.

I am now, at last, safely at my hotel, overjoyed to still be alive. Enjoying reminiscing on my many adventures so far in the bush.

DAY 5:

The morning invaded my sleep with gorgeous sunlight, summoning me out of my bed and down to the shore. For the first time since arriving, I got to soak in the beauty of the Indian Ocean. At first, I ambled down the beach looking for cool shells and other interesting ocean treasures. But finally, I could ignore no longer the call of the sea, and I plunged into the surf, enjoying an invigorating early morning swim. The joy of that moment was fleeting, as the sunny dawn soon gave way to morning rain. I swam ashore, collected my flip-flops, and headed back to my room, praising God for the beauty of His nature and the opportunity to enjoy it, if only briefly.

After showering and dressing, I watched the rain continue to pound outside my balcony. I was antsy to get back to the school to monitor the drilling and help with any new projects, but I really didn't want to drive the motorcycle in the rain. I clicked on the TV in hopes of catching a weather update. This proved futile. Checking the Internet on my computer provided similar results. I learned that weather information from Kenya, or, for that matter, most African countries, is generally not worth the effort. I flashed back to checking weather conditions in Mombasa from back in the States. The results were always one of two things: "rain" if it was the rainy season, "sunny" if it was the non-rainy season. Pretty simple, huh?

The truth is, during the rainy season, it rains pretty much every day in Mombasa. And in the dry season, it rarely rains. So the only real weather questions to ask during this trip are, how long will it rain, and how hard?

I decided, for a change, to enjoy a slow breakfast at the huge buffet which came with my room, along with a myriad of European guests in Kenya on holiday. Speaking of my room, this thing is enormous. The large wrap-around balcony provides a great view of the huge swimming pool (one of three on the complex) and a line of beautiful palm trees overlooking the ocean as the pool's backdrop. Inside the room are two very large beds, a shower and a bath tub, and enough clear space to entertain dozens of people. When I arrived at the hotel several days ago, there was a beautiful bottle of wine and two glasses waiting for me. I had to double check the room rate at the front desk to make sure there wasn't some mistake. No mistake, said the receptionist. I would be staying in one of the bridal suites, with all its amenities, for the quoted price of $75 per day!

"But I'm not a newlywed!" I protested. "Actually, I'm here alone." I didn't have the heart (or the guts) to tell her that I was divorced as of one year.

"That's okay, Mr. Nee-kol. We already know that. We know why you are here in Kenya, and we want you to be comfortable when you return to the Voyager Resort Hotel each evening."

The truth suddenly dawned on me. "Have you been talking to Chris?" I prodded.

"Yes," she confessed with a big smile. I had met Chris Moore, a missionary from Texas, during his first mission trip back to Kenya. He and his wife, Lisa, were supporting the development of the MBEWAU church and school. In fact, within a few months, Chris and Lisa will be moving to Kenya permanently as full-time missionaries. Chris had evidently used his influence to arrange these wonderful accommodations for me here at the Voyager. (I called him later to ask about it, and he thought it was pretty funny. Yes, he had negotiated a good rate, but he had nothing to do with the bridal suite arrangement! "They just know why you're there, Bobu, and they wanna take good care of you.")

"Well," I grinned at the pretty young receptionist, "bless you for that."

"You're very welcome for that, Bobu," she responded with a wink and a smile.

Soon enough, the rain let up, and I pointed my motorcycle back to the bush. By the time I arrived at the school, it was midmorning, and the drill team was hard at work. Already bored with the monotony of the drilling, I was easily distracted by some curious activity taking place on the schoolyard. When I had entered earlier, I noticed a man building something out of wood under one of the huge, shady mango trees. The project looked a lot like a casket. I asked Jackson about this strange sight, and he told me that the man was a well-known, local "*fundi*."

I had heard the term "*fundi*" many times in Kenya before I pieced together its meaning. It is one of those catch-all Swahili words with many layers. I had heard it used to define an auto mechanic, a cement finisher, and even a tile layer. I determined that it means "craftsman"—in this case, a carpenter. I could see that he was truly a skilled craftsman, a *fundi* by every account. He could have built a glorious temple, like Solomon in the Bible. Instead, he was building a simple casket to inter an elderly man in a nearby village who had passed away during the night. Leaving the drilling behind me for the moment, I reveled in this opportunity to absorb myself in watching a true *fundi* at work. Even knowing that his detailed object of beauty would, within days, be laid in the earth and covered with dirt, the gifted *fundi* worked on tirelessly, cutting not a corner. Starting with simple rough-hewn boards, he crafted them into a noble sarcophagus, fit for a tribal king. It was pure joy for me to watch him work.

He worked alone, with not one power tool, equipped only with a hand saw, a hammer, and a plane. No table saw, no joiner, no power sander or circular saw—he did not even use any clamps, even though the top and bottom sections were made by joining two of the boards together lengthwise. I watched as he cut a rectangular opening in the top where one would expect the deceased's face to finally rest. He then fit a small hinged door in place to cover the opening. By now it was early afternoon, but the fundi never stopped working. With the woodwork complete, he took several small pieces of sandpaper and began smoothing all the edges and corners, first with a plane, then with the sandpaper. It was a thing of exquisite artistry.

As the craftsman completed his work, I wandered over to check on my drillers. They had worked relentlessly all day, extending the borehole mere inches per hour. I admired their diligence greatly. They never quit. They never seemed to get discouraged. They just kept drilling. I hate to admit that I would have quit long ago, and not before complaining heartily to my boss about such woefully inadequate equipment. But they never did. I suppose in a way they can't. This is their job, and I can only imagine that they feel blessed to have steady work. The adult male unemployment rate in the coastal region around Mombasa is greater than 70%. That must be the reason nearly every adult male worker I've ever laid eyes on is always smiling—they're happy to be working and able to feed their families in such a poor economy.

The trouble with this reality is that because so few get steady work, there is a much more significant problem of theft, robbery, and general unrest. In the wealthier communities, you'll find the usual displays of pricey, high security. In the bush, security comes in the form of high walls with broken glass affixed to the top, large growling dogs, or roving Massai warriors with spears or bow and arrows. I suppose these security measures are an effective crime deterrent or the region would be in total chaos, which it is not.

Crime does exist, however, and even those doing the Lord's work are not exempt from the threat. I heard a vividly told story of an American missionary's wife who happened to be home alone when some men broke into their compound and targeted their home. In fact, I had met the woman and her husband when they hosted our mission team in their beautiful home overlooking the ocean. They lived within walking distance of The Voyager, where we were staying on our first mission trip with Chris Moore (the trip where I finally arrived after getting stuck in Baghdad, remember that?). We had been invited for an evening of pizza the night before we were to leave Kenya to return to the U.S. The couple told us the harrowing story of the robbery. Susie had hidden in the house when she heard the robbers break in. If she hadn't, her husband confessed, it is almost certain she would have been killed. She was greatly traumatized by the ordeal and had to return to the States to fully recover emotionally. No, serving the Lord is not without its risks, but we thanked God for his protection over our friends!

When I returned to the *fundi's* project, I found him applying a coat of varnish to the entire casket. And now he had some help—one of the young men from the church community was assisting him, and they were transforming the wood, which was very light in color, to a deep tan-brown luster. As I've observed before, the addition of stain or varnish causes beautiful wood grains to appear that are otherwise hidden. While the young man continued to apply the varnish, the *fundi* crafted, and then inserted, the small doorway of the top section. They only applied varnish to the exterior of the casket, and I figured this was because, of course, no one would see the inside of the casket once the body was placed inside.

As soon as I had concluded that, Jackson and Justin showed up with a sheet of spongy, soft, light blue fabric. With direction from the *fundi*, the men lined the entire inside of the casket with this material, attaching it with tiny nails. The morning rain had since given way to a warming sunny afternoon. The lack of humidity now, combined with the heat of the sun, caused the varnish to dry rather quickly. After installing the lining, they lifted the top section, and the *fundi* guided them in placing it on the casket. He secured it with nails, which he only drove in halfway, then nailed a small metal cross in the center of the top piece.

Several of the men then hoisted the casket onto their shoulders. Justin said they were transporting it to the funeral location, and I asked if I could come along. Off we went down the road to this nearby community, a little over a mile away. The casket was by no means light, but there were plenty of men to share the load. While we walked along behind the men carrying the casket, I asked about the deceased. Justin said that he was old and died naturally, and that he was one of the elders in this mainly Methodist community. Interesting, I thought. I am a member of a Methodist church back home. What that could possibly have in common with this bush Methodist community, I could not imagine. But I would soon observe for myself.

When we finally arrived, there were easily several hundred people gathered—two large groups of women, groups of men, groups of children, and a number of commingled groups as well. The area, which has a large clearing among its trees, consisted of about eight to ten mud hut homes. One of the homes, centrally located in the area, was where the majority of the people gathered, filling a covered entranceway and spilling out into the "yard." It was here that the men brought the casket and set it beside the deceased body. Removing the extended nails from the top of the casket and taking off the top, they gently placed the body into the casket, then rested it on a large table. All this time, continual singing filled the air. It was mainly the women, although a number of elderly men joined in as well.

Once the body was rested in the casket, they began a promenade around the casket, which most of the people joined. Justin quietly motioned to me to come with him so that we could join the promenade and view the body as well. He noticed that I had been taking pictures of the activities surrounding this "viewing," and as we approached the casket, he whispered that it would be okay to take pictures of the dead body. I quickly told him I had no desire to do that. I felt that it would be highly intrusive, especially since I was the only *mzungu* in the entire gathering. Anyway, I'd already taken enough pictures of the event to document my first bush funeral.

The gentleman looked extremely old and quite tiny within the casket. It had surprised me, as I had thought as the fundi was constructing the casket that it appeared to be rather small. Now I could see that the casket actually dwarfed the tiny body nestled peacefully in the soft blue fabric. After completing our promenade, Justin had me follow him over to the far edge of the community. Here we found palm leaves lying neatly on the ground, which Justin removed to reveal a perfectly cut rectangular burial plot extending at least five feet into the ground. Knowing the typically primitive tools that are commonly used for digging, this excavation seemed all the more incredible to me. I surmised that some of these men gathered here had worked meticulously to dig this hole in the ground. Perhaps this was all they had to offer this gentleman, but in doing so, they truly honored him by this rudimentary, but needed task. I snapped some photos, then Justin and I covered the grave back over with the palm leaves.

When we returned to the viewing, I paid closer attention to the small groups. I found it odd that most of the women stayed together, apart from the men who formed their own small band. Justin knew most of the men and introduced me to several. I noticed that the women were well-dressed in rural and beautiful, brightly colored blouses, skirts, and headpieces, while the men were wearing their usual drab shirts and pants. The older men were dressed much nicer, more in keeping with the apparel you would expect to see at a funeral.

The younger women were hard at work cooking a large amount of food, and the rest of the crowd stood around talking, singing, or viewing the body. I asked Justin how long this would go on. Well into the night, he said, long after they enjoyed the meal together. Tomorrow would be the funeral service, which would take most of the day. The actual burial would not occur for two more days. This was not the norm for every funeral, but it is typical for community elders.

Just as we were about to depart, we noticed two young white girls approaching the casket. After they had paid their respects, one of the girls noticed me and made her way over to me, saying she was surprised to see another *mzungu* there. "Not more surprised than I am to see you and your friend!" I responded. "Where are you from?" She said they were college students doing missionary training in a nearby village and wanted to see what an African funeral was all about.

"I am with you on that," I said, and I shared with her some photos of the crafting of the gentleman's casket. Like me, she was amazed to see the evolution of this beautifully crafted piece. We chatted a bit longer, then I wished them well on their training and the remainder of their visit. The day had worn long at that point, and Justin and I headed back to MBEWAU.

Back at the school, the drillers were just finishing up for the day. They had managed to extend the borehole beyond 60 feet. They didn't seem one bit discouraged by the continually slow pace. Based on their equipment, perhaps this is as well as could be expected. Who am I to judge? Tomorrow is another day, and maybe they will eke out another 5 to 10 feet. Slow and steady wins the race, right?

DAY 6:

Did you ever notice that funerals seem to come in bunches? It is not two days after the last funeral, and I've already had another opportunity to observe this fascinating cultural event. As I was driving towards the school today, an unusually clear morning, I noticed Justin, Jackson, and Pastor walking along the road, not far from the school. I continued on and arrived at the school just ahead of them. They explained that they had been visiting a family in the nearby community of Mtepeni to pay their respects for the overnight death (again, of natural causes) of a revered matriarch of the entire community. She had been very well-known for a lifetime of service to the community, and the funeral service was expected to be quite large. Justin asked me if I would like to join him later that morning to pay our respects. I wasn't sure if he thought I had a strange penchant for funerals, but I couldn't help but say yes. While I do not "enjoy" funerals any more than the next person, I do recognize them as an integral part of life here on earth. Indeed, it will happen to each of us sometime, right? I saw it as another chance to meet and observe people as they carried out their culture's way of paying tribute to and burying one of their own.

Later this morning, after watching the drill team deepen the borehole mere inches at a time, Justin and I set out towards the tiny community of Mtepeni. There were many more people out and about than I was used to seeing, and as we approached homes close to the community center, the numbers increased. In addition, several autos—new models, no less—were parked off the dirt road. Cars are not unusual in Kenya, but you seldom see them parked in the bush community. They often simply pass through as they transport prominent local individuals. Justin told me that these cars most likely belonged to several county officials who would be attending this funeral, out of respect to this very well-known and beloved lady, who herself was a county official as a younger woman.

On arriving at the home of the deceased woman, the scene was much the same as that of the old man's funeral, albeit with many more people gathered. Justin, who lived only a stone's throw away from this house at the center of the community, was greeted by well-wishers right and left. He introduced me to each one, and I started to feel like a county official myself with all the attention! Justin invited me to take photos, but I held back. As the only *mzungu* at this gathering, I had begun to feel like something of a spectacle. Fortunately, a few well-dressed dignitaries arrived and began making the rounds, shaking many of the same hands that we had just clasped. I was glad for the diverting of the crowd's curiosity.

As the men made their way through the crowd, I noticed the handshakes they received were unique. As each person extended their hand, they would clasp their left hand under the forearm of their right. They only did this with the official-looking men and occasionally with an elderly person. With everyone else, they shook hands normally. What struck me most was that the two-handed method had been used by many of them when greeting me—but not with Justin.

Later, back at the church, Justin explained that this type of handshake was a traditional Kenyan way to show honor to a person, and is usually reserved for dignitaries and the elderly.

"Then why me?" I asked. "I'm not that old!"

He smiled. "No, Bob. To them, you are a dignitary. You are *mzee*—someone deserving of honor, not necessarily old. They are honored that a *mzungu* would come to visit them way out here in this bush community and offer his condolences. It is certainly not an everyday occurrence for them. And I can assure you, much of the talk back there right now among those gathered, even tonight in their homes, will not be about the officials that came to pay their respects. It will be about the *mzungu* whose hand they shook."

I was astonished. "That can't be true. How can I be anything to them? Is it just because I am *mzungu*?"

Justin shook his head. "It's more than that. They feel that they know you."

"But I only just met them today. I didn't even catch most of their names."

"But they know why you are here, Bobu. They know that you came several months ago, and then they saw the electrical power lines extended to the church and school. Now they see you again, and they know that we are drilling the borehole. Soon there will be water at the school, where they can come and collect it for their homes and their families."

"How do they know all this?" I asked.

"Because they know me, and they know Pastor, and they know Jackson, and because we all live together in this community. They ask us many questions."

"Well," I responded, "I am glad that they ask, and I'm glad that you tell them. It's true—soon we will have water, plenty of water. They can all come and get as much as they need. That has always been our plan. But I sincerely hope that they do not think that *I* am the one who is doing all of this, Justin. They need to know that many wonderful people in America, from many different churches, have provided the funds to construct this water well, as well as the beautiful elementary school that Chris has already begun." In fact, as I remembered admiringly, the first floor of rooms for the school was already nearing completion.

"But most importantly," I insisted, "these villagers need to know that we are doing all this so that the gospel of Jesus Christ will be proclaimed in this school, in this church, and in this community. That is who is providing this well—Jesus Christ."

"They will know that, Bobu," he assured me. "We will tell them—me and Pastor and Jackson. We will tell them."

I smiled broadly and gave Justin a great big hug. "Yes, I am sure that you will, *rafiki yangu* (my friend). Now, let us check on the drillers and see if this plan to actually drill a water well is anything more than a pipe dream!" We both laughed.

Back at the drill rig, the work was progressing, still slowly—ever so slowly—but progressing. However, I have decided that I simply cannot stay in Kenya any longer. I've already extended my stay by several days, delaying my trip to Ethiopia. Dean and the others will be leaving Ethiopia at the end of the week, and I still need to join them to visit a medical clinic site that needs a well. I can see that the drillers here are working steadily to accomplish their mission, and although it is taking a long time, they don't complain but continue diligently drilling.

Fortunately, their boss also is not discouraged in the least. He knows his equipment and is confident that they will reach a depth that will unleash abundant water. I reminded him not to go past 150 feet, as I had been warned by a very knowledgeable female engineer at the well equipment installation firm, whom I had also contracted with online. To drill beyond that depth, as my previous borehole driller had insisted, would invite the intrusion of salt water, as we are only 8 km from the ocean's edge.

In fact, that contractor was scheduled to deliver the well pump equipment this afternoon. It includes an electric submersible pump, which is why I had helped them extend the electrical power lines to the school on my last visit. They will also be bringing a ground storage tank, which the community can initially use to draw their water from. Later, we plan to build a tower for the tank and elevate it, allowing the distribution of water throughout the campus, and even—wonder of all wonders—a flushing toilet! One has to dream big, right?

With all of this in place, I feel confident that my drillers will finish the borehole as planned, and as contracted. I suppose I won't get to enjoy the excitement of seeing it completed, but I'm okay with that. Indeed, of the three wells that we had contracted to drill in Sudan on my first trip to Africa, I had only been present for the completion of one. It was certainly exciting, but it just isn't possible in every case. I have to choose the best contractors I can, then trust that they will complete their contracts. Just as I had done in Sudan, I will be leaving capable men in charge of seeing the work through to completion, as well as entrusting them with the funds to pay the companies, as agreed.

Just as I was about to get on my motorcycle and head back to town that late afternoon, Jackson caught up with me and asked if I could come early tomorrow and give him a ride on my motorcycle to the county health department office at the public school. He is going to receive a certificate for having completed a course that will designate him as the health department leader for a wide area centered at Mtepeni. He also requested that I bring my camera. "Of course," I said. "I will see you bright and early."

I forced myself to sound much more confident than I felt. Not that I don't want to take him to get his "diploma" and take photos. Of course I do. But have I mentioned that it is the rainy season? And that during the rainy season it rains almost every day? Sigh. I have endured several harrowing "rain treks" already, and the scariest are when I have to safely transport another person besides myself! Maybe tomorrow will be merciful and stay completely rain-free. I know the odds are slim, though. It has rained every single day since I arrived.

DAY 7:

Looking out to sea this morning, I searched for some sign of the sun. Anything. I'd even take a sliver of light. But no—it was raining so hard that I could barely see the water. I kept an eye on the clock, hoping that it might somehow let up right before I had to go. I had my camera tucked away and was ready to jet, just as soon as I saw even the tiniest relenting of the deluge. I did not want to let Jackson down. I also didn't want to crash Emanuel's motorcycle—or lose it in a mud puddle (a.k.a. "small lake") along the back road to MBEWAU. This is assuming I could even make it past the crazy *matatu* drivers in Mtwapa town. Really, they are my worst fear. These drivers don't bother looking for motorcycles when the sun is shining. I will be utterly invisible to them in this driving rain. How, I fretted, could I possibly drive to the school to pick up Jackson and then turn around and take him to this ceremony? Of course I had prayed about it. But so far I had not seen any doves flying onto my balcony carrying olive branches!

Suddenly, the rain let up just a bit, and I knew it was now or never. I slung my backpack on the front of me, my camera safely inside, and covered us both with my rain parka. My helmet, sadly, does not have a face shield on it, and the rain was driving into my eyes, making it terribly difficult to see. So very carefully, I would quickly glance up and look for pedestrians and oncoming *matatus*. If the way was clear, I'd look down again just ahead of my front tire. I knew that if I could get through Mtwapa town and away from the paved roads, I would only have to conquer muddy roads and the extended water hazards.

Well, thank God—He was certainly, once again, guiding my safe passage. And I only had to drive off the road one time to avoid a *matatu*! When I did, I almost lost my balance skidding into a mud puddle, but I did finally make it to the dirt (mud) road. The road was not as bad as I had expected. It was muddy, for sure, with a lot of big puddles, but nothing worse than I had already encountered. I grinned, mentally patting myself on the back. Here at the end of my trip, I was finally getting the hang of this zany, yet cost effective, mode of bush transport!

Before long, I reached the school property, ready to seat Jackson behind me and prepare for Phase 2 of today's journey. At least the rain had stopped for the moment. As I waited, Justin walked out and asked if he could catch a ride to Jackson's ceremony. "Oh man, Justin, I don't like taking one person on the back of this thing, let alone two of you!" I told him.

"No, Bobu," he said, "It's just me. Jackson has already gone over to the school."

"What?" I exclaimed. "He asked me to be here by 10:00, and here I am!"

"He wasn't sure that you would still be coming. He knows you don't like driving in the rain."

"Well, that is true," I said. "But I wanted to support Jackson on this important day." I restarted the motorcycle just as Justin was climbing on back. "Alright, let's do this."

It was a really muddy and uncomfortable ride, but at least it was short. Jackson saw us drive in and ran over. He was grateful that both of his friends had come, and he apologized for leaving early.

"That's okay, my friend. I really did not want to have to ride both of you anyway!" I said. He laughed heartily and said they were still waiting for most of the dignitaries to arrive.

"I imagine so," I said. "I am familiar with these dignitaries, how they always come late."

"You got it," Jackson smiled. "And I am sure that today will be no exception."

Little did we know that our 10:30 a.m. ceremony would not even start until after 1:00! It was nearly noon before any of the dignitaries even started to arrive. Once the first one showed up, however, it seemed to be a steady stream of important people. Car after car after car pulled up, and well-dressed men and women made their grand entrance.

I couldn't help but notice that every single dignitary was hefty. There wasn't a thin one in the group. This was in stark contrast to everyone else gathered there, including teachers from the nearby school, administrators, and many locals who had come to watch. There were easily twenty or more dignitaries, and all of them rotund. I concluded that these officials eat much better, and more frequently, than your average Kenyan. I figured this was mostly due to the fact that they made more money at their jobs, but I also suspected that they were probably treated to lunch regularly by the townspeople who needed their assistance. Not so different from Washington or Austin, or any state or local governments in the U.S., I thought. I continued to look around at the different body types and muse on their lifestyles, which helped ease the tedium of the interminable time lapse while waiting for the ceremony to begin.

While we waited, some workers erected a large tent and placed many folding chairs underneath. Good call, I thought, as the rain continued to blur the sky. In spite of the tent's protection, the rain collected on its edges and ran off the back in torrents, drenching the last row of chairs every time, no matter how far in they moved them. Did I mention it rains a lot during the rainy season in Kenya?

Finally, it seemed that everyone was gathered, including many of the village schoolchildren I recognized, along with adults who I presumed were their parents. The booming PA system sprang to life, and the long-awaited ceremony was underway. One singing or dance group followed another, performing on the vast lawn in front of the dignitaries, now shaded by the tent from an emerging afternoon sun. When at last it seemed every class in the adjacent public school had performed, an adult native dance team, complete with drums, spears, and other instruments, put on an amazing performance. This, for me, was worth the wait.

Now came time for the speeches. I am convinced that every single dignitary made a speech. I'm not even sure some of them didn't make several speeches! Fortunately, most were given in English, although a few were in Swahili. Finally, it was time to award the diplomas. After many, many recipients, they called our friend, Jackson, and I captured his exciting moment receiving his diploma with my Nikon. After the ceremony, I snapped a few more photos of Jackson and his fellow student friends.

Then I confessed to Jackson that I had to leave to talk to the drillers before they finished for the day. I could tell he was embarrassed that the day had dragged on so long. I assured him that it was fine, as I knew none of it was within his control. I told him I was proud of him and believed he would make a fine area health administrator. Relieved at my response, he beamed brightly and gave me a huge, endearing hug. With that, Justin and I loaded up and drove back to the school.[2]

Upon arriving at the school, I could see that some progress had been made, in spite of the rain. I reminded everyone that tomorrow would be my last day, but that I had arranged for another local missionary, Greg Windell, whom Chris had connected me with on an earlier trip, to continue to check on the progress. He will meet me here tomorrow for the specifics of what remains to be done, including all of the above ground work and the installation of the submersible pump. I arranged for the contractor to deliver the equipment tomorrow that they will be installing, and I plan to leave my remaining Kenyan shillings with Greg to pay the contractors as they complete their assignments. I've already made a down payment to the pump system installer and also paid Earthcore Drilling for about half of the borehole drilling cost.

I also met with Sammy Wambugu, the owner of Earthcore, earlier this week, and we were able to set a "reasonable" schedule for completing the drilling. While I told Sammy that it was taking way longer than I ever expected—and he admitted the same—I felt strongly that he would complete the work in due time. To his credit, he never once asked me for

---

[2] By the way, on my next trip to Kenya, I had the picture of Jackson receiving his diploma enlarged and framed and presented it to him. You could have sailed away on his smile—one would have thought that I had just given him a new house! It never ceases to amaze me how such small things in the eyes of us Westerners seem so valuable to these simple, rural people, regardless of their education level. I hope to never stop being humbled by their reactions and rejoicing along with them. What a blessing to be in the presence of such gratitude.

more than we had originally agreed upon, assuming that the borehole was no more than 50 meters.[3]

I also told him how impressed I was with the two men that were working for him. "They are fine young Christian men, and they work very hard for you," I said. "But you really need to get them better shoes for doing this dangerous work, and some tools as well." He nodded, pleased with the report, and promised to do these things for them.

Back in the States, I had agonized over the selection of the right borehole contractor. I knew that the first contractor that I was trying to work with would have completed the work way before now. But he wanted to drill deeper than was needed, and he wanted much more money for it, too. The funny thing is, I have heard from him several times while I've been in Kenya. He said that he had even come by before I arrived and had seen the drilling equipment. He joked that this contractor is cheaper because his equipment is so bad and he only has two workers. I responded firmly that he is doing a fine job, even if it is going quite slowly, and that I am confident in his work. We will have a good well, when all is said and done.

"We shall see," the contractor chided.

"Yes," I said. "Indeed we will."

In spite of the unseen variables and the time delays, I trust God with the details. He knows the tremendous needs of these wonderful people, and only He can make these dreams and plans to bless them a reality, if we continue to trust and believe. The men and women of MBEWAU truly do believe—they are so steadfast in their faith, it humbles me. I often tell myself to learn to be more like them.

For now, I am thankful for the safety and protection God has given me here, driving these crazy highways and muddy roads every day without a mishap—other than those few off-road ditch excursions! Tomorrow will be a culmination of my efforts for this trip. No, I will not see the work through to completion, and for that I am quite sad. But I am leaving it, I believe, in very capable hands. Now I need to trust God to see it through by enabling Greg, Jackson, Justin, Pastor, the drill team, and the well equipment contractor to do the remaining work.

I got a second chance to swim in the Indian Ocean this evening—something I've wanted to do since my early morning swim several

[3] The well was finally completed at a depth of only 33 meters (110 feet) and provided plenty of safe, fresh water for our school and the nearby community.

days ago. I always try to get at least one swim in here, as the water is so refreshing and the view is simply breathtaking. I have to pinch myself sometimes, to believe that I am really here, having the time of my life serving God in His Kingdom work, while enjoying the company of so many fine men, women, and incredibly cute kids. I'll never forget the beautiful kiddos from the school who keep me entertained with their games and liveliness. It has gone a long way in relieving the boredom of the slow drilling progress!

While I swam, I thought of my first ride to MBEWAU on Emanuel's motorcycle—how scared I was of tipping it over in the mud. And how I got lost just trying to find the place, which I had been driven to no less than four times just seven months prior! I really need to pay more attention, even when (or maybe especially when) not driving. And I thought of how many times I had to ditch the motorcycle, just to avoid being run over—usually by *matatus*, but once or twice by private owners driving hot cars, and one time, no joke, by a city bus!

Yes, God has truly watched out for me. I think I'll take him with me to Ethiopia in two days! Great idea, Bob! I suspect, based on the variety of scrapes I tend to get into, I may need Him there just as much. Especially since this will be my first time in this new and exciting country, and my first time meeting Melaku and Sosi, his wife—the same Melaku I "stood up" last year when trying to leave Iraq. I certainly hope I'll be able to leave Kenya a lot more easily! Ha.

Time to get some shut-eye. This time tomorrow, I'll be on my way to my next adventure. Wish me luck! Better yet, wish me God's continued blessings! That's truly all I need.

> *"I'm there through your heartache, I'm there in the storm, my love I will keep you by my power alone. I don't care where you've fallen or where you have been. I'll never forsake you, my love never ends. It never ends"*
>
> "*Times*" by Tenth Avenue North, from " Over and Underneath" 2008, AllMusic ©

When God Leaned In

"Welcome to the fallout. Welcome to resistance..... The tension is here, between who you are and who you could be. Between how it is and how it should be, yeah. I dare you to move....... I dare you to lift yourself up off the floor"

"I Dare You to Move" by Switchfoot, from "Learning to Breathe" 2000, AllMusic ©

It was a clear, crisp winter night. A seasoned Yankee would probably call this weather an Indian Summer. A Canadian might even call it a heat wave. But to a tried-and-true Texan, this night was cool and brisk. A big ol' Texas moon lit up the countryside like daylight. And stars? Millions. Truly, a perfect night to hear the answer I was seeking from God.

Alright, let's get real. I was not exactly as calm and cool as the weather. In fact, I was pacing through the Texas Hill Country at 10 o'clock at night with a growing desperation to hear God speak one seemingly simple thing—*my name*. Now, I know you've seen the cover of this book and probably assumed that I already have a moniker, Bob, given to me at birth and with which I navigate the world. That is true. But on this night, I was seeking to know a very different name—my *true* name!

Let me add that I wasn't alone on this quest. At this very moment, forty-two Boot Camp soldiers attending this same weekend event were seeking God for their names, too. Sent off into the beautiful conference center grounds, we were instructed to spend time with God and to sit before Him with this question. We could speak a lot or a little, or we could just listen—whatever we felt led to do. I wanted to ask boldly and confidently expect to hear from God on this personal question. But instead, I felt antsy and desperate.

You see, this was not the first time I had asked Him. More than three years prior, I had first uttered this request while gazing out over beautiful Lake Amistad on the U.S. -Mexico border. It was late at night, and I was alone. And God was silent. Not only that, but I asked seven or eight times after that, and still no answer. I began to wonder if I would EVER get to hear my new name.

Let me give you some background. I was introduced to this quest to hear God speak a "new name" from an incredibly meaningful book to me, Wild at Heart by John Eldredge. The book has spawned a journey for men worldwide to meet together to make this same quest every year. The purpose of the conference goes far beyond simply asking for a name; its goal is to help men unearth their buried hearts and to boldly live into the story that God has for each of us.

Eldredge teaches that all men were born with a desire for adventure, to love well, and to know that we "have what it takes." This desire manifests early as young boys play "slay the dragon" and war games, acting out tales of valor and great expedition. Once upon a time, we were fearless, as God intended us to be. But as we grew up and got knocked around by the "real world," we lost that fearlessness—or more accurately, it was stolen from us by the Enemy/Satan/Beelzebub/The Dark Knight, or whatever you want to call the devil.

Within the four-day Boot Camps that Mr. Eldredge and his Band of Brothers Team have designed, each man is guided through the process of recovering his masculine heart while seeking vision for his life from the Holy Spirit. When the demand for attendance at the Random Heart Boot Camps in Colorado far outweighed their available slots each year, they began to provide training materials for other Boot Camp teams to form around the country. Thus, seven men from San Antonio, Texas who had completed multiple Boot Camps trained for many months to establish their own Boot Camp in the Texas Hill Country. Fittingly, they named themselves the Alamo Band of Brothers (ABOB), in the tradition of those brave volunteers who fought and died defending American freedom in a small Spanish mission in San Antonio well over a century prior. Their vision and aim was to instill bravery once again into the first group of forty-two "soldiers" (named Alpha Company) in the struggle to recover their damaged hearts. I was attending the first ever ABOB Boot Camp.

So here I was on a brisk, moon-filled evening—one of the first round of soldiers seeking renewed hearts and new names at this camp. I had asked this question before, but I thought maybe being immersed in a group of men seeking the same thing would help me to hear with a bit more focus. I was open to whatever God wanted to share with me—just hopefully not another given name, like Eddie, Tony, or Raymond. The "new name" is a name that God bestows to define a man's heart and purpose. For example, some of my ABOB friends have God-given names like Warrior Poet, Finisher, and Captain. Each friend recognized their new name as meant just for them—names that fit the new story that the Holy Spirit was leading them into, their specific place in God's Big Story. *That*, on this beautiful winter night, was the experience I was seeking.

Fortunately, I thought, as my anxiety relented briefly, this night feels different. I do feel confident that God will anoint me with a name that I will recognize and endeavor to live into for the rest of my days in this world. It is what I long for, what I dream of, what I have invented and imagined in my head so many previous nights, waiting for the irreplaceable voice of God to speak to me. And tonight, I feel it—it is time.

As I wandered the moonlit countryside, waiting on God to speak, I thought back on the rough road I'd recently traveled. Only six months earlier, I watched in cowering shock as my life fell apart irreversibly. My twenty-year marriage came crashing down around me, leaving me utterly alone and in total darkness. In the blink of an eye, my existence was no longer defined by my beautiful wife and my three lovely daughters, who had been my identity for so long.

Suddenly, unwantedly, I was Divorced. I wore this "scarlet letter" everywhere I went, keenly aware that no matter what other qualities I may have to offer, what jumped out at everyone was this ugly "D" etched into my forehead, clouding my entire life.

Although I felt newly adrift in society, my true friends didn't desert me. They circled the wagons around my desperate heart and cradled me with their support. They made a point to check in on me and continued inviting me to events. I was amazed at their care and general awesomeness. But nothing could be the same for me. I withdrew from "couples' events," found myself dodging my friends' invitations, and, finally, essentially excused myself from our former group. I stopped attending our Sunday School class and even started looking for a new church. I just didn't feel comfortable in my old environment anymore. The longer two people are married, I discovered, the more they become "one." As it should be, I suppose. But when that bond is severed, the suddenly single can find themselves unable to cope with the loss and shame, unable to find comfort in the old circles as before.

So I withdrew. And accurate or not, "alone" was how I began to perceive my place in the world. I worked hard to put on a tough appearance, like I was fine. But I was not. I was alone, hurting, and nothing I could find would fill the huge hole in my empty existence. I was divorced—for the second time, truthfully. However, this one was not my choice in the least. I hated it. I hated it for me and I really hated it for my two younger daughters, both from this second marriage. I truly felt like a two-time loser.

As desperate as I felt for myself, though, I would have taken on double if it meant sparing my daughters from the fallout that was sure to disrupt their lives. Alexandra, the older of the two, had it perhaps a bit easier, as she was off to college and would not have to deal with this head-on. Like me, she focused on the work at hand—earning a college degree while immersing herself in small college Greek Life, the ladies' tennis team, and a new boyfriend—a baseball player. I imagined (and prayed) that she would be okay.

I worried most for Jacqueline, my youngest. She had to face the mess of divorcing parents as a sophomore in a Christian School. Talk about a scarlet letter! I felt deeply responsible for the huge, glow-in-the-dark one that was now prominently etched on her innocent and lovely forehead. Fortunately, she, too, was driven and stayed busy with college level high school class work and year-round sports—cross country (fall), soccer (winter) and tennis (spring)—doing very well as a varsity player in each. She also had a close-knit group of Christian classmates, both girls and boys, who banded together as a "pack" of friends who just enjoyed being together. Indeed, it was these great friends, and their loving, caring parents, who really helped sustain her through these worst of times.

Still, I felt terribly guilty for the inevitable pain and awkwardness poor Jacqueline had to face. The worst part was, there was no way I could fix this. Me, the engineer, so used to putting my mind and effort into figuring out how to "fix" almost any broken object. This relationship, despite my best Mr. Fix-It methods, would remain broken. I finally accepted this when I signed the final divorce papers, issued by my sympathetic, yet helpless attorney-friend. Texas is a "no-fault" divorce state, and there is almost no reason required for ending a marriage, even one with children.

I knew I needed to fight through the pain and be available for both of my younger girls, and also for my oldest daughter, Breanne, who was married and living in Connecticut. I was encouraged to see that, although I had made a mess of my first marriage to her mom, both she and her mom had survived and were doing quite well. My relationship with Breanne was even growing stronger. As a stepchild to my second wife, she had been relegated to a Cinderella-like existence, to a degree. To my shame, I admit that though I had the power to stop this from happening, too often I failed to. I suppose one positive from this divorce was that Breanne was now free of that, and we were free to rebuild a strong relationship. She also became an excellent older sister to her hurting young stepsisters.

Remarkably, even in the midst of so much brokenness and shame, my three daughters began to see me in a new way. My transformation into the joy-filled missionary over the years was a far cry from the broken father that they had known. Even as I was wounded and in the slow process of healing, my Father, I truly believe, was giving them each a unique glimpse at their renewed earthly father. This became a grace on all of us—God was renewing all of our hearts, both in relationship to Him and to one another. I cannot speak for any of my daughters, but I truly had a sense that all of this was being used for our good. I was experiencing the comforting and hopeful words of Romans 8: *And we know that God causes all things to work together for good to those who love God, to those who are called according to His purpose. For those whom He foreknew, He also predestined . . . ; and these whom He predestined, He also called; and these whom He called, He also justified; and these whom He justified, He also glorified.* (Romans 8:28-30, NIV).

Amazing. God seeks not only to restore our lives and our relationships, He also seeks to *glorify* us. I had already experienced so much renewal, so much redemption and mercy from the hand of God, and I was immensely grateful. So why, you might ask, was I hung up on hearing some new name from God? What's wrong with Bob, anyway?

My name, I had learned, is a shortened form of Robert and comes from the German name, Hrodebert, meaning "famed, bright, shining." That's cool, right? I like to think I was named after the brave warrior,

Robert the Bruce, depicted in the movie, Braveheart. However, I'm sure this is not what my parents were thinking in February 1950 when they had to name me quickly, as I was to be released the next day. Thus, I was Christened Robert Allan, after my Uncle Bob (Dad's older brother) and another distant relative, Allan Nicol. Not much meaning there. Back then, if you weren't destined to be a Jr. or a III, you typically named your kids after aunts and uncles.

I'm fine with my name. I've had it for more than sixty-six years now. But tonight's quest was important. We were not seeking another given name from God. Although it *could* be—I have a friend whose real name is John, as well as his God-anointed name, as in "John, the disciple whom Jesus loved". John is truly a loving, caring guy, and he is happy with his "anointed name." But that's not going to work for me. I desire, I covet, a more descriptive name.

There is a Biblical background, by the way, to all this "new name" talk. Eldredge didn't make it up. The quest for a new name comes from the book of Revelation: *"He who has an ear, let him hear what the Spirit says to the churches. To him who overcomes, to him I will give some of the hidden manna, and I will give him a white stone, and a new name written on the stone which no one knows but he who receives it."* (Revelation 2:17, NIV).

A more contemporary version, Eugene Peterson puts it this way: *"Are your ears awake? Listen to the Wind Words, the Spirit blowing through the churches. I'll give the sacred manna to every conqueror; I'll give a clear smooth stone inscribed with your new name, your sacred new name."* (Revelation 2:17, The Message)

I have yet to hear of anyone receiving his name from God written on a white stone. Most hear their name spoken, either audibly or within their spirits. Each time, the new name was unquestionably from God and revealed a facet of their well-defined role now being revealed as they engage in kingdom-building here on earth. As believers, we know our salvation is guaranteed, the future settled. The encouragement of the new name and purpose helps us focus on the work we are given to do in our life's calling here on earth.

The author George MacDonald puts it this way, "The giving of the white stone with the new name is the communication of what God thinks about the man to the man ... The true nature is one which expresses the character, the nature, the meaning of the person who bears it. It is the man's own symbol – his soul's picture, in a word – the sign which belongs to him and to no one else. Who can give a man this, his own name? God alone"[4]

Just to clarify, I don't believe that means we always have to scurry off to a distant developing country, or join the Peace Corps. That's not God's plan for all of us, I'm convinced. There is plenty to do right in our own neighborhoods, especially if travel is not something that you're comfortable with, or living more primitively, or facing true hardship, for that matter. I truly believe that God can find each one of us a place just outside of our "current comfort zone," if we will just ask Him. If we want it bad enough.

So I continued to sit, straining to listen in the silence for a name... just a word, maybe two, dropping down from the heavens. But the only thing I heard was voices in the distance. Some of the soldiers were already "returning to the barracks." Oh, good for you! I thought bitterly. I suppose God already told you your name, and now you're off to happily share it with the group. For a moment, from the depths of my sin-stained nature, I despised those who would say they heard God speak their names. I knew I would either wave it off as folly or think, "What a stupid name!" But I immediately fought the Enemy's volley and sought desperately to be excited for the stories of their special revelations.

Why, I wondered, does God keep me waiting like this? If this is something He knows I want, and surely it is within His power to respond, then why does He keep me in suspense? I could even help Him out with the meaning—I was sure the name would relate to my driving desire to drill wells in Africa. Since God was the one who opened my heart to that particular mission field, wouldn't it make sense that His name for me would go along with it?

I thought back to a story in Wild at Heart. Eldredge recalls a day when, as a young man, he found himself in a small book shop, killing time. He was on the cusp of making a huge decision. He had been accepted to graduate school, a deep desire of his, but he had no money saved up, and a wife and three young kids depended on his provision. He had also been offered a lucrative position with a firm in Washington D.C. He could choose the safe, plush job, operating in fairly elite circles, and be done with the question of easily providing for his family. Still,

[4] "George MacDonald: An Anthology", by George MacDonald, Fount, 1990

he sensed that if he followed his heart to grad school, he would truly realize his dreams.

This dilemma, and the ramifications for his family and his own future, weighed him down, robbing him of sleep. So that morning in the bookstore, he wandered over to the self-help section, then to a random book that he leafed through. The author, Gil Bailie, shared the advice his own spiritual mentor had given him years earlier: "Don't ask yourself what the world needs. Ask yourself what makes you come alive, and go do that, because what the world needs is people who have come alive."

Eldredge was dumbstruck as he suddenly realized that he had lived his life looking for the world to tell him what to do with himself. He thought, "Can a world of posers tell you anything but how to pose?" No, he answered himself, only God can tell me what I need to do. God was answering his dilemma through Bailie's words. He left the tiny bookstore determined to pursue "a life worth living." Within days, he received a call from an old friend offering to pay for his entire graduate school program. His decision to return to school changed the entire trajectory of his life; he became a writer, a counselor, and a lecturer. In doing so, he has profoundly changed the lives of many people.

I carried that quote from Bailie with me as I dashed off to the depths of South Sudan only a month earlier. I left with a broken heart, coming straight from my failed marriage. But there, in the vast Sudanese desert, I experienced my heart come alive with new fervor as I watched men, women, and children celebrate the miraculous gift of clean water, as our newly constructed well began pumping this life blood to the surface. I knew in that moment that this was my life's calling. It became my all-consuming desire to see the joy of the people in these schools and communities experience the blessing that access to clean, safe drinking water provides. It has not stopped thrilling me to this day.

There is really no way, I am certain, that Westerners can begin to experience a similar excitement, save perhaps at that moment of birth when our son or daughter emerges from the womb. I'm not sure we can quite feel the same relief and amazement at a new well, what with our clean, fresh drinking water immediately available with the turn of a faucet. We cannot know the joy that I see these villagers, especially the women, experience. As the primary water haulers in Africa, the women become ecstatic when they see the fresh water spew forth from the new well. They see an arduous journey made shorter, along with the miracle of safe water for their families.

A study conducted by Stanford University scholars on the effect of a safe water source for the African women living in the bush was astounding in its conclusion. When fresh water is available from a well, in addition to the obvious benefits of ease and time-saving, they found that African women also have fewer babies. As the death rate of children is reduced by the clean water (water-borne disease is the primary cause of death among African children), the women feel a level of control over the number of children they birth. They determine that they do not "need" as many children to help them with chores and to care for them as they age. All too often, the fathers have long since disappeared, leaving the usually uneducated moms in survival mode.

Confidence and prosperity emerge from this new water source, and many single moms even begin growing their own crops in their little *shambas* (gardens). Soon they learn to grow more varieties and in quantities that allow them to sell some of their harvest locally, gaining needed income. Eventually, some will even begin to pursue an education, a luxury they had no time for as young mothers with huge responsibilities and never-ending chores. A brighter life emerges—and it all begins with a dependable water source.

I carry this knowledge with me to every new well project, the far-reaching benefits this one simple well can bring. I like to build benches under shade trees near the completed wells to provide a place for the women to fellowship as they wait to fill their large jugs with water. Sometimes they bring laundry to the well site so that they can save the hauling of more water for clothes washing back to their homes, saving even more time in the day. Can you see why I'm excited with every new well? It is more than safe water—it is life improved, fellowship enhanced, and in many cases, death defeated. And it makes my heart truly come alive.

I will, of course, continue to stride forward in this new passion, this newfound calling in my life. I just really, really want to know my new name, the one that corresponds with my purpose. Maybe, I sighed to myself, I want it too much. Maybe that's why I'm not able to hear the name He has for me. It could be me who's blocking the clear path, getting in my own way, as I tend to do all too often, honestly. But then

I think, Come on! He's God! He can reach beyond that, right? On and on the inner battle rages. Oh well, I decide, I'd better get back, name or no name, before they declare me AWOL!

I turned and began making the short walk back to the masses. And then suddenly, just like that— I heard it. God spoke my new name. *What? Are you sure?* I looked around and saw no one. I heard it though, quite clearly. But was it audible, or just in my head? Maybe God will repeat Himself. Worth a try. "Hey God, was that You?" No answer.

Great. Now I have a whole new dilemma. Do I go with what I think He called me, or do I deny that this whole thing ever happened? I only heard one word. I know I said I was fine with that, but…was that the way He spoke to the others—to my friends and fellow soldiers? Or did they get more like a sentence, or a full phrase, at least? Something like, "From now on you will be called..." All in a deep, Darth Vader-like voice.

Now I was wrestling with doubt that was even more painful than not having a name in the first place! The questions raged as I strolled back to "base camp." Did I really hear my name or am I making it up? It was only one word? Nothing more? No explanation? Why would He leave me to figure it out? Arghh! This is so not fair! My head was swimming with unanswered questions.

As I rejoined the group of men, I began hearing animated stories of their "discussions with God." Yep, *discussions*! I only heard—or thought I heard—one word. So what? Does that somehow make them more special, or more "right" with God? Or maybe I could argue in the other direction—that I am SO RIGHTEOUS that I only needed the one word!

On and on the conflicting opinions swirled in my brain as I rejoined the others. I knew I was spiraling, thinking unhelpful thoughts, so I remained silent before my fellow soldiers and "officers" as their discussions ensued. Their stories were authentic and compelling, and I concluded that since I was doubting what I heard was from God—or that I even heard anything—I would say nothing at all. I couldn't see myself trying to convince others when I couldn't even convince myself.

Bob! Enough with the suspense! What did you *think* you heard? What is your new name?!

Alright. I'll tell you what I thought I heard. It was one word: "Deliverer." I wasn't sure how this would work as a name. *Deliverer?* I imagine most people will continue to call me Bob. Can't see my friends saying, "Hey Deliverer, wanna grab a beer with us after work tonight?" Or, "Are you going to the Missions game tonight, Deliverer?" Don't really see that catching on.

And so, I struggled with sharing this "name" with my comrades. I knew that none of my true friends, particularly my ABOB comrades, would ever doubt the sincerity of my hearing God speak my name to me. Sadly, that didn't stop me from remaining in hiding. I should have known better, of course. For days we had heard how the enemy works feverishly to dampen our spirits and tame our hearts. He wants no part of a heart coming alive. And one of his chief tactics is self-doubt. So I withdrew into myself and thought of very little else for the remainder of the sessions, which concluded on Sunday morning.

I suppose I lost the battle that weekend. I spoke not one word about my new name. Not that weekend, not that year (2008); not even, sad to say, the next year, or the one after that. Certainly, it floated constantly in my mind, as I vaguely searched for "the right time" to share what I had heard. But there never seemed to be a right time. I kept the name a secret. I told myself that I can still be God's Deliverer—His *secret* Deliverer. I don't have to announce it to the world, right? Doesn't stop me from living out my new dream of actually drilling wells with my own hands and equipment in Africa, just as I'd do with or without a name! And true to my word, I didn't stop doing what made my "heart come alive," name or no name. To this day (eight years later at this writing), I am still active in a ministry that drills and equips water wells in Kenya, Africa.

I got on with life, work, and my ministry. A year passed, and I was invited to attend my second boot camp—Charlie Company, or Boot Camp 3—by the Alamo Band of Brothers. My friend Tom and I had both attended previous boot camps as "soldiers;" this time we were asked to serve as part of "the enlisted"—anonymous, praying members who would stay alert to assist "the wounded."

You see, as the weekend unfolds, many of the men experience the opening of old wounds in their souls. As Eldredge explains, boys were designed by God to be fearless, strong-hearted, and strong-willed (to Mom's occasional frustration)! But as they grow, men lose that fearlessness, that desire for and confidence in "battle." Our God-given confidence is stolen from us through the pain of shattered dreams, or by an abusive or absentee father. Every man I've ever heard from at these camps has experienced some degree of "stolen valor." In this process, the men have to "own" their painful story before the healing process can begin. In essence, Tom and I were the first responders, staying vigilant to provide prayer and support once these various wounds splayed open.

As the weekend stretched on, the men began to open their hearts and share their deepest fears with almost total strangers. The only way this level of comfort and trust could have been achieved was through the work of the Holy Spirit, and it was incredible to be a part of it. To top it all off, several of our soldiers even heard their "new names" right away. As you've probably guessed, however, I still felt uneasy about sharing mine.

I had, however, been thinking about what it meant to me over the past year. Deliverer. It had revealed itself as more fitting than I had first thought. I saw that I was now thoroughly submerged in my new life of "delivering" water to many people, first in South Sudan, and then Ethiopia, then Tanzania, and eventually Kenya. I was providing access to safe, clean water, which many times, most notably in South Sudan, the people had never experienced before. Figuratively, I did consider that I "delivered" this water to these villages, even if I wasn't physically pumping or hauling.

By the way, I have hauled a 5-gallon jerry can, which weighs about 45 pounds. After walking less than half a mile, I was tired and my arms ached. Yet I have seen women, weighing no more than 100 pounds, carry a full 5-gallon bucket on their heads, with a child on their back, often times barefooted, and sometimes even carrying firewood in their "empty" arm. I read about the rigorous training that our Navy Seals and Army Rangers have to endure, to "pass the test" towards becoming elite fighters. I'm thinking we should add this combo of water bucket, infant, and firewood-hauling to these training programs!

Charlie Company's weekend wrapped up, and I was tempted to let the whole issue of my new name just stay forever my secret. I couldn't see how it mattered if anyone knew, and I was tired of wrestling with it. Would it change the way our ministry worked? Would we get more requests for donated wells? I had finally accepted that "Deliverer" was, in fact, my new God-given name. It made me feel good to know it. I was fine keeping it to myself and getting on with my purpose.

A year and a half passed quickly after Charlie Company, and I heard that my friends were preparing for Echo Company, Boot Camp No. 5. My ABOB friend, Alan, asked me again to serve on the Intercessory Prayer Team. I jumped at the chance, glad that I could attend this one since I had no current plans to return to Kenya for a few more months. I attended a pre-weekend meeting and met four men who, along with Tom and me, would make up a larger, more focused Prayer Team. Tom and I were enthused by this new format, remembering how exhausted we were by the end of the Charlie Company weekend. This time, we would have a full team of prayer warriors to attend to the wounded.

We were excited to be back at the Franklin Family Ranch—2,000 acres of wooded rolling hills, complete with a meandering stream, a lake, expansive grass fields for sports activities, a first-class skeet shooting facility, and enough beds in cabins and bunk houses to accommodate nearly 100 people. In addition, there were many exotic animals from India and Africa that roamed the wooded area. In fact, one of the major attractions of the range is an exotic game hunting lodge. For our ABOB weekends, though, we were content to take guided tours to view the incredible wildlife.

As the name implies, the FFR is a family-owned ranch. One of the unique features of what the Franklin family offers to every group is their hands-on hospitality. Mr. Franklin, who runs the facility with his two daughters and sons-in-law, is the former CEO of a very large and successful communications company in San Antonio. At the ranch, you'll find the entire Franklin family, from Mr. and Mrs. Franklin down to their grandchildren, serving as tour guides, cooks, food servers, and schlepps. Obviously, the Franklins could afford to hire help for all of the menial work, but they don't. It is humbling to see Mr. and Mrs. Franklin, their daughters, and their families cooking and serving us food and then cleaning up after us. As a strong Christian family, well grounded in their faith, they demonstrate the Christ-like concept of serving others, and they do it in such a friendly and warmhearted manner. It makes a great weekend even better.

A we settled in, over forty new "recruits" arrived—mostly from Texas. But there are always a few who make their way here from other states. In fact, at the Charlie Company boot camp, one young man had traveled all the way from Alaska—by car. He drove here. The ABOB team now consisted of six committed Christians who had all attended multiple boot camps put on by John Eldredge and his team in Colorado. Putting on a boot camp is no small undertaking, requiring many months of preparation; in fact, the ABOB team prepared for more than a year for the initial boot camp.

I knew two members of the team before the Band formed, Alan and John, since we attend the same church and Sunday School. I have since come to know and highly respect the other four members: Brian, Jay, Neal, and Jonesy. Each member of this six-man team is successful in his own business. They don't *have* to take time off for weeks on end to prepare to battle the Enemy for the renewal of men's hearts. They *want* to because Eldredge's team did it for them, and they want to serve others in the same way. I am one of the happy recipients of their commitment. I'm also honored to now call them my friends. It is only because of their friendship and willingness to serve, I believe, that I was able to hear and know my God-given name.

I had been content to leave my new name a secret. At this point, it had been almost three years since the night I first heard it, and I still hadn't told anyone. The experience was becoming more distant as time went on, and harder to share. However, I really trusted these guys, and something deep inside of me still wanted it to be out in the open. Make it "official." I still had so many questions, though, about my name.

The Echo Company Boot Camp weekend unfolded in much the same way as the previous four camps. Wounds were exposed, and our prayers were focused and intent. Naturally, I had more than enough to do during the boot camp; but in my few moments of rest and solitude, the question of my name resurfaced. Why was I so afraid to share it? *Deliverer*. Each time I thought of it, I thought of how people might respond. "Sure Bob, you deliver water to poor villagers. We get it. Did you make up this name to fit what you already do in your ministry?" And the fact that I had waited so long to share it had caused me to lose momentum.

I gladly pushed these thoughts out of my mind to attend to the work of the weekend. This is really okay, I told myself. This weekend isn't about me, anyway; I'm here for the soldiers and for the ABOB Team.

And so far, this one was shaping up to be another smashing success. Yes, wounds were breaking open, but just as quickly they were being tended to, either by a prayer warrior or by a new friend and brother. Men nurturing one another—it was quite a sight to behold. The same men that might be deftly shooting skeet or throwing a football around during our afternoon free times were now patiently listening to their brothers—even hugging them—as they revealed their hearts' deep, festering wounds. Such is the "magic" of the Holy Spirit's healing, as it begins to take a new foothold in these men's lives, while they come clean with their suppressed stories. I had no time to dwell on my issues, and truly, this was a good thing.

But in the quiet of late evenings, after the others had gone to bed, I found I couldn't fight it anymore. The time had come. If this was truly the new name I had been given, it couldn't stay my secret. I knew I had to "come out of hiding" and share it with these, my trusted Christian friends. If I ignored this urging, I would essentially have to disavow any knowledge of my new name and forget it forever.

And I already knew I could not dismiss what I had heard and still remain true to my faith. I felt in my heart of hearts that God had bestowed this name on me. My problem? It just didn't seem to speak fully enough to my purpose. I loved delivering water to villages, but honestly, I didn't feel like a "deliverer" in the rest of my life. Most of the year finds me shopping, eating, and living comfortably (albeit in a tiny but modern apartment). I have all the modern features, like heating and cooling, electricity, and even running water. I simply couldn't travel to Africa any more than I was already, since I still had to hold down a job and support my daughters here in the States. I didn't feel like a "full-time" *Deliverer.* If the name referred to water delivery, well, the truth was, it just seemed a bit limited. I was looking for something…*bigger*. Before I fell asleep, I asked God to show me what I was missing.

I awoke the next morning after a restful night's sleep. As usual, I was one of the first campers up and made my way to the big house to make some coffee. I enjoyed my first cup while rocking in a big rocking chair on the front porch, where I had an expansive view of the beautiful hill country.

While I was there enjoying the quiet serenity of the morning, I started musing on what had changed for me since that night when I heard God speak my new name. I was now making three regular trips a year to a number of countries in Africa. My role as a volunteer missionary with CrossWay International was to oversee all of our planned and in-progress water projects.

Okay, I thought—I am steadily involved in this work of delivering water to thirsty communities in South Sudan, Ethiopia, Tanzania, and now Kenya. Wasn't this enough? No. I felt no peace in this "simple" explanation. I knew I wasn't making it up either; it seemed the Holy Spirit Himself had more to say on the matter. I couldn't let it go, and now I felt *He* wouldn't let it go until I knew the meaning of my name in its fullness. This journey had felt a bit like Jacob wrestling with the angel—but at least I woke up most mornings without a severe limp!

I thought about the health and hygiene class that I taught to the recipients of the water wells. Starting with the first well Crossway drilled in South Sudan, I had taught the villagers the fundamentals of how to properly collect, transport, store, and use the water from the wells. This teaching is a vital part of our drilling a well, since the well water must remain clean until it is consumed or used in the home. If not, then little has been improved, since the primary goal of providing a clean source of water is to eliminate sickness and even death from water-borne disease. These hygiene classes were central to the ministry I provided. However, even this puzzle piece did not seem to fit in the larger picture of the story of my name. For now, I would have to pause in this process, as the soldiers began to appear, stumbling like zombies toward the beckoning coffee aroma. I left the serenity of the back porch and joined the group gathering around the popular coffee pot.

After chatting for a bit, I left in search of my fellow prayer partners, who would already be well into the daily prayers for each man at Echo Company Boot Camp. I was looking forward to jumping into this final day. Sundays are always very special. Trying, definitely, but also very rewarding when we witness soldiers responding to the God who loves them. It can be a bloody battle at times, but it is well worth it to see men's hearts come alive and witness their healing. As intercessors, we had the responsibility to silently observe these men, while remaining vigilant for signs of "battle fatigue" at one extreme and exuberant excitement at the other. Regardless of which emotion emerged, we were alert to the fact that the Enemy was never far away, always prowling about looking to steal the new life that was emerging. For this reason, each Sunday the ABOB presenters made a point to caution our new soldiers to be prepared for renewed enemy attack, which could happen as soon as they arrived home or, in some cases, even on the return drive.

After hours of praying, seeing chains broken and hearts restored, we were given one more small space of free time to be alone and rest. It was one of only a few times that each of us on the prayer team was able to relax and experience some "alone time" for ourselves, without having to focus on anyone else. It was a very welcome time for me—"*nice*," as my Kenyan friends would say. Naturally, as soon as I was alone, I felt the old question surface. I took a breath and began by asking the Holy Spirit for more insight about this name thing. Then I let my mind drift, not expecting an immediate answer.

I thought further on this new chapter of my life. Drilling water wells and teaching hygiene classes were both important parts of my new ministry. And besides trying to learn as much as I could about well-drilling and the geology of Kenya, I could think of only two other major commitments I'd taken on since discovering my passion: my continued participation in these Boot Camps, and a class that I was enrolled in at my church. Each was totally unique, with very little overlap with the other; the one thing they had in common was that they both occurred within Christian community.

These two new commitments had been good for my heart, my soul, my well-being. I had been invited to join, too, in both cases. Our senior pastor, David, had invited me to this "seminary-lite sort of class" at our church. He heard that I was making regular trips to Africa for water ministry work and thought I might benefit from the studies. I could use the knowledge while serving in my ministry, and the class could benefit from hearing about my hands-on mission work. It was called The Quarry. At first, I didn't feel I had much in common with the other students. While some were making occasional mission trips, most of them were attending in lieu of seminary to receive a pastoring certification. I was merely there as a sponge, soaking up all this sound Biblical knowledge from truly great teachers.

David, our senior pastor, received his PhD from Duke Divinity School, while Scott, our associate pastor and full-time pastor of our mission church, Riverside, was a Perkins School of Divinity graduate. When I joined The Quarry, they were just beginning their second semester.

I had already missed a good bit of information, but it would run for four semesters (two school years) and then start over again. So while I would not get the information in perfect sequence, I could eventually get all of it. And I had learned by that point to let go of trying to control the order of things happening in my life.

This issue of letting go of control and allowing change to occur was something I was learning to do, step by step. Not only had I learned to rush less to complete tasks, I actually took more time now to consider projects and seek God's advice in taking on new commitments. I was learning to trust God with every facet of my life, even in the seemingly "small" decisions. I found it very freeing as I stepped out on seeking His direction more closely.

I suppose I'm sharing that with you because I've come to realize that we are ALL control freaks to some degree. John Eldredge calls this "our pose." Everyone is posing in some way, not just in controlling our lives, but also the way we mask our true selves with a false persona. I know this from experience—I once decided that I had made posing into an art form, I had become so adept at it. Fortunately, my closest and dearest male friends, including some of my Band of Brothers, saw right through it and helped me to deal with it, head on. As long as we are breathing, we will have some level of posing and need honest relationships to guide us to the truth. Our natural sin nature always leads us astray.[5] In fact, in Jeremiah we read, *"The heart is deceitful above all things, and beyond cure. Who can understand it?"* (Jeremiah 17:9, NIV)

I feel so thankful that I had friends who cared about me enough to tell me the truth, and then followed up with me to make sure I was living it out. I may still pose from time to time, but at least now I have strong insight into who I am and what on earth I'm doing here. I've been empowered by God to grasp the fleeting tail of the life that was meant for me, holding firm with new commitment, determined at every moment to live into my true story—the one God wrote for me from the day he "stitched me together in my mother's womb." I pray that everyone

---

[5] I realize I have talked a lot about Eldredge's works and the Boot Camps in this story. Although his teaching is central to the chapter, I'd like to emphasize that my limited coverage of it here is not intended to cover the topic in any depth. If you'd like to know more, I encourage you to read Wild at Heart by John Eldredge and consider signing up for a Boot Camp in your area or at the beautiful Ransomed Heart Ranch in Colorado.

reading this might bravely face down their pose, too, and discover their God-given purpose!

There in the woods of a serene hill country ranch on a beautiful Sunday afternoon, I mused further on the Quarry class, considering what I would do with the information I was receiving, in this season of learning so much about myself and how I might be better used by God. Surely, by learning that I was a redeemed son of the Most High God and experiencing a glorious overhaul of my identity, I couldn't believe that I had enrolled in this class by happenstance. Even though I still wasn't sure I quite belonged, I thoroughly enjoyed the class.

When I walked in that classroom the first time and looked around, I recognized more than half of the 40 or so students as members of my church, where the class was usually held. We did have one class at a local barbeque restaurant, where Scott dramatically presented the bloody events in Leviticus; then, for another class we all met in downtown San Antonio and followed Scott, once again, our budding "rabbi," stopping at various buildings and monuments so he could provide some historical insight and relate it to Biblical teachings. Fun "field trips!"

Most nights we were given a lecture, and the teacher (David, Scott, or a guest) would open the room to questions and discussion. If we didn't cover all of the material, we'd just pick it up the following week. Unlike a school course, we were not on any firm completion schedule. In fact, it seemed more important to the teachers to engage the class in critical thinking, and believe it or not, many times the students would offer a more "correct" or "consensus" answer that satisfied a difficult question. I admired our instructors, as they welcomed any assistance class members could offer on a complex subject.

After almost two full years, I had gained extensive knowledge of our Judeo-Christian heritage; participated in lectures and discussions of most of the Old Testament, including a study of significant writings by Marvin Wilson; studied vast portions of the New Testament through the writings of NT Wright; attended wonderful guest lectures on topics such as sonship, ancient Hebrew weddings, a synagogue's structure and functions, and the Passover. I had even learned the basics of homiletics and how to prepare a sermon. I loved participating in the class; yet many times I wondered, what in the world was I going to do with all this information? A number of students used it as a "springboard" into seminary. Several classes focused on "our calling," what it looked like and how you could tell if it was authentic. Neither of these was quite what I needed.

By now I felt that I had already received my calling and was living into it as best I could. I knew that David and Scott, our other pastors and church staff, and many of my Quarry classmates, knew of my water well ministry and supported me wholeheartedly. And while I never felt the urge to run off to enroll in seminary, I was excited for those that did. Still, there I sat, sponging up all this great information, but never knowing exactly why I was learning it. I had even asked God on more than one occasion, to help me understand why I was there. So far, He had remained silent on that question, as well.

I was getting used to this silence from God on fervent questions I asked. Maybe this was part of my education in waiting on God and not trying to control everything. I leaned back and soaked in the silence and beauty of the Hill Country, relinquishing my need to know the answers to my questions in my own timeframe.

Then all at once, God broke the silence.

Without thunderbolts or lightning, in one quiet moment, I suddenly knew the answer to question of the class, and the answer to the earlier, all-consuming name question. No dramatic clouds parting or audible voice. I can only say that it seemed like God "leaned in" and connected the dots between my name and my purpose. God opened my tiny human brain, and made way for some bit of wisdom, or insight, perhaps, to flow in. Suddenly I got it.

I knew in an instant that as His "Deliverer", I was sent to deliver more than just clean water to these wonderful people. I was also charged with delivering Jesus' message of love and kindness, forgiveness and grace. I knew instantly why I had joined the Quarry class and why I continued to participate in these Boot Camps. God was training me for a greater mission, to deliver His water, His Word, and His love—to open men's hearts to receive The Living Water that His own Son offers to all of us, everywhere, each and every day!

I sat there, stunned. Just like that beautiful, crisp full-moonlit night when God had called me His Deliverer, he had come through again—this time by merely leaning in—to provide the insight that I so desperately needed. I was excited beyond belief. I could not wait to tell my Band of

Brothers; and this time, I would not wait two years! I'd find a moment once camp was over. For now, I focused my thoughts and prayers back on the soldiers I was here to serve. But as I headed back to the conference room, I was buoyant with confidence and sporting a Cheshire cat smile; I'm pretty sure I was hovering slightly above the ground as I walked.

The leaders wrapped up the weekend with a final charge to the new soldiers before they headed home—back into reality, into the world of work, families, and the Enemy. Then, after our goodbyes and with most of the men gone, I assisted the ABOB Team in the breakdown of the conference room and packing of their movie and sound system for the transport back to San Antonio.

As we worked, I mentioned to Alan that I had something really important to share with the team that tied back to our first boot camp. He noticed the huge smile on my face and glint in my eye and immediately gathered the team together. While I still felt some hesitation in telling my friends about my first encounter with God more than two years prior, today's revelation gave me strength to just do it. With these six strong Christian men now gathered around me, I began by apologizing for turning the focus on myself and away from the forty-two brave men that we'd ministered to for the last four days. But I thanked them for the chance to finally share my story with them.

I took them back to that moonlit Saturday night at Alpha Camp when God gave me my new name. I said it out loud for the first time—"*Deliverer.*" I admitted that I had never told anyone because I was afraid. "Of what, I don't know," I said. "Maybe I was just living deeper into my pose. All I know is that I was silent for more than two years, struggling with doubt."

I looked around at my friends, grinning. "Until today. I finally heard again from God just today—a few hours ago, actually. Originally, I thought the name referred only to my passion to deliver safe, clean water to the poor in Kenya, Africa. But it just didn't seem big enough, or encompass enough of my life. It always seemed to me that there was more that He wanted me to know. But I simply didn't know what that was—until today! God showed me that it is not only water he wants me to deliver. He also desires that I deliver His message, that His Son, Jesus, is the Living Water, and that those I serve need Him as their Lord and Savior. This class I've been attending at church for the last year and a half was really preparing me to better deliver that message. The water I help provide saves lives, most certainly. But the greater message I can deliver—and their acceptance of the salvation of Jesus—brings eternal life."

The brothers were silent. Then two standing on either side of me simultaneously put an arm around my shoulders. Just like that, as if choreographed, all seven of us melted into a "group hug" of sorts.

"On top of all of that," I continued, "participating in these Boot Camps, supporting you six incredible men, has given me ample opportunities to learn from you, while honing my prayer skills and arming me with the boldness I need to accomplish my assigned task. I'm so grateful for every one of you, for all that you have done for me and my ministry without even knowing it. You are all a rich blessing to me. Thank you for inviting me again and again; and thanks so much for your continued friendship! I truly treasure it."

"You got it," they replied as they each hugged me. "We love you, Bob."

"Thanks," I chuckled. "But from now on, you can call me "*Deliverer*!"

> *"Truth spoke in whispers will tear you apart, no matter how hard you resist it. It never rains when you want it to. You humble me, Lord, Humble me, Lord. I'm on my knees empty. You humble me Lord. You humble me Lord. Please, please, please forgive me."*

> "*Humble Me*" by Nora Jones, from "Feels Like Home" 2004, Blue Note Records ©

So, There Really are Camels in Ethiopia?

"Come to the treasure you who search and you'll search no more. Come to the lover you who want and you'll want no more, no. And all you who labor in vain, and to the broken and shamed, yeah. Love is here. Love is pouring from His hands, from His brow. Love is near, it satisfies. Streams of mercy flowing from His side. 'Cause Love is here."

"Love is Here", by Tenth Avenue North, from "Over and Underneath", 2008 AllMusic ©

This time, I wasn't trying to get there from Baghdad. In fact, my first visit to Ethiopia was relatively uneventful. I came straight from the well-drilling project at MBEWAU (remember those Mtepeni Baptist Elders Waking Up fellas?). I arrived three days later than planned, after extending my time in Kenya, hoping—dreaming actually—that Earthcore Drillers might somehow complete the borehole drilling during my visit. Not to be. In fact, it would be more than a month before water would come to the school and local community. Knowing that now, I am glad I left when I did; I would have been frustrated from not seeing the well completed and having to miss Ethiopia yet again.

I was eager to finally visit Ethiopia, not only because I had missed it on my last go-round, but because it's *Ethiopia*—the birthplace of man, they say. So many Biblical stories about the country or people make it a fascination for many, myself included, like the beautiful story of Philip witnessing to the Ethiopian eunuch (Acts 8:26-40, NIV). Also, I would finally get to meet Melaku Abebe, CrossWay's in-country manager. Then I could apologize for "standing him up" on my intended stop-over from Iraq to Kenya the previous year.

Stepping off the plane in Addis Ababa, I was amazed at the beauty and newness of the airport. I had not expected this. Nor did I expect to spend the next 45 minutes obtaining my travel visa at the tiny visa office, which stood in sharp contrast to the vast and surprisingly modern terminal. I took my place at the back of a long, meandering line and settled in for the wait. I noticed with surprise that many of those queued up seemed to speak English, which was some comfort.

Looking around, I realized that most were holding several filled-out forms. I asked the couple in front of me, who I had overheard speaking American English, about my missing documents. They turned and signaled an official and asked where they could get another visa form for "their friend." How 'bout that—not ten minutes after deplaning, I had already made two new friends! The airport official immediately ducked into a room and returned just as quickly with a visa form. "Thank you," I told the couple. "This is my first visit to Addis." I had already picked up on the local tradition of truncating the capital city name.

"Oh, we remember our first trip, and how bewildered and confused we were, believe me," said the lady. "I'm Gillian, and this is my husband, Roger. This is only our fourth visit."

"Fifth, actually," Roger piped in.

"Is it five? I lose track of those things, but not Roger. Okay, so this will take some patience, Bob. You won't believe what they are doing in there—they're handwriting every visa using the information from your form. You shoul d start filling it out, while you're waiting. Not that they will call you anytime soon, ha!" Gillian laughed heartily at her own joke. "I'll shut up now, so that you can finish your form," she said. Roger laughed and rolled his eyes. "What?" she asked him.

"Nothing, sweetie," Roger grinned.

"Oh, no, it's fine," I said. "You guys really helped me out. I would have stumbled into that room, form-less, and been sent all the way to the back of this line." I hurried to complete my form right there in line, even though it didn't seem to be moving quickly at all.

Eventually, all three of us did make it inside the visa prep room, and I was somewhat astonished. Gillian, watching my reaction closely, chuckled. "Didn't I tell you?"

"Wow," was all I said, not wanting to cause any ire in the very folks I was hoping would give me this highly sought-after travel visa. I lowered my voice to a whisper. "I thought it was archaic in Kenya. At least there, they had individual booths with a protective glass and a little sliding window just above the counter from which to talk and receive the documents."

Here in this modern and new airport terminal, however, there were three women sitting at a six-foot wooden table, hastily writing out travel visas—the full passport page type that they stick directly onto the passport visa pages, as in Kenya. Two of the ladies were writing out the visas, while a third lady handed them papers from a small file box, after looking up the passenger name from the form and comparing it with the papers in her box. Strange, indeed. I couldn't imagine what was in her file box that could possibly pertain to any of us in line, as we all appeared to be from somewhere other than Ethiopia. Unless it was some kind of "no-fly" list! Gillian and Roger could not shed any light on this strange process, either, even as "seasoned" visa seekers. It would have to remain a mystery, since none of us were willing to ask, for fear of jeopardizing our chances of getting through this process in real time.

It was now clear to me why so many of the passengers on our large Airbus plane had practically run from the gate exit the minute we disembarked, elbowing one another through hallways, down flights of stairs, through doorways. How curious, I had thought, watching and trying to stay out of their way. Now I was lamenting a bit at not having joined them in that quest for first place in the Gate-to-Visa relay race!

Next time, I thought, I'll be ready! I started planning right there how I would be among the first in the visa line, if not Number 1! First, select a seat as close to the front of the plane as possible, even if it meant grabbing (horror of horrors) a *middle seat*! Then, carry as small a bag onto the plane as possible, checking EVERYTHING else. Surely my computer satchel, bulging at every seam and zipper, weighing in at close to 45 pounds, would never do. I would have to work on that one, as it totally defines the modern-day "take it ALL with you" approach to air travel. I would need faster shoes, as well—my work boots would never do in this competition. And finally, make sure to get all required forms and have them filled in impeccably, with printer-quality penmanship.

This planning session did have a very positive effect of consuming my brain for the next half hour, making the visa wait almost bearable. At last, I heard the word I was waiting for. "Next!" chirped the little grandmotherly-looking lady, dressed in a sack dress and babushka. Stepping up to the table, I marveled at how these three ladies provided direction to us visa-seekers in the nicest and quietest tone imaginable. How on earth do they do that? This seemed to me one of the worst jobs I could imagine, yet they were speaking so quietly, and smiling as they did.

Certainly, most U.S. airports are much more efficient than this one. However, the folks that work there tend to be rude and loud, particularly in Chicago and along both coasts, in my experience. These three grandmas could not be nicer. I was almost expecting them to ask me if I had enough to eat on the plane, maybe even offer me their homemade bakedforth goods!

Very quickly, this niceness gave way to a gentle request for my visa payment: $100 for five days! I could stay one day or ninety, it didn't matter—it would still cost me $100. Ah-ha! It is clear to me now. Send out the granny patrol, smother us with soft-spoken words, then hold out your little old hands, demanding 100 "semolinas" from us all. What a racket! Oh well, at least I now had my visa, which would allow me to stay for months, should I want to.

Gillian had informed me that this was only the first step in a multi-step exit process! Upon leaving the visa room, I was now directed to any of several queues lined up in front of multiple passport-check kiosks. Of course! Why would I even think that they could complete the visa/passport process in one central station? Even in Kenya, where they also forge your travel visas in longhand, they process your passport at the same station. Oh well, at least they were multiple glass-enclosed passport-check kiosks, allowing the queues to be short and the process to be relatively speedy.

At the departure of the passport kiosks, everyone was then directed into the expansive baggage claim area. This part of the terminal was also quite new and very modern. I couldn't help but smile, and even chuckle, as I approached the baggage claim conveyor belt. As with every large airport that I had ever passed through, the common denominator bottleneck was always baggage claim. Nowhere worse than Chicago O'Hare, I recalled ruefully, but indeed, it was not much better here in Addis Ababa. I tried not to look openly amused as I stood next to many of the same men and women who I had seen sprinting from our arrival gate, only to find themselves standing here beside me, Mr. Tortoise!

None of them looked happy. I'm sure that I probably wasn't helping things much with my Cheshire Cat smile. So much for my plans to beat them all in the race to the visa prep room on my next visit. I could file those plans away for good, unless I wanted to be the first to arrive and wait around in baggage claim! The only "winners" were those who had packed light and had no need for baggage claim. That would never work for me as long as I was traveling internationally. So, long waits would just have to be part of the journey.

I glanced around and saw Gillian and Roger standing nearby. Gillian saw me and waved me over. "So now you see, Bob, why we are never in a hurry to get to the visa room," Gillian chuckled.

"Yes," I nodded. "You are truly experienced."

"It only takes once," she responded, and the three of us laughed, totally at the expense of our sprinting fellow passengers.

"I hope our luggage has made it through, after all this," said Roger, 'The Quiet One.'

"Oh, mine is already out here, making yet another trip around the conveyor belt," I said.

"Why aren't you retrieving it?" Gillian exclaimed. "Do you need help?"

"No," I explained. "I just want some of those "sprinters" to get their luggage first, so I don't have to walk right in front of them and grab mine! I suspect this would just upset them all the more. We three seem to be the only Americans here, and I am cautious that they might 'connect the dots' in the wrong way and end up somehow blaming me or you guys for their inconvenience. America doesn't really need more enemies, right?"

"Wow," said Gillian. "That is so astute of you. Roger, we probably need to be more aware, don't you think? ...Roger?"

Roger wasn't answering. He just stood there, mouth hanging open, with a look of mild terror in his eyes.

"I'm so sorry," I said quickly, "I shouldn't startle you two in this manner. It's probably fine! It's just that I have traveled to South Sudan and even Baghdad, and I managed to get myself into several potentially dangerous positions, only because of my lack of awareness or perhaps my naivety. I'm trying to be more aware of my surroundings and how I am perceived by foreigners. I keep telling myself, this ain't Kansas, Toto!"

"No, it sure isn't," agreed Gillian, while Roger remained mute. "This may be just your first trip to Addis, but we're learning from you, just the same.

Thanks for your insight in this regard. We will also try to be more careful, won't we, Roger?" Not much more than a headshake out of poor Roger.

"Well, good," I said, glancing at the thinning conveyor belt. "Looks like most of 'em have collected their luggage and left. I think I'll fetch mine and do the same. My friend will be waiting for me somewhere out there." I gestured toward the outdoor area beyond the terminal glass wall. "At least, I hope he is! I've not yet met him in person."

"We should have room and can take you wherever you need to go, Bob, if you need a ride. Right, Roger?" Roger nodded, but looked doubtful.

"No, no," I assured them. "I'm sure he'll be here. But thank you so much for the generous offer, just the same."

As the words were leaving my mouth, someone hollered my name. I turned and saw a guy waving from the reception crowd. "Melaku!" I shouted excitedly. "Is that you?"

He jogged briskly over. "Bob! So good to meet you, at last!"

"Melaku, what a pleasure to finally meet you," I said warmly, trying to hide the rapid floods of relief I felt at his arrival. "Meet my new best friends in Addis—other than you and Sosi, of course! Gillian and Roger, this gentleman is Melaku Abebe.

After a brief chat, we said goodbye to Gillian and Roger, and I thanked them again for all of their help through customs. We then made the long hike down the switchback walkway to the lone parking lot. Melaku unlocked the trunk of a nondescript Japanese sedan, which I guessed was about 20 years old. I hoped the numerous dings and scratches peppering the exterior were from previous owners and not indicative of Melaku's driving skill!

We jumped in the car, and I soon learned that Melaku was a pretty good driver. I also learned that even well-used vehicles rifled with pockmarks sold for a premium in Ethiopia. Melaku had paid the equivalent of $10,000 USD for this jalopy of a Japanese sedan, which would probably sell in the States for no more than $2,000. "My goodness!" I exclaimed. "For $10,000, I could buy a low-mileage Japanese car, less than four years old."

"What?!" It was Melaku's turn to be surprised. "For that kind of vehicle, you would pay close to $30,000 USD here."

"I don't understand. Why are they so expensive here?"

"Well, for one thing," Melaku said, "there are just not very many decent cars for sale. So the ones that are available demand a very high price. The business people who bring these cars into Ethiopia stand to make a whole lot of money."

"I would think the Ethiopian government would step in and regulate this industry for its citizens."

"Actually, Bob, they are the biggest part of the problem. Not only do they not try to regulate the industry, they charge a large VAT on all imported goods, including automobiles."

"You're kidding! I admit that I am not great at economics, but that has to be one of the worst monetary policies I've ever heard. They are simultaneously scaring away international business partners, while significantly driving up the costs of imported goods for their own citizens."

I knew we were probably not going to solve Ethiopia's financial problems, at least not on this trip! But it made me wish that I could find a way to buy a decent used car in the U.S. for less than $5,000 and just ship it to him.

I stared out the window at the chaotic swirl of the city. "Melaku," I chuckled. "You say that there are not that many cars for sale in Ethiopia. But it appears to me that everyone that does have one must be driving it at the same time! Is this city one big traffic jam?"

"Yes," he sighed, "and it's only going to get worse. Soon the Chinese are coming and will be building major highways all over the city, especially coming and going from the airport."

"Interesting," I responded seriously. "I heard they are getting ready to do the same thing in Kenya. The Chinese seem to be everywhere, building things. I guess they ran out of things to build in China!"

Melaku broke into a hearty laugh. "I think that I am going to enjoy getting to know you, Bob. You know that Sosi and I are already enjoying entertaining Dean, Dr. Kate, and Nurse Susan and her husband, Stephen."

"Of course," I nodded. "But I only know Dean. I knew that he was bringing several people with him, but I have not met them yet." By now, we had left the major city arteries behind, and suddenly, we were shunted onto really crummy dirt roads. For a moment, I thought I may have returned to the Kenyan bush! The high-rise offices, apartments, and commercial space gave way to much smaller, cramped housing. I suddenly grew concerned about whether Melaku and Sosi had space to accommodate all of us. Just to be sure I had the right head count, I casually asked Melaku if he and Sosi had any children living with them.

"Yes, we have a daughter, Beza, who still lives with us. Actually," he explained, "Beza is not our daughter. We were not able to have children. But we adopted her as our own. My mom lives with us as well. But she is on the first floor, and we live on the second floor and also keep an apartment on the third floor."

Melaku grinned and looked over at me. "So if you're wondering, Bob, do we have enough room for everyone? The answer is yes."

"Oh no! I wasn't at all worried about that, Melaku," I quickly protested—basically lying through my teeth. "It sounds like you have it all under control," I added, trying to sound convincing as we pulled up in front of a large sliding garage door. Melaku sounded the horn, and in no time, we heard the sound of locks opening, and the large door began to creak open. Instead of a garage, the door opened into a courtyard with a driveway. There was a car already parked there, as Melaku pulled into this open space, and he had to pull up, bumper to bumper, to allow the young man who had opened the door to close it behind us.

On the right side of the courtyard was a high concrete block wall, and the three stories of apartments rose up to the left and in front of us. We retrieved my two bags from the trunk, and I followed Melaku up the narrow winding stairway at the near end of the apartments, past the first floor—where I remembered that his mother lived—to the second floor. While we were climbing, the young man who had opened the door caught up to us just as we walked out onto the second-floor balcony and walkway, facing the courtyard. Melaku introduced him as Moses, his son. Seeing my confusion as we entered one of the last doors on the second floor, Melaku laughed. "You have caught me—he is not really my son. But he is like a son to me."

"And Melaku is like a dad to me," piped in Moses.

Melaku clapped him on the shoulder. "But he doesn't live with us like Beza."

"It is very nice to meet you, Moses," I offered, dropping my bag just outside the door and sticking out my hand. He was slight of stature, but had a strong handshake and a smile as sweet as his "dad's."

"The pleasure is all mine, sir," he said, which surprised me, both his deliberation and his smiling stare, while he gripped my hand all the tighter.

"So what has Melaku been feeding you about me, Moses?" I had to ask. "Has he told you yet how I stood him and Sosi up, leaving them at the airport without so much as a phone call?"

"Yes, sir, I know all about that," he said. "But he and Sosi were mainly upset that they had not gotten to meet you and hear of your time in Iraq. He never complained about your not calling. I think that you provided him with an adequate reason for why that was just not possible."

"Good," I exhaled. "Now I can stop fretting about that unfortunate incident."

All at once, we were all gathered in one place: Melaku and Sosi, Dean, Dr. Kate, Nurse Susan, Husband Steve, and me, along with their "adopted daughter," Beza. In a strange turn of events, it was Melaku who introduced me to three people from my own area of Texas. I knew that I was going to enjoy working with this crew.

We each had our assignment: Dean was there to preach and teach, as always; Dr. Katie and Nurse Susan would "doctor" for two days at a tiny clinic in Meki, a small town near absolutely nothing in Ethiopia (but still, not as far from civilization as Adoor, South Sudan). (Big) Steve would provide some crowd control for the many who would come for free analysis and treatment. Steve, who was, himself, a contractor, would also evaluate a small facility that CrossWay was hoping to upgrade into a medical clinic. And me? I was checking out the water and sanitary conditions at the Meki clinic for adequacy as the clinic was developing.

Making use of the unused third floor apartment, Melaku was easily able to accommodate all of us, including a few mattresses on the floor of their living room. Dean and I must have drawn larger straws! We got the whole upstairs apartment—and our own bathroom!—to share. The other six shared Melaku's bathroom on the second floor.

By the time I hit the sack, I was totally exhausted. Seems the trip had taken more out of me than I realized. True, it had only been a two-hour flight, but the weariness had accumulated with the required early arrival, after a wicked commute through Nairobi's notoriously horrific traffic. Adding in the long wait at the Addis Ababa Airport and the stress of obtaining the visa, it all amounted to a tiring and drawn-out commute.

I could have easily slept until 9am, and would have, I'm sure, if I hadn't been startled out of my drowsy wits by the blaring P.A. system from a nearby mosque, calling all Muslims to prayer—at 6am, I noted, blearily checking my watch. The chanting droned on, easily drowning the city noise of this bustling metropolis of some 2.5 million inhabitants. In all my previous trips to Africa and even Baghdad, I had never heard the monotone chanting of the Muslim call to prayer. It was not at all enticing.

Now fully awake, I was curious to observe the ritual, as it sounded like it was right outside Melaku's apartment complex. I pulled back the curtain on the nearby window but saw no signs of a mosque—not even a minaret. But a throng of people were already up and about, traipsing about the dirt streets—kids headed to school, ladies and men dressed nicely for work. Most were on foot, save for a few in beat-up autos and delivery trucks, and even a couple of nice sedans. But they all had one thing in common—each one was oblivious to the booming chant filling the airspace.

I felt bad for all of these people scurrying about, having to endure this almost painful sound. And then I felt doubly bad for Melaku, Sosi, and Beza—and Mom—who had to wake up to this noise every day! I asked them that morning how they coped with this incessant chanting, what, five times a day? Melaku chuckled. He didn't realize that I had never heard this before in my travels. For them, it was part of their way of life. And they had learned to ignore it. "But how?" I exclaimed. "It's SO LOUD! And SO BAD!"

"Bob, after hearing it all of your life, believe me, you learn to tune it out," Melaku said, shrugging his shoulders. "You will too," he tried to assure me. "But it may take a few days." (I'll let you know right now, I never did learn to tune it out. Perhaps I wasn't there long enough. The sound was just really startling, even troubling, to my ears.)

I do have to say, however, a part of me admires the Muslim for their faithfulness. I doubt that I could ever see myself interrupting my day, five times a day, to stop to pray. I don't agree with their methods, but they do have an unshakeable commitment to prayer that demands our admiration. I began to think if we all had such commitment to our own spiritual walks, the world would become a much better place.

After Sosi had fed us enough breakfast (both Ethiopian standard, plus American), we all got ready to depart Addis for a few days and head southeast to the town of Meki, where CrossWay had hopes of building a medical clinic and, eventually, a medical training/conference center. We were traveling in two cars. Melaku had traded his sedan with a church friend for the day and was driving a minivan in exchange. Moses had returned, along with an Ethiopian couple (I presumed), in a larger sedan; together with the minivan, there appeared to be plenty of room for all of us, and all of our personal luggage, and a considerable number of pharmaceuticals and other medical supplies! It was decided that Dean, the ladies, and the young couple would ride with Melaku in the van, while Steve and I would ride with Moses. That was fine with me, as it gave us plenty of room to spread out.

Although we were somewhere in the middle of this sprawling city, the area where Melaku and Sosi lived seemed almost rural, if only because of the deplorable condition of the muddy "streets" and the fact that we had to share them with so many pedestrians, as I had observed before—yet again, the many adults, dressed nicely and walking quickly to some form of mass transit, I presumed. Then there were the scores of school children, of all ages and uniforms, traveling in mass groups or with a mom or dad with one or two little ones in tow.

The "street" itself appeared more like a military training ground for tanks and Humvees. The holes and accumulations of large and small rocks were massive and ubiquitous. And there were other vehicles on the "cart path/street" also, from tiny, multi-dented autos to massive lorries, and motor bikes and bicycles, too. Lastly, there were the herds of animals who paid no attention to anyone, and no owners in sight—cows, goats, donkeys, and some chickens, all running wild.

The "road" seemed to grow narrower in many places, as the homes—or I should say, the garages or walls around the homes—were built right to the "edges" of it. As we headed toward the approaching tarmac road, countless *ducas* and small stalls lined every available square inch of real estate, leaving very little room for the horde of humanity, vehicles, and animals to share in this mass movement we could term the "morning commute."

I am amazed as I write this at just how much of this first trip out of Melaku's neighborhood I can so vividly recall. It is now seven years later, and so much of it remains strikingly embedded in my mind's eye. I remember Steve and I saying very little—both in some degree of "urban shock," no doubt. Moses seemed unfazed and undaunted as he deftly maneuvered this large sedan through the menagerie of man, beast, and machine. At this point, I have now made this journey from Melaku's home to the hardtop road perhaps two dozen times, with my seven trips to Ethiopia. I have to say, they never really get any easier.

I would like to say that everything got smoother once we reached the tarmac road. But it would not be true. At least, not for the first couple of miles, as we wound our way through the heavy commute traffic in the city. Once we got outside the city, the traffic started to lighten up a bit. Finally, we could relax and enjoy the scenery. As we meandered through the rolling hills of the countryside, it was quite enjoyable to see how the people lived and worked. We passed by large high-rise construction projects, factories, schools of all shapes and sizes, and a variety of churches and temples. On the edge of one town, I watched as some women laid out large woven mats with a wide variety of beans and peas to dry in the sun.

I was astounded to see so many hard-working people—men, women, and children—working the land. As we drove through this Ethiopian breadbasket, many were already bringing in their day's harvest for market, I presumed. Young boys and girls, some quite small, perhaps four or five years old, were herding goats or cattle along the edge of the highway. Men were plowing or chopping down the harvest with large sickles. A couple of times, I saw something in the field that looked very strange, until I figured out what they were doing. I missed the opportunity to take photos at first, but I was determined to have my camera ready. What a great reward I received for this Boy Scout readiness!

What I was able to finally photograph was a group of several boys hurrying a team of oxen that were strapped together in a line, pivoting around in a circle. They looked like a small Rockettes chorus line linking arms and swirling around in a large, arcing circle. Can you picture that? It finally dawned on me what they were doing. The boys were using the oxen to stomp on the newly harvested wheat spread out in front of them, beginning the process of separating the wheat from the chaff. No John Deere or International Harvester for them!

I never got a picture of the follow-up task after this "threshing process," because I only saw it once in passing. I was too slow to recognize and capture a photo as we hurtled by in our wayward sedan. The separation of the wheat from the chaff as it lay on the ground was accomplished by picking up the threshed material with a pitchfork and lofting it into the air.

I marveled that this same process was going on in Biblical times, and 2,000 years later, I was seeing it happen just the same out my car window! Hundreds of large piles of grain were left to dry in the sun, and fully threshed grain was compacted into neat bundles. I saw the bundles getting loaded onto hand-pulled wooden carts, being hauled to market, no doubt, either by donkeys or really hard-working humans.

After witnessing the widespread, rampant laziness of the majority of the male population in Sudan, I felt a warm attraction to the work ethic of Ethiopians. I had already noticed so many of them bustling about back in the city and suburbs and all along the highway. Sure, there were the packs of young boys just standing around, or playing, of all things, foosball at many locations within these towns, immediately adjacent to the roadway. These were the "city boys," I concluded, with no farming chores to keep them occupied, and apparently left behind by the public-school system. Such a stark contrast to the hard-working "country boys and girls" of these rural areas.

I liked the country. The scenery along our journey, now stretching beyond two hours, was quite stunning. The large expanses of farmland on the rolling hills, along with a backdrop of large, beautiful mountains, presented numerous opportunities for postcard-grade photos. Sigh—if only I were a better photographer.

Eventually we reached the outskirts of the town of Meki, population 60,000 or so, I'm told. We pulled off the highway, then crossed over a small drainage ditch and stopped at a big metal gate with a high concrete block wall on both sides. Moses sounded the horn and before long, the gate opened from the inside. The gentleman who opened it bid us welcome with a big smile as our caravan passed by. We continued driving towards the small, single-story building located towards the back of the walled-in property. As we alighted from our vehicles, a lovely young lady walked out of the building and greeted us with a big smile. Melaku and Sosi greeted her with big hugs and kisses, and then Melaku introduced us to his sister, Sarah, and then to her husband, Wesenu, who arrived after locking the gate behind us.

After escorting Dean to a plastic chair under a big shade tree, to rest out of the hot mid-day sun, Melaku took Dr. Katie, Susan, Stephen and me on a tour of the building. There were four adjacent rooms in this one-story structure, each with a wooden door and two with a single window, with the typical "burglar bars" and no screen. These first two rooms are set up as living quarters for Sarah and Wesenu—one a living room, filled with simple, yet comfortable furniture, and the second a combination kitchen/bedroom. Not a kitchen like we're used to in the West, mind you, but an 'area' that serves a variety of functions, including cooking on a portable electric double burner. No built-in appliances and no sink. The third room appeared to be just a storage area, while the fourth room at the far end was a primitive toilet with a simple hole in the concrete floor. There was no plumbing in any of the rooms, but there was electricity in the first two.

Later, I discovered that CrossWay had purchased this property, and Melaku's sister and her husband were staying there rent-free to watch over it. Their income was derived solely from selling produce from a farm that Wesenu's family owned, a few kilometers out of town. We soon enjoyed a lunch with some of the wonderful vegetables from Wesenu's garden, but I was not able to see the farm until a later visit to Ethiopia.

Melaku and the others joined Dean under the shade tree, and Wesenu led Stephen and me over to see the one structure that I was most interested in. It appeared to be a typical African well hand pump, identical to those that we installed in Sudan previously. But the base of this one sat near the edge of a cylindrical structure with a concrete top slab, approximately one meter above the ground. To operate the pump, one had to climb up the broad concrete steps attached to the outside of the cylinder.

When Wesenu saw us staring in confusion, he opened a metal manway in the top of the cylinder so that we could look inside. It took a few moments for our eyes to adjust to the darkness of the well, but when we could see inside, we were both left gaping at what we saw. Amazingly, this same cylindrical structure that was visible above ground extended at least 80 to 90 feet deep into the earth! Indeed, we were gazing into a hand-dug water well.

Stephen and I had seen shallow hand-dug wells in our home state of Texas, but neither of us had ever seen anything like this. This well was no more than two feet in diameter and was lined with concrete and quarried rocks all the way to the bottom. As a contractor and an engineer, we both had years of experience with a wide variety of construction projects. But the thought of humans burrowing into the ground vertically for 80-plus feet, in a space not much wider than their bodies, was quite difficult for us to wrap our heads around. Each of us could easily imagine primitive tools for the excavation process—it was the removal of the excavated soil and rock, coupled with the sheer difficulty of penetrating the hard rock, that was so hard to comprehend. More than that, at some level there would certainly be water to contend with—if not on the way down, at least at the bottom.

Neither Melaku nor Wesenu had ever seen the digging of one of these wells. Thus, Stephen and I were left to our own imaginations as we struggled to unpack what we were seeing. For now, it seemed, it would just have to remain an astonishing mystery for us both. Shaking our heads, we returned to the group assembled under the shade tree. Great timing, too, as Sarah and Sosi were now bringing out food for dinner.

You could not believe such an exquisite meal could be conjured in such a rustic setting. There were heaping bowls of delicious spaghetti and meatballs, fresh-baked bread, and some of the most flavorful, fresh vegetables I had ever eaten. One could easily imagine themselves at any five-star Italian restaurant in Europe or the U.S., were it not for the primitive wooden table, plastic chairs, sandy "floor," and, of course, the many hungry flies swarming about. But the food was certainly five star. I asked Wesenu, on one of my later visits and after several more of Sarah's wonderful meals, if he realized how fortunate he was to have such a beautiful wife who could cook that well! "Oh, yes," he said with a big smile. "I know I am a blessed man."

After dinner, we set out east towards the Kenyan border. We were on our way to see David Roschli at his factory in a town called Awasa. This amazing Dutch engineer and inventor had designed a vast array of water well pumping mechanisms. Our reason for visiting, though, was to see his percussion hand drilling (borehole) machine. Melaku had told me about it, and now I was interested to see if this was something I could use here or elsewhere in Africa.

As usual, the trip itself would prove just as interesting as the time spent with Mr. Roschli. Moses was driving Melaku and me in the big sedan, so we were limited to a speed of about 55 kph. But there were still so many people, hand-drawn carts, and animals along the highway that we would not have been able to go much faster anyway. Once or twice we saw camels loping along some distance from the highway, seemingly without anyone to control them. I was excited, as this was the first time I had seen any camels "in the wild" in Africa.

Suddenly, Moses screamed and slammed on the brakes. Right in front of us, consuming the entire highway and a good portion of the shoulder and beyond, was a massive herd of camels—perhaps a hundred or more! Then I saw three young boys with sticks and ropes trying their best to herd them off the highway. I looked at Melaku and asked if this was a common occurrence. "Never, Bob!" he exclaimed. "I have never seen this before." Moses simply sat there in stone silence. I couldn't tell if he was startled as well, or embarrassed. I was simply delighted, and I quietly thanked God for providing this marvelous interruption.

Finally, we arrived at David Roschli's workshop. As expected, it was an inspiring visit. Not only is Mr. Roschli a brilliant inventor, but he is a strong Christian with a huge heart for orphans. This facility—actually more like a campus—is also an orphanage, which he built and continues to support, even well into his seventies.

When we first arrived, David was on an errand and would be back soon. But since we had been expected, his next in command, John, was there to greet us and take us on a tour of the campus. He started in the metal shop, where teenage Ethiopian boys from the orphanage were at work, learning to fashion items out of sheet metal. They were mostly small items, like bowls, multi-compartment drawers, and some ornamental-type objects like picture frames and mirrors. But they were all practical, and all crafted to specifications. David had provided the specifications and the templates so that the young men could learn to use almost every piece of equipment, including large and small hand tools.

Once they "graduated" from the sheet metal shop, they were brought into the pump manufacturing shop. Here they would learn to craft larger and heavier metal components that would eventually be built into water pumps. Some of the young men would focus on the electrical aspect of the pumps, the motors and controls, which would provide them with a different skill set. These pumps, as well as many of the sheet metal products, would then be sold, with the profits used to help support the orphanage. The pumps were sold not only within Ethiopia, but outside the country as well. How clever, I thought. Not only were these young men crafting useful items that people would actually buy, but in doing so, they were also learning life skills that they could use to gain sustainable employment out in the "working world." Moreover, they were receiving the opportunity to learn about a free market system and even business management.

As John explained the facets of the training and production facility, I could not help but marvel at such an opportunity for *any* young boy, let alone an orphan. This had to be monumental for them. One day an orphan, out on the street, perhaps, and the next a boy might find himself in a safe place, surrounded by adults that would show him love and respect, while training him to have a real opportunity to succeed in life. Is that not the most beautiful picture of what an orphanage should be?

David Roschli soon arrived, and he completed our tour of the factory by showing us the actual water pumps that the young boys were crafting, from his design, there in assembly-line fashion.

"But, from what I understand, you really came to see the "manual" well drilling apparatus and operation, is that correct?" he asked.

"Well, that's quite true," I responded, "but what we have seen here in your training center is just as amazing, and brilliant. I love how you are teaching the young boys a trade—even multiple trades, it seems, while turning out products for sale. Tell me, sir, are you able to fully fund your orphanage in this fashion?"

"Oh, no," he sighed. "I could only wish. No, it takes a good deal more than the income from our sale of products. But it certainly helps, that's for sure. We still must rely on donations from Sweden and from the U.S. Have you met David Harding, one of our chief supporters and regular visitor to our orphanage and factory?"

I shook my head. "I'm not sure I've ever heard that name before."

"Well, he has just returned to Addis Ababa to visit our other orphanage. I am sure that you will be talking to him, if we get the opportunity to assist you with your plans to drill a new well at your place in Meki."

As we spoke, David led us out of the factory, down the long driveway, and out to a field. On the way, he stopped to show us his "static display" of various types of pumps that he had designed over the years. They were really all variations on the means to power the pumps, other than by the typical hand pump. One had a "stair climber" attached to the pump discharge pipe coming out of the well. David invited me to try it, so I climbed on and began high stepping. It worked just like one you'd find in an American gym. Next to it was one that was powered by a small "merry-go-round," like those in the old schoolyards across the country decades ago. I had only seen one like this before in a brochure for a "play pump."

Just beyond this pump, out in the green grass yard, was a tall steel pipe tripod. David saw me looking at it and said, "You ready to do some real drilling?" He had my attention—how does one drill with only a 10-foot tripod?

As we walked towards the lone tripod, standing idle in the field, we were joined by several young men from the shop. At David's direction, one of them grabbed a *panga* (machete, or multipurpose tool), which would serve as a post hole digger. I watched in amazement as they worked. After digging straight down for about 2 feet and then removing the loose soil, David brought out a handmade metal cylinder with a sharp steel point welded on one end. The other end he threaded onto the end of a 6-foot piece of 1" galvanized pipe. There was a rope that looped up to a pulley, suspended from the top of the tripod. He then tied one end of the rope to the end of the 1" steel pipe. Before having the boys hoist the pipe and pointed cylinder tip up to the top of the tripod, he motioned Melaku and me to come over and examine the tip up close.

What he showed us was more than just the point and cylinder. Inside the cylinder, which was exposed where the steel point was welded, there was a steel ball. David turned it upside down and back again to show us how the ball was free to move up and down slightly, but was stopped from rolling all the way up the cylinder. This, he explained, was the "non-return valve" (or check valve, as we might call it). It is a simple valve that allows flow in only one direction, sometimes using an engineered ball, as in this instance, and other times by use of a flapper mechanism. David demonstrated how the downward plunge of the "drill bit" and pipe would force the ball to the top of its travel, leaving the bottom open. This was how the mud with the soil "cuttings" would enter the pipe, to travel up the pipe, as more and more mud was added, where it would eventually be extracted from the top, onto the ground. "Wow! That sounds so simple," I exclaimed. "May I see how it works?"

"Absolutely," said David. "That's what we plan to do. Guys," he said, turning toward the young men helping him, "let's get started."

Immediately, one of the young men grabbed the pipe and lifted it overhead, aiming the sharp point towards the hole that was just started. The other three boys grabbed onto to the other end of the rope hanging down from the pulley and pulled all the slack out of the line. They then held it loose, after receiving a signal from David, and the guy holding the pipe slammed it down into the hole. Then the three guys would pull the pipe back up until the point was once again overhead of the other guy. He would then, on signal, plunge the pipe back into the ground. As he did that, the three guys on the other end of the rope would open their hands, allowing the rope to slide through.

As the pipe dropped further down the hole, with each plunge, the three guys on the pulley end seemed to be working much harder to raise it up again. Eventually, the top end of the pipe was getting close to the top of the hole. Here, the gentleman that was directing it into the hole stopped momentarily to attach a 90-degree elbow and short piece of horizontal pipe to the vertical (plunging) pipe. Soon, muddy water started spewing out of the pipe as it was dropping into the hole. Before long, they had to stop to add another piece of pipe—and take a short breather.

I asked David if I could try helping them lift the pipe up for dropping. "Be my guest," he responded with a smile. I grabbed onto the rope as one of the boys relinquished his spot (somewhat gladly, it seemed—he was breathing quite heavily). It didn't take too many rope pulls, followed by just letting go as the weight of the pipe was providing most of the downward force. I managed to make it to the top of that second pipe before I was quite exhausted and sweating profusely. "This is really amazing," I said to David and Melaku. "Slow, but amazing. We're actually 'drilling', aren't we?"

"Take a look," said David, gesturing to the hole. Sure enough, I could see that we had 'drilled' down about 15 feet already. And it was producing a straight, clean, 4-inch diameter borehole!

"So how deep can you extend the borehole by this method?" I asked.

"That depends—usually on how deep before we hit hard rock. If we do not encounter too hard of rock, we have drilled beyond 150 feet by this method. Sometimes the rock stops us, and sometimes we are able to penetrate—eventually."

"But this is only a 4-inch hole."

"Oh, this is only our pilot hole," he responded. "We then have to ream it out with a 6-inch bit. But this goes faster, because of the pilot hole."

"About how long does it take to drill a 120-foot hole? Assuming that you can penetrate any layers of rock encountered?"

"We can usually drill them in one week. As long as we can penetrate the rock."

"What happens if you can't?" I had to know. I didn't want to leave this subject unanswered.

"Well, then we have to bring in our big drill and finish the job," David responded.

"Is that a truck-mounted drill rig?"

"Yep, it sure is. A good-sized one, too. But it is kept pretty busy. So, where we can, we like to try to use the hand drilling, as it saves the client a lot of expense."

"That's all good to know, Mr. Roschli," I said. "We may be in the market for a driller soon, as we're considering drilling a deeper well at our planned clinic site in Meki. They have a hand-dug well there. But when we add the clinic and, hopefully, a small conference center, that shallow well will not sustain our needs."

"I see," he nodded. "Then you should talk with David Harding. Either he or our drilling superintendent, Atkelt, can give you pricing and make arrangements. I don't get involved with that."

"Yes sir, I'll do that. And tell me, please, if I wanted to buy some of your hand drill bits, would that be possible?"

"Oh, I'm sure it is," he responded, looking surprised. "Where do you plan to drill with them, Ethiopia?"

"Oh, no, sir," I replied. "I'm thinking about using them in South Sudan. I had not thought of such a thing until you showed me how easy this can be—albeit slow and strenuous. But I believe that this would work well in the soft soils of South Sudan, where the water table is quite shallow."

"Yes, this technology would likely work quite well there. Do you have a drill team set up there?" he added.

"Not yet. But I know a number of people there that we could work with, and I'm sure that it would be well received, since their need for water is great. But their ability to obtain it on their own is almost non-existent. They are totally at the mercy of charities and ministries, as there is no real government that seems to want to help them—even though their civil war ended recently."

"Okay then," he said, "please talk to David about this. I'm sure that he can get you what you need. By the way, how would you plan to get them there?"

"If David can ship them to Nairobi, we will carry them with us to South Sudan on our next visit. Really, we should only need the drill bits, as the tripods can be built out of the small, sturdy tree trunks they have there. Then we would only need to find the pipe."

"That sounds like a good plan, Bob. I wish you well on that, and we'll help you any way we can."

"Oh, you already have, Mr. Roschli, believe me. I have learned so much from our visit today. Thank you for giving us so much of your time, and for showing us this simple drilling technology. I will try to connect with David Harding, perhaps back in Addis, before he returns to the U.S."

"You're very welcome, indeed," he responded. "Please, come visit us anytime."

Darkness was approaching, and I was eager to get back on the road and return to Meki, as I knew that Dean would be getting anxious. It took us almost two hours to drive here in the light of day. Then again, we did have to stop for the "camel parade."

As dusk gave way to darkness, Moses continued to drive without the aid of headlights. There were almost no roadway lights, except when passing through towns where some of the businesses were lit up, spilling some light onto the roadway edge. I remained quiet as long as I could, not wanting to "backseat drive." But all of a sudden, I yelled, "Look out!" as a child darted out into the road from a crowd gathered on the edge.

Moses slammed on his brakes, just as the boy looked up and a hand reached for him and pulled him to safety.

"Okay, Moses," I snapped. "I'm not sure why you refuse to put your headlights on, but I really must insist." Melaku agreed and sternly told Moses to do the same. "I'm sorry for yelling," I added. "But there are still so many people walking along and across this road. At least we can see them here in the towns. But as soon as we leave the town limits, the lights end, and we're back to darkness."

Fortunately, there were no more close calls along the return trip. But that didn't stop me from anxiously watching for people and animals matriculating along the darkened roadway. By the time we arrived back at the hotel, I felt as if I had driven the entire way, and felt quite worn out. But on reviewing the day, I was thankful for all that I had seen and done, particularly our visit with David Roschli.[6] The long trip was worth the effort, I told Melaku. I thanked him and Moses for taking me there, as I now felt confident about the well we intended to drill here in Meki, as well as what I had learned about simple drilling that I could take back to South Sudan with me. All of this made for a very good day, indeed. Although fatigue was beginning to settle in, I was excited about the future here.

On our last day in Meki, we assisted Dr. Kate and Nurse Susan in what they had been doing the previous day and a half—providing free medical examinations and medicine to the locals. My role was simply to help maintain order for all the people that were lined up to see the doctor. I had only to follow Stephen's lead, since he had performed similar services during this time and had a plan in place for maintaining some degree of order. But really, the people were so appreciative of the medical help that they were responsive to any direction we gave them, making our job that much easier.

By midafternoon, the long line was starting to taper off. "Good thing," I thought, as both practitioners appeared to be utterly exhausted as the last of the patients cycled through. I can speak to how exhausting

[6] I learned, in speaking with Melaku several years ago, that David Roschli had passed away. It saddened me to know this. But in my sadness, I found myself so very thankful, as well, for the wonderful afternoon that we had the opportunity to spend with him. I learned so much during this visit. Not only about his many amazing inventions, but also, his love for the neglected in life and his meaningful way of bringing purpose into the lives of so many youth that will carry them through life, I have no doubt. Truly a remarkable man, in so many ways.

working laboriously out in the hot sun can be; but I really don't know at all how demanding it must be to treat so many people in desperate need of medical attention. Still, that didn't deter them from joining the rest of us in handing out treats for all of the children still gathered out in the clinic courtyard.

A short time later, after a heartfelt goodbye to Sarah and Wesenu, we were on the road again, back to Addis Ababa. Just as twilight was setting in, we wound our way through the city to Melaku and Sosi's place. Knowing that we would have to leave early the next morning to drive to the airport, the ladies were anxious to do some souvenir shopping. Ever accommodating, Melaku offered to drive us all to the market area and take us to the best places to get good trinkets at reasonable prices.

We were deep into the recesses of a long, narrow shop, when everything suddenly went dark. The power had gone out, it seemed, at least in this sector of the city. Since we couldn't even see the merchandise anymore, we all made our way back out to the street to wait it out. After fifteen tedious minutes passed, Steve and I agreed that we were more than ready to return to Melaku's house. The ladies, of course, would have none of that. In fact, they were using the unusual occasion to dicker ardently with shopkeepers at the front of their stores, where, at least, it was not pitch black. Finally, the power returned, and we all were able to complete our "treasure hunt" before piling back into Melaku's car.

Later that night, our last in Addis, Dean and I met with Melaku to discuss the next steps for construction at Meki. We agreed that I should make another side trip to Ethiopia on my next trip to South Sudan. In the meantime, I would continue to gather price information and arrange for David Harding's drill team to plan to drill a well at Meki. Not only a well, I told them, but also an elevated water tank on a tower structure and all the distribution piping. When I returned to the U.S., I told them, I would draw up some plans and go over them with Mr. Harding in the hopes of getting a good bid price.

I would only have to wait two months before returning to Ethiopia. The short wait, truthfully, did not give me a whole lot of time to budget and plan the work, but I did manage to negotiate a scope and price for drilling a new well with David Harding. So the plan was to begin the work at about the same time that I was scheduled to arrive in Meki.

This, my second trip to Meki, would be my first of six more trips that I would undertake in the next two years, overseeing first the drilling of the new water well there—or at least the start of that effort—and then the constructing of a wastewater septic tank, shower, and flushing toilet facility. And with each trip, I became more and more infatuated with the beauty and people of Ethiopia. Truly, one of the more interesting and unusual trips I took to Ethiopia was this second jaunt in January 2009.

The journey began unremarkably enough with an easy trip from Tanzania, via Nairobi, Kenya. The flight was all the more delightful when I struck up a conversation with the young lady seated next to me. She was a missionary, returning to Ethiopia, where she would be stationed for the next several years. She told me that she was learning the national language of Ethiopia, Amharic.

"Wow!" I said, impressed. "I wish you good luck with that. From my minimal experience, I have found it to be an extremely difficult language, and I've doubted that I will ever learn more than a handful of words or phrases, if that."

"Yes, thank you," she said, laughing. "It is quite challenging, and I may never master it. Did you know that only around 30% of the entire population actually use it?"

"That's crazy! I know that Arabic is often used, but I really thought that more Ethiopians than that used Amharic. Is that because it is so difficult?"

"I'm sure that's part of it," she said. "But there are so many native dialects—more than 80, I understand—and with regional or tribal variations, there could be as many as 200!"

"Oh my! That's even worse than Kenya, where there are 60 or 70 tribal languages spoken. But at least many more than 30% use Swahili there. Good thing you are still young, with a better functioning brain for this sort of challenge. I'm afraid that I would not be able to learn Amharic. I struggle to learn Swahili, and I think that is much simpler, right?"

"So I'm told," she nodded. "Yes, I believe that all Semitic languages, like Arabic and Amharic, are difficult in that way."

"Ah, so it's like Arabic? My brother speaks Arabic. They taught him in the Air Force. They must have figured that he could handle one of the tough ones—and one that they really needed at the time. This was during all the commotion in the Middle East, and shortly before the Six-Day War, back in 1967."

"Oh wow!" she said simply, possibly to cover up a lack of knowledge of this "ancient" historical event.

"I'm sure it also had to do with his gift for learning foreign languages—one of only a few that he mastered, or cared to, in high school. He took all that our small rural public school offered, like French and German, and then started taking outside classes in Latin, and later, Russian at local colleges."

"That's amazing."

"I know. What's even more amazing, is how he really had no use for college after graduating. He enlisted so that he could pursue language learning in the intelligence department. But when he completed his military service, he had some 18 college credits in hand from his linguistics training. That, and the GI Bill, convinced him to enroll in college. He went on to get a master's degree and then a PhD."

Her eyes widened. "In Arabic, or linguistics?"

"In Middle East History, actually."

"Now that is an incredible story."

"I know," I said. "I never get tired of telling people that story, especially if someone, like you, has an interest in history, or language."

"So what about you?" she asked. "What brings you to Addis?"

With that, we launched into a lively discussion about what had brought each of us to this point in our individual ministries. The two-hour trip flew by, and we were surprised when the announcement of our pending decent into Addis came over the PA system.

"Well, once again, I wish you all the best with learning the language and engaging with the Ethiopian people. They are such a delight, aren't they?"

"Oh yes," she beamed. "You think so too? I thought maybe it was just me. I fell in love with them right away."

"I'm not at all surprised," I responded. "I don't know many—just a handful, really. But they just seem so happy with life, as are most Africans

I have come across. And they seem to be such hard workers, particularly in the rural areas."

"Even more so than Kenyans?"

"I'd say so, from my limited experience. And much more so than the Sudanese. The men there were not very willing to work at all. In fact, I rarely found them working during the several weeks I spent with them. Even when we were paying them to work."

"That's sad," she said, frowning. "I agree with your observations, I have not seen any unwillingness to work here in Ethiopia."

We deplaned and walked together towards the point of departure, separating at last—I to my long, meandering visa line, and she, with her extended visa, direct to passport check. "Lucky you," I laughed, heading to my visa line. She grinned and shrugged. "Goodbye!" she said, then turned and walked away.

I was collected by the smiling and ever-upbeat Melaku, and we drove off through the heavy traffic to his home. After catching up with Sosi and him, I hunkered down for a good night's sleep. My second trip to Ethiopia was underway and starting well!

The next morning, Melaku informed me that Atkelt, the foreman for David Harding's drillers had called him early this morning to say they were on their way to begin drilling.

"I thought you told me that their drill rig was busy for a few more days?"

"It is," he replied, "but they are going to start by hand-drilling, to see if they might complete it before reaching the hard rock."

"Great," I said. "Now I can see for myself how well this method works before I try to take it to Sudan!"

We arrived at the site a few hours later, and Atkelt and his team of three were just starting to drill. Just like we had seen at their shop, they had erected a simple wooden post tripod with a pulley attached from the apex. The pulley supported the pull rope, leading down to the top of the steel drill pipe, which was rising and falling as they pulled it up and then dropped it, over and over.

Atkelt was squatting next to the muddy borehole, guiding the drill pipe as it rose and then dropped again. They had dug a short trench and a small pit before our arrival. This was being used to carry the muddy water that was emerging from the top of the drill pipe, where there was a 90-degree pipe fitting attached. I noticed that Atkelt would hold his hand over the end of the 90 as it was dropping. Then he would remove it as the team pulled on the other end of the rope, raising the pipe well above the ground surface.

This action caused two things to occur over and over. The first was that every time he would let go of the pipe, as it rose past him, muddy water would spew forth from it. The second thing was closely connected to the first; by kneeling next to the borehole, he was continually getting sprayed by this thick muddy mixture of water and borehole cuttings. I immediately felt an admiration and genuine liking for this man.

Even as he was squatting there, getting doused with varying shades of mud-water, he was directing his crew, and encouraging them, as well. The lifting was becoming more and more strenuous as the hole deepened. Eventually, they reached a point where the top of the pipe—where the 90 was—was barely above ground level. With a word from Atkelt, they stopped lifting and dropping, or "drilling."

Atkelt arose and helped the crew pull the pipes all the way out of the borehole. I was again surprised to see that it was more than the 10 feet of pipe that I expected. It was more like 20 feet of galvanized steel 1" pipe. No wonder they were panting hard and sweating profusely in the already hot morning sun.

Walking over and pointing to the pointed bit, Atkelt gave them verbal direction, then approached Melaku, Wesenu, and me as we stood watching nearby. Melaku immediately stepped forward and introduced himself, extending his hand. I then extended my hand as Melaku gestured towards me, still speaking in Amharic. This hard-working Ethiopian boss-man reached out and firmly shook my hand, smiling broadly. "I am most pleased to meet you, Bob," he said in near-perfect English.

"It is I who is pleased at our meeting, Atkelt," I responded. "And I am impressed by your hard work and progress already. I can see that this is not easy, and it is dirty work."

"Yes, it is," he chuckled, looking down at his mud-splattered pants and shirt. "But we are making good progress, I think. So far, we have not hit any layers of hard stone. So that is good."

"Dave Harding tells me that you may try to drill the entire well this way. Is it possible to drill as deep as 50 meters like this?"

"Oh yes, it's possible. It all depends on the rock—where we encounter it, and how hard and thick it is. We have some other bits that can penetrate soft to medium hard rock if it's not too thick. Let me show you."

He led us to his pile of equipment next to their transport truck. Opening a crate, he reached in and pulled out several drill bits. Handing one of them to me, he said, "This one was designed for penetrating the rock."

I could see that it looked more intimidating than the one they were currently using. "Couldn't you put this on now and drill faster in the soil?"

"No, the bit that we are using goes faster in soil, but it cannot penetrate the rock," he responded. "So we will use that one until we're stopped by the rock."

The team had gathered and looked ready to begin drilling again. Atkelt shook our hands again. "We should continue drilling. Please excuse me."

He and his team connected another piece of pipe; this one was made of lightweight PVC and appeared to be about 10 feet long. I remembered that David Roschli had told us that after the first piece of pipe, they change to PVC to keep the weight down, which they have to lift and drop continually.

They began by raising one end of the two pipes, now connected together, creating a total of 30 feet. Again, Atkelt was next to the hole, where he guided the drill bit end of the pipes down the hole, while the team raised the other end using the rope attached to the tripod. Before they resumed the drilling process, Atkelt filled the pipe with water from the drum that was next to the hole. Then they continued as before, hoisting the pipe up into the air and dropping it, with Atkelt guiding it at the hole. It was obvious that the total weight had increased, from the weight of the added water now, even more than the weight of the pipe. But they also had more help. Wesenu, who we had greeted when we arrived, had joined them, and they certainly seem to enjoy his presence as they were smiling brightly and engaging in noisy conversation.

This process continued for a few hours. Sometimes Melaku would assist, and other times I would take my turn at hauling on the rope connected to the increasingly heavy drill pipe. All was going smoothly until we reached a depth of about 60 feet. Here, we ran into a layer of much harder material which they could not penetrate. They changed out the drill bit to that heavier, sharper bit that Atkelt had showed me earlier. But even so, they didn't make much progress.

They took a break. Atkelt walked over to me. "It seems we have encountered a thick layer of hard rock. We are having some success in breaking through it, but it appears to be defeating us because it is so thick. We will try one more time. If it doesn't work, I will call our shop to find out when we can bring the drill rig to complete your borehole."

While he was doing that, I asked Melaku if he could take me back to the hotel so I could lie down. I had not been feeling well since lunchtime. This unsettled Melaku greatly, and he asked if it was something I had for lunch. "I really don't think it was the food," I responded. "I don't feel nauseous. More like a dizziness."

I rested a few hours, and fortunately, I started to feel better. We drove back to the clinic and arrived just as Atkelt was packing up to leave. Apparently, the latest attempt to penetrate the hard rock with their best rock bit was not successful. He hoped to be back within a few days with the drill rig. I told him that would work, as I was planning to stay for another four days. I thanked him for showing me this new drilling method and for all of the team's hard work.

As so often happens on these projects, "a few days" turned into several weeks. Atkelt and his team were not able to arrange to get the big drill and return to the clinic in any timeframe that included me in it. But finish they did, including the installation of the submersible pump, the discharge pipe up to the surface and on up to a tower that they fabricated from steel and installed, along with two plastic storage tanks.

I, on the other hand, continued to feel worse by the hour. I spent half a day more in Meki, diagramming and planning for the future water distribution system and the septic tank and flushing toilet structures that we would need to support the full clinic and conference center. But after trying to ignore the dizziness, I finally told Melaku that I needed to see a doctor. The irony of all this was that on our last mission trip—my first visit to Ethiopia—I was in the company of a very competent doctor and a nurse!

I was sorry to have to leave Sarah and Wesenu after so short a visit. But they were concerned and kind, and I promised to stay longer the next time I visited. Melaku then drove me back to his home in Addis Ababa. After a night of little sleep due to constant shaking, I told Melaku that I really needed to return to the States, for medical help that I would be confident in. He understood fully and never insisted on my visiting a local doctor.

I was able to change my flight back to Nairobi for a flight leaving later that morning, for which I was extremely grateful. But the earliest that I could get a flight back to the U.S. was not for another day and a half, arriving back into San Antonio around 10 p.m. I would try to make arrangements at an emergency room where a doctor from my Sunday School class worked, since I had no regular doctor. In fact, I had not seen a doctor for nearly 20 years, as I was unusually blessed with very good health.

After joining hands and praying with Sosi and Melaku, there in their home, Melaku drove me back to the airport and said goodbye. I promised him that I would return as soon as possible, to continue the work at the clinic.

I remember vividly that long wait at the Addis Airport. Melaku could not stay with me, since they allowed no one to enter the terminal who did not possess a ticket for that day. Such is the case all over Africa, wherever I have traveled, through an airport of any size. The line to obtain my boarding pass was short (and fast, *thank you Lord)*. But as usual, the line at passport control was long and meandering, with many switchbacks, and so, so slow. I filled out my travel departure form while standing there among the horde—no easy task, as the shaking in my body made it difficult to write legibly.

I was quite concerned about my health, mostly because I had no clue what this malady could be. I was not nauseous, although my stomach was uneasy. I didn't have a fever. Thankfully, that ruled out malaria. It was the shaking that had me most concerned. I also was experiencing double vision, making reading almost impossible. Perhaps it was an upset in my nervous system. But, not being a doctor, I could only speculate, at best. I yearned to be home and in the care of an American doctor.

For just a moment, that picture gave me comfort. But as I stood there shaking, trying desperately to write my name in any recognizable way, I was hit with the reality of my situation. I was in a massive airport in a large African capital city, half a world away and at least two days from returning home. I tried to stuff down the mounting desperation and do my best to fill out the paperwork that would allow me to leave—although "leaving" only meant I'd be flying on to another large African capital, where I would have to wait for at least another day and a half before getting on a flight to the States. On the way, I would endure a 5-hour layover in yet another vast airport—Schiphol, in Amsterdam—before settling in for an 8-hour leg to Detroit, where I'd wait in another 3-4 hour layover in that airport. Then—at last!—I'd be on my way to San Antonio, where I could seek medical help. Frankly, when I looked at the entire trip in front of me, I wasn't sure I had the stamina.

I forced myself to dwell on the positives, to find something to hold onto. Okay, so I was shaking badly. But I was certain I didn't have malaria, or significant stomach disorders. I also did not have any major bodily pain. "You're okay, Bob," I encouraged myself. "At least you're still standing!" Although the truth was, I desperately wanted to sit down. But I didn't dare leave this line.

All this self-diagnosis and pep talk distracted me for a time as I inched closer to the passport kiosk. Good thing, as I was starting to get anxious about making my flight, which was about to start boarding, according to the airline schedule. The thought of missing this flight and having to wait another 6 to 7 hours caused my shaking to double.

It didn't help that a general unrest was growing in the line, as some of the passengers started pushing past me, yelling at the airport personnel to get more help or we would all miss our planes. What was once a well-formed, snail-paced line was now turning into a semi-dignified mob scene (if there is such a thing). The building riot was not helping my composure; I was now shaking almost uncontrollably and was concerned about how this might come across to the passport agent, should I ever get the opportunity to stand before one of them. Helplessness began to set in. I knew I had no means at this moment to reach a successful outcome in this situation. What, indeed, could I do to help myself?

As best I could muster, I lifted up a silent prayer to the Maker of the universe. Only He could see me through this. "You know my situation, Lord," I breathed. "I cannot see my way out. I'm drowning in utter confusion, trying to make sense of the escalating unrest. But I understand nothing of what I can hear. My ears have heard no language that I can understand for too long, and I am desperate."

No sooner had I prayed than several men entered the large room, followed by a group of men and women. They quickly pushed to the front of the masses and began speaking loud and distinctly, while pointing and even physically moving people into orderly lines. The men and women just behind them were ushered into several of the awaiting kiosk terminals and began motioning those in front to approach them with their documents. Just like that, I found myself smiling, as I could now see that I would soon be processed through this checkpoint.

While happy for my own fate, I was more pleased to see the very hand of God enter into this room of chaos and bring *shalom*. All of us, Christian, Muslim, Hindu, Jew, and non-believer alike were the beneficiaries of this act of mercy. Small thing, you say? Perhaps. But to me, it was truly awesome. And I felt blessed, indeed, to perhaps have been the one to ask and receive on behalf of myself and all my fellow travelers there that day. Once again, God had "leaned in" and guided me—all of us, in fact—through the command of these security personnel and passport agents. I'm certain that I even saw some tiny wings on their backs as they passed! "Thank you, Lord," I said quietly, just as the sweet young lady in the passport booth smiled at me and said, "Next."

I would make the flight in plenty of time, as it turned out. Thank God that I did not have to wait long to board the plane, too, after finally clearing passport check. And the flight itself was not difficult. I was able to calm down my shaking a bit, avoiding drawing too much attention. As soon as we landed in Nairobi, I made my way to the visa and passport station, which was surprisingly not crowded, as had been the norm. After collecting my checked bag, I quickly walked outside and hired the first taxi driver I saw, who whisked me away—in light traffic, again, much to my surprise. I couldn't help but smile brightly as I pondered how much 'mileage' I was receiving in the way of good fortune. I knew it was only due to God's blessing on me. And all from a simple prayer whispered in a chaotic passport station at the Addis airport!

As my driver pulled off the main road and down the winding entrance road for the Fairview Hotel, I felt like I was coming home. I had stayed here on every trip to Nairobi, and a few days before, I had spent one night between my return from South Sudan and my trip to Ethiopia. As we drove past the large palm trees and beautifully landscaped gardens, I let my mind wander. There, on that short, 30-second drive, time stood still, as I traveled back to the time when Emma McCune and her friends and family members would meet here prior to entering South Sudan or upon returning.

It was 1987, and all of Sudan was mired in a 20-year Civil War. In the midst of describing its horrors, and how Emma herself became embroiled in it all, author Deborah Scroggins presents the Fairview as a lovely respite from the fray.[7] She describes in detail this very entrance road, as well as the beauty of the hotel and its charming, well-manicured grounds. I remembered the story every time I stayed here, and part of me wished that I might have lived in that era and could have met Emma and her friends. What lovely parties they engaged in here!

"Sir, welcome to the Fairview," said the young lady, smiling brightly at me, but as if she were not sure I was understanding her. "*Karibu sana* (most welcome)!"

"Oh, *asante*," I responded. "*Poli sana* (very sorry). My mind was somewhere else."

"That is fine sir," she laughed. "Do you have a reservation?"

"I'm afraid not," I said, grimacing. Her smile gave way to a look of concern.

"Oh my. I'm afraid that we're full."

"Really?" I responded. "I was here only a few days ago—with my blind missionary friend, you may recall." I really hoped to make an impression as, at least, a semi-frequent visitor.

"Yes, I remember you now," she said, lightening up a bit. "But I'm afraid a large conference is starting here in Nairobi tomorrow, and our hotel has filled up."

"Let me tell you why I am back here so suddenly, and why I didn't secure a reservation." I then launched into a "Cliff Notes" version of my truncated trip to Ethiopia. When I finished, after commanding her perfect attention for my entire story, she smiled brightly and said, "Let me see what I can find."

"Thank you, Miss," I said gratefully. "Even a tiny room with a single, small bed will do." I really did not want to have to look for another hotel. I knew this one well and had always found it to be very comfortable and the staff very accommodating. I felt that here I would have my best opportunity to recover in these familiar surroundings.

After a few minutes, she looked up from her computer and said, "I did find a room for you, Mr. Nicol, but it is quite small. Can I have someone show it to you before we reserve it?"

---

[7] "Emma's War, A True Story," , Deborah Scroggins, 2002, Pantheon Books

"No," I said, "that won't be necessary. As long as it has a bed and a bathroom, I'm sure it will be just fine."

"Yes, well, it certainly has both of those," she said, laughing slightly. "Actually, it is an overflow room that we don't often use. But because of the convention, we are totally full. You did say that you will be staying for two nights, correct?"

"Yes, that's correct," I responded. "I have to leave very early on Thursday morning for the airport to catch a flight."

"Okay, we can schedule that for you as well, if you like. If another room becomes available tomorrow, would you like me to switch you into that room?"

"Oh my, that is very sweet of you, Miss. But that won't be necessary. I'm sure I will be fine staying in the cozy little room," I said with a smile.

"The computer says I am to charge you full price for the room. But that doesn't seem right to me. I am going to charge you $70 USD per night, is that OK?" she asked, somewhat hesitantly.

"Oh yes, that is very fair." I knew that the full-size single rooms started at about $110, so this was a very generous price. "Thank you again for taking so much time with me and for all your trouble."

The bellman showed me to my room. By comparison to all the other single rooms, it was, indeed, much smaller. And it was tucked away in a funny place, away from most of the other rooms. But that was quite all right. With the hotel being completely full, perhaps this may even be one of the quieter rooms.

It was getting late in the afternoon, but there was still light. I'd have liked to read or write, but knew that wasn't an option with my incessant shaking. I decided to try to nap, but as soon as I laid down, the shaking became quite violent. Sleep was out of the question. Thus, I arose and decided to get something to eat.

The food at this restaurant was quite good. It was actually one of three restaurants within the hotel, but easily my favorite. I decided to take it easy and just have some soup. It filled me, but wasn't too heavy.

I returned to my room, but knowing I couldn't sleep yet, I decided to go for a long walk. I knew that the evening air would be pleasant, and I needed to tire myself out in some way. After walking around the vast hotel, in most of the well-lit grounds area, I finally returned to my tiny room. I tried to sleep again, and many times found myself drifting off, but I would eventually awake again, shaking violently.

This pattern continued throughout the night and into the early morning. Finally, I had enough. I showered and dressed, and went to eat a light breakfast in the hotel restaurant. As I walked again around the compound, I noticed the beautiful pool area was already filling up, and the padded lounge chairs looked quite inviting. I hustled back to my room and changed into a pair of shorts—that could work as a bathing suit, I decided—and returned to the pool with my smartphone and my earbuds. I also brought the book I had been reading earlier on the journey, but had since given up on it due to my nervous condition which made it almost impossible to read. Some time by the pool, I thought, on this beautiful, mild winter day in a city close to the equator, might do me well.

In fact, it did just that. After lounging for a time, I could feel my skin starting to burn. I dipped into the water, and although it was a bit chilly, it felt rather refreshing as it cooled me down. I went through several rounds of lying in the sun and cooling off in the water, and decided to try reading. To my surprise, I found that I could actually read, although the sun was quite bright and my sunglasses were not bifocal prescription, like my regular glasses. Nonetheless, my shaking had slowed considerably. Then I started to feel hunger re-approaching. Checking my watch, I was astounded to see that I had been poolside for hours. I must have dozed off—more than once, I suspected. As I was sitting there, enjoying my partial recovery, a waiter came by and asked me if I wanted anything to eat or drink. I ordered some light lunch and then went back to my book.

After lunch, I decided to stay at the pool. I had no agenda for the day, other than trying my best to get beyond this horrible shaking, which seemed to be happening in this oasis. The pool area was now full of guests, every lounge chair and many of the upright chairs around the umbrella tables occupied. I ran back to my room for sunscreen, as the sun was now quite hot. Luckily, my lounge chair was still unoccupied when I came back. I laid down again, and, before dozing off, I thanked God for all that He had brought me through on this journey. Yes, I had a setback, and, yes, this "condition" I now had was troubling. But here I was, with a new travel schedule that would see me home in a little more than one more full day. And I had a nice, cozy room in a very comfortable hotel that I knew well. I was even feeling somewhat better, having spent a relaxing day basking in sunlight and chilling in a beautiful pool, with beautiful grounds surrounding me.

"Really, God," I prayed, "I know that you are taking care of me. I will continue to trust you in this, even as you have brought me so far from the fields of Ethiopia, and set me safely on my way home." I still had a long way to go, for sure. But I was finally feeling strengthened. I could do this. Knowing I wasn't alone, but instead, I had the God of all creation watching my back, didn't hurt my psyche one bit.

After a deeply relaxing day at the pool and a nice dinner in the livelier restaurant, where a large number of conventioneers had shown up, I headed back to my room for some sleep. Not that I needed it anymore. But then again, I didn't have a whole lot else to do. It must have been decent sleep, as I don't remember anything else from that night.

Early the next morning I boarded the shuttle for Jomo Kenyatta International Airport, passed quickly through the maze of security and passport check/visa closeout, and then waited two hours to board the KLM flight to Amsterdam. Eight hours after taking off, and another long nap on the plane (thank you, Ambien), we landed in Schiphol International Airport. Upon deplaning, I went immediately in search of one of those "wavy lounge chairs" that I had discovered on another layover here.

I found the area where they were all stationed, but unfortunately, they were already all occupied. Oh no! Now where would I spend the next six to seven hours while awaiting to board my flight back to America? Normally, I would hop on a train and arrive in downtown Amsterdam within twenty minutes. There I would enjoy the sights and sounds—and food—of this vibrant, beautiful city, with all its lovely canals and 13^{th-} to 17^{th-} century buildings. But my health would not permit that today. After walking around for a while, I stopped back at the lounge chair area just in time to see a couple packing up to leave. I hurried over and set my bag down. As soon as they departed, I grabbed one of their loungers. Hooray! I was set.

This lounge chair was not just a luxury for me, but a necessity. On the flight from Nairobi, my shaking condition had returned. I wasn't sure if I'd even be able to rest, and I was afraid to take another sleeping pill for fear of missing my next flight. I would try to read for a while—maybe that would tire me out. I had grabbed the KLM Airline magazine from the flight. Easier than trying to tackle a book, I concluded.

It worked. Before I knew it, I was headed to the gate to board the Delta flight to Detroit. Once there, I would have a much shorter layover before catching my final flight to San Antonio. As I entered the boarding area, I was surprised to see so few people. If it stayed this sparse, I might get lucky enough to grab an entire row for the 8-1/2-hour flight to Detroit. "Stop dreaming, Bob!" I told myself. "There's no way that will happen."

But guess what? That's exactly what happened! This was a Boeing 777, with four seats in the middle, flanked by two seats on either side of the aisles. I was sitting in the aisle seat of the middle section—and no one else came to claim any of the other three seats! "Thank you, Jesus," I whispered. "You rock!" Once the plane was airborne, I gathered all of the pillows and blankets from each of the other three seats and, along with my own, made a comfortable bed, with every intention of sleeping all the way to Detroit. I was not at all hungry. Though I would probably get dehydrated, I expected to wake up at some point, and then I would get some water. I settled in for some awesome sleep.

Unfortunately, this was not to be. I had all the right elements—fantastic leg room, practically a bed on the plane, way better than business class! But I forgot one significant detail—the flight was leaving in the late morning from Amsterdam, and, heading West, we would be "chasing the sun" all the way to Detroit. And at 38,000 feet, the sun is always out during daylight hours. So while I was certainly relaxed, I certainly could not sleep. Bright light shone throughout the cabin, as many of the passengers had their windows open all the way. Why I just didn't just give up and watch movies, I don't know. That surely would have passed the time much faster.

This flight seemed even longer than the 17-hour flight I had taken from Atlanta to Dubai, back in July. In reality, it was barely half the time; but due to my condition, I was completely unable to relax in any position. It didn't help that I had captured so much snooze time on the previous leg from Nairobi, and during the lengthy layover at Schiphol. This did not turn out to be a "short and happy" flight like I had anticipated.

Somehow, I survived, and we touched down into Detroit Metro. I would now get to experience my first U.S. Customs entrance into this very modern airport. I was so used to coming into country through Houston, Atlanta, or JFK that I was looking forward to experiencing something different. Not "bad different"—that would be flying into O'Hare, easily my worst customs/baggage claim nightmare, creating the need for me and six of our students, plus Chris and Jamie, one of the moms on the first mission trip ever, for Real4Christ, to have to spend the night in Chicago—on the last leg of our journey home after ten days in Kenya. But that is a story for another time, perhaps.

As it turned out, Detroit customs was a delight. (And in the years to come, it only got better when they rolled out—and I immediately joined—the "Global Entry Nation," allowing me to whisk through customs in airports throughout the country.) Although the switch-back line was formidable, the number of customs agents was significant, thereby moving the traffic along quickly. Good thing, as my "condition" was not improving, though at least it didn't seem to be getting any worse. I thanked God, at least, for that blessing.

Before long, I was able to clear customs, acquire my luggage, and re-check to San Antonio—a series of tasks I was becoming all too familiar with the more I traveled back and forth to Africa. I was beginning to realize that this process is not something you can really "get used to." But I did find that I could learn to live with it, while engaging in an unending search to determine the best way to travel as efficiently as possible, even though we travelers have little control over what happens once we enter the bowels of these mega airports. We're all just lemmings, heads down and following the feet in front of us into "the abyss." Okay, it's not that bad, I guess. But it can seem that way, depending on one's outlook—and health, I was now learning.

One benefit to this difficult trip, feeling awful while simultaneously dealing with interminable customs queues, was gaining a greater empathy for people who travel with disabilities. Of course, mine was relatively minor, and hopefully only a one-time event. Whatever malady I was experiencing, I was reassured that it was not a physical system shut-down (in this case, neurologic, according to my careful self-diagnosis). Also, I was feeling orders of magnitude better by now. No, I would be fine. But the partially-formed, or the amputees, or those suffering from any variety of crippling diseases had to deal with much worse on a regular basis. While I hoped that they would always experience special assistance and an expedited ingress, it still didn't lessen their life burden. As I was exiting customs and joining the next crowd heading to baggage claim, I thanked God for his guidance of my path thus far, and for some improvement in my current health condition. And I added a special prayer for those just mentioned, that live with their infirmity every day.

With a shadow of guilt, and a stronger sense of thankfulness, I waited for my luggage to emerge while working to steer clear of any feelings of self-pity. In doing this, however, it seemed as if I might somehow be missing a chapter of my life story. Fortunately, it re-emerged just prior to boarding the plane, several hours later, for my last leg to San Antonio. What actually drew me out of my "coma" was the muffled sound of my phone, buried in my backpack under books, notebooks, and an "emergency" change of underwear and socks.

When I finally retrieved it, it was Jacqueline, my youngest daughter. She told me she was worried about me and had been praying steadily once she received news of my condition. She was my only daughter still in San Antonio, and was halfway into her senior year in high school. She asked me when my flight was to land in San Antonio. She had already called her mom, Linda, and they would be waiting to take me to the Methodist Hospital emergency room. Linda had even contacted her sister, Terri, an emergency room doctor who used to work at Methodist. Terri, in turn, called Dr. Wilson, one of her former associate doctors, to alert him to my pending arrival in a few hours.

Now I was even more excited to get home, since Jacqueline and Linda would be there to meet me. It had been several years since anyone had met me on my return from any of my trips abroad. That, and the prospect of getting focused medical attention, would easily carry me through this last leg of my trip, making it feel so much shorter.

In fact, I awoke from a gentle nap just as the flight attendant was announcing our final descent into San Antonio. I was amazed that I had been able to sleep, since I had not taken any sleeping pills for fear of falling too deeply to sleep, or having extreme grogginess if awakened suddenly. Nonetheless, it was sheer delight to have quite missed this entire final leg of the arduous journey of the past four days.

As I was waiting for my luggage to arrive at baggage claim, I called Jacqueline. They were en route to the airport and would arrive at the terminal in just a few minutes. Upon retrieving my luggage, I walked out to the arrivals exit and reached the curb just as they drove up. Jacqueline jumped out, hollering, "Daddy!" and grabbed me, giving me a big bear hug and kiss. "I'm so glad to see you. Are you okay? We have been so worried for you."

"I'm actually feeling considerably better," I said, while shoving my heavy suitcases into the back of Linda's Jeep. "Hi, Linda. I can't thank you enough for coming here to meet me."

"Did you call Dr. Wilson?" she asked.

"I was able to reach him just before boarding in Detroit. He's not on tonight, though. But he said to go the emergency room and check in—they'll be expecting me, and one of the doctors would see me right away."

"Oh, good!" she responded. "Let's go."

When we arrived a short time later at the emergency room entrance, she dropped me off and said that they would be right in.

"You don't have to wait for me," I said. "I don't know how long this could take."

"Daddy, no!" Jacqueline responded, before Linda could speak. "We're not leaving you here."

"But it's a school night, baby. I don't want you to miss sleep. Remember, I know how cranky you can be."

"I'll be fine," she said. "Just get in there and get checked out. Mommy and I will be right in."

I looked at Linda, who gave me a smile. "Just go," she said. "I'll be in as soon as I can find a parking place. Jacqueline, why don't you go with Daddy."

The receptionist at the front desk looked frazzled. I could see why. The waiting room was mayhem, packed with people. Kids were running around, parents were shouting and barking orders at them, in multiple languages. Instantly, I knew I was back in San Antonio. It was late—nearly 11 PM. What were all these young kids doing here? I wondered. Most didn't appear to be sick. Probably just came along with Mom and Dad with one of their infirmed siblings.

As I was checking in, I realized that my hand was still quite shaky, as I was trying to write legibly. The receptionist asked, "Is this why you're here, sir?", an air of compassion in her voice.

"Oh, you noticed," I said, somewhat embarrassed. "Yes, I have been traveling overseas and came down with something. It's been like this for three or four days now and has me concerned."

"Well, we will do our best to get you in to see a doctor as soon as possible. But, as you can see, we're quite busy this evening."

"Yes, I am amazed at so many people here this late," I responded. "Just so you know, I called Dr. Wilson, who is a friend from my church. He told me that he would alert the doctor on duty, and they were to be on the lookout for me when I arrived."

"Okay. That's good to know. Let me tell the doctor that you are here. He may want to see you right away. Please have a seat—if you can find one," she said, looking past me at the assembled throng, many watching the louder-than-necessary TVs mounted on several walls.

I looked around the room and spotted Jacqueline, waving to me. Linda had joined her, and they had a seat for me. But I no sooner sat down when I heard my name called. A doctor in a white lab coat was looking around the room, and I walked toward him.

In the waiting room, he performed a form of triage by simply asking me a series of questions. He also took my temperature and blood pressure, as his clarifying questions continued. I felt more at ease as he started to list all of the things that he was ruling out—malaria, dengue and yellow fever among them. I felt quite proud of my own self-diagnosis, since I had also ruled out many of those same things.

"Have you taken any medications in the last several days?" he asked.

"No," I responded. "I wouldn't know what to take, since I never had any stomach problems or fever."

"I see. How about any travel medications or immunization medicine? Anything for malaria, perhaps?"

"Oh, yes," I nodded. "I always take anti-malaria medication. But, come to think of it, this time it was different. I generally take Lariam or Mefloquine, the weekly dose. But this time I was not able to get the prescription filled in time. My missionary leader gave me some other kind that he gets in quantity to take to the villages in Africa. I had to take two pills at a time, one yellow and one white, three times a day, instead of just one pill a week. I didn't like that at all. For all I knew, they were past their expiration date, since he got them for free. Whereas Lariam is quite expensive—$10 - $12 a pill."

"Do you remember what that medication was?" he asked.

"No, I'm afraid I don't. But I can try to find out."

"Okay, that would be helpful if you could," he responded. "I'm going to order some blood work so that we can try to get to the bottom of this. Please, have a seat, and I will get back to you when I can."

He turned and went back through the door. My concern for ever really discovering what I was suffering from returned with a rush. Apparently, it was written on my face as I walked back to join Jacqueline and Linda.

"What's the matter?" Linda asked.

"Oh, we still don't know," I answered, trying to stay upbeat so as not to worry them further. "At least it's not malaria, or yellow fever. He wants to do some blood work, but I don't know when."

"Did you ask him if he heard from Bob Wilson?" she asked.

"That's why he even saw me in the first place. I just thought that he would take me into an analysis room or something, and order the bloodwork from there." I glanced around the waiting room. "Is it me, or did this place fill up even more?"

"Yes, Daddy, I think it did," Jacqueline said. "This is crazy. Do you think they will call you soon?"

"I hope so," I answered. "But if they don't, you guys should go. You have school tomorrow, Jacqueline, and Linda, I'm sure you have to work, right?"

"Yes, but we want to stay with you until they find out what's wrong," she responded. "Maybe they'll call you in soon."

Unfortunately, "soon" never happened. After sitting for more than half an hour, I sighed heavily. "Please, you guys need to go. I will be fine."

"How will you get home, Daddy?" asked Jacqueline.

"Sam will come get me," I said. "He offered to bring me here, actually, and said to call him if I needed a ride—anywhere, at any time."

"Please keep us posted on anything that you learn, okay?" Linda asked.

"You know I will. Thank you both for coming to get me. It was awesome to see you at the airport. I really appreciate this."

After getting goodbye hugs from both of them, they left. I sat back down to wait. After watching the room nearly empty out and then fill back up again, I realized that these patients were being seen based on some kind of triage. It never seemed to matter what order they arrived here. I was quickly losing hope of ever being called back in.

I finally called Sam. Being the great friend that he is, Sam drove out to the hospital, then took me home. On the way, I told him all about my getting sick in Ethiopia and my long pilgrimage back home, including the interminable wait just now in the Methodist Hospital ER. He offered to pick me up in the morning and take me to the nearest "Doc-in-a-box" clinic, as early as possible. He said that he could get me there as soon as they could take me, but that he had a commitment later that morning, so he would not be able to stay and wait with me. But he would see if one of our other friends, John or Ralph, might pick me up.

With the next day's schedule in place, I slumped into bed. Once again, sleep came, but with some difficulty, and intermittently. By morning, however, I was feeling somewhat better and not shaking quite as much. True to his word, Sam dropped by early and drove me to the nearest Texas Med Clinic. He said our friend, John, would be on standby to get me if Sam wasn't out of his meeting in time to pick me up.

The scene in the clinic waiting room was the total opposite of the one I had just experienced some eight hours prior. Perhaps six or eight other people, all sitting in silence, reading, or talking quietly to their spouse or child. I walked to the front desk and went through the same discussion and information gathering as the night before. I sat down with the others to wait to be called, but I only got through half the magazine I had picked up when one of the nurses called my name. She had me follow her into the clinic, where she took my height and weight. Then she led me into a checkup room, where she took my blood pressure—normal—and pulse—still slightly elevated, but not dramatically.

While she was writing down my vitals, a doctor entered and introduced himself. He proceeded to ask me many of the same questions. After checking my eyes, ears, and the inside of my mouth, and taking down all of the information regarding my medication, he said that he would have the nurse take a blood sample. He said that there were a few tests they could run quickly, but the full scan would not yield results until tomorrow. I told him that this was fine, as I was beginning to feel somewhat better. I could only surmise that this was simply due to being back home in familiar surroundings. He did write me a prescription for some medication that would help me relax and, hopefully, sleep better. I thanked him and returned to the waiting room to wait for John, who arrived quickly.

We stopped at Starbucks on the way back, where Sam joined us after his morning meeting. It was great to be back with two of my very best friends. They told me how concerned everyone was. I was surprised to hear that so many people knew that I was sick and coming home early, since I only told my family and a couple close friends. Sam said that Pastor Donna had announced it in church on Sunday during the service, asking everyone to keep me in their prayers.

I told them I felt uncomfortable, since I no longer felt all that bad. Sam chuckled. "Bob, their concern is genuine, regardless of how sick you turn out to be."

"Okay," I said. "I'll accept that. I have to say that I was truly concerned in Ethiopia, trying to fly back to Kenya. Actually, I was quite terrified. I didn't know if I'd make it through the excruciatingly long customs process, all while experiencing what felt like a nervous system shut down. The shaking became nearly intolerable. But then, I honestly felt God's healing response—to all those prayers, evidently. I had the chance to recover, partially, while resting in Nairobi, waiting nearly two days for my next flight. Without that break, I don't know what I would have done. I probably would have checked into a hospital in Nairobi as a last resort. But that can be a challenging event, I'm told."

"Well, you're here now, and we're all thankful for that," John responded.

"So, what did the doctor say at Med Clinic?" Sam asked.

"He seems to be leaning toward a negative reaction to the anti-malaria medicine I was taking. But they won't know for sure for at least 24 hours, when the blood test results come back."

"Did he give you anything, in the meantime—any meds?" Sam asked.

"Yes, actually, I need to go by CVS and pick up my prescription," I responded.

"Well, let's go now, and then we'll take you home to rest," said John. "We want you healthy again."

I slept on and off for the next day, eagerly waiting the test results. At last, the doctor called. As expected, I was told that there was nothing really out of the ordinary with my blood test results. It had most likely been a reaction to the malaria medication. He said to keep taking the medication he had prescribed and let him know if my health took a turn for the worse.

Within a week, I felt normal again. The blurred vision had disappeared, and eventually the shaking subsided. There seemed to be no lasting harm to my nervous system. At last, my long ordeal was over. I was whole again. Thanks be to God through the prayers of His people!

In the months that followed, I kept close tabs on the progress of the well drilling in Meki. I exchanged many emails with Melaku and with David Harding, back in Florida, and even with Atkelt, in Awassa. It would take Atkelt another 6 weeks to complete all of the work, after waiting for the availability of their LS200 drill rig, and then the fabrication, delivery, and installation of the elevated twin water tank platforms, the foundations, and the tanks themselves and the connecting pipes. But when it was all done, the word came back from Melaku that water was flowing and the tanks were filled! I was overjoyed.

I started making plans to return to begin the next phase of the work there, that of building a septic tank system and a building to house flushing toilet stalls, wash sinks, and showers. All this would be needed once the development of the medical clinic and conference center was underway. I also wanted to extend the water from the elevated tanks to a station just inside the back gate of the complex. Here, we would install several faucets for the public to use to obtain our good well water. Soon, I believed, some relief would come to the people of Meki.

My return was scheduled for June 2009—five months after coming home unexpectedly from my previous trip. This trip was added on to another visit to coastal Kenya, where I planned to oversee the drilling of a well there at the first Real 4 Christ School. [*The reader may recall that this trip to Kenya was when I had my first motorbike adventure—see Chapter 2*] I had been emailing constantly with Melaku and his architect cousin, Dagmawi Lemmagobena, who was helping design the septic tank for the Meki Clinic. I had met Dagmawi in Addis on my previous trip (prior to getting sick). We had exchanged details for the design of the underground two-chamber vault. The benefit of this turned out to be significant, as Dagmawi was very familiar with available local building materials and construction practices. He was able to revise my original design to make it easier for a local contractor to build, and at a reasonable cost.

By the time I left Kenya (after surviving my motor bike adventure!), the hand excavation had been completed and the bottom slab had been poured. When I arrived with Melaku a day later, they were already erecting the cut stone walls of the vault. After the water system took nearly three months to complete, I was astonished by the quick progress happening with the septic system.

As I watched them work, I could see why they had come so far, so fast. With only the supervisor and a stone mason installing all of the cut stones, and two younger guys constantly mixing and delivering grout to them on the walls, the structure was taking shape very quickly. And the workmanship was extraordinary. It looked much more like a small house than an underground septic tank. Indeed, all the lines were true and straight, and the angles, perfect. That, and the variation in the rocks, in size, color and texture, made for very aesthetically pleasing walls. I found myself wanting to add some windows and a door! But such features would certainly not be practical for an underground septic tank. Still, I found this attention to detail and perfection for such a "lowly" structure, whose only purpose was to hold human waste, spoke volumes about the integrity of the craftsmen.

One day, as I was watching them, I noted that they soon would be approaching the surface with the exterior walls. I told Melaku that we needed to insert the inlet and outlet pipes into the walls at the correct elevations, which I would provide. He informed me that the piping was not intended to be performed by this crew—another would arrive after the chamber was complete and backfilled. However, I advised him that we needed to make the connections now, by inserting the pipes in and out so these craftsmen could grout them in place and build the wall around them, rather than break out the wall just after building it. He now understood, but said that there were no piping materials on the site yet, as this was intended to come later. I suggested that we go and purchase them in town, if available. Then I would supervise their installation at the correct location and elevation. He agreed. "We can take a *tuk tuk* into town and see if we can purchase the pipe."

We hailed a *tuk tuk* just outside the gate of the clinic compound. Before traveling very far, we came to a merchant who appeared to have the correct pipe stacked outside his store. We stopped the *tuk tuk* to investigate; indeed, it was the right pipe, so we purchased the smallest length possible, 20 ft. (6 m). Now the question was, how to get it back to the compound? We asked the hardware store owner to cut the pipe in half for us, which he did willingly. But now we still had two 10-foot pieces of pipe to transport by *tuk tuk* back to the compound. The merchant tied them together at several points with small pieces of rope to help us to handle them. The pipes were thin-walled and not too heavy. I was able to hold on to them outside the *tuk tuk* while sitting inside. One can imagine what a sight this was as we drove slowly down the streets of Meki!

Just as we came into view of the clinic, we passed a policeman standing beside the road. As we passed him, he started waving frantically. I thought he was just being friendly, so I smiled and waved back to him. All at once, Melaku told the *tuk tuk* driver to stop. The policeman was now running towards us. Melaku told me to wait and stepped out of the *tuk tuk* to confront the officer. Since they were speaking in Amharic, I could only guess what they were saying. The officer was speaking loudly and pointing to me, then to the pipes, then back to me again. Melaku, being a soft-spoken gentleman, remained in total control as he quietly answered the officer's agitated questioning. Finally, he returned to the *tuk tuk*, climbed in, and told the driver to continue on.

I asked Melaku what that was all about. "Oh, the usual," he said. "The policeman was just trying to extract a fee from us. He said it was unsafe for us to be hauling this load of pipes sticking completely out of the *tuk tuk*." Though he remained calm, I could see that he was quite angry, which is an unusual thing for Melaku. "He saw a white man in the *tuk tuk* and thought he could extract a fine from us. Of course, he could not cite any laws or tell me the associated penalty fee."

"Did you pay him?" I asked.

"Of course not. He soon learned that he would not get a bribe out of me. So finally, he just gave up and told us to go."

"Well, good for you, my friend," I said. "I'm guessing it wouldn't have been that expensive, but I still don't like to pay bribes."

"Neither do I, Bob. At least he seemed to understand when I told him the purpose for these pipes, and even more to his point, what a white man was doing in this town."

When we got back to the clinic, a material delivery had been made during our absence. Parked in the shade of a tree was the delivery vehicle—a handsome donkey, pulling a cart stacked with several bags of cement grout. The donkey stood patiently, languidly grazing on the grass. "Now that's what I call cost-effective delivery service," I joked with Melaku. "We should have hired him to haul our pipe for us!"

I borrowed a saw from the contract foreman and cut one of the pipes in half again. I then took these pipe sections and laid them on either end of the structure. Then I showed the foreman exactly where I wanted him to insert them into the walls that he was bringing up. Since they were getting close to that point, I stood by to guide them, as necessary, in recognizing the critical placement of the inlet and outlet pipes for the effective operation of the septic tank.

Visualizing the construction of this important feature of our utility system for the clinic filled me with great hope for this trip. Having this important task nearly accomplished made me feel newly confident. Before leaving the site, I went over the details with both the contractor foreman and Wesenu of the leech field (septic tank discharge) piping that needed to be performed next. I even went so far as to drill holes in one of the pipes and then laid it on the ground exactly where it needed to be buried. I showed them how the rest of the pipes needed to be similarly drilled, and then made a line in the dirt to where the pipe needed to extend. They both appeared to understand.

Melaku came by as I finished explaining. He told me that we would have to leave shortly to get back to Addis before dark. When he heard that, Wesenu became very excited and started jabbering quickly to Melaku in Amharic. Melaku turned to me and said that Wesenu and Sarah really wanted to show me his vegetable garden. "I would like to see it," I said. "Let's go."

We piled into Melaku's car and began driving south through Meki. After we had traveled for several miles, Wesenu pointed to a road leading off of the highway. We drove past one farm after another, filled with rows and rows of vegetable produce of all shapes and sizes. Finally, Wesenu motioned Melaku to pull over and stop. We had stopped at the end of a large plot of rows of extremely lush cabbage plants. We walked toward a small, primitive structure, outside of which several men were standing. Wesenu talk to them briefly before leading us into the structure. Inside, we found a large pump next to a hand-dug well. Wesenu explained that he had purchased this pump, and was using it to irrigate this entire property. We surveyed the land, and indeed, it was vast and lush. I can add that it was also far healthier than any of the nearby vegetable fields.

"Wesenu," I exclaimed, "your garden is amazing, and it is beautiful!" He beamed a beautiful smile and thanked me.

"Here, please, let me take your picture, with Sarah, in front of your beautiful *shamba*." He started to comply, but then stopped and looked at me, perplexed. Then it dawned on me—I was mixing up my countries and languages. "Oh, sorry," I waved my hand. "I mean, your vegetable garden. '*Shamba*' is the Swahili word for it."

Melaku, standing behind me, heartily laughed at my mistake. "I am sorry that it must be hard for you, Bob, changing from Swahili to Amharic to English, even."

"Oh, not so hard," I chuckled. "I know so little of either of them, I really only make mistakes because I become feeble-minded."

"Oh, ho! Not you, Brother Bob, I am sure of it," he responded, laughing harder.

Wesenu and Sarah stood watching, beaming brightly and holding on to each other, still in their camera-ready pose. It was a beautiful moment. So simple, yet so profound. The lush vegetables provided a gorgeous backdrop to this very down-to-earth couple, who seemed so grateful that we had taken the time to come see the result of their hard work. I could tell Sarah was so proud of her husband, as she held his arm and smiled brightly as we lauded his efforts. Back at the clinic Wesenu was just a guard and caretaker, which, I have to say, he did very well. But out here, he was a master gardener. His investment in the pump and irrigation system, which I could see was significant, had placed him head and shoulders above any of the other *shambas* that we had passed throughout the countryside. It was also highly evident that his crop was well ahead of any of the others, allowing him to get to market sooner.

We drove back to the clinic, where we said goodbye to Wesenu and Sarah, hugging them warmly. I had a feeling that the visit was as good for them as it was for me. At least, I hoped and prayed to God that it was.

We arrived back at Addis well after dark, but Sosi greeted us with a warm meal shortly after our arrival. She, too, seemed happy to see me feeling so much better than when last I had visited. We talked as we enjoyed dinner together, along with their teenage daughter, Beza. I told them, in detail, about my long and arduous journey home, beginning with the excruciating time at the Addis Airport, where I had felt the worst.

As usual, they wanted to know when I would be returning next. What a great feeling, when someone that you are leaving only wants to hear about when you will return! I don't know about you, but it just makes me want to be with them all the more. That's how I feel about my growing number of friends here in Ethiopia and in particular, Melaku, Sosi and Beza. But now, I add Sarah and Wesenu, as well, whom I felt that I had come to know so much better, even if it was only a few days spent with them.

I responded that Dean was asking me to go with him to Tanzania, where he was heading up a Pastors' Conference. He had been talking to Tony and Cath (Cathrine) Swanson, English missionaries from the Africa Inland Mission (AIM) Church. When Tony found out that we do water wells, he asked Dean to help them out with one in Tanzania. So Dean had put me on it. I would be going there with Dean to oversee the well drilling. "Perhaps I can make a trip back to Ethiopia after I'm finished in Tanzania," I said.

"That would be great, Bob," said Melaku. "You know that we would love to have you back here with us. And I am sure that we will continue to need your expert advice at Meki."

"Well, I don't know how 'expert' it is! But I am always glad for the opportunity to come back to Addis and spend time with you all. Let's just see what the Lord has in mind for me, okay?"

As it turned out, I did get to combine another trip to Ethiopia at the end of our trip to Tanzania, some months after returning from this trip. Again, Dean did not come with me, but left Tanzania even before I did, once he had completed with the Pastors' Conference.

Melaku wanted to know all about Tanzania when he greeted me at the Addis Airport, after my arrival and the usual, laborious visa-gathering process. I was so glad to see him, though my stamina was waning after a long day of flying and airports, having left from the Dar Es Salaam Airport in Tanzania before noon. It was starting to seem like every return trip to Ethiopia was immediately following a well-drilling project in another country. My previous visit was on the tail end of the well drilling for the MBEWAU school in Kenya (the trip where I rented the motorbike). This was my third trip to Ethiopia in 2009. I guess that you can say that I was really starting to like this place! Actually, I was enjoying all of the African countries that I was having the opportunity to visit. All except South Sudan, that is, as it was the most difficult to access and had just come out of a long civil war.

We would have plenty of time to talk. And although it was quite late when we arrived at Melaku's home, Sosi had prepared another wonderful meal. It felt almost like coming home, being here with Melaku, Sosi and Beza once again. They made me feel like so much more than a guest—more like an honored guest. Or better, like family. Indeed, in just three short trips, and now this, my fourth, Ethiopia and its beautiful people were beginning to hold a special place in my heart.

The next day, we got an early start on our trip to Meki. Although we tried to get out of the city before the heavy traffic buildup, that's mostly an impossibility in Addis. It's the part of the trip that one simply endures, while looking forward to the drive through the beautiful rolling hills and farms, with distant mountains in the background. I told Melaku, as we left the noise and traffic of the huge metropolis, that I didn't think I would ever tire of making this trip—at least this portion of it. I was always amazed how calmly he dealt with the craziness of the traffic snarls. To be fair, the traffic in Nairobi and Mombasa, two cities I was spending more and more time negotiating, were easily as bad as Addis. And Addis, to its credit, had several multi-lane highways with actual lane markers—unlike Nairobi or Mombasa, where it seemed more of a 'free-for-all' looking for a demolition derby, I would joke.

Melaku and I chatted easily, and I told him that I was excited to see the progress at the clinic, even though it had only been a few months since I had last been there. I was glad that he had Dagmawi making frequent visits to check on the contractors building the toilet and shower facility. From the photos that he had sent, it looked like steady progress had been made. When we arrived several hours later I was delighted to see that, not only had they completed the building exterior, including the metal roof sheets, but even the entire grounds looked better than ever.

Melaku told me that he had asked Wesenu, when he wasn't busy at his vegetable plot, to clear out the underbrush and 'slash' the high grass that had seemed to take over the property. I commended him—the place was really shaping up. And that was despite the fact that new construction was still evident throughout. I told Melaku that I had learned, through years spent on many construction sites, to look beyond the piles of materials waiting to be installed and of excavated soil waiting to be backfilled, to a vision of the site with the construction complete, including the final grading and landscape. I recalled to mind Dagmawi's architectural renderings of the completed facility, with all the lodge buildings and the clinic and support buildings. I could see that this was beginning to take on that image. I hoped I could present this to Dean in the right words, to effectively give him a picture of what an amazing little property this was truly becoming.

Melaku just smiled and even chuckled a bit. "What?" I asked, snapping out of my reverie.

"You amaze me, Bob. Here we are with only a water tower and the toilet building visible, and you are already having a vision of a completed facility."

I had to laugh, too. "What?" I asked. "You mean you can't see that? I realize that the 'beautifully crafted' septic tank is underground and thus, out of sight. Fair enough. But with the work that Wesenu has done, I can now envision the several small lodge units that Dagmawi designed and the finished clinic. I believe it will look just grand when complete."

"Yes, I am sure that it will, Bob. But let's get the latrine finished first."

"That's why I'm here."

"Well then, my friend," he responded, laughing, "let's put you to work."

"I'm ready, Melak," I said, using the clipped version of his name I had heard Sosi use, and climbed out of the car. Without waiting for him, I strode immediately to where most of the day's activity appeared to be happening. This would be at the near end of the main building, where sometime in the recent past, the concrete floor had been placed to add a fifth room. The work was now focused on laying concrete block for the walls. While two men were busy doing that, two other men were building forms and setting rebar for the corner columns.

When Melaku caught up to me, he pointed out that this construction was for a new examination room for the clinic. It would be one of two examination rooms, with the other being the current living room of Sarah and Wesenu.

"So what will happen to them?" I asked.

"They will have to leave. In fact, Dean has already told me that he wants them to find a new place to live soon."

"Really?" I responded, astonished. "Why do they have to leave now? It makes more sense to me that they stay here for as long as possible. Having them here on property is good security, I would think. Plus, having this place up and running as a clinic/conference center is still a long way off, by anyone's estimate. And even when that does happen, we're going to need people like them—Wesenu, to take care of the property, and Sarah, possibly, as a receptionist or host at the clinic. Besides, it just doesn't seem right to kick them off."

"Yes, Bob, I totally agree. And I explained this to Dean. But he seems to think that they are taking advantage of him by staying here for free. And we are actually paying them a small amount to guard the place and take care of it."

"What do you mean?" I asked. "Like keep it clean and free of trash? And to cut the high grass?"

"Yes," answered Melaku. "That is basically what we asked Wesenu to do already."

"Well, now I feel bad," I said, shaking my head.

"Why is that?"

"Because Dean always asks me how the place looks whenever I come here. And up until now, before Wesenu cut all the high grass and cleaned everything up, I have to admit that I told him it really wasn't looking all that good."

"Bob, it's not your fault," he responded. "It really wasn't looking very good, and I even told Wesenu that he would have to do a better job."

"Well, now that he has, I will talk to Dean again and tell him how good it looks. Maybe then he will allow them to stay. In fact, I will make it a point to talk to him as soon as I return, to try to convince him to let them stay."

"Oh, thank you for your concern, Bob," he said. "But actually, they have already found another place and will be moving soon."

"Well, I'm sorry, Melaku, but that really does make me feel bad. And I still don't think it makes any sense."

As we were talking we had wandered over to see the progress of the toilets and showers facility. Since I was here last, the roof had been completed, and they had installed the metal toilet partitions and the doors. Some of the plumbing work had started to take place, as well.

Both sinks were in place and some of the piping connected, but none of the toilets or urinals had been set yet.

I commended Melaku for the significant progress. "Thank you, Bob," he responded. "But it is really Dagmawi who should get the credit. He has been the one to push the schedule and oversee the workmanship."

"Well then, thank you Dagmawi," I said, with a big smile. "Please tell him, for me, that he is really doing a great job. Everything looks really good." I looked around quickly. "Now tell me, Melaku, where is the contractor foreman? I would like to talk to him."

"Wesenu told me that he is off site buying materials," he responded.

"Okay. Maybe we can go and check into the motel and come back later. And tell me, is it the same contractor who did the septic system vault? I recognize some of the same men constructing building block walls who, I believe, worked on the septic tank walls, as well."

"Yes, you are very observant, Bob. It is the same contractor. And yes, we can go now to check in to the hotel."

When we returned a few hours later, we found the contractor supervisor there, so I went over all of the remaining work with him. This included the piping and the underground valve vaults for the pipes extending from the building drains to the septic tank.

I also went over the details for the shower and toilet facility. The rest of my time on this short stay was spent monitoring all the construction work taking place. It also gave me time to check out the completed installation of the water towers. I found some minor problems with the piping, which was not installed well and was leaking. Fortunately, I was able to purchase the necessary fittings in the town at one of the hardware stores. After a day and a half of this, Melaku and I returned to Addis for one more night of Sosi's great cooking before taking me to the airport the following morning.

I assured him I would return again soon, and we would spend some time in Addis. Here, we would purchase the piping materials needed for extending to the clinic and to the exterior public water station. Melaku knew that this was my dream for this place, as with all places where we installed water wells. He promised me that he would assist me to see this through as soon as possible. "But someone is going to have to manage and oversee the upkeep and distribution of the water. We cannot have uncontrolled access to the property to get water, right?" I asked.

"You're absolutely right, Bob," Melaku responded. "We will have to do that."

"All the more reason to have Sarah and Wesenu here to do that as part of their duty. Doesn't that just make sense?"

"Bob, you will get no argument from me on this issue."

"I know, Melaku, I am not trying to be argumentative. I'm just having a real hard time understanding why Dean would want to run off the people that we all know and trust, especially when we're going to need their service very soon. It's a mystery to me. I will certainly ask him about it when I get back."

When we arrived at the airport, before entering the terminal, I told Melaku what a great job he was doing here. "I know how hard it is to manage projects in your own city. But to have to do that in a small town some 130 km away must be really difficult. And it's not your only job, I know. You are also running the English-speaking school for CrossWay here in Addis, and you yourself are attending college to get an advanced degree. When I think about all that, Melaku, I am simply amazed. And you do all of that in such a quiet and gentlemanly way. Everybody that I have met here loves you, and I can see why. You are wonderful Christian man, and I'm proud to call you friend."

"Thank you, Bob. I am likewise proud to be your friend. Please, have a safe journey and come back to see us again real soon."

We hugged, and I entered the airport, ready for my journey home to the States from this, my third trip to Ethiopia. I would return only five months later, and we would be able to purchase the necessary pipe materials in Addis and heat fusion welder for joining them. With help from Melaku and Wesenu, I completed the water distribution from the towers to the buildings. We also were able to install the public water station along the back wall of the property next to the rear gate. This, we all agreed, would make a good location for easy access and egress by the public to get water.

I also had to check on the submersible electric well pump, which Wesenu advised was having difficulty filling the elevated tanks. With the help of some of the contractor's men, we pulled the submersible pump up to the surface. This was the first time that I had seen it since it was installed by Atkelt and his team after drilling the well. As it turned out, when I checked the output curve for this particular pump, I could see that it was marginal at this depth for pumping to the top of the water tank. Thus, we would either have to get a bigger pump, or raise this pump higher in the well.

With our budget being tight, we decided that we would have to work with this pump. That meant that we would have to raise the pump, which we did by some 20 feet. When we inserted the pump into the borehole, it was able to fill the tank at a much quicker pace. The problem with this solution was that we gave up 20 feet of water depth, which could pose a concern during any extreme dry period.

I would make two more trips to visit Melaku and Sosi after this one, and each time Melaku and I would travel to Meki to continue the work started there for the planned medical clinic and conference center. On one of these trips, Dean again accompanied me. Sosi also made the journey, as well as a young new pastor and his wife, who were relocating from Addis to preach and live in Meki. In fact, Dean and I participated in the young man's ordination service at Melaku's church one day prior to making the trip to Meki. (I should say, Dean participated, and I observed.)

By now, Sarah and Wesenu had moved to a small apartment, more than a mile away. Obviously, I was not able to talk Dean out of dismissing them from the clinic property. He assured me that he had this would be good for them and for the clinic, in the long run. While I didn't see it the same way, I know that he has his reasons – and he is in charge. Plus, I know that he does not make these decisions lightly, but considers all the impact that this has on everyone involved, particularly Sarah and Wesenu, in this case. I also know that he prays long and hard before making such decisions. So, perhaps I should consider focusing on my own tasks and leave these staffing decisions to Dean in the future – only offering my opinion when requested. I have to say that they seemed to be doing just fine, from my observations – which I shared with Dean, when he made it a point to ask for my opinion in this regard. And they came right away to the clinic when they heard that we were coming, and Sarah, along with some other local ladies, prepared a nice meal for all of us to enjoy upon our arrival.

While at the clinic site for two days, I was able to do more checking of the work on the toilet facility prior to attending a "ribbon cutting ceremony" at the clinic. Dean had come for the main purpose of speaking at the ceremony, as well as meeting some of the town dignitaries. I remembered that it was a nice, but cramped service, as we were all crammed into that brand-new clinic examination room.

On my very last trip to Ethiopia, I would, once again, make the trip to Meki with Melaku. For once, we were under no pressure to get to Meki at any specific time. This allowed Melaku to stop at a very nice restaurant in a really cute little community that he had always wanted to show me. I could see why he was so anxious for me to finally have the time to do this. I had seen the outskirts of this community a number of times while driving by at 80 kph. But, until now, I never had the opportunity to explore it in any detail—or even drive through it, for that matter. Today, Melaku was treating me to an exciting, if brief, side-adventure. How cool!

The first thing that I noticed about the town was the cleanliness of it. There was not the usual avalanche of plastic bags strewn everywhere, blowing along with the wind or curled around street sign posts. The trees and shrubs, where visible, were neatly trimmed and a vivid green. And there were hills and curves and smooth paved roads. "Where am I?" I marveled out loud.

Melaku chuckled. "I knew you would like this place."

"Why is it so nice, Melak?" I asked. "I have not seen any other community quite like this one in your country. It is lovely."

"They just take pride in their town," he responded. "They always have, it seems, since I have been coming here, anyway."

"Well, I'm so glad that you brought me here. This is delightful. This gives me some hope for Ethiopia. Maybe there are more places like this than you know. Have you traveled extensively within Ethiopia?" I jabbered on.

"Yes, I've done some traveling. And there are other nice places, for sure. But this town is one of the nicer communities in this part of the country, for sure. You know, we have traveled almost halfway to the Kenya border from here, that time we went to Awasa. We didn't see any better, did we?"

"No, we didn't. But Awasa appeared to be nice—what we saw of it from the outskirts. And that big lake nestled in the edge of the town was lovely, as I recall."

We drove a bit longer in silence. "So, why did we come here, Melak?" I asked. "Just to show me around the town?"

Melaku didn't answer, but smiled as he pulled off onto a long driveway leading up to a prominent building. "No, I'm taking you to lunch."

"Wow. This place looks like it has real potential," I said.

"I think that you will like it. It is nicer than any place I have taken you to in Ethiopia so far. And the food here is very good."

The restaurant was vast and welcoming. We were the only patrons in the place, so it seemed all that much bigger. Melaku was surprised to see it so empty. But it was, we finally realized, midafternoon already—approaching 2:30.

We had a delightful meal and received excellent service. I was enchanted, and asked him why he brought me to such a nice place to eat. He said that it was because we always arrive so late, between meals, and then he feels bad that we often work at the site until nearly dark. By then it is quite late, and with Sarah and Wesenu not living onsite anymore, we often overlook lunch.

After our magnificent lunch, we settled back into the car. As we left the entrance road and headed back onto the main street that led to the highway, the strangest thing happened. Just as Melaku was entering the main street, where many people were walking about, a totally naked man with long scraggly hair came walking towards our car. I mean, right towards it. He was carrying a large rock and yelling as he continued toward us. Melaku saw him first and hollered, "Look out!" just as he reached my side and hurled the rock at us.

I had no time to duck before it crashed off of the small panel between the front and rear windows. It made a huge smashing noise. Melaku pulled over immediately. People were shouting and running toward the man, while some came over to our car. I was startled, unable to move from shock. Melaku got out and came over to open my door and inspect the damage. I was just staring at the man, who was now surrounded by a large crowd.

"What was that all about?" I sputtered.

"Oh, that guy is a bit crazy," said Melaku.

"But what was he saying? Was he after me, or was that just random?"

"Well, he probably was aiming for you," Melaku admitted. "When I first noticed him, that was when I shouted to warn you. He was running towards the car. He threw the rock as he was running."

"By the grace of God, he missed the window. I can only imagine how much damage that would have done."

"Oh yes, Bob, that could have been so bad. I cannot even imagine. There would have been shattered pieces of glass flying all over the cab and all over you, my friend. Truly God was looking out for you."

"Yes, indeed," I replied. "He always does, it seems. I have been in some sticky situations since I started making these voyages to Africa. Some, I put myself into, I know, by my own naivety. But others, like this, are more of being in the wrong place at the wrong time."

"Yes, but I know that you have had some other scary situations. Like the time not long ago when you became so sick here in Ethiopia and needed to go home to see your doctor. Also, I remember waiting for you at the airport, when you were to arrive from Baghdad. But you could not get out." He shook his head. "Really, Bob, you should write a book about these events. And how God has always delivered you."

"I honestly hope to, one day. For sure, God is ALWAYS watching me, just as He is everyone, I believe. When He sees me in trouble, regardless of how I got there, He always steps in. I see His hand in so many of my deliverances from danger, or potential harm, or even just difficult situations. My oldest daughter and her husband are always telling me I have good fortune. But I don't think it's fortune at all. I truly believe that it is the hand of God, reaching out and rescuing me, over and over—delivering me, as you say. Yes, perhaps this would make for some interesting reading someday. But for now, we have a clinic to build, yes?"

There were no more incidences on this, what would turn out to be my last trip to Ethiopia. And to Meki, as well, since we always traveled here on every trip as this was where the focus of my assistance was needed. They had made great progress in the development here. The clinic building was taking shape and was functioning as an actual medical clinic, complete with running water—from a faucet in a sink! The shower and flushing toilet facility was complete and fully operational, as well.

There was even a doctor, from a nearby community, who was seeing patients there, several days a week. The hope was to bring him onboard full time, and perhaps, to find a qualified nurse as well. But when I asked how all this was developing, including the procurement of more medical equipment, Melaku said that it was quite slow and taking a good bit of his time. They were under intense scrutiny, also, from the government, which was demanding a lot before they could even have their approval to officially open the clinic.

"Wow, Melak, I had no idea," I said. "You would think that they would be tripping over themselves, looking for ways to assist you, since your only focus is to care for the sick and the needy in that community and region."

"Ha! Tripping over themselves?" he responded, laughing. "That is a funny expression."

"Oh yeah. Sorry. I need to realize that many of our everyday slang expressions are unique to us in America, and the rest of the English-speaking world doesn't speak that way. But still, I can't believe that they would be making it difficult for you. I'm sorry, but that's just wrong."

"Yes, Bob, it really is," Melaku responded, becoming serious once again. "I would expect the same, that they would assist us. But sadly, that is not the case. They always seem focused on finding ways to take more money from us, instead of helping us."

"Well," I said, "Ethiopia is certainly not alone in that. Every developing country I have worked with, or heard about from others, does the same. I've experienced it in Mexico, and pretty much all over Central and South America. And I highly suspect it happens in every country in Africa. But still, it is disheartening, especially when you're trying to bring humanitarian aid that the government has failed in their obligation to provide."

"Yes, Bob. I truly love my country. But I do wonder sometimes why they must act this way. They really should be eager to help us, as you say. Perhaps I will ask them that the next time I speak with them. Maybe then I can better understand, even if I don't accept it."

"Well, be careful, please," I said, rather firmly. "I don't want my rebellious attitude to rub off on you and get you into any trouble. Tread lightly, my friend," I added, smiling broadly.

"Ha ha!" he laughed, quite heartily. "Now I am starting to understand your hidden language better. I promise you that I will, as you say, "tread lightly." Thank you for this advice, my friend. And now, I should get you back to Addis so that you can make it on time for your return flight home."

> *"Twenty-four reasons to admit that I'm wrong. With all my excuses, still twenty-four strong..... But I want to be one today, centered and true. I'm singing Spirit take me up in arms with You. You're raising the dead in me."*
>
> "*24*" by Switchfoot, from "The Beautiful Letdown" 2008 Columbia Records ©

Maybe it's Really Not About the Well

"And you ask me what I want this year. And I try to make this kind and clear. Just a chance that maybe we'll find better days. Cause I don't need boxes wrapped in strings, and designer love and empty things. Just a chance that maybe we'll find better days."

"Better Days" by The Goo Goo Dolls, from "Let Love In", 2006 Warner Brothers ©

"You wanna drill a well—*where,* Dean?" I'm fairly sure my face was scrunched up and my head was cocked slightly. Seems silly now, since Dean is blind and can't see my reaction anyway. One of those curious idiosyncrasies that we humanoids can't help, I guess.

"In Morogoro, Tanzania," came the response.

"But—why there?"

"I'm going to present a teaching conference at the request of a missionary couple who live there," Dean replied. Turns out that Dean "met" this couple online, after he and I had met recently with their boss in Nairobi, the African Inland Missions (AIM) director for East Africa, Marv Smith. He had a young missionary couple working with AIM at one of the Africa Inland Churches (AIC Tanzania), whose soul was to reach the unchurched while serving charitably in their community. This couple was Tony and Cathrrine (Cath) Swanson, from England.

When Dean started planning for the conference, he learned that the Swansons had an ambitious plan to build a Christian conference center near their home in Morogoro—a relatively small hamlet, about 2-1/2 hours inland from the coast by car. Dean told them that CrossWay had installed wells in an even tinier (and way more remote) village in South Sudan, Adoor, as well as our more recent efforts at a proposed medical clinic in Ethiopia, and also at a Christian school near Mombasa, Kenya.

When Tony asked about the possibility of doing the same for them, Dean (he of the enormous heart who never wants to disappoint) said, "Sure, we can do that." Of course, as the engineer, it fell to me to figure out how to accomplish this, and at what cost!

Was I okay with this? Absolutely! I was eager to drill more wells, particularly where we already knew something of the situation there and the ultimate benefit of the water to the community. If Tanzania was the latest and neediest request, then Tanzania is where we drill!

I found myself getting more excited as I worked, long distance, to locate potential drilling contractors in this area. Tony was a big help in that respect. He did some digging and found several potential well drilling companies located in Dar es Salaam, the large port city, which also contained a regional airport.

After several weeks of emailing back and forth between several companies, I began negotiating in earnest with one of them. Finally, we arrived at a price that we could afford, and I began working with them to get a contract and a schedule. Once we established the time, Dean and Tony made the final plans and set dates for the Pastors' Conference. It would be at their local AIM church, using the Sunday School classrooms.

Knowing the contractor's schedule and Dean's schedule, I was finally able to begin arranging for my own travel. I managed to get on the same flights as Dean to Tanzania. But I would be on my own on the return, since I would be traveling back to Ethiopia while Dean was coming directly home from Tanzania. Then, almost at the last minute, Dean asked me to stop off in Liberia on the way over. Dean had recently visited there at the request of a pastor named Isaac Zoedah. It seemed that Liberia, like most African countries, was in desperate need of water wells and sanitation. The plan was for me to go there on a preliminary visit to get an idea of the actual need and our ability to respond.

The major problem with trying to arrange this trip so late was the need to get a travel visa to enter the country through their embassy in Washington, DC. Unlike Kenya, you could not just purchase one on arriving at the airport in country. Not having done this before, I ran into all sorts of difficulties. I was dealing with a private company in Washington who helped obtain visas at various embassies for a fee.

The part that I don't like is having to mail your passport to people that you've never met before.

I got over it, however, and mailed off my passport. But after waiting nearly a week, they informed me that I didn't have enough empty visa pages remaining in my passport, and I would have to pay to have more added. Although I knew this was not true, I didn't argue with them because they still had my passport. And I didn't trust them at all. With this hiccup behind me, I assumed that I would have my Liberian visa in hand any day now. But as the time approached for my departure, I found myself still visa-free. I called them to find out what was happening with my visa. Nothing, they informed me. They were still waiting on me to pay the final visa fee.

Apparently, they had not even approached the embassy for my visa. I told him that it was now too late. I would have to once again change my travel plans, and I needed my passport back immediately. I directed them to send it overnight and just forget about the visa. The next thing I know, their company president got me on the line. He apologized for everything, and said that they could get the visa that very day and overnight it for no extra fee. I finally agreed, but insisted that they overnight it back to me for early morning delivery, as my plane would leave later that evening. I got another call from them several hours later. It seemed that the Liberian embassy would *not* provide the visa the same day unless it was a dire emergency. The earliest they could get it would be 24 hours later.

Exasperated, I ordered them to return the passport as soon as possible. I would now have to make last minute flight arrangements to fly to Tanzania and skip Liberia. Fortunately, I found the flights, but I would not be able to travel with Dean as I had hoped. In fact, he was already on his way to Tanzania.

By now I was accustomed to traveling with Dean. I actually enjoyed it. I know that he saw himself as a burden, but I rather enjoyed being his eyes. I would always tell him what I was seeing in the airplane or the airport, or the view outside the window. He really seemed to like this as well. And I was improving in my descriptive skills. Best of all, we always got special attention and treatment from the flight attendants. I made sure Dean understood that this was special attention. "In fact," I would say, elbowing him teasingly, "I'm personally enjoying this because I get to chat with any number of lovely flight attendants who would otherwise not give me the time of day." This always made him laugh. "See, Dean, there are some benefits to hauling around a blind guy!"

"Alright, Bob," he chuckled, "that makes me feel better, that you can derive some benefit from traveling with me."

"Oh, c'mon, Dean, you know it's more than just the special attention. I enjoy your company and conversing with you—and learning from you. Honestly, it's a pleasure, and never a burden."

But this was not to be one of those "travel together times," thanks to this grand failure to secure a Liberian passport. This made me feel even worse for Isaac. During the last couple of weeks, I had gotten to know him through our constant emailing. He came across as a very gracious and kind man, and I had been looking forward to meeting him and spending some time getting to know his city of Monrovia, and Liberia in general.[8]

Right before I was set to leave Houston to fly to Tanzania, something happened that could have been tragic, had God not intervened. I was staying with my oldest daughter, Breanne, who would drive me to the airport to catch my first flight to London. Earlier that day, my youngest daughter, Jacqueline, had left us to drive back to San Antonio. She and I had driven over on Friday night to spend the weekend with Breanne, her husband, Andrew, and young daughter, Kennedy. This was Jacqueline's first long solo drive, as she had only recently received her driver's license.

On the drive over, I took the same route that she would take to return, showing her clearly where all the turns were and what landmarks to look for as guidance. Before she left, I typed a text message into her phone that said, "I am now on Interstate 10, heading West." This, I explained, could easily be sent by pressing only one button on her phone, so as not to distract her. Around the expected time, my phone beeped with the text, letting me know that she had made all the right turns and was now on I-10. Once she arrived in San Antonio, I knew that she could get

[8] I'm feeling a strange sense of deja vu as I write this. I am, at this moment, in the midst of again pursuing a Liberian visa for an upcoming trip, with a stopover in Monrovia to meet with Isaac. After 7 years of emailing from time to time, we have been able to keep up with one another, even through the horrors of the deadly Ebola plague that crippled his country in recent years and still haunts them today. He has asked me once again to come over to assess their acute water shortages and see if there is some way that we can assist them. I now have a flight arranged to stop over on my return from Nairobi, and I'm looking forward to it. But I will feel much better once I have the visa in hand!

from I-10 to her house. I felt good now about her having to drive back alone and started packing and loading my travel bags into Breanne's car.

Just as we were getting ready to leave, my phone rang—Jacqueline's number! "What's up, baby?" I answered, quickly trying to determine if it was possible for her to have arrived home. It wasn't. Worse, she was crying hysterically and I couldn't understand her. Something about the car and the rain and a wreck! "Are you okay?" I shouted into the phone. "Are you hurt?"

"No," was all she could say coherently. She was gulping for air and sobbing loudly in between.

"Is there anyone there with you?" I asked her.

"Yes, this man—"she sobbed.

"Please, honey, can you put him on?" I begged her.

A man came on and told me that she had been passing his trailer and truck in a hard rainstorm on I-10. "All at once, her car started skidding," he told me. "Then it turned a complete 360° right in front of me. I was able to slow down without skidding, to avoid her. Then her car veered sharply in front of me and went off the road, clipping a highway sign before shooting across a field and into some small woods. That's where I lost her. By the time I could safely slow down, I was well past her. But I wanted to see if she was alright, so I turned around and came back."

I was stunned. I immediately thanked God so very much for saving my daughter from any serious injury. I knew in an instant that, while this could have been absolutely horrible—fatal even—He had spared her for a purpose. I just knew that He had a bigger plan for her. She was destined to do great things for the Kingdom.

After thanking the gentleman profusely, I asked him if he knew if the police had been called. "Yes, sir," he said. "They're already here—a state trooper."

"Can you please ask him if he will talk to me?" I asked.

"Sure," came the answer. "Hold on."

The policeman was also very understanding. "Thank you, Lord," I said again, quietly. He told me that Jacqueline was fine—shaken up, but not hurt, not even a scratch. The car, however, was off in the edge of the woods. "Sir," he told me, "after hitting that sign post and sailing across the field, it went into a more wooded area. It finally came to a stop without hitting anything, and only six feet before it could have fallen into a deep creek bed sideways and flipped over. I've called a local wrecker from Seguin, is that okay?"

"Oh, absolutely," I responded. "Thank you for doing that. I will call my insurance company and give them this information. Please, would you mind putting my daughter back on?"

"Sure," he said. "Here she is."

"Hi sweetie. I'm so thankful that you're not hurt," I said.

"But Daddy, the car?"

"Baby, don't worry, I can fix the car. I don't care about the car. I'm so sorry that this happened to you. This is more my fault than yours. I never practiced driving on wet roads with you, not once," I said. "That's on me. I should have been a better teacher. This is not your fault, do you hear me?"

"Okay, Daddy. Thank you," she choked out.

"Is there anyone that you can call? Have you tried to call Mommy?"

"Yes, but she's in Austin or Georgetown and won't be back until tomorrow," she responded.

"What about Maddie, or Courtney? Can you try one of them? Maybe their Dad can come pick you up until Mommy or I can come get you. I'm at least 2-1/2 hours away. It would only take either one of them less than an hour."

"Daddy, I don't want you to have to miss your trip to Africa," she said. "I would feel horrible."

"Well, thank you, baby. Yes, this one was really hard to plan. But I will if I have to. Please make those calls and then call me back as soon as you talk to one of them, okay?

"Yes, Daddy, I will." She hung up.

All this time, Breanne was sitting by, listening to my end of the conversation and trying to fill in the rest. "Daddy, do we need to go get her?" she asked. "Because I can take you to her if you need me to."

"No, I don't think so, Bree. But thanks," I said. "Linda's only an hour and a half away. But I'm hoping Maddie or Courtney's dad can come get her. I'm waiting to hear back from her."

My phone rang again. Jacqueline was calmer now, and said that Maddie and her dad were on their way to get her and would take her to their house for the night. Maddie could also take her to school tomorrow.

I felt a huge relief. I asked her: was it okay that I go ahead to Africa?

"Yes, of course it is, Daddy. I'm sorry to trouble you. I'll be fine. But what about the car?"

"I'll call the insurance company on the way to the airport. They may need to talk to you, just as a point of contact. You have the policy information. It's in the glove compartment. They will arrange with the towing company where to take it. Everything will be fine with the car, so don't worry about that. I'm just so relieved that you are all right. I'm going to have Bree take me to the airport now. I'll call you in a little while to see if Maddie and her dad have arrived, okay?"

"Okay Daddy. Thank you. I love you—and please be safe, okay?"

That's the way I left the U.S. to go to Tanzania. It was pretty scary, but I knew Jacqueline was in good hands. I got Maddie's dad, Dick, on the phone and thanked him for coming to her rescue. Being a wonderful Christian dad, he said that he was glad to help, especially since it was Jacqueline, whom he and his family adored. He assured me that all would be fine and that Jacqueline could ride to school the next morning with Maddie.

Once again, I thanked God for saving Jacqueline. I saw his hand all over this horrible ordeal, and I was thanking him as much for me as I was for Jacqueline. I knew I would have forever blamed myself if something more tragic had occurred that day. Life happens, of course—rain on slick roads, inexperienced drivers, and the physics of hydroplaning sometimes conspire against us. But here was God, in the midst of it all, crafting good out of life's potential tragedies. Jacqueline was safe with Maddie and Dick, and I was still heading off to Africa. I knew clearly that in all of this, he had more for each of us to do.

Because of the visa debacle, Dean arrived in Tanzania a day ahead of me. I flew into the large port city of Dar es Salaam, which means "Abode of Peace" in Arabic. Though if they had asked for my input, I would not have named it that. I saw very little that appeared "peaceful" and heard even worse stories of the rampant violence and crime from a number of Tanzanians and missionaries by the time I left the country only a week later. It was quite large, too—the largest city in East Africa by population (over 5 million).

The late arrival of my flight from Nairobi required that I spend the night in Dar (as Tanzanians call it). Tony arranged for me to be picked up by a local cab driver and brought immediately to an apartment complex where the ministry maintained a unit for its workers. I was instructed to lock my door and stay inside. Another driver would come for me in the morning. This was fine by me—it was very dark on this side of town, with very little street lighting and even fewer house lights. Indeed, I would do my part to "keep the peace".

I was tired from all the trans-Atlantic and trans-Euro-Africa flights, along with their lengthy layovers. But sleep was difficult due to the surrounding city noise and, more likely, from the uneasiness of staying in unknown territory. I have found that if I arrive at a destination during daylight hours, I have time to take in my surroundings, which gives me a measure of comfort as far as my personal safety. Whereas by arriving after midnight, on a pitch-black night, and being told to bolt my door and stay inside—it wasn't exactly a calming "good night." Nevertheless, after tossing and turning a while, I managed to get some sleep, and was dressed and waiting when my driver arrived the following morning.

I suspected the trip to Morogoro would not be quick. I had no idea what the roads were like, but a map I perused showed a distance of over 190 km, depending on where in Dar we were starting from. Google maps said 3-1/2 hours, but due to the slow, lumbering lorries overloaded beyond belief and huffing up the large hills along the way, the total trip took well over four hours.

However, I must say it was an interesting ride, with lush scenery, a number of quaint villages, and some of the largest and most fruit-laden mango trees I had ever seen. There were also some very picturesque mountains in the distance as we left the coast and headed inland. We passed a large intersection about halfway on our journey, and the driver told me that road led to the famous peak of Mt. Kilimanjaro, on the border between Kenya and Tanzania. With all this beautiful scenery, I didn't really feel the four hours of driving—other than the soreness in my back from sitting so long.

The driver dropped me at the guesthouse where Dean was staying, aptly called Peace Lodge. While we were invited to stay with Tony and Cath, it would be a bit crowded with their other permanent house guests. The plan was for the two of us to stay there until Dean left in four days, and I would move into a small guestroom with a single bed for the remainder of my stay.

Dean was alone in the guest house when I arrived. He was waiting for Cath to come by and pick him up and take him to their church, where they would make final arrangements for the Pastors' Conference, which was to begin the next day and run for three days. While they were doing that, Tony took me to their property, a few miles beyond the town of Morogoro. The property was still undeveloped, but soon they hoped to start construction of their planned conference center. They had named the place *Sanga Sanga*, after the nearby community of the same name. Strangely, the name means "mud hole." I never thought to ask why, since the community is actually very picturesque.

In fact, I was actually taken aback by the beauty of the surroundings. The property itself was not all that pretty, but the view—wow! Especially as we drove farther back and higher up, we were treated to a panoramic view of the cloud-shrouded Uluguru Mountains across the valley. They were so high and lush and green that they were begging to be made into a beautiful postcard, I told Tony, as he watched me snap photo after photo, smiling broadly all the while. Then he took me back down the hill to the place that they wanted the well to be drilled. I could see that it had been carefully chosen, on a portion of the property that was most level. "This," I said, "will make it possible to effectively stage the drill rig that I am anticipating will soon be arriving."

"Oh, yes, the drill rig," said Tony, smiling wryly. "It seems that B.R.A. Company, the driller, are delayed yet another day. They were supposed to be here yesterday, but they are behind on another well that they are drilling on the other side of Morogoro. They have been having some problems with that well. But they hope to finish tomorrow and then move the rig here, according to Godfrey, the supervisor."

"Well, I'm sad to hear that," I responded. "But I'm not surprised. I have found in my experience, both here and in the States, that it always takes longer than I anticipate—even when everything seems to go right. Tell me, is it possible that we could drive there tomorrow, perhaps, to have a look at their operation and talk to Godfrey?"

"That would be fine. We can drive there tomorrow morning after we get Dean set up at the conference. I promised to spend time with him tomorrow, to help kick-off the conference. But I will call Godfrey to let him know when we plan to be there."

By the time we drove back to the guesthouse, Dean was already there. He was resting before dinner. Tony left briefly, then picked us up an hour later and drove us less than a kilometer up the hill to their lovely home. The grounds were full of mature mango, coconut palm, and banana trees, as well as many shade trees. There was also a lush vegetable garden and many bougainvillea trees in an array of colors, as well as other brightly-hued flowers. The house seemed spacious for two people, but I soon learned that they had taken in several small children and teenage girls whose bedrooms were either in the house or in a small building in the yard.

We had a wonderful meal, followed by lively conversation getting to know each other. This lasted late into the night. Finally, Dean confessed what we all were feeling—that we were tired and in need of some good sleep. Dean especially needed his beauty rest, as he'd be leading two sessions the next day, one in the morning and one in the afternoon.

After the short trip back down to our guesthouse, Dean and I said good night to Tony and quickly readied ourselves for bed. There would be no worrying about security here. We felt quite safe. We dropped off to sleep quickly in the cool mountain air, and before we knew it, the sun was peeking over the mountain, welcoming us to a bright and glorious new day. What a difference a day makes!

Cath and Tony picked us up for the day's events. Tony was to help Dean and Cath begin the Pastors' Conference. Once he felt that all was in order and Dean was underway with the morning session, he and I would drive out to see Godfrey at his current project, which, fingers crossed, they would be completing today. The ride down the hill was really pretty; the view down into the valley, with its bustling community, and across to the beautiful cloud-blessed mountains in the distance nearly took my breath away. "This is the prettiest drive to work I believe I have ever taken," I said in wonder.

"It is lovely, isn't it?" said Cath, turning in her seat. I tried my best to describe it to Dean, but my words were really just too small to fulfill that mission. It was not just the gorgeous landscape, but also the simple houses with their fresh, bright paint, and all the people, walking to and fro, dressed in bright colors and carrying all kinds of produce and flowers. Some were carrying chickens, or pushing carts full of chickens and roosters.

"Where is everyone going?" I asked.

"Oh, today is Market Day," answered Cath. "Every Tuesday, we have a local market. Everyone brings their goods to sell. Produce, handcrafts, livestock, flowers, you name it, they try to sell it."

"Everyone seems so happy and excited. Are they always that way, or only on Market Day?" I asked.

"Interesting that you notice that, Bob," responded Cath. "While I do believe that Market Day tends to bring extra hope and excitement, the people of Morogoro and the remote areas of Tanzania are generally a happy people. How does that compare to other places that you've visited, I'm curious to know?"

"Actually, it's quite similar elsewhere in Africa. I found Ethiopia—not the capital city, Addis Ababa, but the towns and countryside—to be full of vibrant, happy people, whether they were coaxing along a herd of goats or cattle or pushing a heavy cart filled with farm goods or lumber, or even rocks. For that reason, I really took to being there. I get that same good feeling here, too, I can tell you."

"That's interesting," said Tony. "And you don't get that same feeling about the people of Kenya? Surely you have spent more time around them, right?"

"Don't get me wrong; I love the people of Kenya—the "real" people, not the posers and government workers. But I tend to categorize groups of people by my observations of their apparent work ethic and their attitudes. No great scientific process, I assure you. It's just what I tend to notice. I tell you, I saw the same thing when I vacationed in Peru almost ten years ago. I admit that I didn't spend much face time with the Peruvian folk, but I still came away with the impression of them as wholesome, hard-working, and generally happy."

"I think that's fair, Bob," Cath responded. "Your process may be spot on, actually. And plenty scientific enough for me, anyway."

"Thanks, Cath," I laughed. "I accept your validation of my process."

After helping to get Dean and Cath situated at the classroom where the training would take place, Tony and I drove off to meet the drilling contractor at his current site, south of Morogoro. We found the place to be quite muddy—at least the access road was. The drilling was actually complete, and the drill rig was already moved away from the borehole. They now needed to bring the air compressor back on site to develop the well. The only hold up was that the truck pulling the compressor was not powerful enough to maneuver through the muddy haul road. There it sat, like a beached hippo in the mud—this big yellow beast of a compressor.

Godfrey was offsite, looking for a bigger truck or tractor. If they could only get the compressor over to the well, they should be done today and ready to move everything to our site tomorrow morning. It appeared like they had a good plan—IF they could secure a dozer. It's not like they could drive over to United Rental, as in the U.S., and just rent a dozer for a few hours.

Tony called Godfrey, who promised that he would mobilize to our site by tomorrow morning. He would move the compressor to this well today and complete the work here. He might even move the drill rig over today. When Tony pressed him further, he said that it would be there by noon. Okay, I thought. We have a plan!

Well, you've read enough of my well-drilling stories to know... so much for plans, huh?! After leaving that drill site, Tony and I went back to Morogoro town, where he ran some errands. Then we drove back to *Sanga Sanga* and waited. And waited. And waited some more. Finally, around mid-afternoon, the really old truck-mounted drill rig came rumbling down the highway and turned onto the property. Tony showed the driver the stake marking the proposed borehole location. The fellow skillfully maneuvered the rig over the location. Then he and his two assistants began setting the outriggers to stabilize the drill.

As they were working, I noticed that the drill pipes that they were unloading were not what I expected. In fact, they were not drill pipes at all, but sections of auger bits. I told Tony that this was unusual. I am not that experienced in drilling, but the only auger bits I am familiar with are large diameter bits used for drilling concrete caissons. But these are generally used for deep anchors or sub-foundations for buildings and bridges, not for water wells. That's not to say that they aren't ever used for this purpose. They may very well be, in certain situations. But why here?

Tony placed a call to Godfrey, who gave him the bad news. The reason that the air compressor was not there was because it was broken down. As best that Tony could cobble their story together, the compressor, which sits quite low to the road, developed a crack in the oil pan when they were dragging it out of the mud (and rocks, apparently), and some of the oil drained out. After dragging it to the drill site, they finished draining the oil, then removed the pan and had it welded to repair the tear.

After reinstalling it and refilling with oil, they apparently left the drain valve partly open. No one noticed all the oil draining back out. When they cranked it up and ran it for a short time, it began smoking, then "coughing," then finally just died. The engine had seized up from overheating.

Tony asked if I could stay here and observe the drillers while he drove into town to meet Godfrey. "Sure," I told him. "This is a new way of drilling boreholes. At least, not one that I have ever seen before. I'm interested to see how this works."

"You don't think it will work?"

"I'm not saying that. It's just new to me, is all. I have seen lots of auger drilling. But not for deep boreholes. Only for drilled foundation casings. I'm not saying that this won't work; but I will honestly be surprised if it does."

"Well, with that vote of confidence, I'm off to have a talk with Godfrey about his compressor," responded Tony, somewhat tongue-in-cheek.

I watched intently as the drill team finished securing the drill rig and installed the first section of auger pipe. The rig appeared to be quite old, but the big diesel engine sounded strong as they started it up and began twisting the auger into the earth there at the proposed *Sanga Sanga* borehole location. Down, down it went, slow and steady. I expected the upper portion to be quite easy to drill, comprised of silty sands and some clay, but no rocks. The drilling did go smoothly for several lengths of 10-foot-long sections of auger pipe.

But then the downward thrust seemed to slow. All of a sudden, the operator started removing the auger, first one section, then another. I assumed that he was going to use another bit—a tri-cone, perhaps, as I noted that at the point he stopped drilling, the drill pipe started jumping around and clanging loudly. I knew this sound—some sort of rock. At this depth, maybe only 25-28 feet, he had encountered rock and determined that the auger bit was not what he should be using.

As they were removing pipes, Tony drove up. He walked over to see what was happening, and I told him what I had observed. I explained about encountering rock. "There, they stopped and removed the auger pipes," I told him. Tony walked over to the operator to find out more.

When he returned, I asked if he was intending to use a different bit and continue on down the hole. "No, Bob," he responded, "actually, Kambona—that's his name, by the way—told me that they have encountered extremely hard granite rock and this bit cannot penetrate. He said that they must wait for the air compressor and use the down-the-hole hammer to defeat the hard rock."

"Really?" I asked, surprised. "Let me see what Mr. Kambona is talking about." I walked over to the pile of cuttings, picking up some of the last pieces to emerge, which would have been from the lowest depth. Indeed, there were very small pieces of sharp-sided white stones that looked like quartz to me. Not being adroit, quite honestly, of geological visual recognition, I tended to put soil types and rock extracted during the drilling process into one of only several small categories.

"I'm not sure that is quite right, Tony," I said, objecting to the thought of quitting so soon. "These pieces of rock are not, in my admittedly limited experience, impenetrable without the use of a hammer. I'm not really sure why he is stopping. We've been waiting patiently for days for them to get here, and now they quit after only 30 minutes of drilling. Please ask him to show you any other bits that he has so that I can see if one of them might work better. They may have to revert to mud drilling, which they may not want to do, as the setup time is lengthy—and hard work, as well."

Tony went off to speak to Kambona once again, who looked over at me with the utmost indignation. Tony showed him the bits of white stone that I had given him, along with my explanation. They had a rather lively discussion, complete with a lot of arm waving and head shaking by the gentleman. Apparently, he was not buying our argument.

Tony returned with a resigned look on his face. "You were right, Bob," he said. "They want to wait for the air compressor so that they can use the hammer. He says it's the only way. I told him what you said about using a stronger bit and mud drilling, which should easily penetrate the encountered rock. But he gave me all sorts of excuses for not mud drilling. I sensed though, like you said, that it is too hard work for them."

"Yes," I said, "I'm guessing that with a big compressor for air drilling, either with a bit or a hammer, their physical work is much easier and tends to go faster. But it just doesn't seem right, since they don't actually have an air compressor now, do they? But they do have a drill—and they do have a mud pump—I see a rather large one on the truck."

"That may be true, but we probably need to discuss it with Godfrey, anyway. This chap does not seem to be in the mood to do much of anything, except wait," Tony said. "Anyway, I need to get back to the church to check on Dean and Cath. They should be finishing up today's session shortly."

Before we could get away, however, an older gentleman rode up on an old bicycle. He had something long and narrow in a sack slung over his shoulder. Tony spotted him and said, "Oh yes, I almost forgot—our guard has arrived."

The man propped his bike by a nearby tree and pulled the sack off of his shoulder. We walked over to him, and after shaking hands with Tony, he proudly pulled out what looked to be some sort of antique long rifle. "Wow!" I said. "Does that thing actually shoot?"

They both immediately looked at me—Tony with a look of, "I can't believe that you just said that," while the man just looked confused, apparently not understanding a word of English. "Never mind," I said. "I really don't need to know that."

The man climbed up onto the drill rig and stood like an armed bank guard, feet set apart, with the rifle cradled in both arms. I couldn't help myself. I had to get a photo. I pulled out my camera and looked at Tony for approval. He nodded his head slightly. Good enough for me! The funny thing was, as I strode over to the drill rig and aimed my camera at the man, he shifted his feet a bit and stood erect, striking a pose, looking away and focusing on something well beyond me— a perceived enemy, perhaps.

As I climbed back into the car with Tony, I asked, "So you really think that this guy can protect the drill rig? And against whom?"

"Well, probably not against someone who is bent on actually stealing it," he replied. "But we don't really have that kind in this region. They're mostly law-abiding. The chap with the gun is really there to keep the honest man honest. Or to deter any idea of stealing something or vandalizing the equipment."

"So, to answer your previous question," Tony continued, "I'm not really sure if that gun will actually shoot. Nor am I even sure that he has any bullets. In fact, I doubt that he has. But I didn't want to ask him because like you have surmised, it really doesn't matter. And we're all probably better off if he does not."

"Fair enough," I answered, as we drove back to town.

Arriving at the church, we walked to the classroom. Dean and Cath were sitting just outside, talking to some of the "students"—young pastors who had journeyed here from a number of locations from around the country, both local and far-off.

"Hello there," said Dean, immediately recognizing our voices. "How's the drilling going?"

Tony and I looked at one another, not knowing who should answer. Cath looked on anxiously, as well.

"Well, the first 30 feet went quite smoothly, Dean," I answered. I stopped there, not sure how to break the bad news.

"And then?" asked Cath.

"Then they hit some hard rock," Tony stepped in. "And they stopped. They said that they need the hammer and the compressor, as they claim the rock is too hard to rotary drill through. Bob doesn't agree, and now, neither do I. So we are on our way to find Godfrey with the compressor."

"And where is the compressor?" asked Dean.

"It's here in town now," Tony answered, "but the engine seized when all the oil drained out of it on their last project, just south of town. They have taken it to a local mechanic shop, where they are repairing the engine, we're told."

"This doesn't sound good for getting this done in the few days you have left, now, does it, Bob?" Dean asked.

"No, it really doesn't, Dean," I answered. "I may look to extend my time here by a few days, once we determine the condition of the compressor and when they might begin again. We are going to talk to them about rotary drilling with mud, as well. I think that they could easily penetrate this rock with a decent tri-cone bit, as big as that drill rig is."

"But the foreman-operator seems to believe that he can only accomplish this with the hammer and air compressor," Tony added. "That's why we need to talk to Godfrey. We're off to find him now. We will meet you back at the house, well in time for dinner, okay?"

"That's fine," said Cath. "We're off now, too. I need to stop at the market briefly. Then Dean and I will be heading home."

Tony drove us to another part of Morogoro town, not all that far from the church. I was surprised to see that he was driving into a neighborhood and not stopping at one of the shops in the town. He drove along a wall and then turned in at a gate entrance.

There before us, in someone's backyard, as best I could describe it, was the large air compressor. The access doors were wide open, and there was a rather large shirtless fellow selectively removing parts and laying them on a piece of plastic next to the engine. Already I could see that he had amassed a large quantity of these parts, both large and small. Indeed, most of the large cylinders were already laying there, dripping oily goo all over the plastic.

Tony parked nearby, in the grass, and we walked over to have a look. Tony glanced over at me. "You weren't expecting this, were you, Bob?" he asked, in response to my look of sheer disbelief.

"I'm not sure what I was expecting, Tony. But not this, no. I could not have begun to imagine this. I can see that this *fundi* knows what he is doing. But this compressor will not be fixed by tomorrow, even if they have all the replacement parts that they need—which I highly doubt."

"So, what are you thinking?"

"Well, I'm assuming Godfrey is not here. All we have is this fellow taking this engine apart piece by piece. I think we need to find Godfrey and ask if he knows where to get another compressor. Perhaps he could rent one back in Dar?

"Okay, I'll call him," he said. While he was doing this, I walked over to the back of the nearby building. It looked like someone's house, not a shop at all. There were several young children running around, as well as a number of chickens. And here was this *fundi*, in the middle of it all, dismantling a huge air compressor right there in somebody's backyard. Perhaps it was his house, I don't know. But it was all so surreal—to me, at least.

I walked over to get a closer look at the engine work. When the *fundi* saw me looking intently at one of the cylinder pistons, he came over and said that this was the one that had seized—broken. He picked it up and showed me some gouges in the piston rings. "Yes, I see them," I said. "But are there more?" Could more than one cylinder fail?

"Yes, that is possible," he responded, in quite good English, which I was also not expecting. "For that reason, I have to take them all apart and check them all very carefully."

I looked at a few of the pistons already removed and lying on the plastic. Looking back at the engine, I could see that he still had several more to remove. I thanked him and moved away, to allow him to get back to his work.

Tony returned from his telephone conversation with Godfrey. "Let's go, Bob," he said. "I'll tell you about my conversation on the way home. We shouldn't be late for dinner."

We climbed in the car and took off. Tony sighed, breaking the silence. "Godfrey said that they would have the compressor repaired by tomorrow."

"Do you believe him?"

"From what we saw, it doesn't look likely. I'm not skilled in engine repair, but that looked rather significant."

"I would agree," I said. "In fact, I would consider it a minor miracle if it happened by tomorrow. From what I saw, if they can secure all the necessary parts, and if they don't have to bore out any of the cylinders, they might have it running again in two days. But even that is assuming a lot."

"I see your point. So what do we do?"

"I think that the guy needs to be honest with us, for starters, Tony. We're not stupid. We're paying them to drill a well, not re-build their equipment. I'm sorry if that sounds harsh, but my time here is limited, and they don't seem to be doing anything that we ask. They could drill that well, I am sure. Even without the air compressor. With the right bit—a tri-cone bit, as I told that foreman—and with that drill, they could easily drill your borehole."

"We should probably meet with Godfrey, so that you can discuss this with him and ask those tough questions."

"Yes, I would welcome that," I said, "and the sooner the better. By the way, why wasn't he there with the compressor? I was hoping to talk to him then."

"Oh, I'm sorry, I thought I told you. He was still at the previous well site that we went to this morning. They are still busy completing that well project, now that the drilling is complete."

"So yes, then, Tony. It would be good to meet with him first thing tomorrow. Perhaps we can meet back at the 'compressor repair shop,'" I added, somewhat sarcastically.

"You liked that 'shop', did you, Bob?" he asked, grinning at first, and then laughing. This only caused me start laughing, as well.

"Now that was a repair shop, if I've ever seen one," I snickered. "With the kids and the chickens running everywhere, I can't imagine how that poor *fundi* keeps track of anything, let alone keep the dirt and dust out of all those tight-fitting engine parts he is disassembling. It's actually quite amazing, when I stop to think about it. But still surreal. How he can ever put all of those pieces back together, some with minutely small tolerances, is beyond my ability to grasp."

"Crazy, and yet incredible—all in one, you say?" he asked, still smiling.

"Absolutely! Crazy-amazing, if he can make it happen! But not by tomorrow, I assure you. That's simply not possible."

"What do we tell Godfrey?"

"I think that we have to tell him to try to find another air compressor. If they take until Saturday, let's say, before they can even try to restart it, and then it doesn't work, then I'll never get to see them actually drill the well, which is what I came here for. And what is so frustrating to me is knowing that they have, right now, what they need to drill," I said, shaking my head.

We finally met with Godfrey the next morning, and some concessions were made. He would try earnestly to find another compressor that he could rent. He would also have the *fundi* continue to repair their compressor. As to why they couldn't just mud drill, as I suggested, he told me that this rock was simply too hard and too thick. They had tried to penetrate it on more than one occasion, but had "always been defeated," he said. Maybe if he had a better bit, he offered, then they could mud drill.

Tony looked at me when he said that, and I just nodded. I couldn't know what the quality of their equipment was. Perhaps all their rock bits were dull or badly worn. And I really didn't know the specifics on their Italian drill rig. It just looked big. Certainly much bigger than any rig that I was looking for CrossWay to buy someday.

After the meeting, Tony and I drove to the church to see how Dean and Cath were doing at the conference. When we arrived, Dean was still in the middle of presenting one of the sessions. I sat with Cath to listen.

I always enjoyed listening to Dean, whether teaching or preaching. He is such an inspirational speaker. Of late, he had been working diligently to memorize large portions of the Bible. He could now recite entire chapters, word for word, and was working to commit the entire book of James to memory. Once he achieved that, he'd move on to other books.

I found that so incredible. I'd always had a hard time memorizing a few verses, or even a single verse of Scripture. Like his students, I sat there captivated by Dean's teaching, even though I knew many of his stories—or so I thought. But he always threw in one or two that I had never heard before, and I would be drawn in once again. What a gift, I thought—and to use it all for the glory of God and His people! I enjoyed watching others in the listening community get pulled in to his stories, as well. They just couldn't help it, I told myself, smiling shrewdly. I knew that he hid nuggets of pure truth within his stories, leaving the listener with something to pack away and carry along with them for future use.

I watched these students as they listened intently, eyes fixed on a man who could not even see them looking at him. When the session ended, many of them waited patiently to talk to Dean. Although you could tell that he was tired, he took the time to pour into all who wanted more information. He was always excited to talk to new believers or, as in this case, young pastors. He never made them feel that their questions were not important. Among many things I admired about him, I marveled at his patience.

Finally, when all were satisfied, Cath said that she would like to distribute some of the new soccer balls that we had brought with us from the States and asked if I'd like to join her. "Of course," I said. "I would love to!" Tony, who had just returned from his own errand running, said that he would take Dean home so that he could rest before dinner.

The two locations that Cath took me to were both well off the paved roads. We traveled down dirt roads that eventually led to barely discernible paths. At the last stop, we drove across a partially plowed field. It seemed to be an area that had already failed to yield any crops and was quite beaten down. The homes that we visited were nothing more than mud huts. In each of them lived a single mom and several children. To see their eyes light up when they saw the shiny new soccer balls was a humbling experience. I had seen this before on my trips to South Sudan. Immediately, they began playing with them right there in their grassless yards. There were no rules, no boundaries, and no age or gender limits. All kids were welcome. The only requirement that I could see was to participate—and to laugh heartily and smile continually.

At the second home, there was an older boy who was badly deformed and mentally incapacitated. When we arrived, we found them in their one room hut. The place was quite dark, as it was late in the day, and there was only minimal natural light trickling in. When my eyes finally adjusted, I saw the boy, who appeared to be of teenage size and development. He was lying in a heap, basically, on the sofa. His mom was next to him, rubbing his arm and wiping his mouth when he could not seem to control his saliva. Scattered around the room were children of all ages.

I saw no male adult. This happens all too often, I had learned, not just in Kenya, but all over Africa. Statistically, African males are highly capable of producing offspring, but not very good at raising them—or in even staying around to observe the process.

Along with the soccer balls, Cath brought a large batch of fresh vegetables gathered from her garden and from the local market. The mom was so appreciative of Cath's generosity, I could tell, although I couldn't understand what they were saying in Swahili. When the children saw the soccer ball, they were suddenly animated. Immediately, they all popped up and headed out of the hut, ball in hand. Cath and the mom picked up the crippled young man and carried him outside, where they laid him out on a grass-woven mat. The other children were already engaged in a lively game, again with no rules other than to laugh out loud and enjoy the moment.

When Cath and the mom gently placed the young man on the mat, they both stayed by him, speaking quietly and stroking his head and arms. He responded in the only way he could, flashing a big crooked smile and making some gurgling sounds that seemed positive affirmation for their acts. As we sat there, another lady joined us, bringing her own brood of children. Cath introduced us, telling me that this was the lady's sister who lived nearby in another mud hut, with her many children and, like Cath's friend, also without a husband—man of the house.

As daylight was just giving way to dusk, Cath and I finally drove away. She filled me in on the woman and her crippled son. She gave me the statistics, but I no longer recall them, regarding the number of single women raising multiple children here in Tanzania. Suffice it to say it is daunting. Couple that with the fact that most of these women are uneducated, and it leaves you with a helpless feeling of "this is as good as it gets." How sad, right?

Into this despair comes Cath, with her presents and fresh vegetables—a warm ray of sunshine in an otherwise difficult life. I told her that, but she quickly pooh-poohed the thought. "Bob, I do what I can," she responded. "I cannot change their lives. I can't offer them a job or any source of steady income, for that matter. That's for the father of those children to do, who, of course, has long since vanished. And here they are, stuck raising their children the best way they know how."

"And let me guess," I said. "The government is no help at all."

"None," she snapped. "It's not like America or Europe, where there would be some level of assistance from the government. This is Tanzania—this is *Africa*, for that matter. People in government are too busy taking care of themselves to ever consider helping the needy. Look at you—*you* are here to help provide water, as you have done so many other places. Why isn't the government doing that?"

"Don't get me started on that, Cath," I said.

But I started thinking again about the well drilling here in Morogoro—or lack thereof. Our problem was not with the government, but with the driller. I was concerned that they might never find a way to drill the borehole. Or if they did, they would want to charge us a lot more money, even though the work scope was not changing. It was due to their ineptitude and, perhaps, the poor quality of their equipment.

I almost laughed when I thought back to Mtepeni and that diesel motor smoking like a steam engine, with that skinny Kenyan boy mounted on top, trying his best to imitate a substantial applied load. No, I have to say that this equipment was far superior to that. Perhaps they really were having some misfortune. Surely things would get better, right? Yeah, but whether I could stay around long enough to actually see it unfold, I was beginning to wonder.

Then again, I had not been there for the completion of the Mtepeni well, either. And guess what? It was working just fine, providing water for the entire school, with plenty more for dozens of local households to collect and use on a daily basis. Thus, I was forced to conclude that my presence was no guarantee of success, nor my absence any portent of failure. I was forced to honestly evaluate just how important I was to this borehole drilling project. I had to conclude that it was less about what I brought to the project and more about the capabilities and integrity of the driller.

Then, I asked myself, how best could my services, however limited, be effectively applied in this unusual circumstance? In what way could I best support Tony, whether present or not, in successfully completing his well? I determined that I should focus my energy and attention on making sure that the driller fulfilled his commitment in a reasonable time frame. That, I concluded, would be far more beneficial than working feverishly to try to cajole him into completing the job on my schedule.

In addition, before departing I would plan to prepare Tony for the inevitable task of verifying each task to be undertaken by the driller to full completion and proof testing of the well. This, at least, would help ensure a viable product in the end.

Once I gave up my need to control this schedule (which I was quickly realizing was out of my hands anyway), I began to relax. Sure, I wanted to see that ailing compressor—last seen with its guts strewn all over somebody's back yard—spring back to life miraculously. Then the task of drilling the borehole, if not completed by my departure time, could at least be headed in that direction. But I'd be ready to roll with the setback as best I could.

Returning back to the guesthouse, I found Dean rested up and ready for dinner. He said that Cath told him that it should be ready about now. I called up to their house to confirm. "Dinner will be ready in about 30 minutes, Dean," I announced.

"How did you get your phone to work here, Bob?" he asked.

"Oh, yeah, that," I responded, somewhat sheepishly, "Tony took me to a phone shop where I bought a Tanzania SIM card and, wonder of all wonders, it worked in my Kenyan phone."

"That's pretty handy," he said. "I wish I had thought to do that. If I only knew. But realistically, it wouldn't make as much sense for me, trying to keep up with swapping SIM cards. It's all I can manage to make calls where I do have access. But I'm glad that worked for you, Bob."

"Oh yeah, makes sense. Having to find someone to swap your SIM cards for you, and just keeping up with multiple cards, tiny as they are, without being able to see the difference, does not seem at all practical in your case."

"Exactly. So, 30 minutes, eh? Is someone coming to pick us up?"

"Cath said to call them when we were ready and Tony would pick us up," I responded. "But I was thinking, it's a really nice evening, and it's not far at all. If you're up to it, we could walk up there, and I could tell you what the scenery looks like. Better than riding in Tony's car, even."

"That sounds fine with me. I might need a ride back, but maybe not. Let's do that."

"Great. Just let me wash my face and change my shirt, and I'll be ready to go."

The walk up the hill, not so steep after all, proved to be quite invigorating. The opportunity to see the beautiful scenery in the valley below and the mountains across it, unfolding slowly before us as the sun was setting, was almost breathtaking. I tried my best, but my intent to describe what I was seeing to Dean fell well short of worthy. Nonetheless, Dean responded very appreciatively at my attempt.

However, what seemed to engage him more was the interaction with various people that we encountered along the way. Some were also traveling on the road, while others were in their yards. But all were intently watching and wondering, no doubt, what two white men, one obviously blind, were doing, for God's sake, walking on their road! How peculiar that must have looked. After all, this is not downtown Dar es Salaam. It's an extremely small rural community, not known for anything. But it *is* highly picturesque, and could easily be a tourist trap if located in the West.

I would simply say, "hello" or "good evening." If they responded back with a "hello," we would endeavor to engage them. But, like our limited Swahili, most of them stopped at "hello," either because they were uncomfortable in speaking English or just didn't know where to take the conversation.

This was all was okay with Dean, as the intent to communicate was generally greeted with broad smiles from them, and even laughter from several children. All of this, coupled with the backdrop of an unforgettable sunset over the mountains in the distance, effectively etched a most beautiful and lasting picture in my mind's eye—even to this day.

Before we knew it, we were at the outer gate leading to the long driveway to the Swansons. The gardener/yard man came out to greet us and open the gate. Tony met us on the driveway. He ushered us into the house, and handed Dean off to Cath, and then asked me if I would like to see his office, since dinner was not yet ready. "Sure. Is it outside?" I said, as we walked to the back yard.

"It's right there," he said, pointing to a storage container about 20 feet away.

"Your office is in a storage container? That's so smart!"

Tony laughed and opened the door. From the outside, it looked like an ordinary container, without the usual walk-in door cut into one half of the huge, heavy steel end doors. But as he unlocked the double latches, the heavy door swung open to reveal a sliding glass door.

"I have never seen this arrangement before, Tony, although I have seen many containers used for shops and even homes throughout Africa," I marveled. "Your concept of the sliding glass door is brilliant. It allows you to see out, even with the door shut, in case you want to leave the office for a while, but not leave your compound."

He turned on the lights, and the interior immediately came to life. A long, built-in desk covered about half of one side. Tony reached across it and opened a short double-door, revealing a window with a screen. There was an identical one a few feet to the right. A third cut-out in the same outer wall contained a window unit air conditioner. You couldn't actually see out of the windows, because there were also outer doors cut into the container corrugations that would have to be opened first. Tony showed me how these worked by sliding open one of the windows and screens to access the window latch, which he then opened, revealing the world outside.

"Wow, Tony, this is really awesome," I said. "I'll bet that you really enjoy working out here—preparing your sermons and stuff, huh?"

Just then, Cath called to us that dinner was ready. "Okay, Cath. Be right in," Tony shouted back, as he began to reclose the windows and then the door. "You can come back here and work with me after you move into the house in a few days, okay? You can see that there is plenty of room."

"Sounds great."

As always, dinner was marvelous—as was the conversation. Dean and Cath talked exuberantly about the response that they were seeing from the Pastors' Conference. I affirmed their observations based on what I had seen just from one presentation by Dean. Tony offered to present one of the topics the following morning, as we were not too hopeful that the driller would be doing any drilling.

"If we do hear that, by some miracle, they complete the repair on the compressor," I said, "and I can get a ride out to *Sanga Sanga*, you can leave me there."

"Are you sure, Bob?" asked Dean. "You don't mind being out there alone?"

"Not at all. After all, that's what I came here for. I would love nothing more than to see some drilling accomplished—beyond the original 25 feet, that is."

"Well, okay," he responded. "Let's see what the driller says in the morning."

"Sounds like a plan," Tony said. "Dean, you look tired. I can drive you and Bob back down to the guest house now, if you want."

"That sounds like a big hassle just for that short distance," Dean said. "We can walk back, right Bob?"

"You bet, Dean," I responded quickly, delighted that he was eager to make the short stroll. "It's a great night for a walk, and I'm sure it will help us sleep better—not that we'll really need that much help, I'm sure."

Both Cath and Tony walked us out to the gate and made plans for meeting the next morning. After saying goodnight, Dean and I began our short walk back. Not only was it very comfortable, weather-wise, but the stars were unbelievable.

As we walked out from the shadow of several large trees next to the road, I breathed a sigh of awe. "Dean, I wish that I could aptly describe the beautiful night sky. Indeed, our loving God has painted a most beautiful and bright canvas. And in this gorgeous setting, the mountains behind Morogoro town are creating a dark silhouette against their brightness. It is as if the mountains are etched in gold."

"Well, you have done a great job of describing it, Bob. Yes, I can see it now, in my mind's eye," Dean responded, graciously.

"Oh, but Dean, you can't even imagine," I said, without even thinking—which I did more than I'd like to admit.

Dean, thankfully, smiled broadly. "Oh, but I can, Bob, I assure you," he said. "In fact, I may even be imagining a sight more dazzling than you are looking at! Have you ever thought of that?"

"Ha! No," I said, chuckling. "That is possible, I suppose. But I have a hard time believing it, since what I am gazing at is so magnificent."

"Okay, then, you have your picture, and I have mine. And since you cannot see mine and I cannot see yours, then we are both left to be content with what we can see. Fair enough?"

"Fair enough," I laughed. "I am truly content—thrilled, even."

"And so am I," Dean said. "So you see, you have done an apt job of describing what you see. And I believe that God agrees, as he has painted, as I have told you, a very beautiful picture for me to see in my mind's eye."

"Oops. Sorry," I said, as we walked together into a ditch and he nearly fell from my grip. "My bad, Dean."

"It's okay, I'm fine. But one of us has to watch where we're going. And that probably should be you!" he added, laughing heartily at his own wit.

"Right. That's part of my job, I know. But I told you that I sometimes have difficulty in multi-tasking."

"Oh, you do fine, Bob," he responded quickly. "And, by the way, I think you do a great job of painting for me what you are seeing and even describing people to me that you see, or whom we are about to talk to. I appreciate that greatly. It's one of the things that I enjoy most about traveling with you. You take good care of me, Bob, most of the time—when you're not running me into a ditch, that is!"

I shook my head, though he couldn't see. "Yes, so sorry about that, Dean. I will try to be more careful. Anyway, we're here."

"I figured that we were getting pretty close, and I recognize the gravel driveway that we're now walking on," he said.

"You can recognize the driveway from just walking on it?" I asked, dumbfounded.

"Well, not exactly, but I can gauge distance pretty well, and I'm sure that many of the homes here may have the same type of driveway. So, no, I'm not that good," he responded. "But, I'll tell you what, would you like me to describe our guesthouse?"

He then launched into his description, which was so accurate that I stopped to compare what he was seeing with what I was hearing him describe. All the while he walked on, right up to the door, leaving me slack-jawed in the driveway.

"Holy cow, Dean! Are you sure you're blind? Have you been holding out on us?" I teased him, as we entered the guest house.

The next morning, Tony and I visited the *fundi* once again. There were still many pieces of engine parts strewn around the compressor. At first, I thought that little or no progress had been made since we were last here, more than a day ago. But on closer inspection, I could see that all of the cylinders were back in the engine. So that was good. What remained to be done was to put all of the connecting linkage and parts back together and insert them in their proper place. How this *fundi* could accomplish that was another source of amazement for me.

I thought back to when my dad, older brother and I had taken apart the engine on my car one summer in our driveway in Pennsylvania. Okay, I have to admit that I was merely the grunt in that endeavor. I fetched tools and cleaned parts in gasoline or degreaser and put them in certain places, as commanded by my brother. Everything was systematic, with separate containers for all the individual parts making up a complex segment grouped together. Even then I was amazed when we started the engine and it actually ran—and ran quite well, after some minor adjustments.

But here, there was no order that I could discern. Nonetheless, the number of parts still scattered here and there were fewer than what I had seen two days prior. Well, this guy does this for a living, I concluded. My brother and dad were amateurs by comparison. Still, some semblance of order would seem to make more sense, I concluded—but decided not to share.

As I was marveling, both at the progress and at the apparent amount of work remaining, Tony was speaking with the *fundi*. Once or twice, the conversation became rather animated, mainly from the *fundi*, since Tony is not prone to raising his voice. But he was holding his own, I could tell, occasionally speaking quite firmly and repeating a long string of Swahili words.

Finally, he came away shaking his head and pulled out his cell phone to make a call—no doubt, to Godfrey. More Swahili words followed. "You really need to take those Swahili lessons, Bob," I told myself. "This is so frustrating, and I feel of so little service."

"Maybe tomorrow, Bob. I'm sorry," Tony said as he hung up the phone. "What?" he asked, noticing the slight smile on my face.

"Tony," I said, searching for the right words. "You are a model of patience. I cannot begin to know all that you have been discussing since we arrived here, first with the *fundi*, and then Godfrey. But I can certainly imagine. I feel bad that I have brought so much trouble to your already complicated mission here."

"Nonsense, Bob," he responded, somewhat surprised. "On the contrary, it is I who am in awe of your patience. After all, you're here at your own expense, trying to assist us on a difficult project that is going nowhere. None of this is your fault."

"Nor yours, my friend," I quickly responded. "And you're having to deal with all of the issues, a number of individuals, each with his own unique personality, and various time schedules. I find myself adding nothing in the way of assistance to this situation we find ourselves in. That does not sit well with me, I can assure you. I'm a fixer, Tony. I often find myself in the midst of tricky problems, not sure how I got there. But with some serious help from the Holy Spirit, I generally find a way out. Not always, but usually."

"Well, Bob, I think that sometimes a situation is simply beyond our ability to fix. This surely seems to be one of those instances. We hired a contractor to do a job, and he's just not doing it. You've been here what, four days now? And they have only managed to drill 25 feet! I am sure that I would be displaying a much higher level of frustration, if I were in your shoes. So that is why I marvel at your patience, my friend."

I chuckled. "Okay, now that we've flattered one another with mutual respect for the other's fortitude, what is the latest from our erstwhile driller?"

"Ha! Well, it seems that he is short some repair items, which he is bringing from Dar. He is now saying that they will complete the overhaul today and resume drilling tomorrow."

"That's where it gets tricky for me, Tony. I was only planning to stay here two more days. But there is no way he can complete the drilling in one day, I am sure of that, let alone install the well casing and other tasks to complete the project. Perhaps I can extend my trip without significant airline fees. I do need to go to Ethiopia, but I don't need to spend more than two days there. Let me see what I can do."

"If that is what you want to do and can do it, that would be great," Tony said. "Of course, we both know that there is no guarantee whatsoever that his repair job will work immediately, right?"

"Yes, you're absolutely right," I said. "We have no way to know that. And, quite honestly, I harbor some strong doubts, though I'm praying to the contrary, that compressor will be back in business anytime soon. That is why I was wanting to urge him to be looking for a replacement compressor that he could rent."

"I forgot to mention that—he did say that he is on the hunt for one while in Dar. I asked him to keep me posted on that possibility, and, you will be proud, I was rather strident with my request," he added, looking, indeed, quite confident as he said it.

"Well, good for you, ol' chap!" I said, startling him with my attempt at a British accent. He smiled at me and shook his head.

"We'll make a 'propa' English gentleman out of you yet, Bob."

We returned to the church, where the conference was just wrapping up. In fact, we arrived at just the right moment, as Cath was wanting to take some group photos. She was excited to learn that I had brought my Nikon camera with me. She asked if I would take the photos, once she got everyone situated. Dean and Cath sat front row center, while the students and Tony stood around them. I took a number of photos so that she could have plenty to choose from.

As we took pictures, men and women from the church began setting food out on several long tables that were brought out into the courtyard. What followed was a great meal, plenty to fill these pastors, young and old, and strengthen them for their journeys home. Some of them would have several days of walking—just as they did to get there.

When the meal was finished, I helped with the cleanup. Cath asked me if I would like to join her later that afternoon to play with the youth from the school. "I want to give them the rest of those soccer balls that you brought from America. Can you help me do that?" she asked.

"Sure," I said, "Just tell me when."

"I know you and Tony have some things to do, and I have to take Dean back to the guest house so he can rest and pack for the trip home. I'll discuss with Tony so that we know where to meet, either in town or back at the house."

I was so glad that Cath asked me to join her. As I looked around at the beauty of the scene in front of me, I realized that even if I were a proper photographer or artist, I could not begin to capture what I was seeing. Here on this large expanse of pure green grass were children of all ages running, playing, and laughing unabashedly, as children do. There were all sorts of balls, and Frisbees, as well, flying everywhere. And there was Cath, standing in the midst of them, along with several of the teachers. I stopped to take a few photos of the scene, and it was not until then that I put the whole picture into focus, with the bright green grass and trees, and the mountains and pure blue sky as a backdrop.

As I was shuttering away, I thanked the Lord of all creation for showing me this perfect picture of life to the fullest. There were even some goats and cows grazing in the far background, just to complete it all. Oh my, but He thinks of everything! [9]

Cath saw me taking photos and came over to sit by me and rest a bit. "Thank you for bringing me here," I said. "This is such a beautiful thing to behold."

"It is rather lovely, isn't it?" she said, gazing with me at the scene before us. "I hope that you got some good photos. I would love to see them."

"Sure," I said, "I'll download them to my computer so that you can see them in larger format, perhaps tonight."

"Oh, that would be grand," she responded. "Now, I want you to meet our older youth group. You can see them congregating over there, under that tree, where they generally meet for Bible study. They are secondary school age, about 14 to 16."

We walked together towards a group of around ten young adults. They were sitting on the ground or on a large dead tree trunk, under the shade of a large, full tree. They already had their Bibles out and were in discussion when we arrived. Cath waited for them to finish and then introduced me, explaining what I was doing here in Morogoro. She then asked me to talk some more about my ministry, which was not yet very extensive, I had to admit. Nonetheless, I took the opportunity to give them my personal testimony story—the abridged version, so as not to bore them.

Then, in an attempt to re-engage them, Cath asked them to tell us what type of mission work they each might one day want to pursue

---

[9] Even as I now write these words, I can see it cast before me, in pure technicolor—God's gracious answer to a prayer of mine. You see, I lost these photos before I was able to transfer them to a "safe place," when the computer on which I downloaded them was later stolen. Stupid boy—I did not have them backed up properly, not being a "real photographer" and all.

and where. It was interesting to hear the wide variety of interests and locations that were mentioned. They began to discuss these things further with one another. Cath reined them back in with questions specific to their current Bible study. I was surprised to see many similarities with group sessions that my daughters would have in their Sunday School classes or youth Bible studies.

All in all, it was a delightful time, and I thanked them for allowing me into their discussion. Cath and I then said goodbye and left to re-join the younger children, still passionately pursuing their own inventive ball games. Finally, as dusk was beginning to settle in, we started collecting the balls and Frisbees, just as parents and older siblings began arriving to gather up their children.

That evening we had another grand meal—thank you, Cath! Back at our guest house, Dean and I settled in for a good night's sleep. Dean would be leaving early the next morning, shortly after sun up, to catch his ride back to Dar and his flight back to Kenya. He would stay just one day in Nairobi with our friend and associate, Ken, before flying home the next day.

After seeing Dean off in the morning, Tony and I headed into town to check on the air compressor repair. Or should I say, "rebuilding?" Once again, Godfrey was not present. But from the looks of things, at least, the *fundi* appeared to have it nearly put back together. He told Tony that Godfrey had brought him the parts yesterday afternoon, and he should have it completed and ready to test within a few hours. Tony told them that we would leave now but be back in a few hours.

He had some errands to run in town and asked if I would like to join him. "Well, I really don't have a whole lot else to do until the drilling actually resumes," I responded. "And if you're going near that common market area, I would like to buy some material."

"Oh really?" Tony responded, surprised. "Do you plan on making something with it?

"Heavens, no," I laughed. "But my sister-in-law, who visited here several years ago, was telling me that I should check out the fabrics here. She said that they are very good quality and for a very good price."

"That's true," Tony responded. "Tanzania is known to have some of the best fabrics in all of Africa. And I know just the place to look."

"Well, good," I said. "Maybe we can run your errands and then go fabric shopping. Ha! That does sound a bit strange, don't you think? Here I have come to oversee well drilling and instead, I'm going fabric shopping!"

"When you put it that way, Bob, it does sound odd. But that is what we shall do! We will make a morning of it."

Tony's errands consisted of a stop at the bank and then off to the grocery store. Along the way, he called Godfrey to ask if he had found a compressor to rent yet. "Nothing has turned up yet," he told me, "but he is still working on it."

"That's good," I said. "Because I still think he's going to need a different compressor. I'm not saying that I don't think the *fundi* is a good mechanic. It just seems to me to be a difficult task to overhaul that big engine under those circumstances."

"I totally understand, Bob."

"Of course, I'm not discounting the possibility of a miracle here," I added. "In fact, I'm really hoping that he proves me wrong. I would like nothing more than to return to drilling as early as this afternoon."

The trip into downtown Morogoro served us well to get our minds off the whole drilling fiasco. But the stop at the local fabric shops took the cake. It reminded me of the times I used to accompany my mom as a child when she would go to the local fabric stores to buy materials to make dresses for my sister. One stark difference, however, were the seamstresses perched just outside the store entrance, in front of almost every fabric shop we saw, working away on their sewing machines. And it was not just women who were doing the sewing. In fact, I saw more men plying this trade than women, surprisingly.

After sorting through bolts of different fabrics, I finally chose two of them. One of them struck me as tablecloth material. I asked Tony to please ask the owner if I could have them sew a hem all around the edge, on four sides, to seal it off. "So you know your sewing, eh, Bob?" he asked with a gleam in his eye.

"Not all about it. But I do know some. My mom and her mother were always sewing stuff—clothes, curtains, even costumes for me and my siblings growing up. My dad's first job that I remembered him doing was selling Singer sewing machines."

I then asked Tony to find out if was possible to finish this work in two days. "Yes, they could," was the answer that was returned. I really liked this material, as it had a lot of safari scenes and obvious African implements all over it in a variety of shades of brown and green. I could just see it on my table top at home. (And in fact, I can *still* see it, as it covers my dining room table to this day!)[10]

By now it was early afternoon, and with all of our errands and shopping, we were both getting hungry. We needed to go out to the well site, but Tony thought it best that we eat first. He said he knew just the place. When we pulled up to the restaurant, I could see why he liked it. It seemed to have a lot of charm. The front porch was an eclectic collection of interesting and unique tables and chairs. Tony asked the owner if we could sit out there. "Of course," she said. "Take any seat you like and I will be right back with menus." The food was quite good, but I decided the chilled Kilimanjaro beers that we enjoyed made it taste even better!

After this pleasant lunch, Tony drove me by the guesthouse to collect my luggage and bring it to their house, where I would spend the remainder of my time in Tanzania. I decided to extend my stay by a few days to give the driller the opportunity to either fix his compressor or rent another one. Hopefully, I would get to see the well actually drilled.

Tony and Cath seemed happy to hear that as we sat around the dinner table. "I hope you can stay through Sunday, Bob," said Cath. "Then you will get to hear Tony preach."

"Is that right, Tony?" I said, turning my head to look at him.

"Yes, but I don't know how fortunate that will make you, Bob," he responded. "Besides, I'm preaching in Swahili, and not the best of that, either. This may not be a memorable sermon at all."

"Well, I may not get much out of it, that's true," I said, "But I'll be impressed, for sure. I look forward to it. You can always tell me what you told us afterwards."

I knew that this plan to extend my stay was not the smartest move I could have made, given the track record of the driller thus far. But I wasn't on a strict time schedule to get to Ethiopia either. I would call Melaku, of course, and confirm that this was the case before making any final flight changes. I guess that I was just hoping against hope that things could turn around for the driller. But even if not, I was really enjoying

[10] The other piece of fabric I bought was much larger and much softer. It, too, was covered with a variety of safari animals. I had a grand plan to have it made into throw pillows, but I have not quite gotten around to that yet. So it remains in a storage box on a high shelf in my apartment. Someday...

being in Morogoro and spending more time with Cath and Tony. And now, getting to stay in their lovely house was a bonus.

If that were not enough, that afternoon Tony invited me out to his office in the shipping container. Now this was a real plus! We had access to the Internet, enabling me to check flight schedules and plan my revised travel schedule. I also sent an email to Melaku, telling him of my plans, just to double check what effect this might have on his schedule.

We got word from the driller that they intended to try to restart the compressor later today. Until they did and we heard back from them on the result, there was no use going back to *Sanga Sanga*. So Tony asked if I wanted to go back and work in the office again. Cath had to leave to take care of some things at the school, and Tony could use the time to work on his sermon.

Late that afternoon Tony got a call from the drilling superintendent. Things had not gone so well with the restart, it seemed. In fact, when they initially ran the big engine, one of the cylinders seized before it even came to full throttle. Looks like we're back to square 1. They would have to tear into it again and rebuild that cylinder. I was now thinking it would be two more days just to get back to drilling—if we were lucky. And so far, that had surely not been the case. Yes, a miracle was starting to look like the only way I would ever see this well drilled.

In the meantime, I heard back from Melaku, and he was fine with my proposed schedule changes. I only needed to let him know my final dates and times for arrival, and he would be there to pick me up. Based on that, I decided to extend for three more days and leave on Wednesday. We finally got some good news when the driller told Tony that he had several leads on rental compressors in Dar es Salaam!

When Cath returned from town, she asked if I would like to attend a Bible study with her and Tony. "Sure," I said. "Tonight?"

"Yes, here at our home. We're expecting two other couples—one is from Zimbabwe and the other from Kenya."

The Zimbabwe couple did not look African at all. Nor did they sound like it, with their proper English accent, similar to Cath and Tony's. But I guess that by now, I should have expected this, as I had met several couple friends of the Swansons from Zimbabwe, and they all looked and talked alike. And they all had similar stories, as well—none of them good.

You see, they had all lived comfortably in Zimbabwe as heirs to land that had been in their respective families for decades, or even centuries in some cases. But in recent years, with the state-directed takeover of all property held by English descendants, many lost their land to former tenants and even squatters, sometimes at gunpoint. This was all part of the ethnic cleansing devised by President Mugabe, who has ruled Zimbabwe for more than forty years. While it was intended to be non-violent, these squatters knew that they had the full backing of the federal government. Indeed, I had heard the news reports from the BBC or CNN, but to meet people that had lived through this, many of them now trying to restart their lives in Tanzania and other neighboring countries, it was chilling to hear their accounts.

The other couple were also missionaries, from Kenya—the Machokos region, outside Nairobi. They were working with Navigators. I recall that their names were Adams and Sarah Mutonga. I remember them because I still get email newsletters from them from time to time, discussing their ministry in Morogoro and their trips back to Kenya, whenever they have a chance to visit. Both of these couples were well-versed in the Bible, as were Tony and Cath, and I could have felt insecure. But none of them made me feel this way. On the contrary, they were all very kind and quite engaging, actually, when they asked about my fledgling ministry.

What a wonderful night it turned out to be, making me so glad that I decided to extend my stay! I could never have guessed that an evening in remote Tanzania spent in the company of couples from England, Zimbabwe, and Kenya could be so enriching. But it truly was every bit of that and more. It even included hymn singing, led by Tony, to begin the evening. That's another first for me, even though I've participated in Bible study groups most of my adult life.

Tony's sermon on Sunday, as well as the entire church service, was really good. The church sanctuary was used for some of the youngest children's classrooms for the Christian school that Tony and Cath had started there. I knew that because Cath had me teach young children earlier in the week about water hygiene; she had heard that I typically do this for receiving communities where I am drilling a new well.

Before the service, Tony introduced me to a young man who spoke excellent English. He brought the gentleman back to the pew where I was sitting, introduced him and had him sit next to me. During the service, he would whisper the translation in my ear. I learned a lot that day, both from Tony's sermon and from the insight provided by this young man. At times, he would explain the meaning behind Tony's words, particularly when it had to do with Tanzanian tradition.

Occasionally, Tony would make light of his improper Swahili, but the charity of the congregation was evident to allow the occasional syntax error. I could also see that they were enthralled by his effort to preach to them in their national language, rather than rely on an interpreter. I was impressed and enjoyed myself immensely during the service. Of course, Cath could have interpreted for me as well, but she was very busy with overseeing the youth Sunday School program during the sermon. That made Tony's effort to see that I was taken care of, in the midst of his final preparation for an entire sermon in Swahili, all the more remarkable. No wonder the community was so kind to him, as he was nothing less than that to me.

The remainder of the day was just as delightful. Tony and Cath took me to the "country club" café, where we met up with two other couples from Zimbabwe. Both had similar stories of escaping from their home country at the hands of the Mugabe regime. But they were happy to be settled here in the beautiful surroundings of Morogoro. One couple had found similar work to what they did in Zimbabwe, working at the only real industry in the region—a large coffee production plant. The others were missionaries who had come into town for a break from their work with the Chaggas, an indigenous tribe of the Kilimanjaro region. It was just another in a growing list of exceptional meals—again, not at all based on food quality (which was actually quite good), but on the excellence of the ensuing discussion with yet more interesting and enjoyable friends of Cath and Tony.

Indeed, from the sum of these one-time encounters with their friends, I could see that this was a mutual admiration society that they were creating. One does not have to spend much time with Cath and Tony to realize the inevitability of such a development. The most succinct way that I can characterize them is charming and committed. They are the kind of people that you just want to be around.

And that's just what I got to do all the next day. It was becoming rather apparent that I was not going to witness any more progress on the borehole drilling, the one I had traveled here specifically to oversee. "At this point," I told Tony, "who knows how long it might take for your contractor to either repair his own or find another compressor to rent?" We were enjoying the morning sunlight filtering in through the trees in his container-office. "I really wish that I could stay to see this project through," I added. "But that could take weeks at this rate. Not that I wouldn't love to stay that long, if I could."

"No, I absolutely understand, Bob, and I'm grateful, really, for you coming here to help me," he responded. "I feel bad that he has performed so poorly that you could not do what you came for. I'm sure that must be very frustrating for you."

"It is," I said. "But I don't want you to feel bad, as none of this is your fault. And I know that I haven't really been able to help. I can, however, leave you with a complete checklist of what to expect once they complete the drilling and start to set the casing pipe and screen, and then finish the well. Since you're not going to install a pump for a while, they can just provide a steel cover with a locking cap. I'll be glad to talk to them about that, as well, and leave you with details showing what that should look like, okay?

"Yes, that would be great, Bob, since I certainly have no experience in this arena."

My morning, and into the afternoon, was spent making this list of tasks that would need to be performed, along with detailed sketches of what it should look like and how they should be installing it to do it right. I then spent a good deal of time going over all of it with Tony until he said that he understood. Of course, he knew that he could always call or email me if he saw something that didn't look right. I wanted him to feel confident that I would stay on top of the process, even if I could not be there in person.

I had one last wonderful, zero-progress day in Morogoro with the Swansons. I even got Tony to take me out to *Sanga Sanga* one more time. It turned out to be a good idea, as we walked the general area where the well was to be drilled, giving me the opportunity to ask about his plans for the water distribution throughout the property.

We discussed such details as where to put the ground storage tank or elevated tank. I also got to ask him about his plans for a sanitary system, as I was assuming that there would be toilets and showers, as well as food preparation, at some point in the conference center development.

"Indeed, there will be," Tony said.

"Well, I have some ideas on ways to treat that waste, beyond a simple septic tank, that could provide reuse quality water for landscape irrigation. If you like, I can make some sketches on what that looks like and how to install it using available local materials."

"That sounds great, Bob," he responded. "See, you're helping in more ways than you thought, even without the well getting drilled. I really like the idea of reusing the water, since we do plan to have a lot of irrigation needs, and I don't want to waste good water on that unless I have to."

"I agree. I will draw those details and make you a bill of materials—once we get back to that nifty office of yours," I teased.

"Okay, Bob, it's a deal. But I believe that I'm getting the best on this one!" he added, with a wink.

"Well, as long as you think that, we're good," I responded, now laughing heartily.

When we got back to the house, Cath was in work clothes and wearing a wide-brimmed hat, working in her garden with two of the local girls that lived on their compound with them. When I walked over to admire her agri-skills, she stopped weeding and gave me a tour. First, she introduced me to the two young ladies. The older girl was just 14, as I recall. Cath informed me quietly later that she had to get out of her dad's house because he had raped her on multiple occasions.

Cath told me also of her own involvement with the local police, trying to get the girl's dad arrested and prosecuted. She was furious that the police had allowed the girl to go back to her dad's house while Cath and Tony were on sabbatical leave back in England. When they returned and Cath found out that he had raped the girl again, she moved her permanently into their home and again went to the police to press charges against the dad.

As Cath did more research, she found that this was a lot more common in the community than she had imagined. She continued speaking out against it, and began a campaign to raise awareness throughout the community. She also began training young girls and their mothers on how to combat it and how to press charges with the local police. She has become a huge advocate of those with no voice—young girls in the overwhelmingly male-dominated society that is Africa, even as we know it today, I'm sad to say. [11]

[11] Cath continued to develop her skills in child protection and is now officially on staff at AIM as the Child Safety Officer, where she does more traveling, mainly to

After meeting the girls, I joined Tony in his office where we discussed in more detail how he might accomplish the well drilling project in my absence. I walked him through the various stages and tasks that would need to be completed for a functional, long-lasting borehole. For each phase, I made simple checklists that he could use to either observe or ask the driller to provide the details thereof.

"If, at any time, you don't see these things happening, or are not getting the right responses, please call or email me, Tony," I said. "I want this to be a good well for you, viable for years to come. Everything depends, of course, on finding water and enough of it to sustain your water needs at *Sanga Sanga*. But I will tell you, that is, most often, a very difficult thing to decipher, when all you really have from deep within the earth is drill cuttings and, at times, fresh underground water bubbling through to the surface. And with air drilling, it is almost impossible to discern. Thus, the level of the water in the well, once the driller has properly developed it (meaning, removed all sand, mud, and cuttings), and how it changes day-to-day, is very tell-tale in this regard."

"This is very helpful, Bob," Tony responded, glazing over my checklists. "I am sure that I will have more questions as the work progresses. I'm thankful that you said to call or text you anytime. So, you should probably expect that to occur, perhaps more often than you would like."

"That's absolutely all right, Tony, I assure you," I responded. "I want, more than ever, for this to work for you, especially since I cannot be here in person—which, by the way, would not be any guarantee of a good water-producing well. But we must work to get the best that this location has to offer, right?"

"Without a doubt," he said. "So, tell me, won't the pump test that you have included here tell us this information?"

"Yes, in the end, this is the best indicator of the well's capacity to produce water and at what rate of flow and recharge. But, as you know, this is done after the well is totally complete, but before the permanent pump is introduced, whether hand or electric/solar. So then it follows that if the well cannot produce any more water than can be determined from the 12- or 24-hour pump test, there is no way to increase it, other than the natural seasonal changes in water table level due to the rain conditions."

---

other African cities, as a speaker at conferences and training centers.

"Oh, I understand," he responded, scrunching his mouth a bit and nodding slightly.

"Well, Tony," I concluded, smiling, "you now know everything that I know about water well construction! My work here is complete. I can leave in peace, knowing all will be fine."

"Ha! I don't believe that for a minute, Bob," he laughed. "But I do feel better about overseeing the contractor's work in your absence."

"I'm sure you will do fine. I only hope that he does not let us down any more than he has already. As long as he completes a good well, all is not lost. But first things first. He really needs that compressor. Any word on that?"

"No, I'm afraid not, Bob. But let me give him a call just to get an update."

Although there was that other private well being drilled, also by Godfrey, when we arrived, the practice of drilling wells in small rural towns and communities is not that common in Africa. Morogoro is no exception to that rule. So the fact that Tony was attempting to drill in even more remote *Sanga Sanga*, and now this beast of a compressor was splayed open in a *fundi*'s back yard, nearby...let's just say that the situation was certainly not looking all that promising.

For two weeks after I left, the reports brought little to no good news. All correspondence from Tony during the time I was in Ethiopia, and then back to the States, was discouraging. Godfrey was searching for a compressor to rent while the rebuilding of his compressor stretched on, day after day. The latest news was that a new crankshaft was now on order, but had not yet arrived! It was getting hard to keep my hopes up.

However it happened, whether through extended dialogue in the community, or by way of social media pleas, or divine intervention (I will choose to believe the latter), along came a gentleman with an even bigger compressor, down the highway and then turning onto *Sanga Sanga* property and right up to Godfrey's drill rig. "I heard that you might need an air compressor," he reportedly said to Tony as he exited his lead vehicle. Tony cannot actually substantiate these words, as he wholly admits to going into a state of total shock, thereby squelching any remote chance of any verbal response, or recall of the conversation. He does somewhat recall sheepishly nodding his head, his mouth hanging wide open. "Y-yes sir, w-we surely do," he believes he responded, finally.

"Well, then, I would like to offer my services, free of charge. We need a good place to test this new compressor of ours, and your borehole project appears to provide just that opportunity." The company's name was Hydrotech Tanzania. I didn't catch the owner's name, but I really wish that I had. I'm not sure that Tony did at this point, but I'm sure that I would have checked the man closely, as well as the crew of men traveling with him, for any visible signs of wings!

Looking over the site, the gentlemen was visibly "disgruntled at the state of Godfrey's drill rig," in Tony's words. Nevertheless, they hooked it up to the compressor and began drilling, initially with a rotary bit, for 20 feet, and from there on, with a hammer bit. In less than an hour and a half, they had drilled to about 60 feet, when suddenly the drill swivel rattled loose from the drill pipe. Someone had forgotten to insert some washers when reassembling it after the last servicing.

They would now have to overhaul the shaft head, since the bolt threads had worn smooth, causing wobbling of the head, which, in turn, ruined the bearings. This effort, Tony reported, took them a day and a half to complete. In the meantime, the compressor team had to leave the site to take care of another well in the region that needed to be developed. But they would be back with the behemoth compressor as soon as that work was complete, they promised.

True to their word, they returned with the compressor two days later, and the drilling resumed from the 60-foot level. Within two hours, they had drilled to 150 feet and started to see a lot of water pressure building from the borehole. Just then, the 350 pounds per square inch of pressure became too much for Godfrey's connecting air hose, and it came apart and started flying all about, narrowly missing several of the 15 men assembled near the operation. Godfrey had to take the air hose into town and have it repaired. When he returned, it was dark, so they continued drilling under the headlights of Tony's Land Cruiser.

By 11 PM, they had reached 200 feet, and by now, a visible stream of water was evident every time they stopped. Besides it being very late for the exhausted team, they were out of drill stem. The compressor crew took the opportunity to detach and leave immediately with their compressor. There was even some discussion about starting over with a new well nearby, as Godfrey was not confident that this borehole would produce enough water.

Tony convinced them all to wait until the morning to see how much water was in the well. They had been drilling in rock for some time, so the possibility of overnight collapse of the hole did not seem likely. Besides, the bottom line was that there simply was no money to drill another well—or even to drill this one deeper. Not only that, but they would be back to having no air compressor.

The next morning revealed that the water level was just over 30 feet from the surface, meaning that there was over 160 feet of water in the well. This was a very good sign, initially. The well pump test, which Godfrey would conduct the next day, would tell them everything they would need to know about flow volume and recharge potential.

The well pump test, however, like every other task on this project, did not go smoothly. (Why was I not surprised?) It seemed that they only had one submersible pump to fit in a 4" well casing, and it was 2 horse power—way too big for this size borehole. Regardless, with an adequate generator, they could still conduct a reasonable pump test. Ah, but therein lay the problem. Their generator was undersized for their pump (imagine that!), so it kept tripping the breaker, Tony said.

To compensate for this, they removed a portion of the pump impeller, thereby reducing the electrical draw.[12] With their newly modified pump, Godfrey and team were able to complete the pump test, revealing a good flowing well with a fairly quick aquifer recharge. This meant that the Swansons should have all the water that they should need from this one well to support their proposed conference center. The only question now was quality. I suggested that Tony get a sample after talking to a local laboratory that could test it for the constituents that I would send him. He said he'd do it before his next trip to Dar, where he would take the sample for testing.

As I mentioned, all of this well drilling took place after I left Tanzania. The actual drilling process took place in only two days, separated, of course, by another two days of breakdown and repair. Okay, so let's say four days total. After extending my trip, I had been in Morogoro for seven full days, not counting travel. One would think that should be long enough to witness a mere two days of drilling, right? That, plus the well

[12] Now this was quite smart, I have to say. I would not have thought of that. But I'll "pack it away" as needed for future projects. I am not at all ashamed to borrow others' good ideas! I believe it's just fine, as long as I give them credit when asked.

casing installation and finishing and the pump test could all have been easily performed within those seven days. But in reality, none of it was! What's with that? The question wouldn't leave my brain.

I remembered knowing at some point that I would likely not see any more drilling on the *Sanga Sanga* well beyond those first 25 to 30 feet. Like Meki, Ethiopia, and Mtepeni, Kenya, before it, the borehole would be drilled without me—and well after I left, in some instances. Such is the nature, I suppose, of trying to connect the trajectory of my short trips to Africa with contract drillers' schedules. I was coming to realize they would rarely cross, and if they did, only briefly. I knew then that I had to find a way to accept this—actually, to expect it. Only then would it not feel so debilitating every time.

This cascade of thoughts whirled through my head as Tony drove me back to the airport in Dar es Salaam. I watched in bittersweet reverie as the beautiful scenery faded, soaking in the last of the beautiful Uluguru Mountains surrounding this lovely hamlet of Morogoro.

My wistful daydreaming came to a halt suddenly, when we were abruptly stopped by a traffic policeman. He took great pains to talk to Tony through the window, and then read, intently, the registration and insurance placards plastered on the windshield, as required. I thought for sure that I must be the cause of this stop, but I really hadn't a clue as to why. The next thing I knew, the cop was opening the back door and climbing inside, adjusting in his seat before closing the door. "Okay," was all he said, and Tony was off again.

I must have been staring at Tony with the strangest look. He glanced at me and said quietly, "It's okay, Bob, he just needed a ride." Now able to exhale, I started piecing it altogether. Of course, there wasn't a patrol car nearby, nor a motorcycle, or even a bicycle. As best I could remember, we were a long way from any town. But what about the other cop, a policewoman, who was left alone to check traffic? She no longer had a companion.

I could tell that Tony wanted to explain this to me, but was not really about to talk about it in front of the policeman, who was staring at us from the back seat. I would have to be content to file away all my questions until the next stop. That turned out to be a busy place, kind of like a full-service roadside rest in America. There were petrol and diesel pumps, several cafes and souvenir shops, as well as large restrooms. We stopped, and Tony and I got out, but the policeman stayed seated. By this time, Tony had had enough. He opened the door and ushered the policeman out, telling him that we would not be leaving for a while and to look for another ride. To my surprise, the policeman responded and got out. He didn't look all that happy about it, but he didn't say anything.

I waited until we got back in the car to ask Tony about the strange trip. He said that it happens all the time. "By law," he said, "you're not required to give them a ride and you can certainly refuse. But I just think that it doesn't hurt to be nice to them, as it may pay off some time, especially when I'm in a hurry and might be speeding. Besides, I usually feel sorry for them, having to stand out there in the hot sun for hours, with those hot, long sleeve uniforms on."

"But what about the lady cop?" I asked. "Now she's left out there all alone. That doesn't seem right, or very smart, to me."

"Oh, I bet that she crossed the road and started looking to stop a car for her own ride not long after we pulled away," he replied. "Or she may have just come on duty and will stay there until relieved, probably by another team of cops. I pass this way a lot, as I told you that I travel to Dar almost every week as part of my work. I only see policemen there about half of the time."

The rest of the trip to Dar was uneventful, thankfully. I really didn't care to experience any more "events" before leaving. I had a wonderful stay with the Swansons and wanted to end on a good note. I had told Cath that morning when leaving that she and Tony were awesome hosts. I really enjoyed my stay, and I told them how I would truly like to return one day soon and see the progress of the conference center at *Sanga Sanga*. Although I felt bad about not helping much with the actual well construction, since it had not yet happened at that point, I didn't feel responsible for that fact.

And who knows? Maybe, in the end, it's not even truly about the wells. Maybe God's trying to show me something deeper here. Do ya think?! Or maybe it's less important that I be the one to monitor the well construction, and more important to simply have it done. I realized I was still learning a lot on these trips, and most of it was not about well drilling. On this trip alone, I learned about the various tribes of this region of Tanzania. I saw firsthand how hard single moms have it here in Tanzania, particularly those with special needs children. I'd be willing to bet you could substitute any African country name here, and the situation would be similar.

I became aware of the plight of white Zimbabweans and the turmoil that they encountered, some at gunpoint. My eyes were opened to the horrors of incest and rape, between fathers and their daughters, no less. I met victims of this atrocity. But I also heard tales from a brave woman who is trying to do something about it, fighting her heart out to intervene and stop this abuse.

I experienced a shipping container put to great use, and truly enjoyed spending time inside the makeshift office for hours at a time! I spent eight days in "Shangri-La," enjoying the beauty that envelops this lovely community of Morogoro and the entire region of Tanzania. I met a number of wonderful people, including Africans and ex-pats, who made me feel special just for talking with them and listening to their stories. I got to spend several days and nights of quality time with Dean, which is always a treat.

And finally, I not only met, but really got to know two wonderful Christians, Tony and Cath Swanson, who are devoted to their task of reaching the unchurched, while meeting so many needs in their community that it just boggles the mind. They are a true gift to this community and are, indeed, the hands and feet of our Savior, Jesus Christ. Well or no well—it wasn't the only thing on my mind as I flew away from Tanzania. I found myself hoping to revisit the friends, the people, and the stories of Morogoro as soon as I could return there.

> *"I'm losing ground and gaining speed. I've lost myself for most of me. I'm headed for the final precipice. But you haven't lost me yet. No, you haven't lost me yet. I'll sing until my heart caves in. No, you haven't lost me yet."*
>
> "*Yet*", by Switchfoot, from "Hello Hurricane", 2009, lowercase people records ©

Journey—Interrupted

"I'm holding on. I'm holding on to you. My world is wrong. My world is a lie that's come true. And I fall in love, with the ones that run me through. When all along all I need is you."

"Sing it Out", by Switchfoot, from "Hello Hurricane, 2009, lowercase people records ©

We had spent hours on the river in preparation, from early morning practice runs to overnight runs. But nothing had prepared us for this. Cindy, my paddling partner, and I were ensnarled in an entanglement of branches in an epic river logjam. It was dark. We were cold. And for the first time in over two days—and more than 220 river miles—we no longer knew where we were going.

Cindy and I were competing in the two-person (mixed) aluminum division of the Texas Water Safari—billed as The World's Toughest Canoe Race and sometimes even covered by ESPN. We were well into the journey, probably no more than 40 miles from finishing the race. But finding our way out of Alligator Lake would not have been easy even in daylight. Here we were, deep into our second night on the river, and not only were we stuck, we were lost—couldn't find the point where the lake emptied back into the river. Plus, there were sure to be plenty of water moccasins in this mess of sticks and river debris; thus, exiting the canoe to disentangle ourselves did not appear to be a safe option. To make matters worse (could they get worse?), the hydraulic force that had pulled us into the jam was now working relentlessly to overturn our boat, creating a huge vacuum that we were fighting strenuously to overcome.

Our strength was fading fast, and though we said little, we both felt the desperation in the air. We had snapped into survival mode, our thoughts now sharpened on staying alive rather than on earlier dreams of finishing the race, or even finding our way back to the river. I tried to shove down feelings of fear and guilt. I had promised Cindy's husband, Terry, our Land Captain, that I would bring her back safe and sound, whether we finished the race or not. Indeed, many would not; Terry had informed us at the last checkpoint that more than one third of the boats had already dropped out, with more dropping by the hour.

It had been a "low water year" due to the near-drought conditions leading up to the day of the race. That meant slower race times, due to extensive sections of low water where "portaging" (exiting the boat and towing while walking) would be necessary. But in the last two days, it had rained quite a bit, and the river was beginning to swell again. On the plus side, the rising rapids had made for more efficient paddling. I had to admit that much. But it had also helped to create this huge logjam that we were presently struggling with all our might to escape.

I was praying like never before; I was sure Cindy, a devout Catholic, was as well. I knew He wouldn't forsake us; God would see us through. But when? I couldn't help but wonder as I felt my strength exiting my body. And how?

It was nearly ten o'clock when we were finally allowed to board the bus. Ken had booked us on this express line, which would take us from Nairobi to our destination near Busia in far-western Kenya—just a stones- throw, incidentally, from the Uganda border town of the same name. The trip would take 10-12 hours with only two scheduled stops. In short, we would travel all night, so sleep was obviously the priority. The bus was crowded, and it seemed that every passenger had brought multiple baggage.

In addition to their carried bags, they were shoving into every free storage space large bags and the purchased items that travelers often bring out of Nairobi, taking advantage of the pricing and availability of needed items. I slipped my large bag of clothes and supplies onto the overhead shelf and held onto my backpack on my lap.

The sea of passengers finally found their seats and settled in for the long journey. I sat next to a young Kenyan man, while Geoffrey and Ken, my two CrossWay associates, sat behind us. Ken had warned me that there would be no bathroom on this bus, but it would stop in three to four hours for the first pit stop and to exchange passengers.

I went to switch on my overhead light so I could read a bit, or perhaps work on my laptop. But I glanced around and noticed every other passenger's light was off—in hopes of catching some sleep, no doubt. I decided to leave mine off, as well. I was already quite aware that I was the only traveler that looked like me on the entire bus. I did not feel the need to draw more attention to myself.

I leaned back in my seat and marveled as the bus driver deftly maneuvered his huge bus through the insanity of traffic that is an inevitable part of life in Nairobi. Either he was very knowledgeable of the traffic patterns, or very lucky. In short order, he had averted all the major traffic nightmares, and soon we were plodding away on the major highway heading north out of the capital city.

Two hours into the trip, most passengers were asleep, including Ken and Geoffrey behind me. A few were quietly chatting amongst themselves. I was quite confident I would not be falling asleep anytime soon—not because of the noise, but more so because of the heat. The young man seated next to me, fast asleep by the window, had wrapped up in a blanket in addition to his overcoat. Puzzled, I glanced around and discovered that most everyone else was also buffeted against some perceived chill. Only I seemed to be dressed for warm weather, a mere T-shirt and a pair of thin safari pants.

Even with this meager clothing, I was still too hot to even think about sleeping, though I was feeling tired. It was also quite stuffy, and I noticed that most every window was closed. Must be that chill my fellow passengers were guarding against. I peeked at my companion again, ensured that he was fast asleep, then reached gently across him and slowly opened the window for some fresh air.

That did the trick. I curled up into as comfortable a position as I could devise and let myself begin drifting off. The next thing I knew, the bus halted, lights popped on, and the sea of people began to stir. Our first pit stop. Geoffrey was still fast asleep, so Ken and I shook him awake, and we followed the passengers off the bus.

The line grew outside the restroom, and a number of travelers purchased food at one of the many nearby stands. Some passengers headed away, while newly arriving passengers stood in line to stow their bags and packages in the large underneath storage compartment. At last, we returned to our seats and the bus chugged off again. Once again, I noticed our window was closed. Once again, I waited until my young friend was fast asleep before reaching over to reopen it.

As I tried to get comfortable, I calculated that I had only slept about a half hour during the first leg of this bus trip. This would call for more drastic measures if I was to be of much value to the next day's project. I had brought sleeping pills for the long plane ride from America, but I worried that if I took one, I might sleep through our final stop. Still, this risk was worth taking if it meant sleep.

I swallowed the pill and was soon sailing into a deep, comfortable sleep when a sharp jouncing of the entire bus woke me up. I asked Ken, who had been violently awakened as well, why we were now on a bumpy dirt road? He said that we were about 10 km into a 50 kilometer detour! "Oh boy!" I thought ruefully. "Only 40 more kilometers of this!"

Fortunately, I was still very drowsy from the sleeping pill. I faded in and out of sleep for the next couple of hours, vaguely aware of the jostling as the bus swung over sections of new pavement and then back onto dirt roads again. More than once I popped awake at the sound of a large truck's air horn, only to be further startled as the huge truck flew by our window with inches to spare! I groggily reminded myself that these were professional drivers, well trained for their jobs. Then I would shoot up a quick prayer before rolling over and drifting off. I finally forced myself to ignore the air horns going off.

I must have become a Zen master of tuning out the noise—before I knew it, Ken was hollering at me to grab my bag and get going. I staggered out of the bus behind Ken and Geoffrey, the only three passengers alighting at this particular "stop"—which I discovered was not actually a scheduled stop. Hence our haste. The early light of morning was nearly blinding as I thudded down from the bus onto a dusty highway shoulder.

We were in a town—if you could call it that. We grabbed our bags and trudged to a nearby general store, where we purchased some *maji buridi*— cold bottled water. Semi-cold, anyway. At least it wasn't warm.

Ken inquired about a taxi to take us the final 10 to 15km that were off the bus path. In minutes, a dilapidated old sedan of unknown make and model wheezed up next to us. Ken noted that this must be our "taxi."

I was frankly in doubt that this contraption could propel itself down a roadway. It was smoking profusely and making a loud rumbling sound, all while shaking somewhat violently.

Ken negotiated the one-way fare with the driver and we started to climb in. Three ladies materialized from a nearby building and started jabbering at the driver before we were even seated. Another deal was struck, and the six of us, plus the driver and his two associates, all began stuffing ourselves—and whatever bags that could not fit into the trunk—into the cab. I sat in the back next to a window, extremely cramped. The driver pulled me out and sat me in the front, in the middle. I had more room to breathe, sure, but from my new vantage point up front, I saw how much of the road was actually visible through the front seat floor board! I was now fighting to find a solid piece of metal I could rest my feet on without the threat of poking through to the ground as we drove. "Keep your feet up, Bob!" I cautioned myself. "This is no time for dozing."

By some strange act of science and technology, as yet untested in the real world, the car began rumbling down the road. We were off… hopefully in the right direction. As we careened along, I had the sense that this vehicle was moving in a non-parallel line to the roadway. It reminded me of my youth in Pennsylvania, riding horses with my friend Johnny. I had the same sensation as the horse would transition from a fast trot into a canter, that they seemed to move at an acute angle to the pathway, while still maneuvering straight down the path.

This carriage felt the same way. I could tell the driver was not struggling to steer in the middle of the road. So I concluded that, along with its other maladies, the car frame must also be warped—one too many accidents, no doubt. I didn't want to ask; I was just happy to be moving in the general direction of "forward," and plus, I had enough to concentrate on as I held my feet off of the rushing roadway just inches below. Up to now, I had thought the worst was behind us with that bus ride. Boy was I wrong.

I can't recall the occasion, nor the exact discussion, that led me to accept Terry and Cindy's pleas to compete in this mixed double class of the annual Texas Water Safari. But I can imagine that it was either following a great day on the water, or more likely, after one too many adult beverages. It had to have been a moment of temporary insanity, for sure, because nothing else could explain why in the world the three of us were out here in the dead of night, driving to a remote location along the San Marcos River, to run our first (and hopefully only) nighttime practice.

At this point, we had completed numerous practice runs, but always during daylight, and often early—usually on Saturday mornings, with some of the longer runs extending well into the afternoon. Cindy and I were getting quite good, I have to say, as our paddling techniques improved and, more importantly, our team approach to maneuvering their light-weight Alumicraft canoe through difficult stretches of the 250+ mile river course was really starting to jell.

We were also getting in better physical shape. Although I cannot say that we were all the way to "ripped," I was content, at 43, to be achieving my best physical shape ever. I knew a ripped physique, at this point, would require a good deal more time and effort, and that was not what I was striving for. I would settle for reaching a level of fitness that could endure the two to three full days of strenuous paddling this race would demand. Both of us were also training daily with specific physical programs. Mine consisted of a mixture of bicycling and Nordic Track workouts, with calisthenics, for specific upper arm and shoulder muscle attention.

We sat wordlessly as Terry drove through the night in his vintage jeep, the canoe strapped to the roof rack. He reminded us of the nuances of this particular segment of the San Marcos. Indeed, Terry took this year's race more seriously than any of the five that he had previously competed in. Most likely because it was his wife and soulmate that I would be paddling with, and he knew the difficulty of finishing this race— having failed to complete on his first four tries.

For tonight's run, Terry had chosen a familiar section, one that the four of us had made multiple times—he and Cindy in their Old Town canoe, and my wife, Linda, and me, in our slower but steadier aluminum craft. But that was always in daylight. Tonight would be a different ballgame. Same river, same turns and minor rapids, but pitch dark and hard to navigate. The key to successful night maneuvering lay in the canoe headlight. Terry had endured a number of failed headlights in his canoeing days. He knew how treacherous it could be if your light failed.

So tonight, not only was he testing Cindy's and my readiness, he'd also be testing his latest and greatest headlight contraption! Terry was always searching for the brightest and sturdiest headlight available. But this was 1993—no searching the Internet for the "brightest and the best!" No, Terry's quest for the ultimate river canoe headlight was old-school research, involving numerous catalogs, magazines, and stores. Having captained Terry's TWS boats in one of his solo efforts and two times with his paddling partner, Bobby, I had seen multiple versions of "the best canoe headlight EVER."

This year's version, however, truly trumped the ones before. Of course, it offered a powerful beam—one with significant candle power. But the key to providing adequate and reliable light through the night lay in the battery selection and the protection of the batteries and wiring from water damage. Since the light would be mounted on the front of the boat, only inches above the water, protection from water below and tree branches above was just as necessary as the strength of the beam and the battery life.

Terry had let me in on his many weeks of developing this latest, greatest headlight. "The monster light," as he called it, would be his crowning achievement, he was sure of it. Tonight was the night we'd see if it lived up to its hype. We reached the "put-in" location and readied the canoe. In addition to The Monster, Cindy and I both wore headlights with an adjustable strap for cinching around our heads. These would be vital, especially for Cindy in the front of the boat, as she would be scouring downriver, looking out for rapids and low-hanging branches. They also helped us find items in the boat without having to let go of our paddles.

I was required to mount the monster light, following his precisely-engineered plan. "And if something goes wrong, Bob, there is a roll of duct tape in the wet-proof bag." I turned on the light then, and wow! Forget canoeing—I am certain this beam could guide airplanes flying high overhead! Terry was excited, even more than Cindy and me. He embraced his wife heartily and watched as we pushed off from the bank and began paddling down river.

We quickly discovered that although the monster light was extremely bright, it was a tight beam, essentially a spotlight—by intention, Terry said, for maximum focused candlepower. Important, to be sure, but we were missing the detail of the entire river, from bank to bank, as we continually searched for the fastest, yet safest, path downstream. In addition, the brightness of the light was creating large dark shadows from all the overhanging tree branches.

We had to get used to discerning the actual branches from the shadows as we swept across the river searching for the best route. It helped immensely that we both knew this river segment—and Cindy much more than I. While Linda and I had made a number of trips down this portion of the San Marcos, she and Terry had probably run it dozens of times. But never at night.

"Everything looks different at night," she said over her shoulder. "It's taking me way longer to recognize where we are and then remember the best route."

"Better you than me!" I assured her. "You're doing great so far."

I trusted Cindy as the leader of this canoe. She is very good at "drawing" the front of the boat—paddling perpendicular to the boat length, on one side or the other, to quickly "draw" the stem of the boat left or right. Even in the dark, I marveled at her maneuvering as she selected the best route, or "line," forward—sometimes at the last moment. Having paddled alongside her and Terry for years now, I knew she was an excellent teammate to have in the front of the boat.

Watching her work like this, on this dangerous night run, made me feel truly fortunate to have been asked to be her partner. Surely, she and Terry would have made a much better team, if winning was the goal. But for this race, our priority was simply to finish. It was a worthy goal, as most novice teams and solo paddlers drop out well before finishing.

I knew that the invitation to be her partner was something she and Terry had cooked up together. Terry said that he was offering in repayment for all the times that I had "captained" him in his quest, both in solo and in tandem, before he successfully completed the race the previous year. The bigger question for me, however, was why on earth I said, "Yes!"

As we got used to paddling at night and the river before us became more familiar, we began to relax and even started chatting during the straight paddling, slower portions of the river. Gradually, all tension drifted away as we began to feel confident that we could do this, that safely paddling at night was actually possible.

"Surely nobody," I said as we relaxed, "barring an extreme emergency, would ever do this for the fun of it, right?"

Cindy laughed heartily. "That's for sure!" Paddling at night was a unique feature of this race—one that caused many teams to fail in their quest to complete the long-distance canoe race. The odds were heavily stacked against our finishing in our inaugural competition, but we also determined that we stood as good a chance as any novice entering the race. "What's more," I added, "we have the best captain a team could hope to have in Terry. And now we have the monster light, too! How could we possibly fail?"

We grabbed our bags from the trunk, then watched as our tottering old taxi wheezed on down the road, still looking quite crooked while somehow managing to follow the general direction of the road.

"How far is Sango's school?" I asked, rolling my heavy suitcase down the dirt road.

"Not far," came the typical African answer. "Just a ways up this road." I adjusted my backpack and fell in behind Ken and Geoffrey, each lugging a medium-sized duffle.

After thirty minutes of walking, I still saw no signs of a school. "We're actually getting close," said Ken. "The road leading to the school is just there." Just as I'm beginning to wonder again what he means by "close," he stops and motions. "Here it is. I told you it was not far!" Good thing, I thought. I would hate to see what he thinks "far" actually looks like.

We continued down the road—more like a trail at this point—and all of a sudden, the typical school buildings began to appear. We heard children playing, and I knew that we had arrived.

We came upon a bustle of activity. Two young men that Geoffrey hired to assist in the well drilling were busy fabricating the steel tower for the new water tank. A contractor that Geoffrey hired was getting ready to insert the submersible well pump into the well. Meanwhile, schoolchildren were running like ants in an anthill, and ladies were chattering and cooking big pots of food on an outdoor fire.

"Where is Sango?" I asked the headmistress.

She waved her hand. "He's off evangelizing. He should be back this afternoon. He was sorry to not be here to welcome you himself. But I am so glad to welcome you here, Mr. Nicol!"

"Please, call me Bob, or, as you like, Bobu. Mr. Nicol is my dad!"

She laughed immediately, totally getting my Western humor. I like this lady, I thought. And I can't wait to meet Sango. I had Skyped with Sango about a month or so prior, he in his office in Michigan and me in my office in San Antonio. Actually, I spoke with Sango and several of his board members with his charity, Love Inspired Outreach.13 Sango Otieno is a Kenyan, and this school, called Sijoa Primary School, where we will be installing a well and water system, was the elementary school that he and his siblings attended. He is now CrossWay's client, as he is paying us to perform this work. He and Dean connected a while back when he found out that CrossWay was drilling wells and water systems in Kenya.

Normally, we would never have agreed to work this far from our home base in Nairobi. But Dean was so impressed with Sango that he agreed to perform the work, at cost, in this far western province. Quite a long bus ride from Nairobi.

Sango has an amazing story. As a boy, his dad insisted that all of his children attend school so they would not have to work as hard as he and their mother did, just to survive. He was a peasant farmer and diligently saved his earnings to be able to pay for his children's education. Sango worked hard and excelled throughout primary school. When he graduated Class 7, he was eligible to take the exams to enter secondary school; he did so well, he was able to get into a very good secondary school. It was on that achievement that his parents bought Sango his very first pair of shoes—they would not let their boy attend high school barefoot!

When I first heard this story, I was struck dumb. I, like most Westerners, have nothing in my culture to even compare this to. Now that one-time barefoot boy is a PhD and a college professor in the U.S., at Grand Valley State University in Michigan. He told me that he loves teaching, but he had always dreamed of returning and helping those who live and attend school in his community. So he formed his charity with a similar purpose as CrossWay's water well ministry. Yes, the purpose is to offer the gift of water—clean, safe, and plentiful water to remote

[13] Please see http://www.loveinspiredoutreach.org to learn more, and https://issuu.comkristievos/docs /sangoandthewell to read his book.

communities in developing countries—but the main goal is to gain a hearing for the Gospel of Jesus Christ. By receiving the gift of water, Sango hopes that the recipients will hear the good news and accept Jesus as their Lord and Savior. Both ministries seek to bring water and bring life—and all the better if it's eternal life!

I still had not met the man in the flesh. But I already loved him as a brother. It seemed that my initial meeting with "the real life" Sango would have to wait just a bit longer now. Ken and Geoffrey wanted me to go with them to buy the materials for the pipes and faucets for the water distribution system for this school. We would need to drive to Busia— Kenya, not Uganda. Good thing, I guess, as I knew that border crossings aren't so simple here. But I was secretly disappointed, as I really wanted to visit Uganda for the first time.

Off we went, retracing the route we had just followed to get here. We found all of the materials that we needed, and here we were, just a 'stone's throw' from the Ugandan border. I asked my friends to drive near it, so I could at least peer into the neighboring country. Of course, it didn't look much different than Busia, Kenya. How, I wondered as we drove away, did they manage to give these neighboring towns the same name? Or better yet, why?

We returned to the school, and I noticed a *mzungu* couple I hadn't seen before. John and Kimberly Hauenstein, a missionary couple, had heard of "Sango and his well" from other missionaries and had driven over 800 km from their Kenyan home near Voi—about halfway between Nairobi and Mombasa—to meet him. Their main missionary tool was the showing of "The Jesus Film" to evangelize throughout Kenya. Thus, they had packed up their projector system and made this incredible trek. They came to assist Sango, expecting that a large audience would be on hand due to the new well and water system for this very poor, but extremely well-run primary school.

After meeting John and Kimberly, I noticed a tall Kenyan gentleman engaged in a lively discussion with Stella, the headmistress, and several teachers. He finished and turned around as I was standing by the Hauensteins.

"Bobu!" Sango shouted, rushing over to give me a huge hug. "I am so happy to see you! I was not sure that you would come, once I heard about the bus ride that Geof and Ken were bringing you on."

"Are you kidding?" I laughed. "Nothing could stop me. I told you that when we Skyped while still in America."

"Even so, *rafiki yangu* (my friend) I couldn't believe you would come. I told Geof and Ken that if I saw you here, I would surely buy you a goat!"

"Really?" I said, turning to look at my friends. "They never told me that!"

"That is probably because they did not believe me." He smiled and winked at Ken and Geoffrey.

"Well, I can understand that," I said. "They probably know that you are quite prone to lying."

"What?" said Sango, his head whipping around. Then he saw my expression and let out another great laugh, hugging me all the more firmly.

"Okay, my friend, let us complete this project and I will have a goat for you."

"We should be done in, what, two more days, Geoffrey? The pump contractor is just finishing his installation. But we still have to install the underground pipe from the well to the tank so that we can test the ability of the pump to fill the elevated tank. You can see that the tower is almost complete, except for raising the plastic tank and painting the steel. And the ditches have been dug for installing the pipes."

"*Sawa*, okay!" said Sango, clapping me on the shoulder. "Day after tomorrow we can turn on the water and begin filling the tank, right? Then I will bring you your goat!"

"I expect nothing less than the finest of goats."

"You shall have it!" he said, laughing loudly as he walked away.

The remainder of the day was spent installing the pipe in the ditch, connecting it to the well pump piping and on up to the tank platform. But not before we all gathered and made plans to raise the large, 10,000-liter tank and set it on the thick wood planks laid across the upper platform steel. Using ropes tied to the top of the tank and laid over the platform to the back side, half of the men began pulling on the ropes as the other half lifted the tank as high as they could into the air, against the front of the tower structure. When it was well in the air, but still below the platform level, several men climbed the tower, crouched under the tank, and again began lifting it higher. The men on the other side of the tower, holding the ropes, would just pull the slack out of the ropes, to hold the tank in place, while the "lifting team" crawled higher up the tower.

Eventually, we raised the tower high enough to slide onto the platform planks. By now a large crowd of students and teachers had gathered, and they let out a great cheer as the tank slid into its final resting place atop the tower. It struck me how significant this must be for them.

Though water was yet to flow, these children and adults could already sense its imminence by the placing of the water storage tank high up on a tower. To us, it was one of many tasks necessary to bring water out of the ground. To them, it was the promise of a wonderful change that was coming into their lives in just a few short days.

I thanked the Maker of the heavens and provider of all water for the privilege of participating in this work. What a blessing it would be, while serving as a platform for Sango to spread the gospel message to his childhood community.

Geoffrey's welder and his helper had now climbed the tower and begun installing the platform top railing that had been left out to allow the tank to slide onto the platform. They also welded a steel ladder in place on the side of the tower. It was an impressive tower, and I complimented Geoffrey and his helpers. Very sturdy, yet cost effective. It would serve the school well for many years, once we finished welding and paintingit.

The rest of the day until dark was spent installing the galvanized pipes in the trenches and connecting to the well pump piping and tower. Though we could not complete it that day, I wanted to get the pipes connected to the elevated water tank. I had seen the well pump when I first arrived on site, and I had my doubts that it had enough horsepower to lift the water from the well bottom up to the top of the tank, where it would discharge. I had snapped a photo of the pump's nameplate, and I planned to search online for the specifications later at a cyber café I had noticed while driving through Busia.

I told Geoffrey of my concern; he had already discussed this with the contractor, who had told him simply, "Not to worry, this pump has plenty of pressure." I hoped that he was right, but I remained skeptical. Regardless, the contractor left after receiving his payment from Ken, but said to call him if we had any problems and he would return to fix them.

It was becoming clear that we would not complete the underground piping today. I told Geoffrey that I wanted to temporarily run a hose, which we had plenty of in our equipment trailer, from the well pump discharge at ground level to the top of the tank. His workers installed it quickly, and we turned on the power to the pump and waited while it brought the water to the surface through the hose and up into the tank.

I calculated that, based on the size of the pump, this process would take several minutes. It always amuses me how those watching the process expect water to flow the moment the pump is turned on. Only after water has filled the pipe the first time, with a foot valve in place to keep the pipes full, will water begin flowing as soon as the power is turned on. This water, however, seemed to be taking even longer than I estimated, and it was only trickling into the plastic tank on the tower. The observers who were still hanging around this late in the day saw the trickle of water and let out another cheer that, despite the problems I was having with the well, once again surprised and thrilled me.

Just then I heard a great scream behind me, followed by explosive laughter. It was Sango, returning from his meetings in town. When he saw the water flowing, he simply could not contain himself. Sango's exuberance was contagious. Soon he had everyone cheering, laughing, and jumping up and down—including Ken, Geoffrey and myself. Indeed, this was an exciting moment. I could not begin to know the joy that it brought this wonderful Kenyan man. He was accomplishing what he had determined to do, years before. His dreams were, indeed, coming true.

All the excitement made it difficult for me to tell Sango of my concerns for the pump. But finally, I had to. The water, while flowing, was doing so very slowly. It would take many hours, a full day, perhaps, to fill the tank at this pace. It was obvious, even without checking the capacity, that this pump was not powerful enough to fill the tank at a reasonable rate. I climbed up onto the tower and removed the hose from the tank to show Sango how slow it was pumping. I ran a simple test to gauge the flow and found it to be less than five gallons per minute. This would not be acceptable.

Not to worry, I assured Sango. The pump contractor had said that he would fix anything that was not working properly with the pump or piping that he had installed. I told him that I would check the specifications as soon as I could get an Internet connection.

When we left the school for the day, Ken drove me to the local cyber café, and I researched information about the installed well pump.

What I learned was that this pump was certainly not big enough to deliver the water necessary to sustain the school and local community. Since Geoffrey had arranged the contract for the pump, I had him call the contractor and give him the bad news; he promised he'd be back within two days with a bigger pump.

The next day was spent installing permanent underground pipe in place of the temporary hose. We also started installing discharge pipe from the elevated tank to several hand wash stations around school. During this time, the welder finished the final work on the steel water tower. Once that was complete, Ken brought out the paint he had purchased, and he and a helper began painting the structural steel.

While all of this was going on, I was rounding up all of the adults, including the parents and school helpers, for water hygiene training. I provide this important training on all of our well projects. We believe that it is not enough just provide safe, clean water. It is equally important for those using the well to understand how to safely collect and distribute the water, whether in their homes or at an institution like this school.

Normally, as in South Sudan and other Kenyan projects, I would have an interpreter with me. Today, Stella was away from school with Sango, and I could not find anyone to help me who was not already busy with the project or teaching. Well, this would be a first!

Fortunately, I had access to a classroom and a blackboard. Thus, whatever concept I was having trouble explaining, I would simply draw pictures and play a version of charades until they figured out what I was trying to draw. That's easy up to a point—drawing buckets of water, faucets, etc. But try drawing diarrhea! Nonetheless, I was able to convey the important message of protecting the water from the point of collection to the end use. I encouraged the adults to pass this on to everyone that would be collecting this water, whether for their families at home or for the operation of the school.

Sango arrived late in the afternoon, just as we were cleaning up for the day. He was excited to see that the permanent piping was now complete all the way to the elevated tank. I also told him the contractor would arrive the next morning with the new well pump and would replace it.

"Good," said Sango. "I am planning to bring your goat tomorrow! We will have a big celebration. And I will distribute my book to all the children and teachers."

"Your book!" I clapped my hands together. "I had forgotten about that, my friend. I cannot wait to see it. I remember you speaking of it during our Skype meeting."

"Yes, so I'm hopeful that the well pump issue will be resolved and we will have much water flowing to the tank. We will have much to celebrate!"

"That is our intent," I responded. "I cannot wait for the party, and to finally receive my goat!"

The next morning, while waiting for the contractor to arrive, I busied myself with helping to install the distribution pipe and wash stations. Stella had selected locations near where the children normally gathered to eat their lunch, and outside the out houses. One was also placed at the base of the tower for visitors and parents to also have easy access to the water.

The contractor arrived with his men, and they set about removing the submersible pump from the well. I took a picture of the new pump nameplate, so that I could check out the specifications. Somehow I was able to access the Internet right there at the school by way of a "magic wifi stick" that Ken had loaned me. This created access to Safaricom, the national (and international, as it is found in most of East Africa) cell phone/Internet provider.

What I found appeared to meet our needs. This pump would be able to push twelve gallons per minute up to the tank. This would allow the tank to fill in less than four hours, which was more than three times as fast as the first pump, and at one third the cost.

Sango arrived at the school just as the contractor was finishing the installation. He was anxious to see how the new pump performed. So was I! But we would all have to wait to gauge its power to move water efficiently. Several of the joints on the piping from the pump to the tank had not been tightened properly and were leaking water. These would have to be fixed before we could restart the well pump test. This turned out to be a bigger job than initially anticipated and ended up consuming the rest of the morning and the early afternoon.

As soon as Geoffrey assured us the leaks were fixed, we restarted the pump. Water was flowing into the tank quicker than with the previous pump, but it still did not seem adequate, nor did it appear to meet the specifications I had looked up. Once again, I removed the supply line into the tank to gauge the flow rate in my primitive way. I determined that it was still only pumping about seven to eight gallons per minute. This would not do.

The contractor also realized that this was a problem, but neither of us could figure out the cause. Finally, I asked him if he had a meter to check the voltage coming into the pump control panel. He grabbed one from his supplies, and sure enough, the voltage showed at less than 200 volts. It should have been 230 volts. Then he noticed that the wires carrying the power into the control panel appeared to be undersized. We checked the voltage at the main breaker and found that it was in excess of 230 volts.

The problem was with the wiring to the panel, which had been installed by a local electrician. The pump contractor said that he might have enough of the correct size cable in his truck, and Sango told him that he would pay him to replace the undersized cables and reconnect to the pump. The contractor was happy to do that, as he wanted to see this work to a successful completion, as well.

Fortunately, he completed the task quickly, and we restarted the pump. Immediately, water started flowing into the tank at a much higher rate than before. When I reran my flow tests, I concluded that it was now pushing water at eleven to twelve gallons per minute. Sango's face burst into a bright smile when he heard this news.

Now we just had to complete the last few wash stations and backfill all the pipe trenches, as well as the drilling mud pit. Sango was excited to see the pump working well. He said that he had to leave for just a bit to run some errands, but he'd be back soon.

When he returned a few hours later, most of the work was complete. Good thing, too, because on a short rope behind him, he was leading a young goat! He gathered everyone under the large mango tree and presented me with my gift. I told him that I was honored, and that this was only the second time CrossWay had ever been given a goat. (The first was a number of years ago in South Sudan, and was also a gift for completing a community water project.)

After the short ceremony, I handed my prize to some men standing by, one of whom carried a large *panga* (machete) in hand. The last I saw of my goat, he was being led behind one of the classroom buildings to be slaughtered, after which the ladies would begin preparing it for the celebration feast.

Sango and Stella met with the students, who were now gathered in the middle of the large courtyard. He told them the story of his life, how he had grown up in this school as a young boy. He then passed out a copy of his booklet to each student, "Sango and the Well." In his book, he gives a lot of credit to his father for the sacrifices he made to send him and his sister to school. And he gives all of the glory to God for everything that he has ever accomplished. What an impressive role model he is for every one of these children!

To emerge from this poor rural school to become a professor in a university in the U.S. is quite a compelling story. And now each of them had his story to read again and again, whenever they needed motivation or felt discouraged or unimportant. The students aren't the only ones to feel awed by this man—I, along with the teachers, parents, and our CrossWay team in the States, are impressed with how Sango conducts himself, and how he continues to give back to his homeland and his people. We all feel blessed to know him and are honored to call him *rafiki* –friend.

We have to say goodbye to Sango tonight, as well as to all of the staff and parent helpers at the school, as we have get a very early (5 AM) start on our journey back to Nairobi. But first, we will celebrate—thanks to my delicious goat-present—and thank God for all his blessings on our water well work for this wonderful school and nearby community.

The night before the race, I couldn't sleep. Even though I knew this would be my last night in a comfy bed for several days—and possibly my last shut-eye for as many days—I still found myself awake very early and could not fall back asleep. Great, I thought, now I'll probably pass out in the middle of the night while cruising down the river. These thoughts, unsurprisingly, did not help me in my sleeplessness.

I turned my thoughts to the daunting race that loomed ever closer, wondering if we were prepared. I thought about our early attempts to paddle Terry's sleek, hydrodynamic missile. He assured us that if we could master this canoe, it would convey us through the course with the least amount of effort. Easier said than done. The first and only time that Cindy and I attempted to paddle his canoe was an utter disaster. We couldn't stay afloat.

In fact, it was difficult to board it without tipping over. While it was very swift in the water, it had a high center of gravity, and we were simply not able to paddle smoothly without rocking it back and forth. At one point, we ran headlong into a logjam and were quickly flipped out of the boat and into the swirling hydraulic below. I honestly thought that one of us was going to drown. We made it out eventually, however, and had to haul the canoe while swimming to the shore. Decision made. This would not be the canoe for us.

We chose instead, to go with their sturdy Alumicraft canoe. It was not fast—quite the contrary. But it was extremely steady in any type of water. And it was durable, something that we would have to rely on sooner than we could have ever anticipated.

It turns out replaying a nightmare experience was just the tonic I needed to drift back into dreamland. I was surprised to awaken hours later from a deep sleep to my alarm. I had spent the night at Terry and Cindy's house, since they live only a 15-minute drive to the starting point at the regionally famous Aquarena Springs in San Marcos—a small college town between San Antonio and Austin where my oldest daughter, Breanne, would one day attend Texas State University. Although the race would not officially start until 9:00, we had plenty of prep work to do after we hauled the canoe to the Springs.

Grabbing coffee, a breakfast bar, and my daily vitamins, I joined Terry and Cindy in loading up the car, as the canoe was already strapped to the rack on top. It was well before dawn as we set off on our adventure.

Cindy and I were silent, perhaps with apprehension, so Terry filled the quiet with stories about his experiences in the final moments leading up to a race. It was easy to find Terry's stories amusing; he has a real knack for storytelling. And I could tell that the fact that he got Cindy and me laughing that frigid morning made him quite satisfied. As our coach, he was helping to get his team's minds off of the daunting task in front of them.

Adding to my nerves was the fact that our longest practice run had only been five hours. This race would require at least ten times that amount. No amount of practice would even come close to the rigor of the actual race. I glanced at Cindy, who sat silent, her face stoic and still. I knew we both wanted the same thing: to get on the river and get this party started. Only then could we stop thinking about it, and just concentrate on doing it.

A number of teams were already unloading their boats and making them ready when we arrived. The Springs actually form into a large natural lake. Within hours after the start of the race, the usual crowd of tourists would arrive to ride one of the glass-bottom boats, viewing the fish, creatures, and flora below. The lake is deep enough that you can't stand beside your boat; thus, the teams and individual paddlers have to start from the shore and then paddle into position.

At the front of the pack are the top qualifying individuals and teams, based on their order of finish in the much shorter qualifying race, held one month prior. We had discussed competing in that event, as it is a good opportunity to test endurance. In the end, we decided to skip it, since it only covered sections of the course that we were already quite familiar with. Instead, we focused on several difficult segments that we had prioritized in our overall race prep planning. Besides, we reasoned, we were never gunning to win this race. Our one and only goal was to finish. Our starting order didn't matter too much.

We jumped out as soon as we parked and joined the teams in getting ready. In short order, we had our aluminum canoe loaded with all of our gear, including food for two days and our initial charge of drinking water. According to the strict race rules, everything needed for the race, including all clothes and food, had to be in the canoes from the beginning of the race. Your named captain (Terry) was the only one who could replenish your ice and water during the race. Thus, anything that you did not want to get totally soaked, like food, was stored in waterproof pouches in the canoe.

Terry gave us some final advice on getting through the crowded beginning of the race. With around forty-three boats in the competition, they had to line us up, six across, just to get all the boats to fit. We ended up with only one boat to our port side, with four more to starboard.

Fortunately, we intended to maneuver to our left, as instructed by our captain, to be in the best position to wend our way through the maze of boats, all heading toward the initial rapids at the end of the Aquarena

Springs pool. The key was to avoid getting rammed by another boat, pushed off course, or catching an errant paddle to the head!

After hugging us both, and giving Cindy a big goodbye kiss, Terry and I carried the canoe and lowered it into the water. He helped both of us into the canoe and shoved us off. We then glided into the thick of the boats and took our place near the back third of the pack, the spot assigned to us by the race officials. We would be well behind all of the qualifying race finishers, and also behind the larger 3- and 4-man teams. The two rows behind us were other 2-man boats and all of the non-qualifying solo paddlers, including kayaks and one-man canoes. I glanced around and noticed several mixed doubles team like us, as well as a couple of all-women teams.

My attention was drawn to the solo competitors, several of whom were women. Having acted as captain for one of Terry's solo efforts, I knew how difficult this race would be for these hardy individuals. As experienced a canoeist that Terry was, there are some things that you just can't plan for. That year I had first captained for Terry, he had the unfortunate experience of breaking his steel rudder cable. He tried several times to repair it, with pieces of broken cable that he found after scouring the banks. But eventually, they all would break, until finally, he was forced to quit. I gazed in awe at the solo paddlers. I expected to see several of them down the river, and I was hopeful that some of them would cross the finish line, as well.

I glanced around at our fellow racers. Cindy and I were dressed like many of the contestants, but certainly not as brightly as some of them. For the cool and overcast morning, we wore our long sleeve shirts and light-colored tights, for maximum UV protection from the hot Texas sun. We also wore baseball caps connected by safety pins and a tether line to our shirts, and our sunglasses were similarly secured with a band. You don't want to risk losing these important items while traversing wicked rapids and overhanging tree branches.

Time seemed to stand still as we sat there, but it was probably only ten or fifteen minutes. At last, an official emerged from the far side of the Springs, delivered last minute instructions, and then started the countdown, finally firing the gun. The race was on!

I had witnessed the gun shots and the first few minutes of this race before, but always from the shore. Being in the thick of this utter mayhem was quite another experience! Over a hundred paddlers in over forty boats are heading for the same narrow entrance; paddles are flying, water is churning, and the noise from the activity on the water and the shouting from the shore is deafening. I silently blessed Terry for giving us a focal point to aim at during these crazy first thirty seconds. Cindy paddled steadily towards our first goal, and I had only to provide power paddling while steering from the stern.

Naturally, there were a number of boats that were trying to take the same line as us. Rather than plowing into them or risk being plowed into ourselves, we paced ourselves to gain some open water before heading into the first rapids. Our efforts paid off. We were able to maneuver through the rapids in single file with the other boats. All at once, the insanity of the race start was over. Hooray! We had survived the first obstacle. Believe me, not every boat does!

Cindy and I transitioned into our "power cruising" mode—the one we had perfected through many hours on the river. Many boats charged in front of us, some trying to pass us as we endeavored to pass others. Our firm mindset was that none of them was our competition. If we could finish, in our minds, we would be winners. I wished nothing but the best to all those exceptional multi-man boats set on winning the race. We would soon learn the hard way that not all paddlers wished us the same good luck.

Our next goal was passing the Rio Vista Dam. Low level or not, this dam presented a challenge. During the Water Safari, the dilemma in crossing a dam is always between "shooting the V" or "portaging." The Rio Vista dam is only several feet high, so it is possible to paddle to one side of the V and jump the canoe onto the top of the concrete dam. You then quickly lower your boat over the dam and set it back in the water for a really short, and often quick, portage. The goal in shooting the V is to keep the stem of the boat from sinking too low and taking on a lot of water, which always results in a submerged boat (and paddlers) and can cause serious injury.

For us, there was no question. Cindy and Terry had maneuvered this many times, and even Linda and I had done it once or twice. While a bit scary, it was not actually that difficult or requiring any great level of skill. You just had to make sure that you kept your boat perpendicular to the dam axis—in other words, heading straight down river. And you didn't need a lot of speed. The thrust of the entire flow of the river gushing through this 6-foot notch would provide more than enough momentum. I knew that we would shoot the V—my only question was what effect the added weight of our supplies would have on the landing.

We were about to find out, as it was coming up around the next corner. We knew a large crowd would be gathered at this point, too, as this was, after the start, the most exciting viewing spot on the course. Most of the contestants would pass through this dam in a relatively short period of time; in fact, it was difficult to watch the start of the race, then drive to this park in time to see many of the boats flying over the dam. For that reason, many veteran watchers (and previous contestants) would skip the beginning of the race and come straight to Rio Vista Dam. If not, you could surely expect to miss the lead multi-man boats.

Sailing smoothly onto the "lake" above Rio Vista Dam, Cindy quickly surveyed the area for any crashed boats, or those in the process of portaging over the dam or re-starting their boats below the dam. Only one team was lowering their canoe over the dam, but well away from the V. There was also a two-man canoe in front of us on the lake, but about to get in position to shoot the V. Glancing back, I saw another aluminum boat with two men paddling. I hollered at Cindy that we should pick it up, to stay well ahead of them while keeping distance behind the two-man boat in front of us.

We didn't have much time to think. As soon as we saw the front boat clear the dam completely, we paddled hard towards the center of the V. I had crossed this dam before in a canoe and in inner tubes, but this time carried more pressure. Quite a crowd was gathered to watch this spectacle. In fact, in previous years, ESPN had one of their camera crews stationed here as part of the race coverage, and sometimes even a national magazine would show up, such as Sports Illustrated, who ran a feature on the race several years prior.

We shot the V in style (for us), and it was pretty exciting. Still, I knew we would not make a good cover story photo or even a video snippet, what with our steady and slow aluminum craft. But that was fine with us. We weren't here to show off, only to make it to the end in one piece. Cindy raised her paddle high above her head, screaming with delight while leaning as far back in the boat as she could without ejecting from her seat. I followed behind in similar fashion, but without the scream

(I think). Our movements helped keep the stem from sinking too low. We did take on some water, but it was not enough to cause us to pull over and dump it out. First obstacle down!

A thrilling start, for sure, but we still had another 250+ miles to go, and many more dams that we would not be able to shoot. The San Marcos River began to look familiar; Cindy and I had run this river, particularly the upper segments, dozens of times.

We came around a familiar bend, under the Interstate 35 overpass, and had a quick change of plans. Due to some reconstruction on the highway, the river was impassable. We would have to portage this crossing. We may have grumbled a bit about the highway department in the process.

Back in the water, we settled in for a familiar ride. The river was shockingly low, even lower than when we had last practiced. We were occasionally dragging bottom, due to our heavy load, but fortunately, we were not having to portage. So far, so good.

Then suddenly, an unexpected disaster. The two-man aluminum boat that had been behind us from the beginning had been gaining on us. For some reason, they chose this meandering, low-level segment of the river to attempt to pass us. As we came around a small rapid, we drifted a bit wide, and they rushed to pass us on the inside of the bend. There was clearly no room for two boats at this bend, and we were still in front of them, yet still they were paddling frantically, trying to catch and pass us.

It was plain to see their boat was out of control. Just as we were about to complete the curve, which would have given them plenty of straight river to pass, they rammed hard into the side of our boat, nearly tipping us over. "What are you doing?" I yelled. "This is no place to pass!"

They said nothing, just kept paddling madly down the river. We would not see them again for the remainder of the race and actually assumed that they dropped out, as bad as they were at paddling. It didn't appear that the collision had caused any permanent damage, other than a big dent in the side of my canoe, so we shook off the nerves and kept going.

We had dumped out the small amount of water we took on at the first dam when we made the unscheduled portage around the I-35 overpass. Imagine my surprise, then, when I noticed water again in the bottom of the canoe. When we moved into shallow water, we stopped briefly to dump it. Not long after, the bottom began filling with water again. I sighed. Those yahoos had done more damage than I had thought. We stopped to dump again, and I took a good look at the dented area. Sure enough, there was a jagged crack in the lower side of the boat. We would have to fix it, or the race was over for us right here.

We were demoralized and started spouting frustration about the jerks that had rammed our boat. Maybe they meant to ram us! To them, we may have been their chief competition, as the aluminum class is usually small. Who knows, we might even be the only two boats in our class! Too bad they didn't realize we weren't in a race against them; their passing could have been much more civil. Oh well, I thought, no use mulling over it. I'll need all my focus to fix this leak or we're sunk—literally!

Before long, we reached the first obvious portage dam, Cummings Dam. Another impassible dam on the San Marcos, one we knew well and had portaged many times. The four of us even did it one time at night, under a full moon. This time we were passing with less leisurely and romantic emotions.

After pulling in to the take-out point and dumping out our canoe one more time, we carried it to a grassy area just off the bank, below the dam. We inspected the damage closer and decided to patch it. As I mentioned, everything you need must be in your canoe already. This isn't a NASCAR or Indy race—there is no pit crew!

Cindy rummaged through our supplies and found a butane lighter and some duct tape. We used a dry T-shirt and the lighter to thoroughly dry the side of the boat at the hole, inside and out. We then applied several layers of duct tape to both sides. After each of the layers, we would apply heat from the butane lighter, hoping it might melt some of the tape's adhesive into the cracks. We repacked the supplies and dragged the boat back to the river, completing the portage below the dam, and dropped the boat back into the water to test our repair job. There was no apparent leakage, so we gladly piled back into the canoe and headed downriver.

While making our repair, a number of boats had passed us by. But we weren't concerned. We knew we'd pass most of them in the upcoming Cottonseed Rapids, especially the novices. Even for skilled paddlers, Cottonseed, with its ever-changing conditions, was a challenge.

True to course, as we were selecting our best line through the rapids, we saw a number of boats that had overturned or gone off course. Several boats were being dumped out on the banks and set back in the water; in fact, we had to change our course just to avoid some of them. Yet again, onlookers crowded the banks, as this was an easy access point from the road, and watching boats maneuver through Cottonseed could be exciting.

Terry had joined the crowd here but was down in the shallow bank area below the rapids: He was visibly upset, so we pulled over to the bank for a short pow-wow. Cindy told him about the boat that had rammed us early in the race, and we showed him the repair job.

Terry was impressed with our makeshift patch. Then he became furious at the guys that ran into us. He promised to catch up with them downriver and let them know the damage they had caused. "In the meantime," he said sharply, "you're going to have to hustle to make Palmetto before dark. You lost more than an hour back there."

"We know," replied Cindy. "Let's stop talking so we can get back on the river."

Terry squeezed her shoulder. "Okay, baby. I won't see you at Martindale, but I'll catch up to you at Staples dam portage. After you portage the Martindale Dam, you should be at Staples by 2 PM." I was familiar with Staples, as we had traversed it often, including starting from there on our night practice run. I was eager to get back on the river as well, and praying we could make up for lost time.

By the time we arrived at Staples, which was a checkpoint for the race officials, we had gained back some time. But we were still almost 45 minutes behind our original plan. We were discouraged, as we had worked hard and paddled furiously all afternoon to get back on track. It had also started raining on us. During the portage, we made a quick stop by a walkway along a restaurant situated along the river bank.

Terry met us there and replaced our water bottles with fresh water and ice. He also cautioned both of us for not drinking enough. I held back my laughter, as I remembered the many times I had yelled at Terry for the exact same thing, when I had served as his captain. He wasn't in the mood to laugh today, I guess. He finished replacing our water, and he said that he would see us next at one of the highway crossings, Fentress or Stairtown, well before we would reach the next major portage at the Luling Dam.

The next several hours progressed much the same. Lots of production paddling, few rapids, and a portage every now and then to keep things interesting. I was amused by remembering how much I used to dread portages while making a fun day run on the river. Now, I was actually looking forward to them, as it gave us a chance to get out of the boat and stretch our legs. And no regrets on losing time, since the portages were part of the race.

By the time we made it to Luling, it was hot again. Our soaked clothes had dried in the scorching sun, then re-soaked with our sweat. Terry met us at Luling, but stayed high up on the opposite bank of this city park, where quite a number of TWS enthusiasts had gathered to watch the boats portage the dam. We made the portage easily, and still had plenty of water to make it to Palmetto State Park, another fifteen river miles. We were starting to realize that we would not be there before dark, as we had planned. Then again, we planned to paddle all night anyway, so we were not that concerned.

The team and I were back at the school at 5 the next morning. We had loaded both the trailer and the drill rig the evening before, so all we had to do was hitch up the trucks and depart. Since Ken was used to driving the CrossWay Land Cruiser, we hitched it to the heavy equipment and drill pipe trailer. Then we hitched Geoffrey's light Isuzu truck to the drill rig. The two young workers would ride with Ken, and I would ride with Geoffrey and share the driving. We waved goodbye to the school custodian, the only one at the school this early.

As is Ken's style, he put the pedal to the metal, and we soon lost sight of him. As we came into a small town up the road, we saw him pulled over at the side of the road. "What's wrong?" we asked, driving up next to him.

"Nothing," he said. "Just stopped to let you catch up to us." He and Geoffrey launched into their usual argument, with Geoffrey complaining that Ken drove too fast and Ken sniffing that Geoffrey drove too slow.

I stepped in, breaking it up. "What's the big hurry anyway?" Ken held out his hands, explaining that it would take all day to drive back to

Nairobi. He wanted to get back before dark, preferring to not have to pull the trailer in the dark.

"I agree," I said. "But we have almost twelve hours of light still remaining. Shouldn't that be enough time for us to get back before dark?" Ken shuffled his feet, and I knew he didn't have a response. He just hates to drive slow.

"Look," I sighed, "if you can slow down just a little, then maybe Geoffrey can speed up a little bit, and we can all be happy, okay?" Both men nodded. "Anyway, we need to travel together, in case one of us has mechanical problems." They agreed that this made good sense and promised to make an effort to caravan together.

The plan worked—for about 10 or 12 km. But somewhere in the next town, as we were winding our way through traffic, Ken took off and left us for good! I guess he'd had his fill of Geoffrey's careful driving. As it turned out, my premonition for needing to stick together would turn out to be well-founded.

With the pressure of keeping up with Ken now dissolved, Geoffrey relaxed and we eased into a good conversation. The long ride was even becoming quite enjoyable. Unfortunately, that ended abruptly when we were motioned to pull over by a policeman standing at the edge of the road. He must have noticed my face—mind you, not the face of a criminal, wanted in Kenya for acts against the state, but the face of a *mzungu*.

By now, this had happened to me quite a number of times, usually in and near the airport. The Kenyan police will stop cars with white drivers or passengers; they'll manufacture some charge, like not wearing a seatbelt or not carrying the right safety devices in your trunk, then threaten you with large fines or taking you to the police station. At first, I was taken aback by this, thinking that we were in real trouble. I soon learned that all they wanted was "*kitu kidogo*"—a "small" amount of money as a bribe. I also learned that the threat of taking you into the police station was quite hollow. Most cops in Kenya don't even have cars.

In fact, the first time I was driving through the big industrial city of Mombasa, I was stopped by a standing traffic cop. He told me that I violated traffic, and then he climbed importunately into my passenger seat and told me to take him to the police station. "Where's that?" I asked.

"I'll show you," he said. So off we went. On the way, when I told him why I was in Kenya, he let me go. Even better, he asked me to pull over and let him out! Which I immediately did. But not before I asked him for directions to where I was headed when he stopped me—to the Likoni Ferry, and the South Coast, beyond.

This traffic stop with Geoffrey was obvious. He only wanted *kidogo*. For some reason, Geoffrey was arguing with him; turns out he wanted to see Geoffrey's driver's license. But Geoffrey was ardently refusing. He confessed to me, when the cop stepped away briefly, that his license had just expired and he had not renewed it. He grumbled that the officer wanted more than the "normal fee" of a few hundred shillings.

"How much does he want?" I asked. Geoffrey shrugged. "Offer him 500 KES."

Geoffrey headed over to the cop, and they began arguing back and forth. I was worried Geoffrey was going to get arrested; then again, the guy didn't have a police car. What was he going to do, walk Geoffrey to the station in handcuffs?

Geoffrey trotted back to the car. "He wants 1,000 KES (about $12 USD).

I pulled out my wallet. "Here is another 500. Just pay him and let's get going."

"No, that's too much," he huffed.

"Look, I'm in no mood to negotiate. You should not have let your license expire. Then we would only be talking about a few hundred shillings, right? Now, pay him and let's go."

I told him to get the cop's name and badge number, too. Geoffrey handed him the money, and as he spoke to him, the policeman looked startled. He turned and stared me down as he showed Geoffrey his name and number badge. I just stared right back at him, secretly praying this wouldn't cause him to change his mind.

At last, we were free. We jumped back in the car and took off (but not too fast). Soon, we pulled into the city of Kisumu, on the northern coast of Lake Victoria. We found a hotel that Geoffrey said had a good restaurant, and we planned to eat breakfast there. But first, said Geoffrey, he knew a place nearby where he could get his license renewed. Off he went, looking for a *boda boda* (motorcycle) rider to take him to the license station.

No sooner had he left than I stalled the truck while trying to back the trailer into a tight spot. I'm already bad at backing trailers, and this rig trailer was single axle—making it especially "squirrely" for a novice like me. Now I was stuck in the middle of a city street and had to unhitch the trailer. I asked a couple of guys standing nearby on the corner to please help me push-start the truck. They jumped in, and fortunately, it "caught" on the first try; I immediately backed up, and they re-hitched the trailer for me. I gave them *kidogo* and thanked them profusely for their help.

Geoffrey returned shortly with his new license, and I recounted my latest little adventure. We went inside the restaurant and ordered breakfast, finally able to relax a bit from the activity of the morning. Two *wazunga* ladies came in and startled at seeing me. They must have been locals or frequent visitors who thought they knew all the *wazungas* in Kisumu.

After breakfast, we tried to start the truck again. No luck. Fortunately, the same guys were still hanging around, so after Geoffrey un-hitched the rig trailer, we once again enlisted their help in pushing the truck. Finally, we were on our way again. This time, I was on driving duty. I had to quickly re-learn how to shift with my left hand and the truck's floor-mounted shifter. Although I had driven both Geoffrey's truck and our Land Cruiser, it had been a while. That's the nature of remote missionary work—picking up a lot of things "on the fly!"

By the time we drove out of Kisumu and back into the countryside, I felt comfortable driving on the left side of the highway—from the right side of the front seat. Good thing, too, because we were headed back onto that 50 km detour, the one I thought might kill us on the bus ride up here!

In the light of day, I could see why the bus trip had sounded so scary. There were long stretches of dirt road, followed by only a few kilometers or less of new paving. On top of that (literally), there was heavy truck and bus traffic. I had to maintain my distance on the dirt road portions to keep from being blinded by all the dust they kicked up.

When I would come to the paved road portions, I looked for opportunities to pass these road offenders. Only trouble was, Geoffrey's truck had little power, and we were pulling the drill rig trailer. Thus, there was not a lot of passing going on.

As it turned out, it was not the trucks and buses traveling in front of us that I needed to worry about. It was those hurtling toward me on the other side that scared me the most. The paved areas seemed to be in the most winding, hilly parts of the detour, and these bus and big truck drivers did not slow down for the curves. More than once, I had to swerve into the edge of the road to keep from being hit by them.

And there was another problem. Due to the new pavement and the lack of shoulders, the drop off from the edge of the pavement could be as much as six inches! I was paranoid that we would fall off the edge of the pavement and break an axle. So in the midst of nimbly navigating this traffic insanity, I tried to keep one eye on the passenger rear view mirror where I could keep tabs on the trailer wheels and the edge of the pavement.

I'm sure by now you're thinking, "That's a lot to handle there, Bob." But wait! There's more! Every couple of miles, they had inserted multiple speed bumps onto this brand new pavement. Three or four at a time!

They were hard to see, and without warning, I would hit them—hard. Several times, Geoffrey hollered at me just in time to let me know they were approaching.

So let me paint you the full picture: I'm driving along on smooth pavement. The road is winding and quite hilly. I'm keeping my eyes wide open for crazy (sometimes referred to as jihadist) tractor-trailer drivers coming at me on my right while keeping a steady eye on the passenger side mirror and the trailer wheels behind. Speed bumps pop up without warning, so I find myself braking and downshifting (left handed, mind you) fairly often. Sounds like the perfect storm, huh?

Well, it was. I was sailing down the bottom of a steep hill on the curve, and a tractor-trailer was charging toward me, more or less in the middle of the road. I swung over toward the shoulder as far as I could go without the wheels coming off the pavement. Just then, a series of three or four speed bumps appeared out of nowhere, and neither Geoffrey or I saw them.

Hitting those speed bumps at such a high speed caused the trailer to bounce off the edge of the pavement and onto the shoulder, some six inches below. There was a loud bang followed by a horrible shaking, followed by the sound of something dragging behind.

I slammed on the brakes, right there in the road, and we jumped out to inspect the damage. The hitch mount had broken on the back of Geoffrey's truck, and the trailer hitch, still connected to the truck by the chains (thank God for the chains), had dragged along and embedded itself into the pavement. We quickly disconnected the chains from the truck, and I drove the truck off the edge of the road. I glanced over the edge and realized that it dropped off to a deep ravine—easily several hundred feet below!

By the time I got back to Geoffrey and the drill rig trailer, there were half a dozen men, women and children standing around. There had been no towns or people for miles. Where in the world did these people come from? I wondered. I didn't have a whole lot of time to muse on that. We needed to get the drill rig out of the middle of the road.

Geoffrey and I started dragging it towards the edge of the pavement, taking special care not to let it get away from us and carom down the side of the mountain! A young man and a younger boy jumped in to help us. We eased the rig to the side of the road, safely off of the pavement, then Geoffrey hollered, "*mawe mbili*" to the young boy. He disappeared for a minute, returning shortly with two large stones.

Geoffrey inserted a stone under one of the wheels, and the young man put one behind the other wheel, to keep the trailer from rolling down the hill. I looked at Geoffrey. "What do we do now?" I was at a loss, unaccustomed to breakdowns in the middle of nowhere. In Africa. We had not seen a decent-sized town in over an hour.

Geoffrey looked unconcerned. "We will find a *fundi*, a welder, and get it fixed."

Right, I thought. We will find a welder. Just like that. "I don't know, let me ask these people," he said, in his unflappable manner.

"Okay, why not?" I answered, trying my best to capture some of his courage, whether real or imaginary. I needed something to grab onto to keep me from shaking off this mountain. "Sure, seems like a good idea to me."

Geoffrey started speaking with the young man that had helped us move the rig off the road. A number of locals (local to where? I still wondered) had gathered around the rig, fascinated by it. Some seemed to be trying to explain to the others what this kind of contraption was used for.

Geoffrey came back over to me. "This young man says there's a small village just a few kilometers away. I think I remember seeing it."

"And there's a welder there?"

"I don't know, but we can drive there and find out." Once again, I was astounded at Geoffrey's calm, matter-of-fact manner. Sure, I conceded. We'll just jump in the truck and drive back to the village, and in no time we'll have the hitch repaired and be back on the road. Maybe Geoffrey was confident, but I was not having it. We had almost been run off a mountain by a massive tractor-trailer, causing us to spill our drill rig in the middle of a busy highway. While moving it off the highway, it nearly rolled off a steep cliff. And now, in the middle of nowhere, we needed to find a skilled welder to repair our truck.

And would we simply leave our trailer-mounted, ready-to-roll drill rig sitting here on this precipice? With these people staring at it? And again, who are all these people and where did they come from? I couldn't have invented this story; it was all too strange, and too unsettling for my taste.

My only recourse in that moment of panic was to send up a prayer to the God of the unfathomable and the mundane. I knew He would hear all prayers, even one about a trailer in the middle of nowhere, Africa. I needed some relief from this drama that had gotten too big for me. Just give it all to God, I told myself. Stop worrying and cowboy up!

We didn't have many choices before us. Geoffrey didn't feel comfortable leaving me here alone to watch the rig with all these strangers. And he couldn't send me off to look for a *fundi*—here in the bush, people wouldn't speak much English, and my Swahili was limited enough, much less tribal dialects. We decided to leave the rig and travel together.

Geoffrey put the young man in charge, asking him to carefully guard our rig until we came back. Naturally, a reward was offered or implied. I let Geoffrey get back in the driver's seat, as I was still shaken up from our little incident. As we drove away, I glanced at the group of strangers again. There were no houses or huts that I could observe, yet within minutes of the incident, all these people appeared. I concluded that God must have sent them to us—guardian angels in the form of bush natives! This made me feel calmer about leaving our expensive drill rig in their hands, while we went on our search for a *fundi*.

In less than ten kilometers, we saw a small village just off the highway, but no obvious way to reach it. The construction of this new highway had cut off the access road to the village. We finally noticed a road leaving the highway in the general direction of the village, but we would have to climb up a steep bank from the asphalt pavement. Geoffrey, who is normally timid in these situations, gunned the gas pedal and mounted the steep climb on the first try. Maybe today's events made him brave!

In no time, we found the "main street." And wouldn't you just know it? Halfway down the badly rutted dirt road, we stopped in front of—you guessed it—a welding shop! The *fundi* approached me, staring at me in curiosity. Geoffrey came around the truck, greeted him, and led him to the back to show him our problem.

As they talked, I looked around. A young lady, presumably the wife or daughter, and two young children were also looking at me very strangely. I glanced up into the town and observed every other person in sight also staring at me. Geoffrey walked over then and could see I was agitated. "It's okay, Bobu. They are not used to seeing a *mzungu* in their town." He laughed. "Once again, you will be the subject of discussion around every dinner table here tonight!"

I relaxed. "That's okay," I grinned. "I'm getting kind of used to that."

"We are in luck. The *fundi* can fix the hitch. He will start on it right away."

Incredible. I would never have guessed that there would even be a welder in this tiny little town, much less that he could fix our hitch.

"*Munga ni mwema*! God is good!" I said.

"*Wakati wote*! All the time!" returned Geoffrey.

I watched the welder work. It seemed he was welding several pieces of rebar together, end-to-end. Then he connected one end of these bars to his big welding machine, way in the back of his shop. To the other end of the bars he clamped one end of his welding cable, and then clamped the other end to the truck bumper. Then I figured out what he was doing—he didn't have a long enough welding cable to extend from the big welder through the shop and out to the street. So he had to use the rebar to extend and connect his ground cable. I shook my head in amazement.

The ingenuity of these Kenyans is incredible. I looked up the road and noticed a small store. "Hey, Geoffrey," I said, "How about I go get us something to drink while you stay here with the *fundi*?"

As I walked toward the *duka*, I could sense that everyone in town was still watching me. I began to notice people appearing in the shop entrances, gawking at me. Man, I thought, this must be how Kobe Bryant feels walking in downtown L.A.! I laughed at the thought. "Enjoy it, Bobu—this might be the closest to fame you'll ever get."

I opened the door to the *duka* and asked the pretty young girl at the counter if she had any sodas—*baridi sana*, very cold? She giggled and pointed to a beverage cooler in the corner. I grabbed two sodas from the cooler and carried them back to the counter. "Wow!" I grinned. "These are really *baridi sana*! How much?"

"One-fifty bob," she replied. That would be 150 KES. I gave her 250 KES, knowing that they usually charged a bottle deposit fee. She looked at the money, confused. "For the bottles," I pointed, "and also *kidogo* for you."

"Oh!" She smiled brightly. "*Asante sana* (thank you very much)!"

I walked back to the welding shop under the staring gaze of the entire city, I felt. Geoffrey and I chugged our cold sodas, sitting on a bench in the shade of the welding shop, watching the *fundi* perform his magic.

I marveled at the entire scene. How on earth had we found our way, within thirty minutes of breaking down, to this tiny village—and one with a capable welder? Surely God had a hand in all of this. Indeed, He was showing me something new. He was rewarding us for trusting him.

Less than an hour ago, I was quite distraught. And for good reason, I had concluded. If only we had stayed together, as a two-vehicle caravan, then this side trip would not have been necessary. Ken could have parked the Land Cruiser next to Geoffrey's truck, and our welder could have repaired the broken hitch with our own large welding machine that was in the back of his truck!

I took another sip of my soda and smiled. On the other hand, I thought, I would not have had the opportunity to visit this cute little village. Surely it's not on any travel adventure destination list. Even if it were, I mused, who could find it? Nor would I have experienced the curious gaze of the watchful villagers; nor enjoy the sweet smile of the pretty young *duka* girl; nor share a refreshing cold soda (which I rarely allow myself) with my friend, while playing "peek-a-boo" with the welder's two children who had, by now, quite warmed up to me.

I was no longer distraught. In fact, I was feeling pretty good—glad, even, that we had encountered this breakdown. Was that crazy?

Perhaps. All I knew was I felt extremely blessed to be experiencing these things.

The welder came around from the back of the truck and announced that he was finished. Geoffrey and I walked over to inspect the work.

Indeed, the bumper hitch looked stronger than ever. He had done a masterful job. I asked him how much I owed him and couldn't believe it when he said, "500 shillings." I saw that Geoffrey was about to start negotiating with him. He can't help it—it's all part of being a Kenyan, I realized a long time ago. But this time, I put a hand on his arm and said to the welder, "That's fine." I handed him 1,000 shillings (about $12) and told him to keep the rest—it was *kidogo*.

We could have been swept right into his big gap-toothed smile! I would have given him 5,000 shillings, and it would have been well worth it. Geoffrey would probably have hit me! I felt like I wanted to pay *somebody*, though, for this wonderful experience that rose out of tragedy. So I quickly thanked God—for ALL of it.

We drove past the *duka* to turn around. As we passed by, the young girl waved at me, sporting her lovely smile once again. I waved back, and as we drove away, I felt a tinge of melancholy. This had been such a delightful experience, and I wasn't sure I wanted it to end. But reality quickly set in, and I knew we had to get back to the rig and be on our way.

I gazed out the window, then suddenly sat up. I had not taken one photograph of the village, the welding shop, or any of the people! Oh, how could I have forgotten to do that? I photograph everything! I couldn't believe I had missed this one completely. Even now, thinking about it gets me upset. I guess I'll forever have to be content with picturing it all in my mind's eye. And you know what? I have to say, remembering it now, that that is really not so bad!

The rain started up again somewhere after the Luling Dam portage–softly at first, then with some intensity. The dark sky seemed to hasten the arrival of nightfall. By the time we paddled into the Palmetto State Park checkpoint, it was totally dark and pouring rain. It was going to be a long night.

We donned our individual headlights once it grew too dark to see our way. At Palmetto, we planned to get out the monster light and install it on the stem. Terry was waiting for us at the checkpoint, tapping his feet anxiously. He watched as we installed the monster light, then beamed as brightly as his famous light the second it switched on, illuminating the entire park, it seemed. He exchanged our water and ice jugs, and we set off again into the rainy night. What fun!

We settled in for the next several hours, knowing it would be quite repetitive—a lot of production paddling until we reached the interception with the larger Guadalupe River near the town of Gonzales, some thirty miles downriver. I hunkered down as the sky continued to pour on us.

Even without the rain, paddling at night was very stressful. Like many sections of the San Marcos, this portion involved constant turns, with only a few extended straight-aways. Cindy had to stay on high alert, constantly panning downstream, searching for the best line around large rocks, tree stumps, small islands, and through constant small rapids. My job was to follow her, of course, and navigate the rear of the boat, taking best advantage of the available current while striving to not lose momentum by over- or under-steering.

It seemed like we were the only ones on the river. Since Palmetto (since Luling, now that I thought about it), we had not seen another boat. Had they all stopped for the night, pulled up on a bank or sand bar, nestled soundly in sleeping bags under a dry tent? Doubtful! No, we concluded that the reason we had not seen anyone was because we were now far in the back of the pack, where the number of vessels really start to thin out. The lead boats would be far ahead of us by now, always staying neck and neck in contention for the prize of being the overall winners.

With 260 river miles to traverse and only 43 vessels, averaging 20 ft. long (ours was 17 ft., while the 4-man boats were upwards of 30 ft.), that leaves a lot of miles of open spaces, right?

I wasn't in the mood to do the math just then. I simply concluded that we were alone and would probably remain that way for the rest of the race. There wasn't really a lot to talk about, though, even if we did have another boat in our midst. After all, it's a competition to most of these racers—just ask the guys that rammed us this morning!

We had just settled into a rhythm when suddenly, on approaching a highway bridge, we saw a light on the bank. Then we heard a familiar voice yelling to us through the loud din of the heavy rain. Terry was waving, motioning us to pull over to where he was standing.

"This rain doesn't look to be letting up anytime soon," he said as we paddled towards him. "You can pull your canoe up under this bridge and get some relief from the rain—and try to get some sleep."

As much as we wanted to press on, it really was raining sheets now, and the thought of getting out of it, even for a short while, was appealing. I'm surprised there are not more boats here," he said. "Except for the lead teams, who of course never stop, I'm sure many boats are looking for shelter at this point." He shook his head. "I've never paddled in the rain at night. You remember, Bob—my first solo try? When I had to pull out at Gonzales with that broken rudder cable? And right after that, it started raining like crazy?"

"I remember. Linda was with us, and we went back into Gonzales and got a hotel room for the night. And we *still* got soaked, just running from the cars to the hotel room!"

"That's right," added Cindy. "And we all talked about how miserable it would be if we were out there paddling in that storm. Well, now we know!"

"You guys try and get some sleep," said Terry. "I'll catch up with you at the Gonzales checkpoint, about ten more miles—right after the Gonzales Dam. You remember that portage, right?" We nodded as we continued to get ready. "And don't forget that you'll meet up with the Guadalupe River, just upstream—about two miles from the dam."

"We got it. Thanks, Terry," said Cindy.

"And thanks for finding us this shelter, Terry. It really is nasty out there. It may be hard to sleep, as wet as we are. But it sure beats staying out there and just getting pounded."

We were really glad to finally be out of the rain. But everything in our boat was soaked, including our change of clothes and towels. We had no sleeping bags, like some of the contestants carry, since we had no plans to stop for the night. Even if we did, they would have been soaked. So we just settled into our seats in the boat, facing one another, and made a pillow from our sack of wet clothes.

It was impossible to fall asleep, even though I was quite tired. I was shivering from the wet and the cold, and I couldn't will myself to stop shaking long enough to drift off. I must have fallen into some semblance of rest, as it seemed that time had passed before I shook awake again.

Ever so softly, I whispered to Cindy, to see if she was awake. Yep. Also too cold to fall asleep. It had stopped raining, though. "Wanna get back on the river?" I asked.

"Yeah." She jumped up. "Let's go."

We repacked our soaked clothes, switched on the monster light, and carried the boat back down the steep bank and set it in the river. Then we climbed in and headed back downriver. While neither of us got much sleep, we agreed that our bodies felt better from the rest. But we had lost several hours, hours we had not anticipated spending on the bank and not on the river.

We shouldn't worry, as we weren't competing to win. But we also knew that we did not want to spend a second night on the river, nor did we want to even consider crossing the treacherous San Antonio Bay in the dark. So the pressure was on to have a productive remainder of the night, along with a really productive day, if we were to stave off these two unwanted scenarios. We vowed to each another to make it happen.

On through the darkness we paddled. The rain had stopped—thank you God!—and the monster light was working like a dream. We laughed about how great Terry would feel, to know that his "invention" was a success. We were also grateful for the absence of any more logjams.

With so many positives working in our favor, we were able to paddle productively while not expending valuable calories stressing over difficult passageways. Sooner than expected, we came to the confluence of the Guadalupe and the San Marcos. Weird, I thought. The San Marcos seemed way bigger than the Guadalupe, here in the wee hours of the morning, under the powerful eye of the monster light. It seemed, briefly, that the two rivers were lined up, and it was really hard to see the flow of the natural water, since it widened so much right where the two came together. We remembered Terry instructing us to keep left at this junction.

We paddled left, and in a few hundred feet, it was obvious that we were on the downstream Guadalupe. This was confirmed minutes later when we arrived at the dam. We knew this portage, having paddled this stretch of river during one of our practice runs. But, of course, that had been in broad daylight. Now it was extremely dark, due to the passing storm, and also very wet. It wouldn't be the last time we'd thank God, yet again, for the monster light!

We managed to pull the canoe out of the water, although with great difficulty due to the muddy bank. The portage was much more difficult with the dark and the wetness, and the path around the dam was through high grass, up to and even over our heads, and hard to see through. But we made it, finally, and found a less muddy spot on the other side of the bank from which to re-launch.

Back on the river, we had only a few more turns, and then we'd come to the next checkpoint at the city park. Terry would be waiting for us there.

As we made our way back to the drill rig, I agonized over thoughts that it may have disappeared while we were gone. My fears vanished as soon as we bounced over the speed bumps that had started this whole mess. There sat the rig, just as we had left it, with the young man, small boy, and a few others standing guard. I exhaled in deep relief, then felt ashamed at my worry. God knew we needed this equipment to provide water for those that cannot provide for themselves. Why would he allow our main tool to be destroyed or disappear?

Still, the hitch had broken and caused us to lose valuable daylight. Why had that happened? I knew well that sometimes bad things happen to "good people," and certainly, I could think of worse things than our recent mishap. Why would my friend, Bruce, as an example, one of the smartest and most gifted, funny, and wonderful fathers and husbands be taken from us by brain cancer at such an early age? Stuff like that is a whole lot harder to wrap my head around.

Life happens to all of us. But I also believe and have seen God regularly step into our daily lives and perform miraculous acts. Whether or not we perceive His actions, or choose to acknowledge them, well, that's a different story. I have seen and experienced miraculous events; I cannot be convinced otherwise. And even in this occurrence, I was experiencing the hand of God in action.

True, we had something bad happen to us, when the hitch broke, and the drill rig narrowly missed rolling off the cliff. But it didn't! That was

God's grace. And who knows, maybe the hitch had been failing for some time, and one more jolt was all that was needed to complete the break.

Okay, so it happened in the middle of nowhere. But what if it had broken loose in a crowded city, like Nairobi or Mombasa? Worse yet, what if it was while we were towing it onto the ferry to cross the strait into Mombasa?

On first blush, our situation looked devastating, with none of our associates or our big welding machine anywhere near to help. But God brought us some "angels" from out of the bush (literally), and instead of confirming my fears at having them around, they ended up being a huge help. As they watched our rig, I got to enjoy the excursion into the tiny village to look for a welder.

We found such a welder and in the process, were treated to a most inviting and friendly community that provided good entertainment while the repair process was taking place. And now, here they still were, those angels, carefully guarding the drill rig and equipment. Everything was just as we had left it. Doesn't sound so bad, now, does it? I have no doubts that the hand of God was all over this!

The guardians greeted us warmly as we drove up. Geoffrey positioned the truck in front of the drill rig, and then, with their help, we hitched up the rig and secured the chains. I made sure Geoffrey had plenty of shillings, in small denominations, so that the young man could share the *kidogo* with all his helpers. We thanked them heartily, even sharing hugs, and said goodbye. Once again, we were off.

No sooner had we gotten back on the highway when Geoffrey got a phone call from Ken. They were near Kericho, some 50 km ahead of us— and they had broken down! A flat tire, no spare, not even a workable jack to remove the flat tire. Of course they don't have a decent jack, I thought. With badly worn tires, a drive halfway across the country, who would think to check the truck jack for workability?

Oh well, at least I had thought to buy a used but powerful hydraulic jack, just for this purpose, and had it shipped to Kenya along with the drill rig. The only trouble was, this nifty jack was—you guessed it—packed safely in the bed of Geoffrey's truck, right behind me. I let out a deep sigh. I could tell I was going to have to insist that "caravanning" be a CrossWay Policy from now on. No more "free-wheeling."

I figured they would bum a ride into Kericho, a fairly large town, where they could find a tire *fundi* to fix the flat. We would continue on our way towards them, and help as needed, depending on their situation when we arrived. Indeed, as we neared the end of the detour, Geoffrey noted that they must have fixed the tire and continued on, as the Land Cruiser and trailer were not where he had expected to find them.

Back on good highway, with no further stops, we could at last make some decent time. The detour, difficult as it had been, had taken us through pretty scenery of rolling hills, dense forests, and a number of quaint villages. But I was blown away by the next thirty kilometers, heading into Kericho. We had drifted into high tea country, where a vast portion of Kenya's world-renowned teas are grown. The plantations were expansive and lush, with beautiful tea bushes gently waving, groves of taller hardwood trees scattered among them. Time sped by as I soaked in all the beauty, and before I knew it, we were driving into Kericho—a pretty town, with lots of paved streets and nice homes and businesses.

Just then Ken called again. I couldn't believe it—they had broken down yet again! The truck had overheated on the other side of Kericho, thirty kilometers away, and the radiator was leaking badly. They had removed the radiator and were bumming a ride back into Kericho to find a *fundi*. We would meet them here when they arrived.

We wound our way through the town and pulled into the parking lot of a big city park. Pretty soon, Ken and our welder came walking up with the leaking radiator. Ken had received directions to a radiator repair shop from the fella that gave them a ride back into town. They were heading there now. We decided that I would stay with the truck and rig while the three of them took the radiator to be repaired.

I kicked around the truck awhile, but it was getting hot. I locked everything up and walked across the street to find something cool to drink. I didn't want to wander too far, or I would lose sight of the rig.

Kericho was teeming with pedestrians shuffling about the city streets. I found a small store and, keeping one eye on the truck and rig, I bought some chilled bottled water and then quickly returned to the truck. I sat nearby in the shade of a full, leafy tree and took a swig of my cold water. Shutting my eyes briefly, I willed myself not to fall asleep. If anything happened to the rig, it would all be on me!

I rested for a couple of minutes, when suddenly I heard a rustling sound. I opened my eyes and was startled to see two monkeys staring at me from about twelve feet away. Actually, there were quite a few monkeys in this park. Most of them were playing games with each other or soliciting food from some of the visitors. I took special notice of a couple of monkeys who were getting quite vicious with each other as they fought over a bit of food they had been given.

I glanced back at my two visitors. Now there were seven or eight more monkeys who had joined their two associates in crime. Looking down, I discovered the object of their attention—the half-empty package of cookies (biscuits, as they're called in Kenya) which I had purchased along with the water. I reached for the cookies, and they began creeping closer.

I must confess that some of them were quite large and intimidating. I knew I did not want to get into a squabble with them. I was greatly outnumbered, and had nothing to defend myself with.

I decided to lure them away from me using the cookies. I tossed a few cookies off to one side, away from both me and the monkeys. It worked, sort of. A few of the monkeys flew after the cookies, but several of them stayed close to me. I tossed a few more cookies in the other direction. Success! The remaining monkeys charged after them, and I jumped up, dropped the rest of the cookies by the tree and took off running towards the truck.

Only when I reached the truck did I look back, praying that they hadn't followed me. One of them had grabbed the bag of remaining cookies and the rest were chasing him around the park. Whew—crisis averted! Only then did I peer around sheepishly to see if anyone had observed my daring escape from the raging man-killer monkeys! No one seemed to have noticed. I decided right then and there that I would not be sharing this story with Ken and Geoffrey.

I glanced at my watch. It had been an hour and half since the three of them had left me. Just then, I saw them walking up to the truck. "Where's the radiator?" I asked Ken.

"We will have to pick it up at the repair shop on the way to the Land Cruiser," he replied. "It should be done by the time we get back. We were just coming to check on you."

I kept my mouth shut about the monkeys as we climbed into the pickup. We picked up the radiator, then drove 25 km out of Kericho to where the Land Cruiser was parked, along with the trailer, beside the road. The three of them quickly re-installed the radiator.

I crossed my arms and turned to Ken. "I guess I don't have to tell you how much time we've lost today by not traveling together in a caravan, do I?"

Ken hung his head. "No, Bobu. You're right." Then he looked up with a bit of a smirk, retorting, "But Geoffrey still drives too slow."

"Well now, because of all our troubles on the road, there is no way that we're going to make it to Nairobi before dark," I said.

"Maybe not," Ken said. "But I would like to try."

"Well, I don't think it's a great idea to drive at night with no trailer lights," I replied. "But let's see how far we can get. *Twende*? Shall we go?"

"*Twende!*" Ken chuckled.

"Let me drive, Geoffrey," I said as he handed me the keys. "Maybe I can keep up with Ken better." I figured the remainder of the trip would be on good highway, recalling our all-night bus trip five days earlier.

Ken slowed down a bit, and we made good time; soon, we were approaching Nakuru, one of the last major cities before Nairobi. Dusk was rushing upon us, and it was obvious that the final few hours of driving would be in darkness. As I was making the decision to stop in Nakuru for the night, I completely lost sight of Ken. I guess I should no longer be surprised, at this point. Just like that he was gone!

I asked Geoffrey to call Ken and tell him I wanted to find a hotel and get a good meal and some sorely-needed sleep. Ken said that he preferred to push on, claiming that he needed to get some important work done tomorrow morning. I took the phone from Geoffrey and asked Ken to be careful and to drive slow, and that we'd pray for their safety. He thanked me and said that he would.

I hung up the phone, ready to get some food and some sleep. I asked Geoffrey if he had ever been to this city before, and if he knew of any decent hotels. "The Hotel Kunste," he replied. "I will direct you. It is not far." Soon enough, with Geoffrey deftly remembering the way, we were driving through the gate and main entrance. Not fancy, but nice and clean.

As we were checking in, Geoffrey was asking one of the attendants where we could park our vehicle, with the trailer attached. We wanted a place out of the way, but still under the security lights, since a lot of the equipment on the trailer was quite exposed, as well as the back of the truck. The attendant said that he had such a place and would direct us there.

After completing the check-in, and before we went to our rooms, we followed the guard around to the back of this large hotel complex. There we found a number of vehicles, including several large lorries. This, we agreed, would be fine. We selected a double space that would allow us to simple pull into, and then pull back out in the morning without even having to back up—something that neither of us was very adept at.

After showering off the day's sweat and dirt, we meandered to the large dining room, where many people were gathered. Apparently, there was some sort of convention going on, which made the atmosphere quite lively and enjoyable. The food was also quite nice, as were the *beridi sana* beers that we enjoyed with our evening meal.

I was not yet ready to turn in, even though it was getting late. I was worried about Ken and wanted to make sure he and his two guys had arrived safely in Nairobi. I called Geoffrey's room and asked him to call Ken. After several minutes had gone by, he called back to say that Ken was not "picking" (answering his phone). "Keep trying," I asked, "and let me know as soon as you've made contact." I then prayed, more fervently this time, that God would please see them safely home.

About thirty minutes later, Geoffrey rang my room. He had just spoken to Ken. And what do you know? They had run out of petrol! "Of course they did," I exclaimed. "This has been a most difficult trip for us all, hasn't it, Geoffrey?" I wondered what God was trying to say in the many trying events we had faced that day.

"They're hiking to a petrol station and hope to be back on the road in a short while," Geoffrey added.

I was tired now, worn out, but of course I couldn't sleep. The thought of Ken and the guys stuck somewhere with no gas kept churning in my mind. Where had Geoffrey said that they had broken down at? I was trying hard to remember, thinking I needed to write these things down. It was at that moment that I decided to try writing a travel blog, to tell the world about this astonishing journey—or at least my friends and family. Truly, I thought, you couldn't make this stuff up!

Hours later, the room phone blared in the silence. I had indeed fallen fast asleep, crashing hard on top of my notebook computer, with the screen light still blazing! The guys had made it safely to Ken's house, and they would all stay the night since it was well after midnight.

I thanked Geoffrey, and then I thanked God for everything. For Ken and his helpers, for their safe, if late, arrival; for good outcomes in our day's many misadventures; for the quiet and comfort of this hotel; and then, thinking of the broken hitch, for the angels that he sent to us, and the wonderful little village with the capable *fundi* who applied his craft to make the necessary repairs that allowed us to continue on.

Finally, I added a big thank you for showing me that He will always bring us through the storm. Perhaps not how we envisioned it. But often times even better than we planned!

The rain had stopped by daybreak, and now the sun was coming up—*hot*. At least we should be able to dry all of our wet clothes and gear, I thought. That's one reprieve. We were heading on down the Guadalupe River, and I hoped that with its much higher flow, thanks to its joining with the San Marcos component, it would help to propel us downstream. Just stands to reason, right?

As the day wore on, the sun's rays began to feel hotter and hotter, and we were soon neglecting to drink enough water—even though, naturally, Terry was continually imploring us "drink more water!" every time he saw us. No matter how much we drink, he insists we need to drink more. "I'm drinking as much as I can!" I told him. "I hope you're familiar with *over-hydration*?" But I knew Terry was right—at this point, I was not having to pee. At all. Which was a bit disturbing. Not the not peeing dilemma, mind you, but that I knew I would have to admit that he was right!

Finally, Cindy and I reached the Cuero Dam. This dam had been destroyed by a flood some thirty years prior and was presently under re- construction by the local property owner. I had visited this dam while captaining Terry on one of his Water Safaris. Cindy and I had come here to watch Terry and his partner, Bobby, come through this point. We arrived before them, as planned, so I was able to explore the construction progress and peer into the ancient turbine building, with the three French turbines still in place.

As a civil engineer, I was fascinated with the progress. Cindy told me the owner intended to rebuild the dam and get these turbines working again. "After 30 years?" I said. "That's crazy!" But as I looked into that turbine room and saw the three turbines sitting there, waiting, perhaps, for some industrious (and perhaps eccentric) person to dare to restart them, I began to see the possibilities. These turbines could be restarted.

But the dam? Another story altogether. This guy, Parker, certainly had a large dozer. But that was it—one dozer, parked up on the bank. I could see that he was working the bank on one side of the river, but there wasn't much progress. The concrete dam was almost obliterated in the flood, leaving no more than a quarter of it extending out into the river, adjacent to the turbine house. How he would extend it across the remainder of the river, with only a single dozer, I could not begin to imagine.

No, we would be safe. Just as Terry and Bobby came around the bend that day, and without even slowing down, swept easily around the far bank, over the tiny hydraulic, and continued on their way, I expected that Cindy and I would have an equally uneventful passage at this broken-down dam today.

But as we drew around that same bend leading to Cuero Dam, something was not right. We instinctively knew to draw right and slide around the dam remains. But oh my! Just as we paddled ever closer to the dam, we could soon see that there would be no "drawing right." For there stood the dam—stretched all the way across the river!

Apparently, someone forgot to tell Jimmy Parker that this feat was impossible.

Then we heard the turbines whirring above the sound of the crashing water. Not only had Mr. Parker re-built the dam, he had restarted the turbines! Instinctively, I looked up to find the telltale overhead power lines. There they were. My goodness, I thought. He did it. How about that?

Let me take a moment to highlight what this guy had accomplished. Talk about having the last laugh! No telling how much money he was collecting from the local power company for the power he was now generating. Actually, it wouldn't be hard to calculate. The most efficient energy source on earth has always been hydroelectric energy. According to the law—the 1978 PURPA (Public Utilities Regulatory Policies Act), one I knew well from my early days just out of engineering school—building fossil fuel and geothermal power plants was now not only possible, but highly profitable.

Through the power of this law, which managed to slip past the powerful energy giants, anyone who generated electric power could sell it back to the local power company. And they had to buy it, at "full avoided cost," which is the actual cost to the power company of developing and producing that same power themselves. The seller would be paid a percentage of that cost, typically 85% to 95%, depending on what they could negotiate with the power companies—who had to, by new law, negotiate "in good faith" to reach an equitable agreement for both parties.

PURPA is the reason we have so many wind turbines dotting the land across this country, usually privately owned, producing power for the local energy company and significant compensation for the owners. Today, non-utilities represent 7% of the total electrical energy produced in this country Alright, enough with my "Bill Nye, Science Guy" lesson! Back to the river.

As greatly as I admired Mr. Parker's feat, in this moment, I could only curse his success. Now we would have to portage a dam that we had assumed we could easily skirt. Not only that, but due to the extent of yesterday's rain, the outtake was a muddy mess.

Not only was the ground muddy, but the mud was deep. With each step we sunk, sometimes past our calves, making the half mile trek seem like endless miles of quicksand. The sun was at its peak and the sky clear as glass. It was hot as blazes!

We finally—*finally*—made it back to the river below the dam, drenched in sweat and caked in mud. The canoe felt like it weighed 400 pounds. Finally reaching the river, we just walked out into it and collapsed into the wet coolness. Oh my, that felt so good. But eventually we had to re-enter life as we then knew it.

Somehow, we summoned the strength to climb back into the canoe and paddle on. I looked back and saluted the grittiness and determination of one Jimmy Parker. Truly amazing, to say the least. But in my salute, I may have extended one of my fingers in the process. I don't rightly recall!

Hours passed of monotonous rowing down what I could have sworn was the same half mile stretch of river, over and over again. Around every new bend lay another quarter to half mile straightaway. Our paddles sliced through the water, left, then right, then left again, involuntary and robotic. A friend of Terry's had calculated the number of paddle strokes that it would take two people to complete the 260-mile race. The grand total? Over 100,000! By any calculation, that number is large, I'm sure.

But I can guarantee you it *feels* like that many!

At one point, I may have started hallucinating. I asked Cindy if we had gotten turned around. "No, why?" she asked, amused at my dumb question. "Because I swear we're paddling uphill!" I wheezed. Soon after, she began to feel the same sensation. Finally, to convince ourselves that we had not been "sleep-paddling" and somehow turned completely around, we stopped so I could satisfy my curiosity with a leaf. The leaf showed us that, yes, we were still paddling downstream. We both agreed that it might be best if we focused on something else.

Be careful what you wish for, didn't Mom used to tell me? I had been wishing for something to chase away the monotony—and boy did I get it! In the distance, we saw fish jumping down river—lots of fish! As we edged closer, we could see that they were offended at the disruption. First one, then another, then a mess of them started snapping at our paddles. "Man!" I shouted. "These boogers have teeth! Since when did piranha invade the Guadalupe?!"

"They're not piranha," she said, half laughing. But I could tell that she was as startled as I was. "They're alligator gar."

"So that's what they look like," I said. "Wow, are they always this vicious?"

"I've only seen them a few times. But never this many, nor this vicious. We're going to have to keep them from jumping into the boat."

"Now that's a startling thought," I said. "I almost wish that you hadn't said it, actually. But you're right, of course."

We began popping them with our paddles in hopes of chasing them away, since it was clear that we would not be outrunning them. We finally either pummeled them enough or drifted far enough downstream that they gave up the attack. Whatever the reason, I was relieved to escape.

"My goodness," I finally said, as we appeared to see the last of them. "I would not want to encounter that school of ninja fish in the dark."

"Oh my!" Cindy responded. "Neither would I."

"Okay then," I said, "I'm no longer bored with this segment. Please, bring back the monotony!"

We settled back into a rhythm, and soon the river changed into a long series of switchback-like segments. We were circumventing the enormous DuPont Chemical Plant near Victoria, and it felt like we were getting nowhere with each turn. Later, when I examined the USGS map, this area appeared just as we had experienced it. If it could have been traversed with a straight shot, it would probably have taken less than twenty minutes of steady paddling. Instead, it took us hours and added quite a few river miles.

Evening was quickly approaching then, and we knew that we would not make our second night's milestone either—to cross Alligator Lake in daylight. (I shivered at the thought of anything further having to do with "alligators.") This was a very wide portion of the river that looked more like a lake. With daylight, one could navigate by dead reckoning and recognize the outlet. But at night, it was next to impossible.

Soon it was dark enough that we had to put on our headlights and set up the monster light. Once again, Terry's amazing monster light broadcast our way down river, as in midday brightness. Prior to reaching the lake, Terry once again had us pull up on the bank to get some sleep. We didn't want to, but he reminded us that even if we got through Alligator Lake, we would still have to deal with the vicious San Antonio Bay at night. We didn't really want to do either of those things, so we grudgingly agreed with him and started looking around at his chosen KOA for us this night!

It seemed perfect. He had chosen a public park at one of the last checkpoints. There were picnic tables near the water, so he suggested we try to sleep on them, to get us off the ground and away from insects. One of the biggest "land problems", outside of mosquitoes, is fire ants. They are everywhere in Texas (except for the deserts, perhaps), and particularly along riverbanks. It seemed like a great idea. Cindy and I each created our own meager padding made from our dirty clothes—at least they were now dry. We could thank the heat of the wicked hot sun for that.

By now, however, with darkness having taken over for several hours, the temperature continued to drop. The concrete surface grew colder and colder, until it seemed like it was sucking the heat right out of our bodies. Eventually Terry, who was standing by, where he could observe our ever-increasing shivering, spoke up.

"You should probably get back on the river," he said. "I've been watching you both shaking more and more, so I know you're not sleeping. In fact, you're probably expending a lot of energy that you could put to good use by paddling."

"What do you think, Bob?" Cindy asked in an extremely shaky voice, one I had not heard before. When I answered in a similarly shivering manner, we immediately jumped up and made ready to return to the water. We thanked Terry for the rest that we were able to receive, both agreeing that it was worth it to relax our aching muscles, at the very least.

In world record time, we packed up the canoe, carried it to the water's edge, and after turning on the monster light and donning our headlights, we launched down river. Terry hollered that he would see us at the next checkpoint.

Still shivering, making it hard to talk or understand one another, we had some difficulty in negotiating several of the turns. Then came the split, just above Alligator Lake. Terry had reminded us to stay right, or we would miss Alligator Lake altogether. While that may seem like a good thing, because of the meandering nature of the left river course, it added a lot of river miles. For this reason, most experienced teams, and the more daring novices, like us, take their chances with the much shorter Alligator Lake course.

All at once, it seemed like the river just went away! Like it dried up or something. We were not yet in the lake portion, so we thought. But were also not sure where we were on the river, either. I remember stopping and pulling up on a shoreline, which could have been a bank or an island. It was that hard to tell in the dark.

We decided to explore. We took turns wandering around on this piece of land, while one of us stayed with the boat. We were trying to determine the best course around—or through—this land, in hopes of finding the lake, which we hoped would be obvious.

As we were doing this, we heard a voice behind us. It was a solo paddler. "You guys lost?" he said.

"Is that you, Ted?"

"Oh yeah. Hi, Cindy!" It was Ted Slaughter, a fellow that Terry knew from way back, who had often paddled the Safari, both solo and as part of teams.

"Yeah, we're looking for the main course into Alligator Lake. We've never run this portion of the course before. I'm thinking now that maybe we should have," she added.

"Well, come on and follow me. I know this part pretty well. But it does look a bit different in this low water, I have to say," replied Ted.

"We're right behind you, Ted. Thanks!" said Cindy, exuberantly.

"No problem. I would do just about anything for you and Terry," he responded over his shoulder. "Man, that is one bright light! Maybe I should let you go in front."

"No, we're fine following you, Ted," Cindy responded. "But we'll provide as much light for you as we can."

In no time, Ted had guided us out of our labyrinth and onto Alligator Lake. Now we could finally relax a bit as we made our way across. All we had to do was follow Ted to the outlet, which was one of our main concerns all along. Much more so than finding our way in, so we had thought.

As we were nearing what appeared to be the end-of-lake shoreline, we saw Ted scanning back and forth, searching for the river outlet. He said that it was not looking the same, and he was having a hard time finding it.

The next thing we knew, we were being sucked into this giant logjam, which had, apparently, taken over the river outlet. We started looking quickly for a way to portage around it. But it was too late. We were stuck. Neither of us remembers what happened to Ted, but in the process of our new survival preoccupation, we totally lost track of him.

We were paddling mightily just to keep the huge hydraulic from turning the boat over. We knew that we had to get out of the boat, because we were expending so much strength fighting the current while going nowhere. Although fearful of deadly water moccasins, we had no other choice.

Hopefully, I thought, this portion of the jam would be too turbulent for them, as well. Not being all that well-versed in snake life, it just made sense to my engineering mind that if you were a moccasin and wanted to make a nest in a log jam, you would tend to look for something a little less dynamic. Cindy, who is also an engineer, seemed to reach the same conclusion. We simply had to choose the lesser of two risky options. The one that won out was risking a possible poisonous bite over the more imminent threat of drowning. Not really that hard when you break it all down, huh?

Fortunately, the water was only about chest-deep when we did finally climb out. At least we could stand. But now, how to get the boat free from all the branches and the huge logs that were entangling us, while we struggled just to remaining upright in the midst of this huge hydraulic?

Cindy ended up on one side of the rushing water, and I was on the other, the boat between us. Cindy tells me that she remembers at least one other team being caught in this same mess. That part, I told her, I honestly do not recall. Neither of us, to this day, remembers how we were able to finally get out of it.

Terry had often recounted stories of paddlers that would start hallucinating due to the lack of sleep and the heightened stress from tremendous obstacles. I wasn't seeing things yet, but I knew I was stressed out by the extreme difficulties, reaching my limits of bravery and conditioning. I was utterly spent. My growing fear was the pressure I felt to stay strong for Cindy. As strong a woman as she was in her own right, I had promised Terry to take care of her, no matter what happened. I'm not sure he could have anticipated this level of danger when he asked me to promise that, but I knew I couldn't give up now. I was struggling mightily to keep my fear at bay.

But still, the battle raged on inside. I was done, I realized all at once, not sure if I could even finish the race. I felt physically capable, especially since I knew that we were getting close. But the psychological toll of all these hardships and setbacks had worn me down. Stuck mercilessly in this logjam, I began to despair of getting free and getting back on our way. I could sense Cindy's anguish mounting as well. If only we could find our way off of Alligator Lake, we might have a hope of finishing.

As our frustration and fears mounted, we individually lifted silent and desperate pleas to the only one who could help us get past this blockade alive. I vividly remember begging God to carry us through this huge impasse, and please deliver us from any more obstacles. I gave it all to Him. I know of no other explanation for how we finally succeeded—I'm convinced of it, even now, as I write this, years later.

Surely that last terror-filled plea brought the Maker of the universe right into our canoe. I can't explain it any other way, other than it was suddenly over, just like that! No more logjam. No more snarling branches entangling us, our canoe or our paddles.

"I've got the front of the boat cleared," Cindy shouted suddenly, as she climbed in and drew hard to her left. I followed her lead and pushed off the remaining snarl of branches, leapt back into the stern, and suddenly we broke free of the impasse and paddled into calmer water.

Just like that, there was clear water ahead. "What just happened?" I asked, stunned.

"I don't know," she responded, equally amazed.

"So, where are we?" Like she would know better than me, somehow.

"I don't know," she repeated. "But I think we're out of Alligator Lake. Everything looks clear up ahead."

"I sure hope so. I'm not sure I could take much more of that. And we're on the right channel, you think?"

"Uhh, well, I think so. But don't really know that for sure, either. I guess we'll soon find out."

We didn't see or hear from Ted again, until after crossing the finish line. I remembered thinking about him, how he had guided us into, and then through, Alligator Lake. But we lost track of him as we were fighting for our lives with that treacherous logjam. I sent up a quick prayer, asking God to guide him safely on—to finish another in a long career of successful TWS finishes for him.

I thanked God for sending another angel for Cindy and me when we had truly lost our way. Knowing what little I do about Ted, and only through stories from Terry and Cindy, I suspect that he might be surprised to know that God used him in this unusual manner. And, while he might not even believe it—or claim it, for that matter—we knew it to be true. Right now, that was all that mattered.

I have to say, it took me a good while—and several river miles—to totally accept that we were finally through Alligator Lake and heading back down the Guadalupe towards the bay. All I could do was say, "Bless you, Father, for hearing our prayers. I had almost given up back there." We paddled on in silence, but joy was pounding in my soul. Invigorated from having eclipsed Alligator Lake, no doubt, we felt new strength for the major difficulty that still loomed ahead—San Antonio Bay.

The room phone was clanging loudly, jarring me from a deep sleep. It was the front desk. I had asked for an early wake-up call, wanting to get on our way before the city woke up so we could beat the traffic on our way out of town. Waking Geoffrey proved to be a bit more difficult. After calling his room several times, I went and banged on the door while calling his name—but not too loudly, as it was quite early. Finally, he cracked the door. He was up, but had been in the shower.

We met a few minutes later in the café, ate a light breakfast, then went out to check on our equipment. We found everything in the truck and on the rig trailer just as we had left it the night before. The same guard who had assisted us in finding this space came to guide us out. But when we switched on the ignition, we discovered the battery was dead.

We would have to push start it, which meant unhitching it from the trailer. The guard found a helper, and together with Geoffrey, the three of them gave me a good push. I was able to catch it in gear and restart the engine, but not without several tries. All three were panting heavily from the strain. I gave the guard a nice reward for his guarding and assistance, and a small one, too, for his friend. Geoffrey climbed into the truck, panting.

"Let's go, Bobu," he said between gulps of air.

"You sure, Geoffrey?" I asked. He looked puzzled. "Aren't we forgetting something?"

"What?" he asked, a bit agitated.

"Do we maybe want to take the drill rig, too?" I asked, with a wink.

He erupted in laughter. "Oh yes! We really should take the drill rig!" Still laughing, he got out and backed me up to make the hitch. No doubt this acute lack of oxygen so early in the morning had momentarily robbed his brain cells of their recollection capacity. Finally, he climbed back into the cab, still smiling, and shaking his head.

"It's *sawa*, Geoffrey," I said, laughing as well. "Today will be a good day."

"Yes, Bobu, I am sure of it as well," he responded, in his ever so constant positive Kenyan attitude—one that I so long for and fight daily to grasp.

With that, we were off. As we left the confines of the city, the highway rose steadily, until we had a good view of Lake Nakuru in the distance. I asked Geoffrey if he had ever seen the famous pink flamingos of Lake Nakuru, that I had read about recently, and heard about often.

"Oh yes, Bobu, there are SO MANY of them, and they are so beautiful. You need to see them."

"Yes, I should like to do that one day," I responded. "Just one more thing that I would like to experience here in your beautiful country. I will have to add that to my extensive and continually growing list."

"Ha, you will, for sure, Bobu! You should really take some time to do more fun things when you come here. You always work so hard, helping our people to have *maji* (water). I know that is so important to you, and we are grateful for your generosity and your passion. But why not take more time and enjoy yourself a bit, while you are here?"

"One day I will, Geoffrey, as I want to so badly," I responded. "But I only have so much time when I come here, as you know. I have a job back home, and there are only so many days that I can be away. I am grateful indeed, for the blessing of this work, and my boss, Alan, who is also a great friend and so supportive of my ministry. He affords me this extensive time off to come here, as you know. I am already making three trips every year, and will continue to, as long as I can afford the expense."

"I thought that you have donors in America that pay for your travel cost, do you not?" he asked.

"Oh yes, to be sure, I have a number of wonderful, generous donors who help support me in my passion. But most of that money goes to drilling wells and water or sewer projects. I have several supporters who directly support me, beyond the well ministry. I do use some of that money to travel here. But not much. Mostly I pay my own way."

"So that is why you have to continue to work, to pay for these trips?"

"Well, that is for sure. But, as you know, I still have one daughter in university, back in Texas. And her older sister, my second-born, recently graduated. As it is here, college tuition is very expensive—perhaps even disproportionate to individual income in America, as I know how much college costs here in Kenya. So, I have resigned myself to quite a number of more years of employment, as the Lord (and my friend, Alan) provides in order to pay off their mounting student loans. Unfortunately, that is how it is done in America. University tuition is ridiculously expensive and the actual money owed by students, and their parents, is now over ten billion USD—more than a trillion Kenyan shillings!"

"But I do long for the day when I can spend as many weeks or months as I would like when I come here. Then I can help with several water projects and still have time to travel—and to relax, just a bit. That will be nice."

"One day you will do that, Bobu, I am sure," he responded.

"But you know, Geoffrey, even now, I am able to see and experience some of the vast richness and the beauty that is Kenya, particularly when we travel afar, as we did to complete Sango's well. And the joy that I experience when I see your people receive the gift of clean, fresh water—well, it is quite beyond my limited ability to even describe. My words are just too small."

We had planned for an easy four-hour drive back into Nairobi. It seemed highly probable, as we soon we had already covered the first 100 km of the remaining 240. We were now on the outskirts of Naivasha, a very popular tourist spot for Kenyans and foreigners alike. This lovely city was nestled on the shores of beautiful Lake Naivasha. No wonder one of my well-drilling missionary friends lives here instead of Nairobi.

I was grateful that we'd had such a smooth trip. No more of this breaking down business! I glanced down at the dash. "I know we're close, Geoffrey, but we really should get some petrol." He knew of a station coming up, and we pulled into a large petrol station—a "truck stop" is what we would call it in the U.S. Its size was quite large compared to most I had seen or experienced. Maybe not on the caliber of a Texas Buc-ee's, since what "gas station" in America is? But even so, quite large.

The attendant came to fill our tank, and we stretched in our seats. I noticed he kept bending down to look under the truck. Finally, he dropped completely out of sight. When he popped back up, he walked over the window. Bad news. We were leaking oil from the universal joint, from the looks of it. Geoffrey and I got out to look. Sure enough, there was a sizeable puddle of oil, expanding steadily with each drip from the underside of the truck. I tried to control my frustration. Would we not have one day where something didn't break or throw us off of our well-laid plans?!

Geoffrey asked the attendant if there was a *fundi* who could look at it. He said there was, and he went off to fetch him. Not long after the *fundi* came back with the attendant and climbed under the truck to examine the leak. When he came back up he told us that the crank case seal was leaking badly and could cause a more serious problem at any moment.

Geoffrey asked him if he could get the parts to repair it, and of course the answer was yes. Don't they always? Still, there was something about this *fundi*—and the attendant—that inspired trust. He said that he could have a boy on a motor bike go for the parts, where he knew that they would have it, while he would begin with the disassembly. Geoffrey asked him how much the part would cost. The *fundi* left to call the auto supply shop.

When he returned, just a few minutes later, he said that the part and the repair total would cost 4,500 shillings. "How long will it take?" asked Geoffrey.

"No more than two hours," came the answer. Geoffrey pulled me aside and told me he didn't have this much money. I asked him if he thought it was a reasonable price; it sounded really cheap to me, about $50, but I only had bloated U.S. repair costs to compare it with. I'm sure that it would cost four times as much at home.

"Yes, Bobu, this is a fair price and I trust this *fundi*," he responded.

"Okay then, I trust him as well. Then let's fix it. I'll loan you the money. And anyway," I added, "you have a good deal more than that coming to you when I reimburse you for the use of your truck for the last two weeks. I can get more shillings when we get to Nairobi."

"Thank you, Bobu," said Geoffrey. "I had forgotten about that!" Geoffrey spoke with the *fundi*; when he returned, I asked, "What shall we do for two hours?"

"Well," he responded, "we can kill some of that time by eating lunch. They have several cafes here at this petrol station."

"You know, you picked a really good place to stop, Geoffrey! Or maybe God led you here. After all, He would know that your truck needed repairing, right?" Geoffrey just smiled. "And do you really think that every petrol station around here has an honest and capable *fundi*?"

"No, Bobu," he responded, chuckling, "I don't think that they do. Yes, I believe that God did guide us here."

"Well," I said, clapping him on the shoulder. "Let's go thank Him while we get something to eat."

As the darkness gave way to bright sunlight, it reminded me, once again, that there was a God, and He was certainly in charge. This was a good anchor for me emotionally, as we were steadily propelling toward our last major hurdle—the six-mile wide San Antonio Bay, a daunting challenge.

The finish line lay just on the other side at the aptly named community of Seadrift, Texas (population 1,300). This fishing village was located on the north end of the San Antonio Bay and was home to a large Vietnamese fishing community. In 1979, upset by the proliferation of Vietnamese fishing boats, a band of white fisherman burned a number of the boats and firebombed a Vietnamese house, leading to a large fistfight. This melee ended in the shooting death of one of the alleged white perpetrators. Two Vietnamese men were accused of the murder, but later acquitted on the grounds of self-defense. (This story was told in the 1985 movie, "Alamo Bay," which I haven't actually seen.)

Other than that, Seadrift is just a quiet, nondescript inner-coastal community. Previous visits had given me the impression that Seadrift had surely seen better days—judging by the run down, hollowed-out "business district." Today, however, I will welcome our first glimpse of Seadrift, no matter how run down.

But first, San Antonio Bay loomed before us. And before that, we would have one more dam to contend with—Salt Water Dam, a barrier against salt water intrusion upriver. It was a variable height dam, set by the water level, so we never knew how high or low it might be. The question to portage or shoot the dam would be totally dependent on the vertical drop and type of boat. Fortunately, our aluminum canoe was flexible to paddle, allowing us to change routes or plans very quickly, whereas the larger 4-man boats were not nearly so nimble.

Terry had learned from other teams ahead of us that the Salt Water Dam's level was low enough for us to shoot and relayed that information to us before we reached it. Sure enough, as we approached the dam, we only needed to find the point of maximum velocity and head there. We found it quickly and shot the dam with ease. Paddling on, ever closer to the goal!

The last checkpoint of the race came near the tiny town of Tivoli, a few miles beyond the Highway 35 bridge overpass. "Here's your ice and fresh water," said our Captain as we pulled over. He seemed more enthusiastic than usual. "No time to rest. I just came from Seadrift. San Antonio Bay is smooth as silk, hardly a ripple. I have never seen this before, or even heard of it happening. You have to go now, before the wind picks up. The wind will make it most difficult to cross."

I flashed back to all the stories that Terry had retold of crossing the Bay in previous Safaris. All the teams, large and small, had their stories. Some canoes now carried as many as six paddlers and were hand-crafted of ultra-expensive carbon fiber—nothing short of sleek, hydrodynamic wonder-vessels. But when it came to the Bay, no vessel was guaranteed safety. I was now reminded of teams that had capsized in high waves and swirling wind, and often times in total darkness. Drowning on San Antonio Bay was always a close threat. If it were possible to cross this Bay with no trouble, I wanted in on that.

Terry challenged us to keep going, not even wanting us to exit the canoe, if possible. With that it hit home with me—just how unusual the Bay's stillness must be. As weary and aching as our bodies were, we dug in and soldiered on, encouraging ourselves that the end might only be hours away now. We had been through two plus days of unrelenting struggle. We did not want an angry bay today. We focused our minds on the image of a glass-like lake and let it push us on towards the finish.

We had never practiced the stretch from Tivoli to the bay and across. Terry didn't recommend it. "Why put yourself through that ordeal?" he would say. "It varies depending on the time of day, the weather, and the tide conditions. Just know that it will NEVER be easy." Today, miraculously, a small window of opportunity was open to us. At this point on our arduous journey, we really could not afford to miss it.

Geoffrey and I grabbed lunch from the petrol station food court and sat down in the open-air dining area. We enjoyed great scenery, too: the station was built on a high overlook, facing away from the city of Naivasha, towards the mountains. An expansive savannah encompassed the entire foreground.

What a blessing this was to behold. Here we were, broken down again; yet once again, God was showing us His grace, and the magnificence of His incredible canvas in this postcard-perfect setting. Had we not stopped here for petrol, and had an observant attendant not noticed our leak, and had he not summoned an experienced *fundi* who offered an affordable repair, we simply would have missed all this. Think what you will, but I cannot help but see these characters in our story as more angels sent from God in heaven.

The dining area was nearly vacant, but it soon began to fill with travelers stopping for a break. Geoffrey and I busied ourselves with people watching. We noticed a few visitors pointing out to the savannah. I strolled out on the deck to investigate the object of their fixed attention—an animal, no doubt, since this was beautiful, wild Kenya. Sure enough, some 300 yards away lounged a large herd of impala, a few zebras, and an array of large birds with long skinny legs and huge beaks. They looked like a cross between a flamingo and a pelican. I was enchanted by the menagerie.

I ran back to grab my camera, and Geoffrey jumped up to join me. I forget that most Kenyans usually don't get the chance to enjoy their own native wildlife. Americans, Europeans, Asians, and Aussies travel to Africa for the wildlife safari excursions, but those safaris tend to be cost-prohibitive for most Africans. I was excited for Geoffrey to see these beautiful animals, particularly in such a gorgeous setting.

I got upset, however, when I realized I had left my telephoto lens in my overnight bag in the back of the truck. The truck was now perched two meters up in the air, with some major parts either removed or temporarily disconnected! I would have to content myself with taking long distant shots and enlarging them later on my computer. At least I brought my field binoculars.

Suddenly, a huge tractor trailer pulled noisily into the parking lot, and the crowd now turned to observe this wild beast of a vehicle, mouths hanging wide open. The trailer portion had been reconstructed into a huge RV, and it was brightly painted, with huge windows all along both sides and across the front. Some of the passengers sat up front, above the top of the tractor. Just then, a door opened far in the back, and a stairway leading up to a sleeping area was suddenly swarming with passengers exiting the bus. They were an eclectic group, varying in age from twenty-somethings to geriatrics, and spoke almost no English as they rushed by us.

The sign, emblazoned on the side, read "UK to Cairo in 40 Weeks." I'm no geography scholar, but how in the world does one get from Great Britain to Africa by RV? If they started in the UK and headed for Africa, I couldn't imagine the time it would take to drive—where?—through the

Chunnel, across Europe, through Turkey, and around the east end of the Mediterranean Sea to finally arrive in Egypt? Sounded crazy to me—though to be fair, they did have 40 weeks, apparently.[14]

A man about my age stepped off the bus. "American?" he asked.

"Why, yes," I replied, surprised to hear English.

"Ever see anything like this before in your travels?" he asked, nodding toward the bus.

"Never. And I'm surprised to see this, um, giant mobile home, would you call it?— here of all places. Why Naivasha?"

"Oh, yeah. Well, we're on our way to Nakuru—for the flamingos, of course. Surely you've heard of the pink flamingos?"

"Of course," I said, leaving out the part about my finding out only earlier that day. "My Kenyan friend is well-acquainted with these famous birds." I was much more interested in finding out more about this strange tour. "How long have you all been on the road?"

---

[14] They only met in Great Britain, I later learned, and then flew directly to Tangier, Morocco where they loaded onto this "trailer park on wheels." They headed south, along the entire west coast of Africa to Cape Town, then back up the east coast. This trip to Western Kenya was an excursion off of the main south-to-north route, to see the animals and beauty of the Masai Mara and here in Naivasha. How fortuitous that we happened to be here at this truck stop on this very day to intersect with them! Though you know how I feel about coincidences…

"Not sure," he sniffed, "six or seven months, something like that. There's others to keep track of that stuff. Me, I'm just along for the ride," he chuckled as he sauntered away.

"Some ride," I hollered after him.

Geoffrey had gone to check on the truck. I hung around the touring trailer, hoping that I might find another passenger that I could engage. I had all sorts of questions about their exciting adventure. The one American on the trip had gotten his fill of conversation, it seemed, and I wasn't hearing any more English among the group. I was disappointed to not be able to hear more about their trip first hand, especially since they happened to be right here, of all places!

The passengers re-boarded the touring truck and took off in search of the pink flamingos (based on the limited information my "friend" had given). I watched them drive away, thinking that it would be fun to follow them on the remainder of their journey through their travel blogs. But in reality, I never did go looking for them. I guess that must mean that I simply tucked this experience away as no more than an oddity, rather than an event worth tracking.

Geoffrey returned, just then and announced that the repair was finishing up in about a half hour. We sat down in the coffee shop, and naturally, this being "African time," thirty minutes rolled into an hour before the attendant came looking for us. "Your truck is ready!" he announced, with a big grin.

Finally, we could be on our way, with some assurance that we might be trouble-free for the remaining 150 km or so of the journey. We also knew that Ken and the young men were safely ensconced in Ken's home in rural Ruiru (outside Nairobi). This was a comfort to us as we prepared to journey on.

We paid the bill, just as presented earlier—4,500 KES (about $50 USD. I don't know about you, but I still find these prices amazing.) Geoffrey said that he would drive, and I was glad to sit back and stare at the scenery, which was captivating, like so much of this beautiful country. I had a good view of Lake Naivasha, and I vowed to one day return to this city and spend some time sightseeing both the city and the beautiful lake nearby.

While taking in the beauty of this region of Kenya, I thought of all that had happened on this latest adventure. Looking back, I can't say

I was sorry about all the unplanned stops. Maybe it was God's way of causing us to slow down and just take in life for a while. The truth was, I needed help "slowing down" in life, and I highly suspect that He knew that. Our mishaps had seemed to be interruptions as first, but through them, I had seen a lot of new, remote places, had encountered memorable people, while enjoying some incredibly beautiful scenery. Doesn't sound like these interruptions were so terrible after all!

More than that, these "interruptions" were teaching me patience. Indeed, I never once saw Geoffrey act frustrated or inconvenienced when we were stopped for any reason. We Westerners seem to always feel the need to be making progress toward our goals, and when we don't, we take on stress. I was learning through these circumstances that accepting interruptions can actually be a blessing—if we take it as from the only One who transcends time. Indeed, He richly blessed us with some unforgettable experiences in each of these otherwise unexplainable disruptions.

Drilling a bit deeper into this new perspective, I can say that I wasn't once in any real danger. Not even from the "marauding" monkeys, who were more of a funny story than a real threat. I lost some time. Maybe a few hours—perhaps even half of a day - out of a lifetime? So what? That which I gained made it more than worth it to me. God willing, I prayed, I will begin to embrace these unexpected interruptions. And maybe, just maybe, I would gain a measure of patience that I could take into my busy Western world!

After an hour, I took over and drove around Nairobi, from Northwest to Southeast, right to Ken's place near Ruiru. The only real difficulties we faced on the last 100 km were the rapid, rushing pace of the highway leading into Nairobi, and the suddenly very narrow rural roads leading to Ruiru. My speed sometimes caused Geoffrey to be concerned, I could see. But I protested that I was simply trying to match the flow of traffic.

It was the narrow rural roads that scared me the most, after our mishap on the mountainous detour, but I began to relax after a bit. Here, at least, the shoulders were not nearly so far below the tarmac. I didn't even flinch when the rig trailer veered off of the pavement, a few times, although Geoffrey was visibly tense. Then again, it wasn't my truck!

Beyond Tivoli, the Guadalupe was lined with very shallow banks and minimal trees. We could peer into the backyards of the homes that sat on the east side of the river. Exhausted, we stared at the lawns, imagining ourselves enjoying a chilled iced tea under a nice shade tree.

The foliage along the bank became thicker, lusher, and all at once, a wide variety of brightly colored flowers popped out against the rich backdrop of the multiple hues of greenery. Had we crossed over into a tropical river course? My eyes drank in the colors. But suddenly, this beautiful scene took on an ugly hue not unlike some Class B scary movie!

The alligator gar were the only animal challenge we had faced so far. But now, we started noticing actual alligators along the shore. At the site of them, with the thought of others looming in the river, the vision of this beautiful flora quickly faded. Just then, alligator gar bobbed up near our boat, some quite large, and all of them snapping at our paddles. As if swatting at gar wasn't enough to deal with, we all at once came under attack by some of the biggest horse flies I had ever seen. They were relentless and bit viciously.

I stopped paddling for a moment, grabbed a wet T-shirt, and began swatting them away from us both. It helped for a moment, until their reinforcements showed up and swarmed in new ferocity. We had a choice: jump in and stay underwater long enough that they'd leave, or try to outrun them. I glanced down at the razor-sharp teeth of the alligator gar and decided on option two.

For the next five miles (it felt like five but was actually more like two), we beat the water, paddling like crazy while I swatted the flies off with the T-shirt. Soon, tugboat horns pierced the air, and we knew that we were approaching the bay. We were actually looking forward to the dreaded bay now, praying for some relief from these nasty flesh-eating horse flies.

As soon as we reached the bay, both Cindy and I, without saying a word, dove into the water. Safely there, we remained under until we were breathless, then bobbed to the surface for a quick gulp of air, and then right back under. It worked. The flies gave up and went in search of other flesh. Cindy and I laughed like maniacs as we climbed back into the boat. Somehow, those lush, floral backyards had lost their allure.

We chugged our cool water, grateful to be on the final stretch. As we idled, we watched a huge tanker being towed right in front of us, on its way to the Gulf. It lumbered along slowly, but we were suddenly nearly swamped by the waves it made. We held on tight and struggled to keep the canoe upright. We were not complaining about the waves, however, since they were practically the only movement in the entire bay.

Propelled, no doubt, by the savage horse flies, we had made record time on this last leg and were now in the bay. It was as calm as Terry had said — "smooth as glass." We didn't even install the splash guard that we had brought with the usual expectation of high waves in San Antonio Bay.

We paddled lazily, pulling through the quiet, still bay water, our journey almost anticlimactic after all we had come through. This was supposed to be the most difficult passage; indeed, the bay never bowed to TWS paddlers. It had not been selected as the last challenge by chance—it was the final opportunity for nature to win the battle over man. I'd heard stories of such harrowing discouragement that teams disbanded and gave up after 60+ hours of paddling, and less than an hour to go.

There were no other boats on the bay, and it almost felt like we were cheating as we glided through glass. Why was the bay so calm? Would it stay like this for long? No. I knew it would break up soon. The wind would pick up or a storm would blow in and churn The Bay to lethal proportions. And the boats that followed would have a most difficult time. That's The Bay as we have all come to know and respect it.

I could only conclude in silent awe that God was, once again, watching out for us. If He could calm the storm out on the Sea of Galilee, surely he could calm the San Antonio Bay! And He had done it just for us.

Well, almost. Our friend and solo paddler, Ted Savage, came across about an hour behind us, also enjoying a silk-smooth bay. Good for him, I thought, after some of his previous encounters with a much more imposing bay run.

On the flat, quiet bay, stroking the water easily as we made our way "home," I breathed a prayer of thanks to the One True God. He knows all of our needs, even before we see them coming, and responds accordingly—but in His time and in His chosen way. Therein, I truly believe, is where true faith begins—when we can honestly say that we trust Him to be there for us, regardless of our situation, whether good or bad, and regardless of how we arrived in that moment, whether by "happenstance" or of our own making.

As we paddled steadily toward the finish line, my mind was going nuts trying to capture all that had happened to us in the last three days.

It felt like some crazy slide show, where my mind was throwing up pictures of every memorable moment—good and bad, scary even. And I was the audience of one, watching in amazement while asking myself, "Who came through all this stuff?" And the answer kept coming back to me after every slide and question: "You and Cindy did."

"No way," I whispered. No way! But yes, "way!" We had done it. Actually, the four of us—Cindy, me, Terry, and God. We had paddled 260 river miles, 100,000 paddle strokes, three full days—choose your metric.

We arrived in 16th place, with an official time of 71.5 hours. The judges handed us each a small plaque that simply read, "Finisher." Had we come in a few hours earlier, we would have finished around 12th place and received a trophy instead of a tiny wall plaque. (Although we were the first 2-man mixed team to finish.) Oh, and speaking of 12th place, guess who won that? The bozos that rammed us in the first hour of the race! Guess that's one way to get ahead…

In the end, 27 boats finished the race within the 100 hours allotted, with the 27th team finishing in 98 hours and 5 minutes! A total of 19 boats were officially listed as DNF (Did Not Finish). [15]

But as I've said before, it was never about winning for us, either the race, or our class, or even a trophy. Winning, for Cindy and me, was finishing. Competing in this "event" turned out to be the real prize, with what we experienced, what we gained, and what God showed us of His majestic beauty, His response to our cries, His showing us the way, and in His total care for our needs along the way. Yes, we were truly winners— and *blessed* winners, at that.

Paddle on!

> *"Some day I'll pass through the great sky above. And the first thing I'll ask is how well did I love. Did I leave the world any better than it was before? Of all the things I've done, could I have done any more?"*
>
> "As Long as I'm Here" by Brandon Heath, from "Leaving Eden" 2011, Reunion Records ©

---

[15] For official race results, see: TWS http://www.texaswatersafari.org/history/1993-tws/

EPILOGUE

Indeed, I was on a journey, a life journey, and a beautiful one. It was a journey in which I was gaining a lot of experience seeing God come through for me. Nine years ago, I had started this journey from a place of brokenness and despair, but He was shining through for me in new hope, new adventures, and new fulfillment in building His kingdom. I didn't know what lay around the next bend, but I knew with God on my side, whatever came my way, I was going to make it through.

My hope is, that by reading my stories – seeing my failures laid out before you, as open and honest as I know how – might stir something within you to, perhaps, search for more also. You never know what you might find. I said "yes" to a blind missionary – to help him on one journey. In doing that it changed my life forever and brought me hope for each new day.

You cannot imagine the joy on the faces of people as they see clean, fresh water coming forth from a hand pump for the very first time. Some of these people, particularly in South Sudan, were elderly – grandparents even. Imagine that! And I am truly sorry, but all my best words are still too small to be able to paint a true picture of what that looks like. You really just have to experience it for yourself.

And while everyone cannot run off to Africa, I know, I am sure God has a place for all of you in His bigger-than-life story. He's been pursuing you your entire life. Like I was, you just may not be aware.

Consider saying "yes" to God and taking that first step. I cannot tell you that it will be easy. In fact, it may be quite difficult. But "*if God starts something in you, he will see it through to completion.*" He has so promised as much in Philippians 1:6. (NIV). You can trust Him on that. I did, and I am forever grateful that I did.

So journey on, my friends, journey on.

ACKNOWLEDGEMENTS

So yeah, where does one start? From the beginning, I suppose – right? It was my Dad, Charles (aka Charlie or Bud) Nicol, Jr. that first started encouraging me to write a book. Every time I would bring home a new story of my trips to Africa – and actually, long before that, too – with stories of strange events happening to me, or because of me, he would simply say, "You gotta write a book, Bob." I would just smile and say, "Yeah, some day in my spare time, Dad." While this would manage to end that discussion, I have to admit that after hearing it numerous times, I actually started to think about it – more and more. Then my Mom, Dorothy Louise (Williams) Nicol, took up the cry, also encouraging me to write, even while Dad was still alive.

So I did start the process of, perhaps, developing my stories into a potential book. It happened on one long return trip from Kenya - requiring two 8 to 9 hour legs (to Europe – Amsterdam, most often) and then on to the US, followed by another domestic leg, back from NY- Kennedy, Detroit or Atlanta, to San Antonio. Plenty of "dead time" that I could only fill with so many full-length movies and cat naps. I began by simply listing a number of incidences/events wrapped around or entangled within these constant trips to Africa – generally three and sometimes four a year. Then, a paragraph or two about each. Finally, I picked one – my first trip to South Sudan, with Dean Chollar, whom you have now met in several of the preceding stories.

No sooner had I started to write, when I realized that my grammar and sentence structure was woefully inadequate. I presumed that any editor worthy of their credentials, could "fix" this problem and create a readable book. But, would anyone care to read it, outside my immediate family and closest circle of friends? I knew that I needed to engage an editor that knew me – and preferably, a Christian, since the intent of the book was to bring glory to God, while highlighting the ever-present need for clean water in developing countries.

I immediately thought of one person, Anna, my former associate at Crossway. Anna Ochoa is a gifted writer in her own right – and now blogs, beautifully and thoughtfully, on-line (You can check this out at sympathyforthesavoir.com). She would often receive my mission trip blogs and, with my open permission, re-write them to put them into a publishable form. The first time she did this, after asking me if she could, I was amazed at how much better these stories read, while not changing the content appreciably. When I asked her how she learned to write so well, she revealed that she was an English major in college. "Perfect," I said. "I have been thinking about writing a book. If I ever do, will you edit it for me?" To my total surprise she said, "of course, that sounds like fun."

That was years before I ever really started formulating any of my "stories" into a possible book. But when I did, I had not gone very far, before I reached back – using an old email address that I had of hers, as both of us had long since left Crossway. To my utter surprise, she responded. Same email – same great sense of humor, coupled with sensibility. No, she wasn't in Paris, writing for some continental magazine as I had expected, after seeing some of her Facebook posts from there. And yes, she remembered agreeing to help me edit a book, should I ever decide, in earnest, to write. To my ultimate glee – she said "yes" once again! She would love to be my editor! I was ecstatic. I could sense that this could now, quite possibly, actually happen. We agreed to meet for dinner and the rest, as they say – is history. Two long years later, here we are. You are now reading the results of our efforts and I truly hope that it has been enjoyable for you.

Thus, I thank you, Anna. You are an amazing young lady, indeed. So many hours you poured into these stories, ALWAYS making more sense of them for the benefit of our readers. I am forever in your debt – and of course, I can't begin to pay you what you're worth, though still you edit. You bless me beyond words. I so wish that I could return the favor. But alas, you know my grammar too well and thus, we both know that this would be nothing less than an absolute disaster. Besides, with your gifts and your heart for God, your blogs are already as good as they could possibly be. Please, just keep bringing them to us.

Getting back to my Mom and Dad for a minute, they have both now passed on to eternity and neither got to see my finished book.

In fact I never told Dad that I was writing it, for fear that I would never actually complete it. In fact, I told very few people, for the same reason. I did tell Mom, but not until her last few hours of life – on the morning that she passed on to be with her Bud – and Jesus. By then she was too weak to speak, but her eyes lit up when I told her. I then asked her if I could read some of it to her. Again she smiled brightly, which I took as affirmation. So I sat on the edge of her bed and read. From time to time she would seem to react - a look of concern or as broad of a smile as she could assemble, depending on the words she was hearing. However, before I could finish the first story she fell asleep. There was never another opportunity to continue reading to her. I wonder if they have Kindle in heaven! I'll just bet they have something way better!

There are still so many more people that I need to acknowledge. However, I simply cannot include everyone, as in doing so, I would miss so many. I will have to settle to highlight just a few. Indeed, some of my immediate family members you have already met, in some degree, in these stories. In particular, my older brother Doug, a writer of our family's history, as a certified genealogist – and also, of books on ancient coins, where he is a world expert. My wonderful and gifted daughters, Breanne (Mrs. Andrew Ward), Alexandra (Mrs. Bryan Catalani) and Jacqueline (Mrs. Philip Carson), were all introduced to some degree, depending on their role in these stories. I love you ladies, and so love watching your splendid lives unfold before me, beguiling and overwhelming me with your unique zest for life and your profound love for others.

To all my most cherished and closest friends, my Emmaus Reunion Group buddies, John Gaines, Sam Bright, Alex Huddleston, Ralph Hayles, and Don Stephens. You were all there for me, in a huge way, in some of my darkest hours of despair and self-critical hopelessness. You have continued to serve me in this way – with accountability, always balanced alongside your open encouragement. Words cannot express my heartfelt gratitude for your constant and sincere support – that continues even to this day.

To my ABOB friends, as well – Alan, Jay, Brian, Neil, Jonesy, and John and to my Quarry Class instructors, David and Scott – all of whom you met earlier, in one of my stories. You have provided me with distinctly different and unique ways of learning about our God and how to know Him better and serve Him best by serving one another and providing for "the least of these". I so cherish ALL of our many times together, whether at Franklin Family Ranch or Alamo Heights United Methodist Church – or wandering around downtown San Antonio, seeing both modern and historic buildings through new eyes.

To my "boss-friends", Alan and Allison Pyle (how many can say that they genuinely love the people they work for). You always grant my requests for extended leave to make these constant trips to Africa, even though it often causes an increased workload for you or operational constraints for the company. But you know my heart for Africa and the African people, and you genuinely support it – in so many ways, including your heartfelt prayers and financial support. Even beyond that, you have made work-a-day life exciting and fun again, with the program that you invited me in to help to develop. You cannot know what a blessing this has become, at this, the twilight of my engineering career. I so love that it mimics my mission work with its focus on providing quality drinking water and effective sanitation for the hard-working men and (several) women at oil drilling sites throughout Texas and adjoining states.

To the many men and women "of Africa", whom I have come to know and love – and cherish as my brothers and sisters in Christ. These include expatriates Chris and Lisa Moore, missionaries with Real4Christ, whom I was privileged to serve alongside for several wonderful years – and even now, look forward to spending time with (as you often host me for days/weeks at a time in your lovely home, in Diani Beach, Kenya). You continue to amaze me with your love for children, your devotion to winning souls for Jesus, and your unbelievable efforts to create incredible Christ-centered schools, complete with church worship centers and medical clinics. Through knowing Chris and Lisa, I have come to know and enjoy serving beside Justin Dida, who has become our full-time drilling supervisor and my closest Kenyan rafiki, and our dedicated team of Peter Myoki, Fred Chai, and our gifted drilling expert, Geoffrey Ndungu.

Along with these mighty men, I have to thank Pastors Rasto Mwangata and Erick Chondo, and wonderful, long-time rafiki,

Ken Gatithi and Jackson Mwangala. As I said above, I could name so many more that have helped me in so many ways. Some of them you have already met in depth – in these stories about my efforts in Tanzania (with Tony and Cath Swanson) and Ethiopia (with Melaku and Sosi Abebe), as well as Kenya (with Dr. Sango Otieno). I now add my recognition to all of them, as well. You ALL held me up and, in so many ways, protected me – saved me even, from sure damage or destruction, at times. All the while, you humbled me with your profound faith and trust in Jesus Christ and your relentless pursuit of justice and improved living for those that you so willingly serve – the men, women and children of Africa.

I am incapable of closing without thanking Dean Chollar, founder and head missionary of Crossway International. You came to me in my deepest days of depression and offered me a chance at new life – a life that could make use of my educational training and years of experience – to help bring life-giving water to some of Africa's most forgotten (not by God, of course, but by their governments). Though sightless, you saw deep within me, a heart to seek the oppressed and in doing so, pursue new life for them, in Jesus Christ. I believe that God has given you this incredible gift, to see that which those of us around you, cannot begin to see with our working eyes. In doing so, I am forever grateful that God directed you to me, and had you pursue my heart relentlessly – but in a beautiful way, without preaching or cajoling. Okay, so maybe there was some cajoling. But I'm sure that I needed it. Anyway, I'm so grateful that you did. Mungu akubariki, rafiki yangu. (God bless you, my friend.)

Where did I do all this writing, you might ask? Well if it wasn't at home, or on a long-distant flight, or in sundry places in Africa – like the Moore's home or my favorite Nairobi "launch pad/decompression zone" – the Africa Inland Mission Mayfield Guesthouse, then it was probably at one of several restaurants in San Antonio. My favorite local writing spots: Panera Bread in Lincoln Heights and CommonWealth Coffeehouse. At both places, I found the staff to be very warm and accommodating and the atmosphere quite conducive to hours of writing. It didn't hurt a bit that the food was quite nice, as well. So if you happen to see me there, crouching over my tablet, who knows? I might just be working on more stories.

Just another day of quiet writing at my favorite
local coffee house, CommonWealth.

Photos

The women and young girls, mainly, still have to carry the water back to their huts. But now it is much shorter and the water is safe to drink.

Geoffrey and his team screwing sections of PVC screen together prior to inserting into the borehole.

A young family in front of their mud hut.

Joseph "the woodcutter" trains young Sudanese men to safely cut with a chain saw.

Our tukol village. Dean and I stayed in the center hut, while Tim, Harry, Isaiah and Joseph enjoyed the other two. Solid comfort.

The nearby river provides a water source for all of drinking water, as well as washing, swimming, fishing, and recreation for thousands nearby.

The completed well draws many to collect the precious water for their families.

I brought many new soccer balls for the village children. But this is a special one, signed by my daughter's high school soccer team. I present it here to Michael, the village chief.

The community present us with a gift, as well – a young goat. Not being able take it with us on the plane, we donate to a needy family in the community

One of the prominent Saddam Hussain's many palaces. This particular palace served as the headquarters for the U.S. Military forces, including the office of U.S. Commander, General Petraeus.

I was amazed at how much water, like this large moat around the palace, that covered large portions of the enormous base.

A detailed frieze depicting elephant hunters decorates a wall leading to one of the palaces.

At least some of the equipment has been set in place, like this large feed pump and the multi-media filters, behind me.

Here in the completed water treatment building, sit the membrane filtration units. Note the lack of any connecting pipes or electrical wire conduit, making startup quite impossible.

The Motorcycle Diaries

Clockwise, from above, the diesel engine, with the belts for rotating the drill, and the "fuel tank" suspended on a stick. Then, one man cranks the engine to start, causing a huge plume of smoke. When it dissipates, we find the other man in place on the drill head, helping create downward force.

Many line up daily to collect water at the school.

Caught in the act of helping to build the perimeter security fance. The initial school classrooms are under way, behind me.

The neatly excavated gravesite.

The craftsman works diligently in the school yard, building the casket.

A large crowd gathers to pay last respects and mourn the death of a county official.

Such a glorious view of Mount Kilimanjaro, rising above the clouds, which I was able to capture on one of my many flights between Nairobi and Mombasa.

Large herd of camels briefly interrupts our journey to Awasa.

"So, There Really Are Camels in Ethiopia?"

Large herd of camels briefly interrupts our journey to Awasa.

Heavy manpower required to raise and then, drop the drill bit and pipe into the hole, sending just a bit deeper with each drop.

Construction of the septic tank structure nears completion.

And when more materials are required, just need to hire a trusty transport.

Helping with some of the plumbing (water taps for the community).

One of two elevated water tanks that completes the new water system.

Maybe It's Not Always About the Well

The drill foreman cranks up the old drill rig and begins drilling with the auger bit, under the watchful eye of Tony and an associate.

Along comes the gentleman with this very big air compressor, looking to help.

The air compressor sends off quite a large blast of air, sending dust skyward, as the air drilling begins.

The driller's compressor remains in the back yard in Morogoro town, as the fundi mechanic works to put it back together again.

During one of many "breaks in the action" I take the time to teach safe hygiene practices to the students and their teachers.

Journey Interrupted

The Sijoa Primary School boys help excavate for the water lines.

Ken puts the finishing touches on the water tank support structure.

The students enjoy fresh water from the new well and piping system.

Quietness abounds as the students read Sango's amazing story.

With some assistance, I retrieve a water sample
from the elevated water tank.

True to his word, Sango presents me with a goat on my final day in country.
Several hours later, were dining on 'mbuzi'!

Braving the World's Toughest Boat Race

On June 12, **Bob Nicol** (SAN) and partner Cindy Alford entered the 31st Annual Texas Water Safari, billed as "the world's toughest boat race." The race began in the springwaters of the San Marcos River, and ended 260-miles later, across the 7-mile wide San Antonio Bay.

Braving enormous log jams, water moccasins, other snakes and critters, strong tides, frontal winds, and sometimes even an alligator or two near the race's end, Nicol and Alford finished the race in 71.5 hours. Despite a large hole ripped in the side of their canoe only three miles into the race, the team managed to finish second in their class and 16th overall.

The race was filled with non-stop paddling (up to 36-hours in a stint), navigating through the darkness, and periods of heavy rain. With sore muscles, raw palms, and bruised backsides, Nicol and Alford were honored at a ceremony at the finish line along with the other successful crews.

Just finishing the grueling race is an accomplishment, as 20 of the 47 boats entered dropped out or were forced out due to excessive damage to boat or crew!

Congratulations to Nicol and Alford!

Copy of an article that appeared in Bob's employers monthly magazine that summer

Texas Water Safari

'rinted in the USA
'SIA information can be obtained
ww.ICGtesting.com
'V052018280624
'CB00028B/1197

9 781643 141107